C/NP

D0884670

Penrose Memorial Library

Whitman College

MRS. PENROSE MEMORIAL

The
AMERICAN HERITAGE
Book of THE
PIONEER
SPIRIT

The
AMERICAN HERITAGE
Book of THE PIO

WALTERS ART GALLERY; © 1951 UNIVERSITY OF OKLAHOMA PRESS

WITHDRAWN

By the Editors of AMERICAN HERITAGE
The Magazine of History

Editor in Charge: RICHARD M. KETCHUM
Chapter Prologues by ALLAN NEVINS
Narrative by ALVIN M. JOSEPHY, JR.
PETER LYON
FRANCIS RUSSELL

Published by AMERICAN HERITAGE PUBLISHING CO., INC., NEW YORK
Book Trade Distribution by SIMON & SCHUSTER, INC.

NEER SPIRIT

AMERICAN HERITAGE
The Magazine of History

PUBLISHER
James Parton

EDITORIAL DIRECTOR
Joseph J. Thorndike, Jr.

EDITOR
Bruce Catton

MANAGING EDITOR
Oliver Jensen

———

Staff for this Book

EDITOR
Richard M. Ketchum

ASSISTANT EDITOR
Stephen W. Sears

EDITORIAL ASSISTANTS
Margaret Di Crocco
Joseph L. Gardner
Mary Sherman Parsons
Margery Palmer Zeller

ART DIRECTOR
Irwin Glusker

DESIGNER
Elton S. Robinson

———

© 1959 by American Heritage Publishing
Co., Inc. All rights reserved under Berne and
Pan-American Copyright Conventions. Repro-
duction in whole or in part without permission is prohibited. U.S. copyright is not
claimed for color plates on pages 12, 14 (left),
15 (right), 18, 28–32, 65, 68, 70, 72–80, 97–104,
113 (bottom)–115, 121 (bottom)–128, 161 (top)–
165 (top), 166, 185–189, 225–232, 241–247, 290–
293, 296–300, 304, 377 (top), 378–382.

Printed in the United States of America
Library of Congress Catalog Card Number:
59-13275

E
178
.5
.A53

Table of Contents

© 1951 UNIVERSITY OF OKLAHOMA PRESS

FEB 4 '60 direct, Mrs. Penrose Memorial, $11.90

88300

COURTESY SECOND BANK-STATE STREET TRUST CO.

THE WAY THEY GO TO CALIFORNIA.

Introduction

After Theodore Roosevelt came back from his years in the West, his thoughts turned again and again to that land of vast silent spaces and to the men who had conquered it. At the same time he looked ahead, certain that the past contained the essence of what must shape the approaching future. "Our country," he said, "calls not for the life of ease, but for the life of strenuous endeavor. The twentieth century looms before us big with the fate of many nations. If we stand idly by, if we seek merely swollen, slothful ease, and ignoble peace, if we shrink from the hard contests which men must win at hazard of their lives and at the risk of all that they hold dear, then the bolder and stronger peoples will pass us by and will win for themselves the domination of the world."

America's story is made up of many elements. But through it have coursed two main streams, whose waters have lapped at the edges of all the major issues, which have nourished and carried a people forward to a destiny that was beyond all imagining when the story began.

One of these is an idea that goes back to the rim of recorded time. It was first a dim, gnawing hope, then a firm belief that the succor of all mankind lay in a magic land off to the west. Once that land was found it drew men to it like a magnet. Cabeza de Vaca, leading the first overland expedition on North American soil, expressed the dream of all those who followed: "We ever held it certain that in going toward the sunset we would find what we desired." The habit of westering came easy to those who had sailed so far to reach a promised land, and for four hundred years men gained hope and new courage when they felt the west wind across their faces.

It is easy to say that it was gold or precious stones or land that drew men on, for it was all of these. Yet it was more—and here was the second great stream of American history. There was something that literally drove men westward, goading them across the endless mountains, through steep passes, across searing plains and desert, into the face of terrors known and those unguessed. It was vision, it was courage, it was at times the sheer joy of overcoming fantastic obstacles. And it was also the conviction that what they were doing was different from anything that had happened before, that nothing would ever be quite the same again, and that the world would be a better place for what they had accomplished. "Eastward I go only by force," Thoreau said, "but westward I go free." The sleep of a hundred centuries was stirred up in that surge toward the sunset, for out of it emerged not only a new people and a new nation, but a force that changed the globe.

The pioneer spirit went deeper than buckskin breeches and a long rifle. Far from being confined to those who made the westward journey, its contagion spread to everything Americans did—to their inventions, to their arts and politics, to the exuberant, confident way they talked and thought. And it was as often evident in a philosopher or teacher as in a mountain man—in a sailor or missionary as in a scout. In going about their daily tasks, many Americans also made history, and those who stood out above their fellows were men and women who did not admit the impossible.

Among these individuals—and they were that above all else—may be found the usual human quota of villains alongside heroes, of sinners frequently outnumbering saints. And for every name we remember there were dozens whose extraordinary stories are forever lost. Theodore Roosevelt, a man who knew the challenges of our land frontier as well as those of the twentieth century, perceived that the highest form of success came "not to the man who desires mere easy peace, but to the man who does not shrink from danger, from hardship, or from bitter toil, and who out of these wins the splendid ultimate triumph."

If we are face to face with destiny today, we have been there before, and the same rules apply.

RICHARD M. KETCHUM

BEYOND THE HORIZON

E very nation needs a frontier—a sea frontier, a hinterland, or some spiritual substitute. In every people the sense of wonder, freedom, and adventure must somehow be constantly fed anew, and from Ptolemy to Lindbergh daring men have blazed new paths to satisfy that craving. As the Phoenician ventured westward from the Levantine shore, so modern man now plans his ventures into outer space. Down the centuries poets have sung of the pioneer impulse—of something lost behind the mountains, of unknown faery seas forlorn, of men who pull out, pull out on the long trail that is ever new. Europeans of the fifteenth century were nourishing their hopes of a larger freedom on tales of discovery in Asia. By letters, word of mouth, and the first printed books, they learned with delight from Ser Marco Polo, Friar Oderic, and other travelers that cities existed with "walles of silver" and "roofes of gold"; that Kublai Khan heaped in great storerooms his ingots, his masses of pearls, and his hillocks of diamonds; that Cambaluc, later called Peking, and Cipangu, now known as Japan, were seats of opulence and power that made Europe seem squalid. As the century advanced, learned and speculative souls wondered whether this bright region of spice isles, Oriental fabrics, and advanced arts might be found not by old routes that the Turk was closing, but by sailing westward. They wondered, too, what islands they might find on the way. The harsh face which the Known turned to men made them long for the Unknown.

The European world was one in which poverty, greed, hate, and war were even more strongly compounded with courage, hope, and idealism than today. It was a world of happy beginnings—Erasmus, archetype of the Renaissance, was born in 1466; Caxton established his printing press in Westminster ten years later; Michelangelo entered the household of the Medicis some dozen years later still. But it was more noticeably a world of men and women burned alive for witchcraft; of cruel punishments for crimes inspired by want; of ecclesiastical corruptions breeding general disgust—never, wrote Erasmus, "were divines greater fools, or popes and prelates more worldly." The feuds and interventions that made Italy a bloody cockpit were teaching young Machiavelli the cynical lessons he was to put into *The Prince;* the miseries of the German poor were soon to explode in the Peasants' Revolt. Never was a new world more needed.

Its discovery seemed to happen suddenly, through the inspiration of one bold mariner, a former wool worker of Genoa named Columbus; but actually that discovery had long been in preparation, and many remarkable men had helped shape events toward it. People in the Middle Ages loved to repeat the legend of St. Brendan of Galway and his sixth-century voyage to a wonder-island in the Atlantic. Western Europe did not know the hard fact that Norse seamen in the ninth century, before the compass was invented, had groped their way to Iceland, then a little more than a century later had planted settlements on the Greenland shore, and had, about 1000 A.D., touched on the North American coast, or Vinland. But the notion that the world was round was gaining credence. Anyone who looked at the earth's shadow on the moon in eclipses could see, as Aristotle did, that it was circular. Classicists caught echoes of Eratosthenes' measurement of the circumference of the globe; and readers of Marco Polo's book took note that he described eastern Asia as opening not on vast marshes sheltering hideous monsters, as fable had it, but on the navigable Ocean Sea—perhaps the same one that washed Europe.

In the compilation on geography which the French bishop Pierre d'Ailly called the *Imago Mundi,* printed in the 1480's, the prelate quoted a bold passage by Roger Bacon using Aristotle's conjecture that a sea voyage of relatively few days might separate Spain from India. Fishermen told stories of far-off lands in the Atlantic sighted by seamen blown off their course. Visitors to Iceland (and Columbus was one of them) doubtless heard of the Greenland, perhaps even of the Vinland, voyages. In the very year 1492 the German geographer Martin Behaim shaped and mapped a globe to illustrate the earth. He and Columbus had never heard of each other, but they shared a common stock of ideas. And while ideas of geography advanced, so did the mariner's craft. When Portugal failed to capture Tangier in 1437, Prince Henry the Navigator decided that her future lay in the oceans. Brazil, Angola, and Goa are among the monuments to that decision. On Cape Saint Vincent he founded a splendid research institution, with expert geographers, astronomers, and mathematicians; he promoted trading companies which dealt in slaves, soap, and textiles; he bought gold dust fetched across Africa by caravans; and above all, he urged on his sea captains. Bartholomew Dias, when he rounded the Cape of Good Hope in 1488, proved that Prince Henry's dream of a direct sea route to India might become a profitable business reality; then Vasco da Gama, persevering to Calicut, brought back a rich cargo.

Christopher Columbus' moment in world history is one which familiarity can never deprive of its magic: the moment when, on the evening of October 11, 1492, sailors aboard Columbus' little ships saw a light flickering on what the next dawn disclosed as a coral island. Certain he must be near the mainland of Asia, he named the naked savages Indians. Surely not far away were Guinsay with its 12,000 stone bridges, and Zaitun with its hundred pepper ships a year! Nothing he saw shook his conviction that he was in the Orient: but not so the Hispanic sovereigns when he sailed back with his Indians, his gold, his spiny iguana, and his story of three mermaids he had seen. King John of Portugal leaped to the conclusion that the new lands belonged to his domains in Guinea, while Ferdinand and Isabella, along with the learned Peter Martyr, surmised he had found a wholly novel realm.

The bright dawn of discovery too soon gave way to the brazen noon of conquistadors eager for wealth and empire. Little by little the vast expanses of the Mundus Novus were unveiled, appealing to greed as well as nobler motives. The picture of white sails on blue seas, with one of the world's great enthusiasts peering from his deck, gives way to that of bearded, hard-faced men in helmets and cuirasses chasing natives with sword and musket. Balboa, a rough blade, smuggled himself into a provision cask, got to Colombia, captured an Indian chief, and carried off his daughter. The most poetic hour of his life came on September 25, 1513, when he climbed a hill on the Isthmus, stared westward, and then called up his men, who *Look'd at each other with a wild surmise—Silent, upon a peak in Darien.*

But this discoverer of the Pacific brought with him fierce dogs which he set on the Indians; and in his first set battle, as Peter Martyr records, drove the savages before him, hewing from one an arm, another a leg, a third his shoulder, and from others their heads. With him on the hill overlooking the

Pacific stood Francisco Pizarro. Later Pizarro, narrow, treacherous, and cruel, advanced in Peru slaying natives, even burning some alive; and after exacting from the Inca one of the greatest ransoms ever recorded—a large chamber filled nine feet deep with gold and another twice filled with silver—let the monarch be brutally strangled.

Yet it is little wonder that the bloodstained chronicle of the conquistadors, with its many romantic elements, kindled the imaginations of Irving and Prescott. Pizarro found in a mountain region of sublime grandeur a civilization, with its advanced agriculture, monotheistic religion, beautiful pottery and metalwork, traditional poetry, caste system, and rigid government headed by the Inca, like no other in the world. Mexico sheltered a less impressive but more flexible culture. To Bernal Díaz, the chronicler, the temples, palaces, gleaming causeways, lakes, and floating gardens of Mexico-Tenochtitlán seemed like "enchantments of the legend of Amadis." Here in the Abode of the War God, maintaining his rule of terror by human sacrifices on a colossal scale, Montezuma lorded it over a domain of 10,000 square miles. And what a succession of dramatic scenes the conquest by Cortés offers! His presentation to Montezuma at the entrance to the grand square; the seizure of Montezuma; the accidental discovery of the royal treasury; the rising of the Aztecs; the *noche triste* in which a third of the fleeing Spaniards were killed or taken; the return of Cortés with a larger army for the final subjugation of Mexico— few tales indeed hold so much pageantry and savage drama.

These were iron men, and equally stern was the stuff of their first French rivals far to the north. France, not Spain, was the leading power of sixteenth-century Europe. Superior in population, armed strength, and leadership, France could never accept the papal line which divided the New World between Spain and Portugal. Jacques Cartier, a sea rover from the Breton coast, which had long been a nursery of fishermen-explorers, began coasting the shores of Newfoundland, Anticosti, and the St. Lawrence several years before de Soto set forth. But his voyages came to no more permanent result than did the epic marches of de Soto and Coronado into the mid-continent. Upper North America, wrapped a great part of the year in snow and ice, with no allurements of gold and pearls, tobacco and chocolate, slumbered on. Yet Cartier's brave example was not lost. Men remembered it when a new century brought across the sea two greater men: Samuel de Champlain, the real founder of New France, and René Robert Cavelier, Sieur de La Salle, most brilliant of all the many French explorers.

Champlain, who at the beginning of the seventeenth century nursed the feeble colony at Quebec into vigor, was a singularly high-minded and statesmanlike leader. He fostered the heroic missionary activities of the Jesuits; he explored what he could of the interior, joining Huron war parties for that purpose; he did something to put agriculture and fur trading on a solid basis. The indomitable La Salle, threading the Great Lakes and descending the Mississippi, established France's claims to the West before he, like de Soto, found his grave there. He dreamed of a great empire for his country, and nobly did he labor to give his vision a basis.

The remarkable strength and enterprise of these men of Latin blood opened the New World; their courage, tenacity, and energy never failed. But New Spain and New France, for all the heroism they represented, were crippled by one common handicap—despotism. Not until a different people, under an aegis more flexible and free, reached its shores, would the new-found world yield to large-scale, permanent settlement.

ALLAN NEVINS

Breaking the Ocean Barrier

METROPOLITAN MUSEUM OF ART

Columbus, tall and freckled, had red hair that turned gray "from his labors." Sebastiano del Piombo's 1519 portrait shows him at about the age, 41, when he discovered America.

We departed on Friday, the 3d of August, in the year 1492, from the bar of Saltes, at 8 o'clock, and proceeded with a strong sea breeze until sunset. . . ." Thus begins the journal of the most famous voyage in history.

Long before Cristoforo Colombo wrote those words, Europeans had talked of sailing west to India. In 1474 the Florentine scholar Toscanelli urged King Alfonso V of Portugal to send his fleets to China by way of the Atlantic, and his map showing Cathay at the western end of that ocean greatly influenced Columbus. But what the idea needed most, Columbus himself brought to it—single-minded persistence, courage, superb seamanship, and a sense of divine mission.

After being shipwrecked off Portugal in 1476, Columbus worked as a chart maker in Lisbon, made a number of voyages, and became a master mariner, while the obsession of sailing westward grew. When he failed to interest the Portuguese in financing him, he left in 1485 to try his luck in Spain. There he underwent "seven years of great anxiety" trying to counteract fables of sea monsters and opinions by men like Aeneas Silvius, later Pope Pius II, that the frigid and torrid zones were uninhabitable, before he won the support of King Ferdinand and his red-haired Queen, Isabella.

When finally the *Niña, Pinta,* and Columbus' flagship the *Santa María* set out from Palos on August 3, 1492, the three caravels were as fateful for history as any fleet that ever sailed. But for the unsuspected continent lying athwart the Atlantic, it is unlikely that they would have returned, for no ship of the time could have made an unbroken run to Asia. Counting on a three-week voyage, he sailed from the Canaries on September 6, setting a course of "West; nothing to the north, nothing to the south." Despite floating plants, circling birds, and other signs of land, the crew was tense and restive by the fourth week. Then at 10 P.M. on October 11 Columbus saw a moving light, and four hours later the cry of *"Tierra! tierra!"* went up from the *Pinta.* A sailor, Rodrigo de Triana, had caught the first glimpse of an American beach gleaming white in the watchful moonlight.

Dawn flames the sky as Columbus is rowed to the Santa María *to begin his 1492 voyage. This painting shows his ships as conceived by the Flemish artist Andries van Eertvelt.*

NEW-YORK HISTORICAL SOCIETY

UFFIZI GALLERY, GIOVIANA COLLECTION

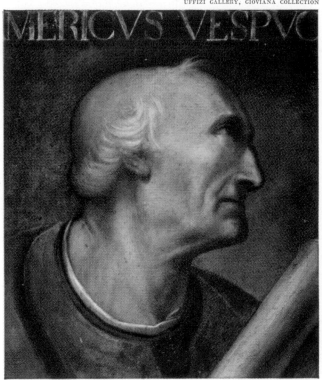

The Cabots

For over 200 years Sebastian Cabot (above) was considered the discoverer of North America. Then, in the eighteenth century, documents came to light showing that it was actually his father, John Cabot, who in 1497 touched on the New Found Land. At the same time as Columbus, John Cabot conceived of a western route, and his first voyage convinced him that he had found Asia's mainland. Not until his second journey a year later could he have realized that it was in reality a new continent; but whether he then returned to England is not known, for with this voyage he vanished from history.

John Cabot was a Venetian who, failing support in Spain and Portugal, had come to England with his sons and settled in Bristol. When, in 1509, Sebastian followed his father westward, he was well aware of the extent of the New World barrier, and he hoped to discover its hidden Northwest Passage. He sailed with two ships to Labrador and then north to Hudson's Strait, which he thought to be the passage. There, in the numbing cold and encroaching ice packs, his men mutinied and forced him to turn back; but before returning to Europe he skirted the North American coast as far south as Delaware. The 1544 map based on this journey supported England's claim to the lands he had seen.

Amerigo Vespucci

In two voyages to the hemisphere which now bears his name, Amerigo Vespucci sailed to Brazil and coasted more than 6,000 miles along the shores, almost to the southern limits of modern Argentina. Unlike Columbus, this gifted navigator and astronomer realized that South America was part of a new world, but he was the unfortunate victim of two fraudulent accounts of his voyages that clouded his reputation for 400 years. One of these claimed that Vespucci had preceded Columbus in sighting the American mainland, and the acceptance of this forgery by the German geographer Waldseemüller caused him to apply Amerigo's Latinized name to the southern continent of the New World.

Yet the name is not wholly amiss, for Vespucci first formulated the concept of an American continent. He was born in Florence and in his youth probably knew the aged geographer Toscanelli. As a business agent for the Medicis, he settled in Spain and finally went to sea as a middle-aged man. His first voyage, in 1499, was under the Spanish flag, his second, two years later, under the Portuguese; but unlike most other explorers his chief interest was scientific. He hoped to find the western strait, but also to test his lunar method of determining longitude and to discover the south polar star.

UFFIZI GALLERY, GIOVIANA COLLECTION

NEW-YORK HISTORICAL SOCIETY

Ferdinand Magellan

Of the great captains none overcame more handicaps than did Ferdinand Magellan, whose five ships left San Lúcar on September 20, 1519, in search of a Southwest Passage. His food supplies had been sabotaged, three of his five captains were plotting against him, and his eighteen-month voyage was an epic scarcely equaled before or since. Alone, against discouragement, sickness, mutinies, pitiless equatorial heat, and antarctic gales, he held his course over uncharted seas and reached the Philippines, only to be killed there by natives.

As a young man Magellan had taken part in the Portuguese campaigns for empire in East Africa and India and returned crippled and impoverished. Lacking favor with King Emanuel of Portugal, he finally left home and sailed on his great voyage under the Spanish flag. The indomitable captain went first to Brazil, followed the coast south, and while wintering in Patagonia put down a mutiny of the dissident captains. Underway again, he found the strait that bears his name and threaded his way to the blue-rimmed South Sea he called Pacific. Grimly pushing across its vastness, he finally reached the longitude of the Spice Islands, which he had once explored for Portugal, and became the first man to travel around the globe.

Giovanni da Verrazano

In 1524 the Florentine navigator Giovanni da Verrazano wrote from Dieppe to King Francis I of France, describing his recently completed transatlantic voyage. Long envious of the wealth Spain was drawing from the New World, Francis had sent Verrazano to claim a share of it for him, and the captain's letter provided him with the earliest existing description of the shores of North America.

Verrazano sailed from Madeira in the caravel *Dauphine*. After a 49-day voyage he reached the low-lying shores of North Carolina and from there followed the South Carolina coast in search of a harbor. Not finding one, he turned north, skirted the shores of Virginia and Maryland, and finally reached New York Bay, where he found the harbor dotted with the canoes of Indians. After a few days there he weighed anchor, and passing Long Island, came to what would later be Newport. Still heading north, he steered along the New England coast to Cape Breton, and from there sailed home. Verrazano's explorations aroused great enthusiasm. He had opened up the New World for France, even though it would be another decade before Cartier took the French ensign along that path; but Verrazano was not to share in the glory. Two years later he vanished forever.

Hernando de Soto stumbled onto the Mississippi in his quest for gold.

Men of Iron Push Inland

Except for what Cabeza de Vaca had seen, the continental interior of North America was unknown until the fourth decade of the sixteenth century, and it was still thought by many to be an appendage of Asia. Then began the independent but simultaneous explorations by de Soto and Coronado of the southerly parts of this area. The most extended ever undertaken in the United States, these two expeditions ranged from Florida to the borders of California and reached as far north as middle Kansas.

As a young man Hernando de Soto had been a lieutenant of Pizarro's. He made his fortune in Peru, and on returning to Spain could have spent the rest of his days as a wealthy noble, but restlessness drove him back to the New World. He was convinced that somewhere in Florida lay greater riches than Cortés or Pizarro had unearthed.

De Soto sailed from Spain with nine ships and over 600 men-at-arms. On arrival at Tampa Bay in May, 1539, nearly half the company had horses with them, but the quagmires and thickets of Florida trapped the mounted men, the natives were primitive and hostile, and almost at once the overburdened expedition found itself in difficulties. Fortunately for de Soto, he met a last survivor of Narváez's expedition who, after eleven years of living with the Indians, served as interpreter.

As de Soto pushed north through Florida and across Georgia, his ragged men were buoyed up by rumors of gold ahead. On the banks of the Savannah River he met the Indian princess of Cutifachiqui, who treated him most graciously, furnishing food and shelter for his men and presenting him with ropes of pearls. These pearls—probably a fresh-water variety—were abundant in the region, and those the princess gave de Soto were the only treasure he was to find. Many of the men wanted to stay on in that pleasant land and establish a colony, but the leader's mind was fixed on the golden north. Most ungallantly he decided to take the princess along as hostage.

De Soto used the natives for forced labor, and his policy of holding chiefs as hostages, in imitation of Cortés and Pizarro, here had the effect of arousing rather than subduing them. Soon he was battling infuriated Indians under the escaped chief Tuscaloosa, and though the Spaniards in winning slaughtered 2,000 Indians, it was a victory made disastrous by their own losses. An even worse disaster occurred at the village of Chicaça when the ambushed Spaniards lost most of their horses, clothing, and equipment, yet no catastrophe could shake de Soto's determination. He could have turned south to Pensacola Bay where supply ships were waiting for him. Instead he ordered his reluctant scarecrows to head north.

Years of privation and hopeless wandering lay ahead, and only half the men would ever return. Obsessed with a dream, de Soto pressed on, across wilderness and rivers, in summer heat and winter snows, through the Carolinas, over the Blue Ridge to Tennessee, down again through Georgia and Alabama. Finally, clothed in dented rusty armor, animal skins, and pampas grass, the Spaniards reached the Mississippi somewhere near its junction with the Arkansas River—the first white men ever to set eyes on its broad waters. Little as it meant to him, this was de Soto's most durable achievement.

He wintered across the river, but when in the spring of 1542 he attempted to send south for reinforcements, he found the barrier of mud and cane-brakes impassable. Discouragement finally over-whelmed him, and he died a few days later of a fever. His body, wrapped in a shroud weighted with sand, was dropped secretly into the river to keep it from the Indians.

At about the same time that de Soto and his men were pushing through what is now Georgia, another well-equipped expedition was being put together in Mexico. As governor of that land's New Galicia, Francisco Vásquez de Coronado had heard of the legendary Seven Cities of Cibola off to the north, whose inhabitants wore emeralds and chains of gold. Cabeza de Vaca's recent account had reinforced such tales, and a rather devious priest, Fray Marcos de Niza, reported to Coronado that he had actually seen one of the Seven Cities.

Spurred by this, Coronado in 1540 assembled 225 horsemen—soldiers of fortune and cadets of the Spanish nobility—as well as 60 foot soldiers, servants, and 1,000 Indian allies. As the imposing army stepped off toward the north, the leader was out in front, sparkling in gilt armor and casque.

The first city they saw turned out to be a pueblo settlement occupied by Zuñis; the others merely adobe villages. Although these could be, and were, conquered and used to provide winter shelter, they provided little else.

Reluctant to forgo his dream, Coronado listened to an Indian captive called "The Turk" who told him of a far-off city called Quivira, built of gold, where the trees were hung with little golden bells, where jugs and bowls were made of gold. This gilded illusion would take Coronado across Arizona, New Mexico, the Texas Panhandle, Oklahoma, and to the geographical center of the United States in Kansas. His scout detachments would discover the Grand Canyon and the Colorado River, while he himself would cross the Great Plains amongst herds of buffalo, and in the end discover and pacify the chief Indian towns and tribes of the Southwest.

However, the gold-and-silver Quivira pursued so elusively across river and prairie proved in reality to be nothing but a shabby cabin settlement of the Kansas Wichita tribe, and the disillusioned Coronado lacked de Soto's strength of mind. Having been hurt in a fall from his horse, he exaggerated his injuries as an excuse to give up the search he had ceased to believe in, and returned to Mexico in the summer of 1542 empty-handed, the gilt worn off both his armor and his reputation.

The Long Walk

John White's water color of a Florida warrior was painted about 1585. Ingram thought the ornaments worn by the Indians were gold.

The marathon North American traveler in the sixteenth century was without question the English sailor David Ingram, who in 1568 with two companions walked over 3,000 miles from the Gulf of Mexico to St. John in New Brunswick. Although he never stayed more than three or four days in any one place, his journey took him almost a year. Today it is not possible to trace his exact route, but he may have crossed the coastal prairies of Texas and Louisiana and he must also have crossed Mississippi, Alabama, and Georgia. In all probability he kept to the east of the Appalachian chain, for in the account he later wrote of his travels he mentioned the abundance of pearls—such as de Soto had found in Georgia—and his description of rivers "some foure . . . some eight, some tenne miles over" could only apply to the Maryland and Delaware country. At some point he headed for Maine, hugging the indented shore line, since he had met natives who indicated to him by signs and drawings that there were ships on that coast. When he failed to sight any, he finished his journey as he had begun it, on foot.

Ingram and his companions were seamen aboard the *Minion* on John Hawkins' third expedition to the Indies. The fleet of six ships, one of which, the *Judith,* was commanded by Francis Drake, had been engaged in bringing Negroes from the African coast to sell in the South American market. As usual, Hawkins combined privateering with trade, but this voyage turned unlucky. In an engagement with the Spanish fleet off Vera Cruz the commander lost four of his ships, including his own flagship, and was forced to transfer himself and his men to the *Minion.* Drake's *Judith,* the only other ship to escape, sailed back to England, leaving the overloaded and underprovisioned *Minion* alone in the Gulf of Mexico.

Rather than starve at sea, a number of the men preferred to take their chances with savages and Spaniards on land. Hawkins landed those who wanted to leave—about half the men, 114 in all—on the shore thirty miles north of Tampico.

Two men drowned in the surf landing and the next day eight more were killed by raiding Indians, who stripped the others of their clothes, but let them go free. The survivors then split up, one group heading south to the secure certainty of Spanish captivity, the other making for the unknown north. After a day or so some two dozen of the northern party became alarmed at the emptiness ahead of them and turned back. Eventually both southern groups were taken prisoner by the Spaniards and turned over to the officers of the Inquisition in Mexico City.

Ingram, with his companions Richard Browne, Richard Twide, and about twenty others, continued north along the coast. Browne and Twide finished the hike with Ingram, but the rest—whether they attached themselves to the Indians or died in the wilderness—were never heard of again.

It was not until a dozen years after his return to England that Ingram prepared a brief account of his travels for a royal commission engaged in collecting sundry information about the New World. An unlettered man, he did not express himself easily, but his narrative does provide a few glimpses into life in the American wilderness.

He mentions the parrots and red-feathered flamingos, the rabbits, the deer, the foxes, and buffalo with "eares like a Blood hound." Unlike later travelers, he fails to mention snakes or mosquitoes, but notes the summer lightning and the tossing storms of the autumn equinox in a passing sentence. What fear or hope he felt in the wilderness, what he suffered and whether he sometimes regretted not having turned south with the others, we shall never know. He scarcely mentions his companions. The three men dauntlessly trudging north through the forests and along the Indian trails escape us.

In his years at sea Ingram had touched on the coasts of Africa and South America, and the impressions of those regions had in the placid atmosphere of the English homeland become overlaid and combined with his fading memories of North America. In his report he introduces penguins and white bears to the Carolinas, elephants and leopards to some indeterminate region. Overawed by the presence of officials like Sir Humphrey Gilbert and anxious to please them, Ingram passed on old forecastle tales which he doubtless considered true, of treasures of gold, a "rich Citie, a mile and a halfe long," and native kings wearing four-inch rubies and carried in chairs of crystal and gold.

Richard Hakluyt published Ingram's account in the first edition of his *Principall Navigations, Voiages and Discoveries of the English Nation* in 1589. But the elephants and penguins, sedan chairs, and nuggets of gold "as big as a mans fist" lying in the rivers were, on consideration, too much for the erudite stay-at-home geographer, who suppressed any mention of Ingram in his subsequent editions.

There is little of the first person in Ingram's narrative. What he was trying to do, perhaps on instructions from the commissioners, was to describe in as much detail as he could the ways and habits of the Indians. He deals briefly with their ceremonies, their music and dances, the relations between the sexes, the size and shape of their dwellings, their religion and their attitudes toward death. The southern Indians he found short, olive-skinned, and naked, those of the north more tawny and with clothing of furs. He noticed the feathered headdresses, the shaved heads, and the copper bracelet ornaments that he took for gold. Those tribes with whom he came in contact abhorred the cannibal Indians, and he speaks of the latter as having teeth like dogs. The petty chiefs he calls kings, and the villages become enlarged by time to cities. He tells of the Indians making fire by rubbing two sticks together, of playing on trumpets made from the teeth of animals. His is perhaps the first English mention of corn on the cob, "a kinde of Graine, the eare whereof is as big as the wrist

of a mans arm." Some of the Indians worshiped a devil named Coluchio, and he claims that he and Richard Browne and Richard Twide once met this Coluchio "with very great eyes like a blacke Calfe," and that it fled at the name of the Trinity.

Ingram's awkward sentences give only hints. The ground was "most excellent, fertile and pleasant." There were "great and huge woods of sundry kind of trees . . . all kinde of flowers, as Roses, and Gilleflowers," and "Vines which beare Grapes as big as a mans thumbe."

He must then have seen the bunches of wild grapes tangling the thickets, traced their autumn scent after the first frost when the leaves had withered. In the dove-gray, striated landscape of Essex he remembered the brightness of American wild flowers like gillyflowers, whose names he had never known. Even when the details had become lost, he recalled the red-brown rivers of the south, the hard granite coast line of Maine, and the vast intermediate land across which he had trudged through all four seasons of the year in that wondrous land across the sea.

White painted not only the Indians, but the flora and fauna of the New World as well. Like Ingram, he was particularly impressed by the flamingo.

HUNTINGTON LIBRARY; COURTESY *Life*

A French Foothold

By the time Jacques Cartier made his first voyage to Canadian North America in 1534, the Newfoundland Banks were common ground for European fishermen. But the Frenchman's interest lay in the great gulf beyond, which might prove to be the elusive Northwest Passage.

Cartier's initial voyage was not much more than a reconnaissance for King Francis I, who was eager to set up a New France beyond the Atlantic. Cartier explored as far as the mouth of the St. Lawrence and planted a cross at Gaspé.

On his second voyage the following year, with three ships and 112 men, he intended to take possession of the lands along the vast unknown river in the name of France and make preparations for a permanent settlement. This time he sailed up the St. Lawrence as far as the Island of Orleans. When Indians from the village of Stadacona—later Quebec—told him of a large settlement called Hochelaga farther up the river, he set out for there with some of his men. After eight days he reached the palisaded wooden town below a broad hill that would later be the site of Montreal. He was received almost devoutly, the Indians bringing their sick for him to touch.

The crew he left behind at Stadacona built a stockaded fort, and there Cartier and his men spent their first Canadian winter in a cold and under conditions they had never believed possible. The Indians, at first friendly, turned distant and hostile; a November cold wave bound the ships in ice; and by midwinter most of the French were down with scurvy. Twenty-five of them died of it, and when the ice broke, the survivors sailed back, abandoning one ship for lack of men to handle her.

Cartier made his third voyage six years later, leading an advance party of colonists organized by the Sieur de Roberval. He cleared some land and built a fort called Charlesbourg-Royal just above Quebec, but discouraged by the winter and the jailbird quality of most of his colonists, he gave up the project and returned to France.

This striking 1547 French map, in which north is at bottom, pictures Cartier's landing on Labrador in 1534. Included in the pastoral scene are the explorer (wearing a cloak), his crew, a priest, and, improbably, several ladies.

Champlain's New France

It was two generations after Cartier's abortive attempt at resettlement before another Frenchman probed the length of the St. Lawrence. Some fur traders may have reached the Saguenay River, but it was 1603 when Samuel de Champlain, retracing Cartier's route by canoe, passed the island of Montreal. Nothing remained of Hochelaga or of the tribes that had then lived in the region, and at the Lachine Rapids—"the passage to China"—just beyond Montreal he turned back reluctantly, not to appear on the St. Lawrence again for another five years.

Samuel de Champlain, soldier, sailor, and explorer, became the first Canadian. He was to make eight more voyages between New France and the mother country, but from the moment he first saw it his allegiance was to the land he adopted.

In 1608, under the patronage of the Sieur de Monts, whose previous colonial efforts had misfired, Champlain set sail again for the St. Lawrence with the idea of establishing an upriver colony and fur-trading post. His old soldier's eye recognized the formidable potential of Cape Diamond, the future citadel, and at its base he established his little settlement. So was Quebec founded, the first continuously occupied settlement north of Florida.

With the Indians of the vicinity, the Montagnais, the Algonquins, and the more distant Hurons, Champlain formed an alliance both natural and necessary for the fur trade. It was this alliance that led him with a war party the next summer against the Iroquois, following the St. Lawrence and Richelieu rivers to the lake which now bears his name. The party found the Iroquois confidently encamped on a promontory near Ticonderoga, and Champlain with two armed companions kept out of sight until the opposing battle lines had advanced within arrow shot. Then suddenly he stepped forward in plumed casque and breastplate to confront the astonished enemy. Leveling his arquebus, he fired at the three leading chiefs, killing two of them. Shattered by the man-thunder, the Iroquois broke and fled; but this casual victory, which made relentless enemies of the most redoubtable of the Indian natives, cast ominous shadows into the French future.

PRINT DIVISION, N.Y. PUBLIC LIBRARY

Explorer, soldier, colonizer, Samuel de Champlain laid the cornerstone of France's empire in North America. In 1608 he founded the great fur-trading center of Quebec, shown in the background of this 19th-century retrospective portrait.

Traveling on foot and by canoe, Champlain in his indefatigable journeys explored Lake Ontario, Lake Erie, and Georgian Bay of Lake Huron. On three earlier sailing expeditions he had charted the New England coast from Passamaquoddy Bay, Mount Desert, and the mouth of the Penobscot to Cape Ann, Boston Harbor, and Cape Cod. He blazed the trails, and in his moccasined steps came the *coureurs de bois.*

In 1628 the Company of One Hundred Associates, under Richelieu's direction, endeavored to build up Quebec by sending on a large flotilla of supplies and settlers. Unfortunately the flotilla was captured by a hostile English fleet under Captain David Kirk, who the following spring took possession of the powerless Quebec citadel. Champlain, his dream broken, was taken to England.

When peace restored Quebec to France, Champlain, at the age of 66, returned undiscouraged to reconstruct his tiny colony. Full of plans for the future and for attacking the encroachments of the Iroquois, the English, and the Dutch, he died of a stroke two years later.

Below, the French employ siege tactics against a strong Iroquois fort near Lake Oneida in 1615. Receiving no effective help from their Huron allies, however, they were driven off. Champlain was wounded, and on the retreat suffered severely "while being carried bound and pinioned on the back of one of our savages."

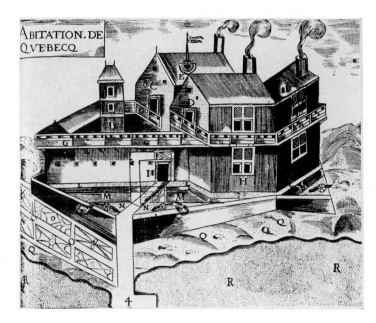

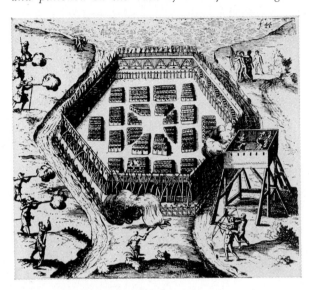

Champlain built the fortified Abitation of Quebec (above) at the foot of Cape Diamond. After suppressing a mutiny, the leader of which "had his head put on a pike in our fort, as an example to those who remained," Champlain saw scurvy kill 20 of his 28 colonists the first winter. Below, Champlain, at center, helps crush an Iroquois force at Ticonderoga in 1609. The French earned the lasting enmity of the Iroquois by siding with their traditional enemies, the Algonquins and Hurons. The engravings on this page are taken from Champlain's Voyages.

Black-Gowns in the Wilderness

Massive Father Jean de Brébeuf, best-loved of the Canadian Jesuit missionaries, once looked up and saw a great cross in the sky, "large enough," he remarked forebodingly, "to crucify us all." It was a vision that anticipated his own martyrdom and the deaths of so many of his associates at the hands of the implacable Iroquois.

Unostentatious as was the arrival of the Jesuits in Quebec, they brought to this new world of self-seeking a disinterested zeal that was almost unique. Through love of God they would save the souls of the ranging savages, convert and baptize them in the true faith, and turn their war lust to peaceful ways. Adaptable as their order itself, they were prepared to learn the Indians' language, live in their villages, share their customs, and when death came to bear up with a fortitude even the Iroquois would admire.

The first missions to the Huron country achieved merely a superficial toleration, and the black-robed priests were often tormented, accused of sorcery, or threatened with death. Eventually, however, they established five missions and later made considerable progress in taming the Hurons' belligerency and in guiding them to a more settled agricultural life. What the fathers hoped and prayed for was a vast area of settled Indians living in peace with each other and loyal to Church and Crown.

Unfortunately for the Jesuits, they would be forever plagued by the echo of Champlain's arquebus. The long-memoried Iroquois, accustomed now to gunfire and provided with their own guns by the accommodating Dutch, were prepared to take a final vengeance on their blood-enemies. In 1649 they scattered and destroyed the Huron nation, carrying off Father Brébeuf and his frail companion Father Lalemant to the slow-torture death that was the fate of any missionary the Iroquois captured.

HOUSE OF THE IMMACULATE CONCEPTION, MONTREAL

Jesuit Father Jean de Brébeuf (left) struggled selflessly, but with little success, to Christianize the Five Nations. Finally, in 1649, Brébeuf and his companion, Father Lalemant, were captured and killed by the Iroquois.

The 1664 composite engraving at right shows the martyrdom of the Jesuits in New France at the hands of the Iroquois. The figure kneeling at left is Father Jogues; tied to stakes at center are Fathers Lalemant and Brébeuf.

Black-Gowns were much favored by the Five Nations for ceremonial burning.

Sometimes with Indian waywardness they would spare a captive, such as Father Isaac Jogues who was seized by an Iroquois war party while on a missionary journey to the Hurons. Few men have ever exceeded the fortitude of Father Jogues, who after being tortured and mutilated was allowed to live on sufferance in a Mohawk village. There, impervious to the threat of death, he baptized children, prisoners, and the dying and did his best to convert his captors. Finally managing to escape with the help of a Dutch trader, he reached France where the Queen herself on meeting him kissed his mutilated hands.

Early the next year he returned to Montreal and was sent to negotiate with the Mohawks over a tentative peace proposal and to found a mission in their country. He returned safely, but on his second visit the fickle Indian mood had changed. He was ambushed and axed as he stooped to enter a chief's lodge. Like Jean de Brébeuf, he had long had a premonition of his fate.

DU CREUX, *Historiae Canadensis*, 1664

Marquette and Jolliet

From time to time the western Indians brought news of "the great river named Messippi" to the Jesuits, and in 1672 Father Jacques Marquette joined the young cartographer Louis Jolliet, who had been commissioned by the governor to organize the first expedition in search of it and of the still nebulous passage to China. The two set out from Michilimackinac in the spring with two canoes and five *voyageurs* and proceeded up the Fox River until they reached the Mascouten and Miami villages at the end of the then known route. Guided over the portage to the Wisconsin River, they journeyed on for ten days before glimpsing the Mississippi near the present Prairie du Chien.

The great river they floated down was smooth and gentle, and the Indian tribes they encountered were friendly. When they reached the junction with the Missouri, the clarity of the river was shattered in that surging muddy current, and as they held their course the heavy southern summer enveloped them with stagnant air and swarms of insects.

Near the mouth of the Arkansas, where the river widened, they met some Quapaws who told them that the sea was ten days away, but that if they went on they would encounter unfriendly tribes and even less friendly Spaniards. Having proved to their satisfaction that the Mississippi entered the Gulf of Mexico, the two Frenchmen turned back, following the Illinois branch this time until they reached the mission at Green Bay. The first white men to explore the Father of Waters had in four months made a voyage of 2,500 miles.

27

ROUEN LIBRARY

Sieur de La Salle

An Inspired Explorer
Discovers
the Key to Empire

It was left for René Robert Cavelier, Sieur de La Salle, nine years after Marquette and Jolliet, to follow the course of the Mississippi to its mouth. La Salle had long been haunted by that continental river, not merely as a waterway to be explored, but as the key to a western empire. He knew that if a chain of French forts could be erected along its length, the English and the Spanish seaboard settlements would be sealed off and France would rule the continental interior.

To dominate the Mississippi watershed became his passionate goal. For it he willingly sacrificed his time, his career, his fortune, and the fortunes of his relatives and friends. Nothing could hold back this dynamic, intrepid man who seemed almost totally undisturbed by accidents and misfortunes.

In the winter of 1681–82 he set off from Fort Miamis on Lake Michigan for the Mississippi with a flotilla of a dozen canoes, a number of Indians, and 23 Frenchmen.

It was April by the time he reached the triple branching of the delta. Here he divided his flotilla into three groups, each following a separate channel until they could meet together in the Gulf of Mexico. There on that shore La Salle erected a cross with the royal arms, claiming the river and all the western country for France. While on his way to the mouth of the Mississippi on a later expedition, he was ambushed and shot by his own men, a victim of his indomitable ambition.

AMERICAN MUSEUM OF NATURAL HISTORY

HENNEPIN, *New Discovery*, 1698

Left, the vanguard of La Salle's first exploring party leaves Fort Frontenac in 1678 to hazard Lake Ontario. La Salle (scarlet cloak) followed with the main body. Above, the ill-fated French explorer and his colonists land on the coast of the Gulf of Mexico in 1685, far west of their Mississippi goal.

OVERLEAF: *In 1682 La Salle visited the Taensa Indians near present-day Natchez. This painting and the one at left are the work of George Catlin.*

AMERICAN MUSEUM OF NATURAL HISTORY

This fanciful primitive painting, done about 1800, shows Columbus landing in the Bahamas.

THE
EUROPEAN
IMAGE
OF AMERICA

BIBLIOTHÈQUE NATIONALE

The Great Khan's palace, from a 14th-century manuscript on Marco Polo's travels.

For nearly two millenniums legends of sea monsters, fabulous islands, and the world's precipitous edge dominated European thinking about the Ocean Sea to the west. Only a few men, like Aristotle, had suspected that those waters might lead to Asia, whose gold and gems, silks and spices, Marco Polo described so alluringly upon his return from Cathay in 1295. No one, except possibly the Norsemen, dreamed that whole continents obstructed the westward passage —not even Columbus, who died convinced that he had found the western approach to Japan. With realization that this was actually a bright new land came Europe's sudden awakening to its opportunities. To satisfy the tremendous curiosity of stay-at-homes, reports and pictures, based more on fancy than on fact, poured from the pens of authors and artists, forming the first intriguing image of America. These illustrations served people of the time as news photograph, map, advertisement, and explorers' boast. Eventually America became the subject of elaborate allegories, filled with the symbols of native grandeur, untold wealth, and figments of the imagination in every conceivable form. Whether fact or fancy, it scarcely seemed to matter. What strife-torn Europe saw and marveled at in these pictures was a bright promise that bolstered men's courage for the perilous voyage across the Ocean Sea.

Beyond the Ocean Sea

NATIONALBIBLIOTHEK, VIENNA

*adbuiar. defcendenfau ad hiemale folfticiu. fimilt-
tade fac auftlib? h ignozantef pagani. tra illa uo
cant feam. 1 beata q̃ tale miraclm pfter mortalib?
Itaq; rex danor̃ e multis aliis reftat÷ hibi ftinge
fit in fuedia 1 i noruegia æ i ceris q̃ ibi ft̃ infulis.,
Preta una adhuc regione recitauit a multis i
eo repta oceano q̃ dr̃ winland. eo q̃d ibi uitef fpon
te nafcant̃ uinu optimu ferentef. fla 1 fruges ibi
n̄ feminataf habundare n̄ fabulofa opinione f; eta
epim̃relatione danor.   Ite nob retulit be
memorie pontifex adalbt̃ i dieb̃ an deceffouf fui
q̃fda nobilef de frefia uittof cã puagandi marifi*

About 1000 A.D., according to the Norse sagas, Leif Ericson explored the North American coast. The first known mention of Vinland, a land of wild grapevines and self-sown wheat, appears in the seventh line of this 11th-century manuscript (above) by Adam of Bremen.

Sometime before 1492 Columbus received a chart made by the Florentine physician Toscanelli which showed an abbreviated Atlantic, unbroken between Europe and Cipangu (Japan) except by islands such as the Azores and mythical St. Brendan's. This long-lost map, reconstructed below, encouraged Columbus to sail west to lands "most fertile in gold."

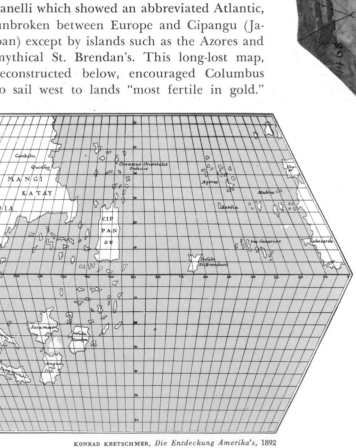

KONRAD KRETSCHMER, *Die Entdeckung Amerika's*, 1892

At the extreme left of this 1468 chart, far out in the Atlantic, Majorcan mapmaker Roselli drew two islands—Antilia in red, and Atanaga in green—suggesting knowledge of land to the west. Europe's towered cities, royal house flags, and the green Alps are at the top. Below is the coast of Africa, with its snake-like Atlas Mountains, nomad tents, and a bright Red Sea, appropriately parted for Moses (lower right).

I R C V

ra Incognita

ā Can Emperator de lo̅
ro̅ q̄ se intitula e̅rey d̅
e̅s y sañor delos sennor
la 2. Nº 15

a en.1500.milla c̅a̅
latras y gente de̅bu̅
stributario tiene
la a causa q̄ no
el rey dsta isla
erto de toro hech
palatio son to=
rā Can ayda=
lla una grāde
nente locu̅eta

Esta tierra fue descubierta
porel marques̅ de̅ valle
de guaxa don hernando
cortes

Golpho dela nueua españa.

In this North American section of Sebastian Cabot's 1544 world map, an angry leopard and some Indians fill

BIBLIOTHEQUE NATIONALE

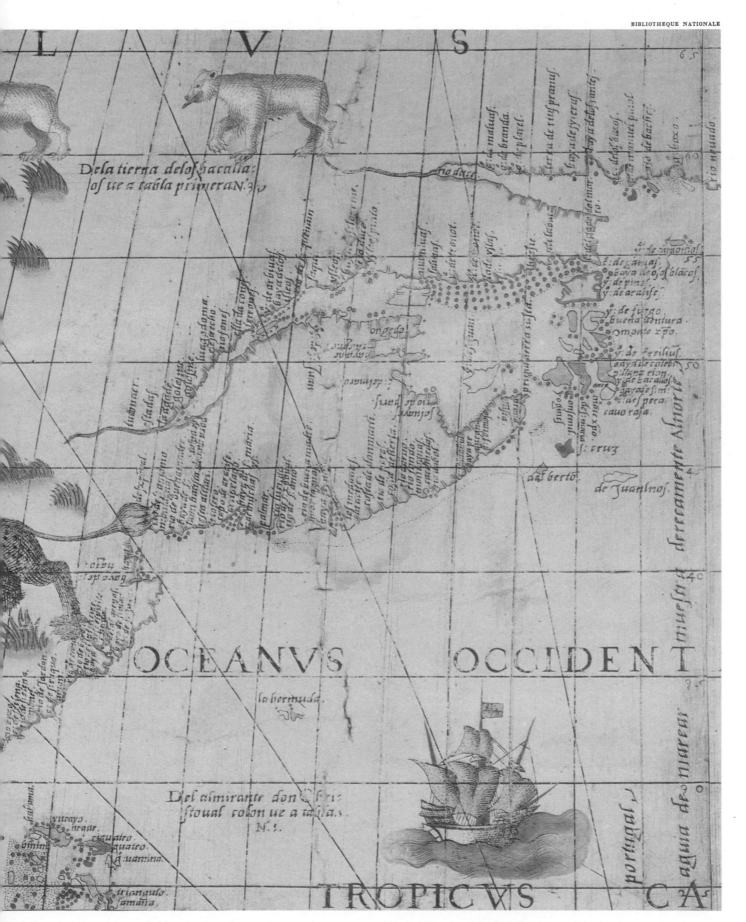

nknown territory. John Cabot's 1497 landfall at Cape Breton is indicated at upper right as "prima terra vista."

Utopian Dreams

"On the borders of Canada" lived this unicorn, according to a 1673 account. It had "black eyes and a deer's neck: it feeds in the nearest wilderness."

Europeans saw the American wilderness as a fertile field for the conversion of savages to Christianity, as shown in this detail from a 1546 French map.

Explorer Amerigo Vespucci's tales inspired Sir Thomas More's *Utopia,* about a mythical island off South America (above), where peace and prosperity reigned.

STOKES COLLECTION, N.Y. PUBLIC LIBRARY

NEW-YORK HISTORICAL SOCIETY

An 18th-century German artist confused East and West Indies in his engraving of America (above), combining elephant and pagoda with his version of Indians.

At left, an Indian chief disgusted by the greed of squabbling conquistadors knocks down the scales weighing his tribute of gold. This wry comment on the Spanish conquest was engraved by de Bry about 1600.

RESERVE DIVISION, N.Y. PUBLIC LIBRARY

A new land meant a new set of opportunities for material reward, and the cartouche below from a Dutch map of about 1650 shows traders bargaining with Indians for furs, gold ingots, and casks of tobacco.

FRANS HALSMUSEUM

The 16th-century Dutchman Jan Mostaert probably based this painting on reports of Coronado's expedition through America's Southwest. The armored Spanish column and fleet (extreme right) are accurate, but the naked savages, fauna, landscape, and the caged hermit (above right, in the fanciful pueblo) are figments of his imagination.

OVERLEAF: When Pierre Descelier prepared a world map for the French court in 1546, he included Cartier's great discoveries in a whale-shaped North American continent. In his map south is at the top, and the St. Lawrence is the only prominent river. Decorative details, darkened by age, and scalloped coasts disguise geographical guesses.

TROPIQVE DE CANCER:

LA MER OCCEANE:

MER DESPAIGNE:

MER DE FRANCE:

CANADA

ISLAND:

QVE:

LE DESTROECT DV LABOVREVR

JOHN RYLANDS LIBRARY, MANCHESTER, ENGLAND

The Fascinating Red Man

In 1662 the Duc de Guise dressed for a French court pageant as an "American king" (above) with dragon-skin armor, feathered headdress, and gem-studded scimitar.

The symbol of America in allegorical engravings was a female Indian with feathers and kilts, who, in this 18th-century example, brandishes a spear ferociously.

Below left, a 1505 German woodcut illustrates Vespucci's tales of cannibalism. The other woodcut is the first known version of Columbus' 1492 landing.

STOKES COLLECTION, N.Y. PUBLIC LIBRARY

RESERVE DIVISION, N.Y. PUBLIC LIBRARY

Jacques Le Moyne painted the first eyewitness view of Indians (above) on a 1564 expedition to Florida. He found a column with French arms, planted in 1562, wreathed with flowers, worshiped by the natives.

A 16th-century Dutch artist captioned his engraving at left: "Cruel America has devoured many men; she produces gold, is skilled with bow and tames parakeets."

OVERLEAF: America's vitality and violence fill this 18th-century allegorical painting by Tiepolo, which adorns the ceiling of a German palace. Symbolic America, buxom and befeathered, straddles a Mississippi crocodile. Around her swarm people from every country, and a cornucopia overflows with exotic fruits.

NEW YORK HISTORICAL SOCIETY

OVERLEAF: WURZBURG RESIDENZ; COURTESY HIRMER VERLAG MUNCHEN

FOOTHOLDS OF THE FOREST

A S DESPOTISM crippled the colonies of New Spain and New France, so freedom lent vigor to the pioneer communities that grew into the United States. And when England moved into America, the basis of colonization shifted from conquest to trade. Small as the English population was compared with the French and Spanish, it had three tremendous advantages in the race ahead. Its large body of seafarers gave it naval power; its merchant adventurers and other traders fostered industry at home and commerce overseas; and its spirit of individual enterprise, unfettered initiative, and democratic good nature gave strength to those frontier communities that survived the first hard years. These advantages are symbolized by three striking figures: Drake the captain, Hakluyt the promoter, Raleigh the colonizer.

Sir Francis Drake might seem at first blush as flamboyant an adventurer as any of the conquistadors. We see him climbing a tall tree in Panama to be the first Briton to descry both oceans at once; capturing Nombre de Dios despite a severe leg wound that filled his footprints with blood; dining on shipboard to the music of violins and carrying with him two artists who pictured in colors the coasts he traversed; circumnavigating the world, to be knighted by Queen Elizabeth on the deck of his treasure-laden *Golden Hind;* playing out his game of bowls on Plymouth Hoe before putting off to rout the Armada; and still a fighter, dying on the Spanish Main. But this royal admiral was far more than an adventurer. He disciplined the Navy to a fine edge; he revolutionized sea warfare by the use of cannon fired not from decks but from rows of portholes; and he taught unity by ordering his officers "to hale and draw with the mariners."

But the Navy would have been worthless without commerce, and commerce rested on British industrial enterprise. Richard Hakluyt made it his task to inspire the English to find realms for trade and settlement in the newly discovered parts of the globe. His fascinating collection of voyages explains why the Muscovy Company, Levant Company, East India Company, and later the Hudson's Bay Company spread English goods around the world, why peaceable English traffickers first carried the nation's fame to the Mogul in Agra and the Tsar in Moscow. One main object of British colonization was to develop overseas populations which would sell raw materials to the homeland and buy finished wares—a basic principle of mercantilism. Hakluyt's effective propaganda for expansion was no mere pounds-and-pence affair. He appealed to love of adventure, pride in England's glory, and other ideal aims, his pages leading men to consider peril, poetry, and profits all at once.

Most important of all was the strong English impulse toward nation-founding embodied in Sir Walter Raleigh. The time was ripe. Both capital and labor had become fairly fluid in the England of late Tudor times. Belted by salt water, the country had suffered less from wars than its continental neighbors and had no need for great standing armies. Rising living costs had made many people restless; the fencing-in of common lands and the expan-

Sir Walter Raleigh, champion of an English America.

sion of sheep raising drove sturdy young yeomen from the soil; younger sons of the gentry looked about, as always, for new employment; and the patriotism that Shakespeare expressed so well made men burn to augment England's power. The increase of unemployed men, "swarms of idle persons," gave rise to the belief that outlets must be found for a surplus population. On all this Raleigh hoped to build.

Tall, handsome, vivid, eloquent, as good at writing as at fighting, Raleigh belonged both to the old age of gentlemen-adventurers and the new age of practical colonizers. Two of his agents explored the shores which were named Virginia in honor of Elizabeth, the Virgin Queen. It was Raleigh who destroyed the nest of Spanish and Italian pirates on the coast of Ireland; who gained credit for bringing the potato to England and for popularizing the use of tobacco; who, penning good poetry of his own, befriended Christopher Marlowe and was respectfully called "The Shepherd of the Ocean" by Spenser; who wrote a classic book on his exploration of Guiana, where the British flag yet waves; who developed the fish trade between Newfoundland and the Channel Islands; and who, above all, laid the first imaginative plans for peopling America. With less Spanish and Indian hostility, more capital, and better luck, the romantic appeal of these plans might have been matched by quick practical success.

The tale of the colony of Roanoke and the three shiploads of men, women, and children whom Raleigh's friend John White took thither in 1587 ends in mystery. Governor White went home for supplies, to be delayed for three years by the Spanish war; and few scenes in our early annals are as pathetic as that of his return. He stands looking about the desolate fort, thinking of his favorite daughter Eleanor Dare and her baby Virginia; his trumpeter sounds the old English calls, one by one, but the wind and waves alone reply. Raleigh died on the scaffold in 1618, a victim of James I's meanness; but before he felt the axe, he knew that English settlement in Virginia was finally a success, for in that year Jamestown had 600 people. He had written Sir Robert Cecil about America, "I shall yet live to see it an Englishe nation," and so he did.

It was on practical business principles, colonizing zeal, and freedom that Jamestown, Plymouth, and Massachusetts Bay built and grew, sheltered by the navy that the Tudors had made the strongest in history. Virginia, initially a joint-stock undertaking in which any colonist might buy his share by personal service, prized free enterprise; and while the Virginia settlement took root under the stern practical control of Captain John Smith and the yet sterner laws of Sir Thomas Gates, its real prosperity began when liberal Sir Edwin Sandys and others instituted individual ownership of land and other property. The Massachusetts colonies prized both religious liberty (for themselves) and free enterprise, the Pilgrims soon shaking themselves free of communal economic controls. All the settlements knew they must trade or die, and in their very beginnings at Plymouth the Pilgrims sent home a vessel laden with good clapboard. Virginia shipped 40,000 pounds of tobacco to England in 1620 and two years later 60,000.

Wherever Englishmen settled, a scene of industry appeared, and everywhere—almost immediately—they looked westward. The Virginians and later the Marylanders moved inland up the rivers and tributary creeks, hewing down the forest, establishing tobacco plantations or farms of wheat and corn, and creating county governments for their loose, townless plantations. The Massachusetts folk pushed westward in more compact fashion, planting town after town, each with its Congregational church, town meeting, and well-drilled defenders; but they also threw out daughter colonies to greater distances, like the groups that followed Thomas Hooker to the Connecticut Valley, alleging the need of their cattle for more room, the exceptional fertility of the soil, and "the strong bent of their spirits to remove thither." Partly to accommodate surplus colonists in Barbados and the Bahamas, themselves looking westward, English patentees founded the Carolinas in the 1660's. Agriculture and stock-growing thrived; furnaces, iron mills, and workshops sprang up; the New England coast became lined with shipyards whose vessels made a triangular trade with Britain and the West Indies profitable.

Freedom had a many-sided meaning in these colonies. Every man was free to hew out his own estate by industry, enterprise, and speculation. Lord Baltimore, a loyal adherent of the Stuarts, gained a feudal grant of the Maryland country that his fellow Catholics might freely follow their faith. Roger Williams stood for freedom in all things and made Rhode Island a somewhat unruly home of libertarianism. To abate the persecution of those followers of the Inner Light, the Quakers, William Penn set up his model commonwealth in a great proprietary grant. The offer of land, religious toleration, and political freedom which he published in Dutch, French, and German brought him 10,000 thrifty settlers within a decade who soon flooded the West India markets with their bread and beer. Every colony, before long, had its own legislature with a stubbornly independent popular assembly, the precedents of political freedom stretching back to the Mayflower Compact and the Virginia burgesses of 1619.

It was inevitable that colonies so well nurtured by freedom, social democracy, and unfettered individual enterprise should soon obliterate rivals in their midst. The Swedes who had settled on the lower Delaware were simply absorbed by their powerful neighbors. The Dutch who had taken the western shores of Long Island and the whole Hudson Valley posed a more difficult problem, but one that was quickly solved by a combination of the English Navy and troops from the English colonies.

All the virtues of the Walloons and Dutch, all the zeal of the Dutch West India Company, were set at naught by the absolutism which fettered New Amsterdam. A series of despotic governors enforced the most arbitrary decrees. They imposed commercial regulations so harsh that ship captains and merchants avoided the city; they harassed the people with petty restrictions and burdened them with high taxes; they put Quakers to torture; they willingly abetted a company policy which enriched a small group of great landholders and fur-trade monopolists at the expense of the common folk; and they did practically nothing to assist religion or education. The inhabitants grew restive, and when an English fleet appeared in 1664 off New Amsterdam, the colony swiftly and happily became the Province of New York —a province of cosmopolitan population and lusty commercial vigor.

By 1700, when the French were just founding Louisiana, the colonies that stretched from Maine to the Carolinas numbered between 225,000 and 250,000 people—in many ways the freest, busiest, most hopeful people on earth. They lay between two frontiers—the sea frontier on one side, the forest frontier on the other. Their strong political and cultural allegiance was with Britain, the motherland to which they looked for protection. But their natural instinct, their practical ambitions, and their hopes for growth bade them look to the West with its free land, abundant natural resources, and countless satisfactions of the pioneering urge.

ALLAN NEVINS

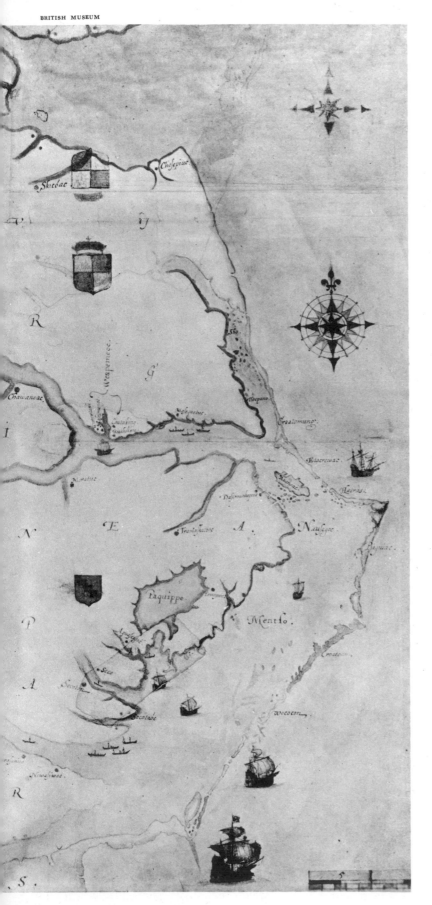

Lost Colonies

Before the successful colonizations there were the failures, scattering bare traces of fort and cabin along the North American coast like empty seashells. Or sometimes nothing remained but the blankness of a legend-embroidered mystery. Such an abandoned shell was the Popham colony in Maine, such a mystery the Lost Colony of Roanoke.

In 1584 two captains, Amadas and Barlowe, had planted the arms of England on the Carolina coast, claiming the continent for Sir Walter Raleigh under his patent from Queen Elizabeth. Some 23 years later the newly formed Plymouth company, whose leading spirits were Sir Ferdinando Gorges and Sir John Popham, the lord chief justice of England, sent a party of 120 colonists to what was then Northern Virginia and is now Maine. They sailed from Plymouth in the *Gift of God,* commanded by Sir John's kinsman George Popham, and the *Mary and John* under Raleigh Gilbert. According to the gossipy diarist John Aubrey, the colonists had been selected from all the jails of England.

When they landed at Sagadahoc near the mouth of the Kennebec, the pleasant August weather made the countryside seem benign and beautiful. They built Fort St. George and within it a storehouse, a church, and a dozen or so shelters. They even constructed a thirty-ton pinnace, *The Virginia of Sagadahoc,* the first ship to be built in North America. George Popham became the colony's governor.

Indian summer found the fort completed; but the early Maine winter chilled the men's mood. Spite and dissension split them, and before the end of the year all but 45 had returned to the mother country. During that first winter Popham died and was succeeded by Gilbert. Then Gilbert went back to England to claim an inheritance. With its last possible leader gone, the colony lost the will to live, and the settlers had no stomach for another Maine winter. By the time the Kennebec had frozen over once more, Fort St. George had been dismantled, and the colonists were back in England.

The Lost Colony of Roanoke is part of American

John White made this water-color map of the Virginia-Carolina coast c. 1585. Lane's colonists first touched at "Wococon" on the Outer Banks; "Roanoac" Island is at center.

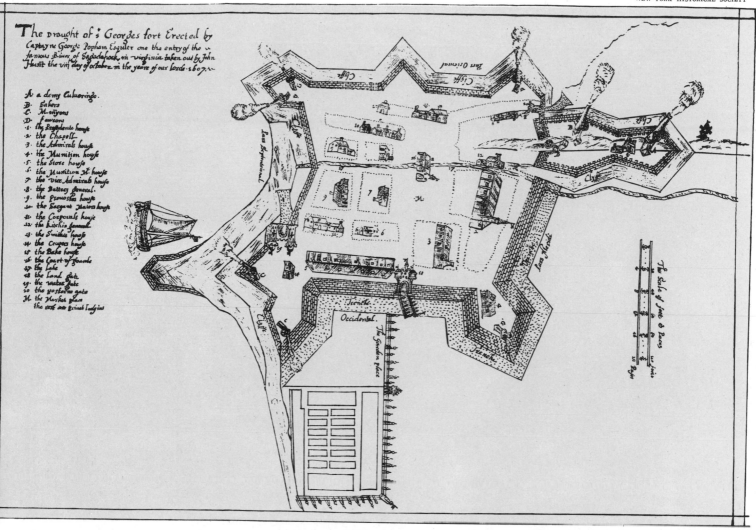

This "Draught of st Georges fort" is dated 1607. It seems unlikely that the fort George Popham built in the Maine wilderness resembled the European-style citadel shown here.

folklore. To that island off the Carolina coast came John White in 1587 with a company of about eighty men, seventeen women, and six children as Sir Walter Raleigh's second colonization effort. An expedition under Ralph Lane two years earlier—the first English settlement in the New World—had ended in failure.

White arrived in the spring, but by August he was "constrayned to return to England." Shortly before he left, his granddaughter Virginia Dare was born, the first New World English child. White was not to see America for another three years, and when he finally reached Roanoke again, he found no sign of his colony beyond a few moldering chests, some broken armaments, and the letters "CROATOAN" cut in the trunk of a tree. Of his company no trace remained. So the story of the Lost Colony has come down to us in all its pathos.

That brave drama was played out unobserved, yet the scenario was not as completely blank as the myth would have it. There is a Carolina tradition of a gray-eyed tribe claiming descent from the lost colonists, and recent investigations have shown it probable that the island originally called Roanoke was 75 miles south of the present one. If so, White came back to the northern, not the southern Roanoke, and what he found there was merely the remains of the Lane expedition.

The colony, lost by him, may have continued to exist on the southern island—now called Cedar Island—until in its unrelieved time it was absorbed by the local Indians.

THE PORTRAICTUER OF CAPTAYNE IOHN SMITH / ADMIRALL OF NEW ENGLAND.

Ætat 37. Aº 1616

John Smith, strong man of the Jamestown colony, New World propagandist, and author of A Description of New England.

The Remarkable Captain Smith

But for Captain John Smith the Jamestown colony would have sunk back into the surrounding swamp, one more abandoned outpost. His was the strength of will that tips the balance from failure to success, and justly, if inaccurately, he is remembered as the founder of the first permanent English settlement in North America.

In impulse he was an Elizabethan adventurer with a quixotic yearning for the heroic past. Small in stature, a tenant farmer's son, Smith had sold his schoolbooks and apprenticed himself to a merchant in the hope of going to sea, and when the merchant tried to keep him at desk and quill, he ran away. At twenty he quit England altogether to fight the Turks in Hungary. A bold, penniless young man, his beard scarcely sprouted, he spent several years wandering across strange lands with tongue-twisting names, his fortunes varying from castaway to hero to prisoner to slave. He was swindled by strangers, tossed overboard into the Mediterranean as a heretic by Rome-bound pilgrims, rescued by a privateer in which he signed up as a sailor and received his share of prize money. When in 1601 he reached Hungary, he joined the army under Prince Sigismund and made a name for himself by instructing the Hungarians in the art of flame bombs and liquid fire. Smith became a hero when on behalf of the prince he accepted a challenge to single combat from the opposing Lord Turbashaw. In borrowed armor, Smith ran Turbashaw through with a quick lance thrust and cut off his head. The same fate awaited two of the dead man's lieutenants who were bold enough to take up the challenge. For that bloody afternoon Smith was made sergeant major of his regiment, and Sigismund later granted him a coat of arms with "three Turkes heads in a Shield."

Then suddenly the wheel of fortune turned against Sergeant Major Smith. Sigismund's army was shattered by the Turks at Roterturm, and Smith, wounded, was taken prisoner. From a Hungarian hero he was reduced to a Turkish slave, manacled, and sent the dusty miles to Constantinople and the auction block, where he was purchased for a young lady, Charatza Tragabigzanda. Charatza's kindness to him he remembered long afterward in giving the name Tragabigzanda to what is now Cape Ann in Massachusetts. Possibly Charatza's relatives felt her kindness excessive, for Smith soon found himself transported to a slave gang in Tartary. One day he managed to kill his master and escape, and working his way north, he reached the river Don, where another woman, "the good Lady Callamata" as he called her, helped him on his way. He wandered across the Ukraine, through Poland, and finally back to his old acquaintances in Hungary. Then, after a quick tour of Germany and Spain, he was off to the wars in Barbary.

The year before his death Smith wrote an account of his life: *The True Travels, Adventures, and Observations of Captaine John Smith.* For 300 years its facts were accepted, but in the mid-nineteenth century American skeptics began to look coldly at the three Turks' heads, Charatza, Lady Callamata, and the rest. So great was the reaction against Smith's veracity that even his familiar story of Pocahontas was rejected.

Twentieth-century research, however, has refurbished Smith's name. Although his account of his years in Hungary and Turkey may seem blatantly improbable to sober minds, recent scholarly investigations have borne him out in plan and event. Except for the captain's own idiosyncrasies of spelling and occasional slips of memory, his *True Travels* can be accepted as such whether he deals with the Old World or the New.

It was inevitable that Smith should cross the Atlantic, although his position in the initial Jamestown venture was a relatively subordinate one. Jamestown was not settled with the idea of establishing a self-supporting agricultural community. The six-score adventurers who made up the original company had the usual fancies of easy riches, fist-sized nuggets of gold lying in the wash of the river banks, and the old will-o'-the-wisp passage to the treasures of the Orient. Too many of them were gentlemen for whom manual labor seemed a form of degradation.

It was in May of 1607 that the colonists arrived, and the site they chose was unfortunate—a low finger of land extending into the James River and surrounded by swamp. Captain Christopher Newport, who had commanded their squadron of three ships, spent the next two months exploring Chesapeake Bay in search of the Northwest Passage, then sailed back to England. With his departure, Jamestown repeated the history of all the embryo settlements, suffering in turn from sickness, hunger, and hostility of the natives. By mid-September half the men were dead, and those who were left scarcely had strength to bury them. Autumn frosts found the community still under dilapidated canvas, their low peninsula thinly fortified, and the majority ready to give up and go home.

Such a challenge would always bring out the leader in Captain John Smith. Any return was for him out of the question. He organized trading expeditions, he forced the Indians—at gunpoint if necessary—to deliver food to the starving settlers, and finally he took over the management of the colony. Without him Jamestown would have collapsed and the derelict survivors faced annihilation.

During the "Starving Time," as that terrible winter was called, the captain scoured the country in search of food. In December, traveling along the upper Chickahominy with an Indian guide, he found himself ambushed and surrounded by Pamunkey tribesmen. Although wounded, he tried to work his way backward, firing his pistol and using his guide as a shield. He killed three Indians and held off the rest; but on stepping back he suddenly sank waist deep and helpless in a bog. The triumphant Pamunkeys dragged him to their vindictive chief Opechancanough, and he in turn forwarded him to his brother, the great Powhatan, who controlled all the tribes of Tidewater Virginia. After several conferences with the captain, Powhatan had two large stones brought in. Smith's head was forced down on them, and several braves stood by ready to beat his brains out.

Then occurred the episode so well known to generations of American schoolchildren. In Smith's words: "Pocahontas the Kings dearest daughter, when no intreaty could prevaile, got his head in her armes, and laid her owne upon his to save him from death." Pocahontas was then thirteen years old. It may well have been that she acted on secret instructions from the wily Powhatan, for he knew if he killed Smith he could expect gunpowder retaliation, yet if he did not there would be trouble with his antagonistic brother. In any case, two days later Captain John Smith was noisily initiated into the tribe, given the name of Nantaquoud, and sent back to Jamestown with a dozen guides.

For another year and a half he held the sagging colony together by the force of his will and example. Hunger, disaffection, the hostility of the natives —all these he bore unflinchingly. And in spite of hardships and disappointments he formed an affectionate and unshakable image of the New World landscape that he would carry with him the rest of his life. When in the summer of 1609 a fleet of supply ships arrived with a new royal charter, Smith found himself superseded by smaller men. The melancholy history of Jamestown after the captain returned to England is a measure of his accomplishments.

Smith saw the New World once more, five years later, when he made an exploratory voyage mapping the coast from northern Maine down to Massachusetts Bay. This region pleased him more than any other. He called it New England, because he saw in it a renewal of old England, where every port and town of the mother country would finally have its namesake in the new. Such was the vision that he embodied in his book *A Description of New England,* a book that did more than anything else to offset the bad name given the region by the Popham colony failure. It was this same book that turned the thoughts of the Pilgrims, then in Holland, to the New England coast.

Later, Smith was in touch with agents of the Pilgrims. He would have liked, he hinted, to serve as captain in their company, but they replied thriftily that it was cheaper for them to buy his book. What he dreamed about in those after years was a colony of his own, of sturdy, self-reliant men and women who would build up a new civilization in the land he had named. Yet for all his wishing and planning, it was his fate never to fulfill himself, never to sail west again. The *Generall Historie of Virginia, New England and the Summer Isles* that he wrote in London was a landmark in English historical writing, but for him it was a thin substitute for the air and soil of New England.

These two engravings from his Generall Historie *show Captain Smith in action against the Virginia Indians. At top, brandishing a pistol, he captures a king-size chief; below, after shooting three Indians, he is captured "in the Oaze." This misfortune led to his dramatic rescue by Pocahontas.*

SMITH : *Generall Historie of Virginia*, 1624

C. Smith taketh the King of Pamavnkee prisoner 1608

C: S:

How they tooke him prisoner
in the Oaze 1607   C: S:

Smith bindeth a saluage to his arme,
fighteth with the King of Pamaunkee and
all his company, and slew 3 of them.

Pilgrims' Progress

Edward Winslow (above) made the Pilgrims' first treaty with the Indians and, with William Bradford, chronicled the Plymouth colony's early experiences. Below, a Dutch painting shows Pilgrims in Holland boarding the Speedwell *at Delft Haven to join the* Mayflower *company in England.*

Brownists, they were called derisively by their orthodox contemporaries, after "Trouble-church" Browne, the fundamentalist clergyman whose searchings in the Bible had found no warrant for priest or bishop. Puritanism was not enough, and the Church of England, become as opprobrious as the Church of Rome, must be abandoned. True believers should deliver themselves from evil and establish their own congregation of Saints, so they carried their dissent to Holland and later to the shores of Massachusetts.

Most of the men were rural artisans and laborers from the vicinity of Scrooby, self-righteous in their vision of themselves as the elect. Although their theological arguments are no longer especially relevant, their denial that the state may compel uniformity of belief is. Because they valued their inner rights as individuals above outer security, they had the courage to endure the heartbreak of exile and, if necessary, death.

As the seventeenth century began, the fragmented Brownist congregations started making their way piecemeal to Amsterdam, where, after the manner of non-conformism, dissent soon parted from dissent, and one splinter group finally mi-

grated to Leyden to become the genesis of the Plymouth colony. For a dozen years the Pilgrims lived in Holland, and inevitably a new generation began prattling Dutch. Another generation, the troubled elders felt, would lose its English identity. Captain John Smith's *Description of New England* opened their eyes. It was time to go.

The ill-named *Speedwell*, which left Delft Haven in July, 1620, with fifty Leyden Pilgrims aboard to join the *Mayflower* on her voyage to New England, was an unseaworthy tub. After turning back twice, she was abandoned, and as many as possible of her Pilgrims squeezed aboard the *Mayflower.* Unhappily, merchant adventurers had outfitted the latter with no higher purpose than that of making money, and when they could not collect enough local Saints to fill up the company, they met their quota undenominationally. Of the 102 *Mayflower* passengers the majority were Church of England Strangers. Yet Saints and Strangers had one common unity—they were drawn from the lower classes, and they had initiative, ambition, and impatience with the stratified society they were leaving behind.

The delay in sailing brought the *Mayflower* into equinoctial storms, the turbulent North Atlantic driving her each day closer to winter. Crew and company in the damp stench of those close quarters grew hostile. Strangers muttered against Saints, and the large group of indentured servants muttered against both. Whatever its later implications, the celebrated Mayflower Compact signed at the end of the voyage was conceived to maintain order and discipline against the anarchy of such resentment.

Their first landfall at the tip of Cape Cod revealed a pale line of dunes and scrub oak beyond a bay dotted with wary flocks of scaup and scoter and bufflehead. The wind-scored spit furnished water and a few buried baskets of Indian corn, and brought the colonists their first brush with the Indians—but no site for a settlement. Six weeks of futile exploration passed before they finally settled on the harbor-hill of Plymouth across the bay.

That winter of death—the familiar pattern of the settlements—saw half the company in their graves before the *Mayflower* sailed back in the spring. Other hard winters would follow, years of death and hunger and plans gone awry; yet as summer burnished the landscape again and crops sprouted, the basic fact became clear—the Pilgrim gesture had endured.

BETTMANN ARCHIVE

Myles Standish

The literate and satirical Morton of Merry Mount had pinned the title of "Captaine Shrimpe" on this irascible little man whose chunky face so easily turned redder than his hair. For Captain General Myles Standish of the Plymouth colony's dozen or so militiamen the name was maliciously apt. Self-important in helmet and breastplate, he looked the florid crustacean as he inspected his ineffectual cannon on top of Fort Hill, awed or threatened transient Indians with displays of military pomp, or explored the surrounding country. Yet for all his martial airs he was a man of parts and capacity; he knew his soldier's trade and he knew how to deal with Indians. A more tactful man might have dealt more easily, a weaker would have been overwhelmed. When his anger against the Indians flared, treachery and murder would seem justified means to him. But in the toe-hold years he kept the colony safe.

Oddly enough, though he commanded the defenses of Plymouth for thirty years, he never became a church member. He liked to boast, on the coincidence of his name, that he was descended from the Standishes of Standish, an old Catholic family—but it was part of the captain general's vainglory. Beyond the fact that he once soldiered in the Low Countries, nothing is known of him. Soldier he remained, loyal enough to be made treasurer and assistant governor of the colony. As Captaine Shrimpe he managed to have the last word when he raided Merry Mount, destroyed that gay rival trading center, and packed the hedonistic Morton off to England under arrest.

John Eliot and the Praying Indians

According to the 1628 charter of Massachusetts Bay, the "royall intention and the adventurer's free profession, the principall ends of this Plantation" were "to wynn the natives of the country to the knowledge and obedience of the onlie true God and Saviour of mankinde." It was not a profession which many of the earlier settlers shared. For those transplanted Englishmen the Indians were devils or a subhuman nuisance—"The veriest Ruines of Mankind," the illustrious Cotton Mather called them.

The Reverend John Eliot of Roxbury's First Church was one of the very few to take the intentions of the charter to heart. To him the Indians were human beings created by God and souls to be saved. This conviction expanded in his inner self until it dominated his life. As he wrote in later years, "Pity to the poor Indians, and desire to make the name of Christ chief in these dark ends of the earth—and not the rewards of men—were the very first and chief moves, if I know what did first and chiefly move my heart, when God was pleased to put upon me that work of preaching to them."

At Natick, eighteen safe miles up the Charles River, Eliot established an Indian settlement according to principles laid down in the Bible. Natick was laid out for some 800 inhabitants. Except for the temporary assistance of an English carpenter, all the work was done by Indians. A circular fort was built, followed by a rectangular meeting house. There were several other dwellings of the English kind, but for the most part the Indians preferred their wigwams.

Once every fortnight during warmer weather, Eliot visited his "Praying Indians." Summoned by two drums, the congregation assembled in the meeting house. And there in the church he had helped build with his own hands, in the smoky, rush-lit room with the noise of running water outside and inside the high-pitched buzz of mosquitoes, Eliot would deliver one of those massive seventeenth-century sermons, expounding the Scriptures in the Indian tongue that he had painfully learned. The Indians came to regard him as a father. Beyond the dogma which they scarcely understood they sensed the goodness of the man.

So they served him with only occasional backslidings, and when the times of trouble came, most of them held loyally to him.

Eliot's translation of the Bible—*Mamusse Wunneetupanatamwe Up-Biblum God* (The-whole Holy his-Bible God)—was his most cherished achievement, the goal of all his studies. From his first days in New England he had seen it as his sacred duty to bring the word of God to the Indians. Only when they could read the Bible could he be assured of the permanency of their faith.

For ten years he labored at his self-appointed task, in the long summer evenings, through the waning autumn days, with winter biting at his study door, testing each sentence, each verse. With his other burdens, it is a marvel that he found time to carry it on, for he had his church and in all weathers and all seasons he made visits to friendly Indian settlements. In 1663 the final chapters of Revelation were printed, 1,500 copies of Eliot's Bible were run off, and 200 were bound in stout leather for immediate use by the Indians. It was his most durable monument.

Eliot's vision of a Christianized Indian fellowship was shattered by the outbreak of King Philip's War. The colonists dumped his Praying Indians onto Deer Island in Boston Harbor, leaving the women and children and old men to shift and starve for themselves. Eliot did what he could to aid them, and through all their wretchedness they still remained firm in their affection for him.

At the war's end the Indians were allowed to leave Deer Island for their homes, but only a poor minority survived. Whatever creative spark Eliot had managed to kindle in them had gone out. He was to live another fifteen years, a patriarchal figure, one of the last links with that first generation from across the ocean. A saying grew up that Massachusetts could not come to an end as long as the Reverend Eliot lived.

He reached the conclusion that much of his work had been in vain. "There is a cloud," he wrote finally, "a dark cloud upon the work of the Gospel among the poor Indians." Cotton Mather, pursuing a fancy of which he was fond, discovered that the anagram of Eliot's name was Toile.

HUNTINGTON LIBRARY

John Eliot, spiritual father to the Praying Indians, saw his monumental Algonquin translation, Up-Biblum, *completed by the Cambridge Press of Boston in 1663. Financed by a London missionary society, it was the first Bible printed in this country. This anonymous portrait is dated 1659.*

Unyielding and highly vocal on the issue of liberty of conscience, Roger Williams became too much of a problem for the Massachusetts Bay oligarchy to bear, and he was banished by the authorities in 1635. His book on the subject, printed in England, was deemed treasonable and was burned by order of Parliament.

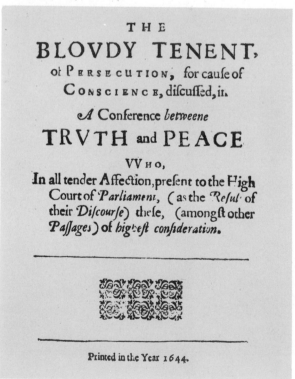

RESERVE DIVISION, N.Y. PUBLIC LIBRARY

The Way to Zion

To the Boston magistrates of 1631 Roger Williams seemed a singularly ungrateful and contumacious young man. On his arrival they had offered him their best—the post of Teacher in the Boston church—and not only did he refuse it, he then and there denounced the corruption of their church and invited elders twice his age to repent. Furthermore, he let it be known that magistrates had no right to punish swearing and Sabbath-breaking or exact oaths for civil matters. Governor Winthrop could not believe his ears.

From then on Boston was through with Roger Williams, though his personal magnetism might have carried the day in Salem or Plymouth if there had not been the matter of the King's patent. John Cabot had taken possession of North America for the Crown almost 150 years before, as every schoolboy knew, and the King's patent had granted this segment of it to the Massachusetts Bay Company. Now, after all that time, here was a know-it-all newcomer maintaining that the Crown could not give away what did not belong to it, that the land belonged to the Indians. Worse than this was the treatise he wrote denouncing the patent, a copy of which he even sent to King Charles, whose archbishop was already considering ways to void the Massachusetts Bay charter. This was too much. Governor Winthrop, who would nevertheless continue to be Williams' personal friend, decided that the logic-chopping young clergyman must go. In the midwinter of 1635 Roger Williams, leaving his family behind, was formally expelled from Massachusetts, the twentieth person in the colony's short history to be banished.

With a companion he followed the Indian paths south through sifting snow in the stark January weather, which, when he recalled the journey in his old age, he could "feele yet." His long trip was broken by interludes with the Indians, from whom he acquired a serenity of faith which never left him. "They have," he wrote later, "a modest religious persuasion not to disturb any man, either themselves, English, Dutch, or any, in their conscience and worship; and therefore say, 'Peace, hold your peace.'"

After crossing the Seekonk River, he headed for

the neutral woods of Rhode Island and came finally to the estuary of Narragansett Bay called Great Salt River. Here, justly, he arranged to buy from the Indians enough land for a settlement, which he named Providence out of gratitude for his survival.

"I ask the way to lost Zion," was Roger Williams' noble phrase. Less noble but in its way as apt was one contemporary's observation that Providence was a place where "all the cranks of New England retire." The selfish and the selfless came to the new settlement, malcontents, idealists, dissenters from dissent, Quakers. Williams was enough of his era to denounce the Quakers' doctrines, but their right to be there he never questioned. "None," he wrote, "bee accounted a Delinquent for *Doctrines*."

In the wilderness settlement and perhaps most deeply in his relations with the Indians, Roger Williams discovered the man that he was. His prickly self-assertiveness gave way to a severity of purpose. He who could not stomach entrenched authority became on his own patient, diplomatic, tolerant in argument, and understanding. The old Narragansett chief Canonicus, who distrusted whites, came to love Williams as a son, and when he was dying, asked for the Englishman to close his eyes. Williams' sharp ear quickly picked up the "Barbarous and Rockie" Narragansett speech. As trader-clergyman he shared the Indian life, slept at their forest firesides, experienced their dangers, and ministered to them. Above all other Englishmen they came to trust him. He became the ambassador between them and the Massachusetts Bay garrison of Boston, and the latter, as Winthrop well knew, came to find Williams' negotiating skill with the Indians indispensable. Even King Philip, who had once contemptuously twisted a button from John Eliot's coat, respected Williams' person. Although Providence was partially burned in Philip's war, Roger Williams could walk safely wherever he chose.

Through his long life he saw with increasing clearness a world irradiated by God's hand, in which each soul had its equal value beyond the compulsion of external authority. Self-interest might divide even Providence, but it would never touch him. For the Protestant ethics of acquisition he had no understanding. Wealth, success, material prospects, status, power—these things were transient as smoke. His vision was of free men standing under the shadow of "eternitie."

CULVER SERVICE

Anne Hutchinson

Governor Winthrop had scarcely settled with Roger Williams when he was faced with the problem of Mrs. Anne Hutchinson. That sharp-tongued woman with the hair-splitting theological mind and sense of personal revelation was challenging the Massachusetts Bay theocracy. It seemed to Governor Winthrop that a mother of fourteen children might better occupy herself than instructing clergymen about the Bible; but Mrs. Hutchinson felt differently. Almost on her arrival in the colony she had organized a women's club where sermons of the preceding Sunday were discussed and dissected. Before long she had even drawn men into her group. She maintained that she was guided by the Divine spirit. This Covenant of Grace, as she called it, she contrasted with the Covenant of Works, composed of such external things as church membership, prayers, and obedience to authority.

Her Covenant of Grace split the colony. Her followers began to boycott or even interrupt the sermons of orthodox ministers. And her undoubtedly magnetic presence attracted the young and engaging Henry Vane, who became her leading disciple and succeeded Winthrop in 1636 as governor.

In the following year, however, when Governor Winthrop returned to office, he saw to it that Mrs. Hutchinson's errors were condemned and she herself brought to trial. She was excommunicated and expelled, and with the help of Roger Williams she settled in Rhode Island and later moved to New Netherland. There, in 1643, she and her family were massacred by a Mohegan war party.

The Indians' First Stand

Benjamin Church (above) and King Philip, by Paul Revere.

BOTH: AMERICAN ANTIQUARIAN SOCIETY

By the second half of the seventeenth century, the westward push of the New England settlements had gained such momentum that clash with the Indian tribes became almost inevitable. The resultant King Philip's War cast the mold for bloody conflict that was to be repeated endlessly over the next two centuries.

Petty tribal rivalries had divided New England's Indians into piecemeal victims of the settlers. Not until Massasoit's son—called by the English King Philip—did a chief appear who had the ability to build an intertribal alliance against the encroaching whites. Philip's war was the final doomed gesture of the New England redmen.

Massasoit, though always faithful to his forty-year peace treaty with the Pilgrims, had banned any missionaries from his Wampanoags. Philip added hostility and resentment to his father's reserve. He had been warned that even though he might harm the colonists, they would in the end destroy him. Philip believed that might be true, but only if he failed to strike in time. So with patience, adroitness, and cunning he plotted a federation of tribes that reached from Long Island Sound to the Penobscot. For four years he made his preparations and mapped his strategy.

The trial and execution of three of Philip's braves in 1675 by the Plymouth magistrates was the excuse he needed, and in mid-June war broke out. From Springfield to within sight of Boston towns went up in flames. Before the militia could effectively counterattack, the western garrisons were besieged and in some cases annihilated.

Terror reinforced all the colonists' earlier prejudices, and John Eliot's Indians lived in danger of their lives. Sometimes they were murdered out of hand, at the least seized and locked up; yet in spite of ill will, suspicion, and harsh treatment which was to grow harsher, the great majority of them remained loyal. And when some of the more practical-minded colonists decided to raise a scouting party from among them, sixty volunteered. The Praying Indians, resuming their forest ways, killed over 400 of the enemy.

Before that balance was finally turned, however, thirteen towns had been leveled, perhaps a thou-

The 1810 engraving above gives a tidy, if highly imaginative picture of King Philip's War. Below, Josiah Winslow, son of Edward Winslow (page 58), was governor of the Plymouth colony and commander in chief of the armies opposing Philip.

sand colonists had lost their lives, and the public debt had risen so high that in places like Plymouth it was greater than the colony's whole property valuation. On the other side, 3,000 Indians were killed. The Narragansetts were ambushed and annihilated by a combined Massachusetts-Connecticut force in the Great Swamp Fight.

The war lasted until the middle of the following year. Philip was finally surrounded and brought to bay at Mount Hope Neck by a force under Duxbury's Benjamin Church. A Praying Indian named Alderman fired the shot that finished him. Church's men found him lying in the mud—"a doleful, great, naked, dirty beast"—and they cut off his head and brought it to Plymouth, where it stood impaled on the Fort Hill tower for the next quarter of a century, its eye sockets a nest for wrens each spring. Over Eliot's distressed protests the war captives, including Philip's wife and young children, were sold into slavery in the West Indies.

With King Philip, there passed the last and greatest leader of the New England tribes. He understood, as his father never had, that the Indian forest way and the English settlement way could not endure together. The brave, relentless Philip preferred to confront rather than retreat from the wave that overwhelmed him. When he was cornered in the Rhode Island swamp, he sent his companions away and died alone.

PILGRIM HALL, PLYMOUTH

65

New England's Expanding Frontiers

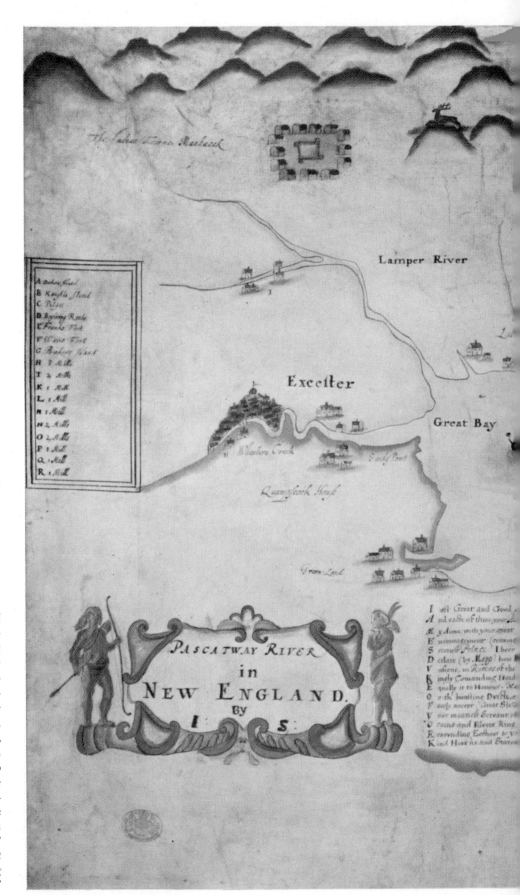

This lively pictorial map, painted on vellum by an unknown 17th-century artist, illustrates the northward expansion of the New England colonies into the Piscataqua River region of New Hampshire. The settlement at the mouth of the river is Portsmouth. At center is Dover, at left, Exeter, and at upper left, an Indian town. In dedicating his work to James II, who came to the throne in 1685, the artist hoped to "Declare (by Mapp) how Englands strength doth lye Unseene, in Rivers of the New Plantations"—strength, he was sure, that "Neither Spaine Or the Boasting Dutch, can shew the like againe!"

66

Oyfter River

Back River

Colater

Mathews Creeke

Little Bay

Wilelmans Cove

Black Point

Long Reach

Stratch of Back Much

Strawbery Bank

Greet Iland

Stoape Creeke

Champernones Iland

Pogos Creeke

Brabord Harbour

Mannestow River

York Town

A Seale of 3 Miles.

NEW-YORK HISTORICAL SOCIETY

Peter Stuyvesant brooked no interference with his New Amsterdam rule. If anyone should object, he said, "I will make him a foot shorter, and send the pieces to Holland."

The water color below shows Dutch New Amsterdam about 1653. At the tip of Manhattan are a weighing beam and crane, in the background a windmill and blue-roofed church.

MUSEUM OF THE CITY OF NEW YORK

Old Silver Nails: Too Late and Too Tough

The mutilated Father Jogues, passing through New Amsterdam on his way back to France in 1643, was reminded of the Tower of Babel. Eighteen languages were spoken within a furlong of the fort by the French, Walloons, Germans, English, Irish, Portuguese, Swedes, blackamoors, and Indians! The inhabitants of the polyglot town were mostly tough, rootless traders who had flocked there as men would later flock to the gold fields.

A decade and a half before Peter Minuit bought Manhattan from the Indians, Henry Hudson had sailed up what he called the Great River of the Mountains in the unending search for the Northwest Passage and given the Dutch their excuse to drive the New Netherland wedge between Virginia and New England. Almost imperceptibly, peltry-minded Dutchmen fanned out over the Hudson Valley, and New Netherland became a series of trading posts along the Hudson.

The first colonists were sent over in 1624 by the Dutch West India Company. This vast and close-fisted corporation regarded New Netherland as a secondary venture and its colonization an irritating expense. The Company's object in North America was to cash in on furs, and as the directors complained to the Netherlands States-General five years later: "The people conveyed by us thither have . . . found scanty means of livelihood up to the present time; and have not been any profit, but a drawback, to this company." Colonists, in any case, were hard to come by. The Dutch preferred their neat brick cities and their flat familiar countryside to any tempting of fate across the ocean.

Director Kiliaen Van Rensselaer, a shrewd Amsterdam jeweler with a calculating mind and a useful lack of ethics, had his own solution. Let the company make grants of river land to patroons like himself, who would transport and settle fifty indentured colonists there. Though he himself never left Amsterdam, he extended his own grant along both banks of the Hudson for eighteen miles, so that Rensselaerswyck, with its bound tenantry (self-contained even to a private executioner), became a feudal dominion facing the wilderness.

Rensselaerswyck, the nearby frontier Fort Orange below the hill at Albany, and New Amsterdam were the three salients of the New Netherland triangle. New Amsterdam was and remained the controlling point. If the government had been better, the colony might have grown more quickly, but what could be said for replacing an upright man like Minuit with such director-generals as Wouter Van Twiller and William Kieft? An ex-clerk, Van Twiller was irresolute in everything except looking out for his own interests. Patroons and their uppish ways, the Indians, the encroaching English, all were too much for him. His successor, Kieft, was a bankrupt and a tippling busybody more concerned about what time New Amsterdamers went to bed than with the major affairs of the colony. Not only was he a more energetic embezzler than Van Twiller, but his senseless handling of the Algonquins brought on a war that almost ruined New Netherland. The burghers elected an advisory committee of twelve whose advice to Kieft was to go home.

Last and most durable of New Netherland's director-generals was sturdy, pig-eyed, one-legged Peter Stuyvesant. Old Silver Nails, as they called him for his silver-studded wooden leg, was a tougher man than Washington Irving's genial caricature makes him out. So were the times. "I shall be as a father over his children," the new director-general told the assembled burghers on his arrival, keeping them standing outside for an hour with heads uncovered to emphasize the fact.

He could be a bully and, as in his dealings with the Quakers, a bigot; but stiff little autocrat that he was, he was also an able administrator and—if he were not opposed—even agreeable. Opposition from the nine elected councilors set his wooden leg tapping the floor, and he would bellow "in foul language better befitting the fish market." To protesting councilors he announced loftily: "We derive our authority from God and the Company, not from a few ignorant subjects."

Though New Amsterdam expanded under Old Silver Nails, and the neighboring villages of Flushing, Brooklyn, and Flatbush developed, the colonists became increasingly disaffected under his arbitrary rule. The English eyeing New Netherland's borders began to seem more a welcome than a threat.

Big Tub's Times of Trial

Big Tub, the Indians called the governor of New Sweden on Delaware Bay. Well they might, for Johan Printz, seven feet tall and weighing over 400 pounds, was probably the largest man who ever crossed the Atlantic. Formerly a colonel in the Swedish service, Printz ran his tiny colony as if he were still commanding a regiment. Accused by the colonists of brutality, he hanged their spokesman before denying the charges.

Hard, foul-mouthed martinet he might be, yet he had the tenacity to hold together his settlement of riffraff colonists for ten years in spite of meager supplies and the home government's neglect. He fortified the site of Wilmington and set up Fort Elfsborg (nicknamed Fort Myggenborg, or Mosquitoburg) on the east bank of the river to put the small English settlement there in its place. On Tinicum Island he built Fort New Gothenburg and a residence, Printzhof, in the log-cabin style of architecture then new to America.

Although New Sweden extended from Cape May up the Delaware River to the falls at Trenton, there were only 100 settlers in the area when Printz arrived and only about 500 at the colony's end. Its original aim was to furnish a refuge for persecuted European Protestants, but when the settlement became a reality, the more practical matters of fur trading and tobacco raising intruded. Printz had been instructed to remain on firm, friendly terms with the English and the Dutch, but he found this difficult. Both were undercutting him in the fur trade, and the Dutch had even built Fort Casimir below the outflanked Wilmington fortifications. Sweden, engrossed in European wars, sent neither supplies nor settlers. Five times in two years Printz wrote in vain to Stockholm, and the only real relief ship sent out to New Sweden foundered off Puerto Rico. Printz had had enough. After tendering his resignation several times, he finally sailed for home without waiting for its acceptance.

The new governor, Johan Rising, seized Fort Casimir, but this was merely what wily old Peter Stuyvesant in New Amsterdam had been waiting for. With seven warships and 700 soldiers he sailed up Delaware Bay to enforce the surrender of the helpless Swedes.

In the primitive painting below, based on Washington Irving's Knickerbocker's History, *a sour trumpeter heralds for Stuyvesant the capture of Fort Casimir by the Swedes.*

Gigantic Johan Printz (right), painted by an unknown contemporary artist, manfully tried to govern the Delaware Bay colony of New Sweden despite its neglect by his government.

NEW-YORK HISTORICAL SOCIETY

NATIONAL PORTRAIT GALLERY, LONDON

The Duke of York

Closing the Dutch Gap

From an angle of Fort Amsterdam, Peter Stuyvesant watched the English frigates swing past, their gun ports open. He had asked the British commander for a parley, and the answer came back to hoist a white flag first. Nine years after the director-general had presented his ultimatum to the Swedes, history turned the tables on him.

Following the Restoration, Charles II decided to do something about the New Netherland wedge. The province that the Dutch had usurped would make a convenient proprietorship for his brother James, the Duke of York and Albany. With Stuart unconcern for the re-established peace between England and Holland, he sent Colonel Nicolls to Manhattan with four ships and about 400 soldiers, and New England added a number of militiamen.

Backed by a hundred soldiers and twenty small cannon, the stubborn Dutchman wanted to defy the English, but 93 of New Amsterdam's leading citizens signed a petition begging him to surrender. Even his son Balthazar signed, and the dominie added that it was a sin to shed blood to no purpose. "Let it be so," the old man finally said. But as the white flag fluttered up the masthead he added: "I had rather be carried to my grave."

This map was done after Holland recaptured New York in the third Anglo-Dutch war. It shows the tenuous position of New Netherland, sandwiched between English colonies.

72

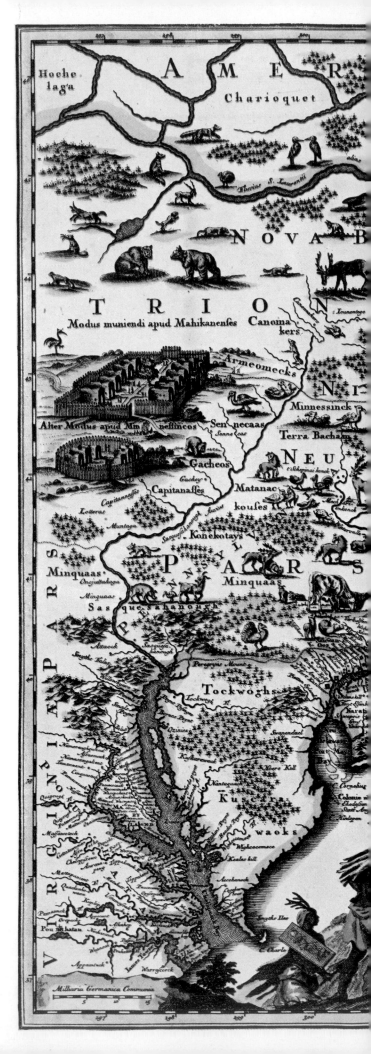

HISTORICAL SOCIETY OF PENNSYLVANIA

William Penn's Great Experiment

Pennsylvania was fortunate in its late founding. The earlier, ill-considered expeditions, with their tattered beachheads swept by hunger and disease, had been succeeded by a planned and orderly immigration. Ocean routes had been established; supplies were adequate. In Pennsylvania the new arrivals suffered from neither the climate nor the Indians. Mosquitoes were the chief complaint.

Yet William Penn, though he came in an easier time and spent only four years in his colony, is as enduring a part of the American tradition as any figure in the colonial period. If one looks for the basic reason among a multiplicity of smaller ones, it is in his selflessness. Others crossed the ocean for some elusive gilded dream, or to escape from established conformity, or to further the interest of their minority sect. He came to the New World with the philosopher's concern for the ideal state, the practical man's driving energy, and the Quaker's faith in attainable goodness. His vision was of a government based on people's wishes, changeable according to their needs in a land without war or class barriers, where the poorest man could live in non-sectarian peace and support himself in decency. As absolute proprietor of Pennsylvania's 28 million acres, Penn could have made himself a New World feudal lord. His only use for such power was to divest himself of it according to his inner light.

He had seen that light as a young man of 22, when he had gone to Ireland to supervise his father's estates. One evening in Cork he happened to attend a meeting of Friends. Among the soberly dressed people, this elegant son of the King's admiral suddenly became aware of the light glowing in his heart, and he stood up in the humble meeting speechless, his only testimony the tears rolling down his cheeks. From that moment he was a Friend, a Quaker in the taunting terms of the day. He would alienate his father, demolish the court career that the admiral had fixed for him; he would face hostile mobs unresisting and see the inside of jails. But the light that was kindled in an obscure

William Penn successfully created a colony in the image of his ideal. This contemporary pastel portrait by Francis Place is considered to be the only authentic likeness.

Irish assembly would guide him all his days.

Although most of his new Friends, including the luminous founder George Fox, were humble in origin, he never repudiated his old court friends. There must have been a singularly winning quality about him, for even the Stuart kings—despicable as his non-authoritarian illumination must have seemed to them—continued the love and concern for him that they had had for his father. He in turn, regardless of circumstance, gave them his loyalty and love.

In a practical sense it was Penn's high position in the world for which the Quakers were the most indebted to him, which time and again released them from persecution and jail and finally gave them a land across the Atlantic where they and all others might live at peace.

That a Quaker and a Whig should have received such a magnificent land grant as Pennsylvania from an absolutist king is in itself extraordinary. It may well be that Charles II, in his affection for the Penn family, wished to send Penn to America to save him from a coming purge. Ostensibly the King granted him the domain in payment of a debt to the admiral, naming it in the latter's honor, but debts were never of much consequence to the Stuarts, except that they considered too frequent hints at repayment a kind of *lèse-majesté*. Charles did, however, need a plausible excuse to give his Privy Council for awarding the younger Penn such a charter. The debt, plus the possibility of exporting recalcitrants at the same time, made the grant seem reasonable. As Penn himself noted, "the government at home was glad to be rid of us at so cheap a rate as a little parchment to be practised in a desert 3,000 miles off. . . ."

In the *Frame of Government of the Province of Pennsylvania in America* Penn drew up the document which, of all his many writings, was closest to his heart. His thought derived from Plato and Aristotle, his governmental forms from More's *Utopia,* Bacon's *New Atlantis,* and James Harrington's *Oceana*. But it was from his worldly experience and sound Quaker common sense that he could write in his preface: "Let men be good, and the government cannot be bad; if it be ill, they will cure it.

But, if men be bad, let the government be never so good, and they will endeavour to warp and spoil it to their turn."

All Penn's knowledge, enthusiasm, and faith were applied to his Pennsylvania project—his law training at the Inns of Court, his administrative work in Ireland, his court experiences, the insights he had gained in meetings and debates. Even before he sailed, he wrote his famous conciliatory letter to the Indians.

Some years earlier Quakers under his auspices had already settled in West New Jersey—later Delaware—and several companies had gone directly to Pennsylvania. Wrapped up in administrative details to the end, he himself sailed belatedly in the *Welcome* in 1682 with a group of a hundred Friends, after receiving George Fox's appeal to "make outward plantations in America [and] keep your own plantations in your hearts." The *Welcome* arrived in October, in the pellucid American fall so different from the misty English autumn. The green- and gold-flecked countryside was finer even than Penn had anticipated, the soil rich and well-watered, birds, animals, and great towering trees in abundance, and beyond all, the forest.

After three days of negotiating and exploring,

Penn reached the site his commissioners had picked for his capital, the high land between the Delaware and Schuylkill rivers marked by a few surviving buildings from the old Swedish settlement. In laying out his new city, Penn was haunted by old London memories of plague and fire. Here he would have no rancid alleys shadowed by encroaching gables, no violent and festering slums, no wooden perils. This would be a planned city with straight wide streets and symmetrical brick houses, each house with its garden, and the intervening spaces taken up by orchards and fields. It would be "a green country town which will never be burned and always be wholesome." Naming his city, he compounded the Greek words for love and friend.

Twenty-four miles north of Philadelphia he commenced building the stately, three-storied Pennsbury Manor, which he intended for his ailing wife left behind in England. His principal administrative task after his arrival, however, was buying land from the Indians and redistributing it to settlers.

In spite of his inexperience with primitives, Penn had an extraordinary facility for getting on with the Indians and winning their trust. Shortly after his arrival he met a large Indian gathering, come to see the new sachem from overseas, and

Describing Philadelphia, Penn wrote, "of all the many places I have seen in the world, I remember not one bette

76

signed his justly famous Great Treaty with them. Two years later, land difficulties with Lord Baltimore in adjoining Maryland forced him to go back to England.

He arrived in London to find King James' drive against dissenters in full swing and the jails again full of Friends. It was a delicate situation for him, to appeal to the King for the Quakers without antagonizing him in regard to Pennsylvania, and though Penn was successful, he could not hurry matters. The 1688 revolution found him still in England, this time suspect because of his Stuart loyalties. He now faced arrest for high treason, and his beloved province was taken from him. Although he eventually managed to clear himself and reclaim his proprietorship, fifteen long and frustrating years elapsed before he was able to cross the Atlantic again.

In that prolonged interval Philadelphia had become the second largest city in the colonies. Pennsylvania, despite a certain amount of internal conflict in the government, was thriving. Settlers—just as Penn had wished and foreseen—had come from France, Holland, Germany, Scotland, and Ireland, as well as England, while peace with the Indians remained enduring and secure. Again Penn traveled about the country, the years having cost him none of his zeal or ability. But his mind ranged wider than his province. He called a conference of the governments of New York, Massachusetts, Virginia, and Pennsylvania to set forward a plan of union of the English colonies, with a broadness of conception scotched by the narrowness of Whitehall. Two years after what he had hoped was his final voyage, a bill before Parliament to bring the proprietary governments under the Crown sent him back to London once more.

These last few years of his life were disappointing. Swindled by one of his trusted subordinates, he was escorted by bailiffs to a debtor's prison. His son William, sent to Philadelphia as his surrogate, proved vain and profligate. Finally no solution was left but to return to the Crown the province which had been so carefully planned and nurtured by him. "Oh Pennsylvania!" he wrote to his old secretary James Logan in America, "What hast thou cost me? Above thirty thousand pounds more than I ever got by it, two hazardous and most fatiguing voyages, my straits and slavery here, and my child's soul almost. . . ."

For what he had created, though, William Penn had no regret.

LIBRARY COMPANY OF PHILADELPHIA

seated." When Peter Cooper made this handsome view about 1720, the city was the commercial center of the colonies.

James Oglethorpe

James Oglethorpe: the Georgia Idea

The Member from Haslemere had never seen anything like it, even at the siege of Belgrade. Like most people of his age, James Oglethorpe had taken for granted that men who owed money should go to jail—until he visited a debtor friend in the Fleet. The bestial horror of that dank prison, the waste of manhood, the corruption and futility of it all, sent him back to Parliament a changed and angry man. What way was this, he asked the House, to deal with Christian Englishmen? Across the Atlantic there was still the empty land of Georgia below the Carolinas, where, with a little help, debtors and other poor could live in self-supporting decency by tilling the soil, raising hemp, cotton, and silk. Were there not mulberry trees in abundance merely waiting for their introduction to silkworms? Not only that—a staunch Protestant settlement on para-military lines would set a useful buffer state between Carolina and the Spanish territories to the south. Let the honorable members give the matter their soberest consideration.

Oglethorpe and other prospective trustees finally petitioned the King for a tract of land "in the south-west of Carolina for settling the poor persons of London." With its granting in 1732, Georgia became a polite London fad, a fashionable crusade preached from pulpits on Sundays, discussed in coffee houses, even rhymed in couplets. Donations came in, not only of money but of seeds, books, weapons, Bibles. Oglethorpe felt Georgia was going to be the greatest philanthropic experiment of the age. It was going to be a different kind of colony, with settlers carefully selected from "sober, industrious and moral persons." These would receive free passage, tools, and equipment. Holdings would be limited to fifty acres. Slavery and hard liquor were banned.

The Georgia idea quickly broadened to include all "poor, humble and neglected folk." From the Continent came such later stalwarts as the Lutheran

RESERVE DIVISION, N.Y. PUBLIC LIBRARY

Oglethorpe's promise of a new beginning in a new world filled Europe's downtrodden with hope. Among those who responded were persecuted Lutherans from Salzburg, shown in this 1732 engraving as they departed for the wilds of Georgia.

Salzburgers, driven from their homes by the Archbishop of Salzburg, who were given a separate settlement at Red Bluff where they could preserve their customs and language.

The first Georgia-bound shipload of 35 families sailed from Gravesend in the autumn of 1732, the zealous Oglethorpe among them. He had forgotten nothing, even to silkworms—although the Georgia mulberry trees unfortunately turned out to be a different species, and the worms died. During the voyage he gave the men calisthenics and instructed them in military discipline. At 36 years of age he had the satisfying feeling that he was beginning life all over again.

After their arrival in Charleston, Oglethorpe moved the company on up the Savannah River to a broad sickle bend where he laid out his city of Savannah in spacious Georgian squares. Like Penn, he was scrupulous in his dealings with the Indians, paying them for their land and establishing fair trading prices. Returning briefly to London the following year, he took with him several chiefs and his Indian friend Tomo-Chi-Chi.

Tomo-Chi-Chi and his picturesque companions caused as much sensation in London as had Pocahontas over a hundred years before. Parliament voted additional funds for the Georgia enterprise, and settlers' applications poured in. Oglethorpe was hailed as a moral hero and empire builder.

On his return to Georgia, however, Oglethorpe's chief concern was with the colony's defenses against the Spanish threat to the south. In an attempt to anticipate this, he made an unsuccessful attack on St. Augustine, but when the Spaniards in their turn attacked, he was able to turn them back. Yet while Georgia was fighting for its life, the other colonies stood aside. It would take another generation for any conception of colonial unity to develop.

79

AMERICANS EMERGE

WHEN James Fenimore Cooper described Natty Bumppo, or Leatherstocking, striding from the forest on the shores of Otsego Lake, long before the Revolution, he gave the world a purely American figure. In dress, speech, and ideas Leatherstocking belonged completely to the frontier. By 1760, when the thirteen colonies held about two million people, a great part of them lived in the back country, often within sight of the Blue Ridge or Appalachians.

The older coastal settlements had a European civilization, with periwigs, class lines, and much the same talk as London. Not so the men of the back country. Fur traders had learned the inland trails from Indians; southern stockmen had followed them with their "cowpens," northern hunters with their packsaddles; and the small farmers came in their wake, frequently squatting on the land with no concern for titles. They cleared their acres, fought the Indians, joined hands for house-raisings or other frolics, but remained stiff individualists, cherishing a democracy which made the indentured servant equal to the nobleman's son. They were often narrow, ignorant, aggressive, and undisciplined, and they possessed their share of shiftless ne'er-do-wells, but their society had the wild freedom of the forest.

The men who looked westward were more likely to think of themselves as Americans than New Yorkers, Pennsylvanians, or Virginians. They wanted elbowroom and untrammeled liberty. Hence they felt a sharp antagonism for the coastal groups that made laws, regulated trade, tried to protect the Indians, and ran troublesome boundaries. Just east of the Appalachians the natural pathways ran north and south—not to Philadelphia, Annapolis, or Williamsburg. Here people were breeding a new race, all the various stocks—English, Welsh, Germans, Huguenots, Dutch, Scotch-Irish—mingling and intermarrying. Here they developed a new kind of emotional religion, taking sects and ministers for what they were worth, and caring little whether a Presbyterian, Methodist, or Lutheran awoke their fervor. Here coastal politics seemed far away, and the Crown still more remote. The people were loosely, unconsciously American, and it needed the French wars and the Revolution to crystallize their nationalism and give them solidarity. To the pioneers and back-country farmers looking to their own future, the French and Indian War was a contest for the West; while to imperial-minded Britain that conflict was the Seven Years' War that checked France in Europe and gave India and Canada to British arms.

When Frontenac reached Quebec in 1672 to give New France much-needed strength, leaders in Paris had already decided to confine the English colonies to a coastal strip while they took possession of the best parts of the continent. On a June day the year before, Daumont de Saint-Lusson had staged an impressive ceremony at Sault Sainte Marie. Before braves of fourteen tribes he unveiled a metal plate which declared Louis XIV potentate of all the lands and waters stretching to the Pacific. Eleven years later La Salle buried at the mouth of the Mississippi a lead plate proclaiming the sovereignty of Louis over the great river and its tributaries, from their sources

Daniel Boone, engraved from Chester Harding's 1819 portrait.

to the Gulf. Thereafter, decade by decade, the French added to their chain of posts from Quebec to New Orleans and tightened their network of alliances with Indian tribes.

The early wars with France in which the colonies were involved all started in Europe, were fought in America mainly for strategic citadels like Louisbourg and Quebec, and though they ended to British advantage, were inconclusive for the New World. But in 1754 the rival forces girded themselves for a final contest which would sway the balance of the world. This time the war began not only in America, but in the West, and it was begun by the young Virginian George Washington, who was intensely interested in expansion to new frontiers.

The French and Indian War, which opened with Braddock's march in 1755 and ended after Wolfe's capture of Quebec and Hawke's destruction of the French fleet at Quiberon Bay some four years later, was to a great extent a wilderness war. Its most striking preliminary scene was the exchange of warnings between Washington and the French over the title to the upper Ohio. "They told me, That it was their absolute Design to take Possession of the Ohio, and by G— they would do it . . . ," Washington wrote. Who held the Ohio would eventually hold the Mississippi, and who held the Mississippi would eventually hold the entire continent beyond the Alleghenies. But for three factors the old dream of Frontenac that France would gain the heart of North America might have come true. These factors were British sea power, the genius of William Pitt, and the irresistible weight of combined British and provincial forces.

In particular, it was an army mainly American which John Forbes, Henry Bouquet, and Washington led across Pennsylvania in 1758 to seize the ruins of Fort Duquesne at the Forks of the Ohio, and to found in its stead the place they called "Pittsbourgh." The resolute Forbes had 5,000 men from North Carolina, Virginia, Maryland, and Pennsylvania serving with his British regulars. He cut Forbes' Road across the Alleghenies and guarded it by blockhouses so efficiently that it soon became a noted artery of western migration. Taken back to Philadelphia a dying man, he was fittingly buried in the province for which he had done so much.

The era of the American frontiersman had now begun. To the Mississippi the West lay open to him, for he paid little attention to the Proclamation Line by which George III tried to stop migration beyond the Alleghenies.

By 1763 the type was well fixed. From the Mohawk Valley to the Georgia uplands were hunters, Indian fighters, fur traders, and primitive farmers inured to the perils of the wilderness trail, its lurking savages and fierce beasts, its summer heat and winter ice. They could find a sure way through the endless forests whose towering branches shut out the sun, through almost impenetrable thickets of brush and briars, across sloughs and deep streams. They knew how to clear the trees, rear log huts, and scratch crops into the soil between the stumps. Women shared the stoic courage and patient endurance of their men, and the children were brought up to regard the family as a close-knit clan in facing hardship. Their faults, like their virtues, were products of an environment full of roughness, sink-or-swim emergencies, and bitter deprivations. "In spite of their many failings," wrote Theodore Roosevelt later, "they were of all men the best fitted to conquer the wilderness and hold it against all comers."

These pioneers had to deal with two clearly defined regions, the Old Northwest and Old Southwest—each with its particular difficulties, political, geographic, and economic, each with its characteristic set of Indian tribes. For various reasons the Old Northwest was not at first fruitful to the newcomer. The war with France was swiftly followed by the sudden bloody uprising of 1763 called Pontiac's Conspiracy. From Venango in northwestern Pennsylvania to Green Bay in Wisconsin, forts and settlements were attacked. Every post in the vast region was lost except Detroit, where the English commandant and French citizens withstood a siege, and Fort Pitt. In the end the Crown mustered its forces, Bouquet routed the savages near Pittsburgh and pushed on into the Muskingum Valley, and Pontiac and other chiefs submitted. But fear of the northwestern forest Indians persisted. Sir William Johnson and his veteran Indian-trader deputy, George Croghan, worked amain to keep the tribes in hand, but men hesitated.

The Northwest was soon to be a land of doughty pioneer heroes, but until after the Revolution speculators were more active there than settlers. Washington in 1770 visited the West with Croghan as guide, and finally obtained 33,000 acres with long frontages on the Ohio and Great Kanawha. Benjamin Franklin was one promoter of a company which, securing a grant of twenty million acres between the Alleghenies and the Ohio, proposed to found a new colony of Vandalia.

Far braver and bolder was the story of the Old Southwest, where that area's first venture in state-making, Kentucky, had a solid basis before independence was won. The farther reaches of the South saw their share of remarkable frontier figures, like Irish-born James Adair, who lived with the Chickasaws "as a friend and brother," traveled to their remotest Tennessee villages in the 1740's, knew 2,000 miles of trail and self-made path, and penned a book with fascinating pictures of Indian life. Equally remarkable were the fearless Lachlan McGillivray, a Highlander who, as Indian trader, gained an extensive influence over the Creeks, and his son Alexander, who became a chief in the tribe. But the founding of Kentucky was the greatest pioneer achievement of the time.

Interacting elements made this feat possible. One was the geographic fact that at the bottom of the great valley which under various names leads down through Pennsylvania, Maryland, and Virginia, the western mountain wall breaks down into the Cumberland Gap. One was Lord Dunmore's epochal victory over the Indians in 1774, which forced the Shawnees to open Kentucky to settlement. Another was the Crown's promise of 200,000 acres in western Virginia and Kentucky to land-hungry veterans of the French war. Most important of all, however, was the emergence of a rugged group of leaders. By far the most famous was Daniel Boone, honest, truthful, simple-mannered, a fearless wanderer and pathbreaker. Asked in old age if he had ever been lost in the forest, he said, "Well, once I was *bewildered* for three days." His description of the beauty and fertility of the Kentucky country fired Judge Richard Henderson's imagination, and Henderson's dream of a colony directed by his Transylvania Company was to be partially realized. Another leader was James Harrod, who the year before Lexington and Concord settled the town of Harrodsburg.

Behind Daniel Boone through the Cumberland Gap in the quarter-century after 1775 came, it is estimated, more than 300,000 people. While the Old Northwest was still hardly settled, Kentucky in 1790 had 74,000 inhabitants, and the Southwest Territory beyond 36,000 more. The pioneers would soon fill a great new country beyond the mountains; but the question was whether they could keep it in integral relation with the older America.

ALLAN NEVINS

Westward Lay the Vision

Somewhere, John Lederer was certain, there must be a pass through the western mountains. What lay beyond them was a mystery; very possibly a great inland bay of the Pacific cutting into the heart of the continent, if only one could find the way. Governor Sir William Berkeley of Virginia was set on finding it, which explained his willingness to commission the newly arrived German doctor to explore the unknown territories to the west.

Lederer was only 22 when he came to America to satisfy a curiosity that he liked to think of as scientific. In Europe he had read about the Indians and their customs, and in Virginia, afternoon after fading afternoon, he looked to the hill country on the horizon, enticing him like an unread book.

Between the spring of 1669 and the fall of 1670 Lederer made three westward exploring trips. Although he never did succeed in finding the pass through the mountain barrier, he learned to know the Indians and observed them with a scholar's eye, later writing an account of his travels in Latin. He was the first European to explore the Piedmont and the Blue Ridge Mountains. When his companions failed him he traveled alone.

On his first expedition he started out with three Indian guides from the York River, and after moving northwest for a week and covering about ninety miles, reached the "Apalatæi." Pushing over rocks and through thickets, he climbed a mountain of extraordinary height—probably Hightop—"from whence," he wrote, "I had a beautiful prospect of the *Atlantick*-Ocean washing the *Virginia*-shore; but to the North and West, my sight was suddenly bounded by Mountains higher than that I stood upon. Here did I wander in Snow, for the most part, hoping to finde some passage through the Mountains; but the coldness of the Air and Earth together, seizing my Hands and Feet with numbness . . . I returned back by the same way that I went."

Lederer's second and most important expedition was a seven-week journey southwest through Virginia and North Carolina to the Catawba River. He started out with a Major Harris and twenty dragoons, but after a couple of weeks of bushwhacking

HENRY FRANCIS DU PONT WINTERTHUR MUSEUM

Sir William Berkeley (left) governed Virginia for 34 years, ably developing the colony's economy. He promoted Lederer's 1669–70 expeditions in the hope of finding a feasible route through the Allegheny Mountains to the promising unknown beyond. At right is a typical frontiersman, as drawn by Frederic Remington.

Collier's, 1903

the latter lost their taste for "discovering the Mountaines" and left Lederer to go on with one Indian.

He turned more to the south as far as the Uwharrie Mountains, across the Indian trading ford on the Yadkin River, until he reached the Sara Indian encampment where the southern mountains began to lose their height. Unfortunately for his reputation he wrote what could only have been a hearsay description of the land beyond the Catawba, including a nonexistent "Ushery-lake."

A month later he made his final trip with a surveyor friend, Colonel Catlet, nine mounted colonists, and five Indians. His route this time was directly toward the Blue Ridge, slightly north of his first trip. The party left their horses when the going became too steep and climbed a high mountain—possibly Mount Marshall—where they looked down over the sweep of the Shenandoah Valley. But always toward the unknown horizon they could see more ranges, blue in the distance, including one "prodigious" mountain that the colonel estimated was 150 miles away. There was no sign of any inland sea, nor any passage through the rock mass. On that cold and windy summit they gave one last westward look before turning back, drank a health in brandy to King Charles, and named the mountain for him.

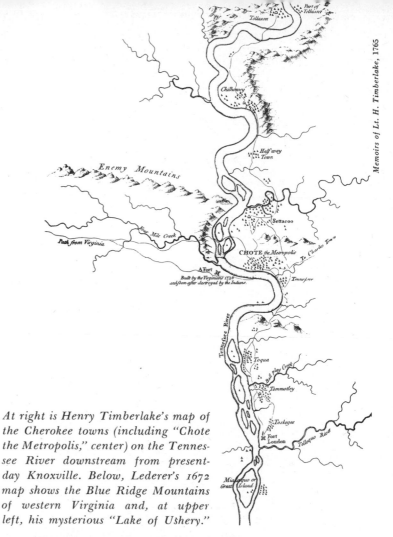

Memoirs of Lt. H. Timberlake, 1765

At right is Henry Timberlake's map of the Cherokee towns (including "Chote the Metropolis," center) on the Tennessee River downstream from present-day Knoxville. Below, Lederer's 1672 map shows the Blue Ridge Mountains of western Virginia and, at upper left, his mysterious "Lake of Ushery."

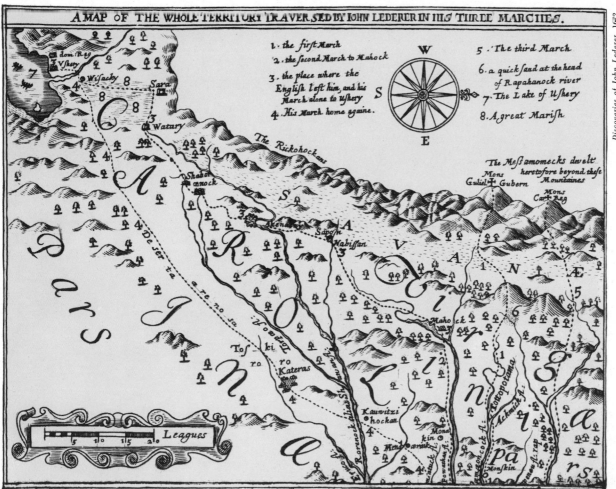

A MAP OF THE WHOLE TERRITORY TRAVERSED BY IOHN LEDERER IN HIS THREE MARCHES.

1. the first March
2. the second March to Mahock
3. the place where the English left him, and his March alone to Ushery
4. His March home againe.

5. The third March
6. a quick sand at the head of Rapahanock river
7. The Lake of Ushery
8. A great Marish

Discoveries of John Lederer, 1672

85

The Over-Mountain Men

The jagged line of the Appalachians divided the land like the Great Wall of China. Against that granite wall a tide from the eastern settlements began to press—the wanderers, the land-hungry, the castoffs, the indomitable. First came the traders, then squatters and settlers. Over the Blue Ridge they trudged, across the Alleghenies, the Cumberlands, the Great Smokies, the tapering mountains to the south. The last of the seventeenth century saw the barrier probed, the early eighteenth century saw it pierced. The Warriors' Path was becoming the settler's Wilderness Road.

Most of the crossings were as unrecorded as they were bold. The year after Lederer's expeditions, when Captain Thomas Batts and his companions crossed the eastern continental divide and reached the westward-flowing New River, they found trees in the mountain passes scored by English initials. Anonymous frontiersmen were establishing themselves beyond the Blue Ridge. In the mid-eighteenth century a young Virginia officer, Ensign Henry Timberlake, made a voyage in a dugout canoe on the Little Tennessee and Tennessee rivers, recording in detail the customs and habits of the Cherokees. His *Memoirs* are a literate and sprightly account of his travels, of much historical worth; but the over-mountain men, engrossed in the immediacy of the wilderness, left few records for history.

There is of course the record of Governor Alexander Spotswood's Golden Horseshoe junket of 1716, to see if a highway could be run between Virginia and the Great Lakes. There are folk heroes like "Marco Polo" Salley who went down the Ohio and Mississippi until he was captured by the French, and then—it is said—was adopted by a squaw and sold for a pipe and three strings of beads. There were wanderers like Thomas Walker, who in 1750 penetrated the great pass, Cumberland Gap.

Indian fighters such as Boonesborough's Bland Ballard and Simon Kenton could scarcely sign their names. Nor did they care. They hated the plow and settled ways. Bland Ballard found his deepest happiness in danger. He soldiered with George Rogers Clark and at the disaster of Long Run escaped by killing an Indian and seizing his horse. Later he was twice wounded and made prisoner, but he lived to the age of 94. While other Kentuckians were staking out land claims, he devoted his life to protecting the settlements from the Indians.

During a Shawnee attack on the scarcely completed Boonesborough, young Simon Kenton rescued the wounded Daniel Boone, carrying him back to the stockade under heavy fire. An adventurer almost from childhood, Kenton came to Boonesborough at its beginning, and Boone made him a permanent scout, for few men could track Indians with his skill. He was a scout in Dunmore's War and at Chillicothe, and was captured on the Ohio. Danger was a tonic to him. He was in Anthony Wayne's western expedition, and at 57 marched with Shelby's Kentuckians in the War of 1812.

Buckskin-clad Bland Ballard (left) was already a veteran of two Indian campaigns when, at the age of 23, he joined George Rogers Clark in a punitive march against the Shawnees in 1782. His portrait is attributed to Chester Harding.

Simon Kenton (right), one of Kentucky's most redoubtable scouts and Indian fighters, once saved Daniel Boone's life during an attack on Boonesborough. Kenton made a steady diet of Indian war from the Revolution to the War of 1812.

KNOEDLER ART GALLERIES

MASSACHUSETTS HISTORICAL SOCIETY

TENNESSEE HISTORICAL SOCIETY

Daniel Boone

John Sevier

Their axes echoed in the valley. Boone's men were making fast time. Where the old Warriors' Path had curved through the Cumberland Gap and vanished in the forest, the Wilderness Road to Kentucky and the future was being hacked out.

Although the Indians had beaten back Daniel Boone's little party two years before and tortured and scalped his boy, he had no doubt this time. The Transylvania Company's land treaty of 1775 with the Cherokees was of some protection, he had thirty riflemen to back up the treaty, and he knew the hills and valleys ahead. His road was going to Boonesborough, the settlement he was planning to build on Otter Creek. Behind him and his riflemen, along the trail he had blazed, the first few families were making their way; while ahead of him and all unknown, almost within ring of the axes, a war party was gathering. Yet the tiny Kentucky outpost would meet this threat tomorrow and others in the years to come. Somehow, through all raids and disasters, Boonesborough would survive, the genesis of the fifteenth state.

As a young man Daniel Boone had ranged the forests like an Indian, and even when he was eighty it was said of him that he could not live without being in the woods. No one sensed the land or the Indians more deeply. He was the wilderness hunter who became the prototype of the westward-ranging frontiersman.

John Sevier, greatest of the Indian fighters, fierce and sudden cavalry raider, was a vengeful shadow even to the shadowy red men. As a young man he could outride, outshoot, and outswear any of the men who followed him. Yet beyond his woodsman's ways and woodsman's dress he possessed an elegant assurance that may have been his French inheritance. Xavier had been the Gallic version of his name, but the Tennessee frontiersmen called him Nolichucky Jack.

After the Revolution the North Carolina Assembly passed an act ceding the state's over-mountain counties, with their impoverished and importunate ex-soldier inhabitants, to the national government. In turn the rejected counties formed their own State of Frankland, or Land of the Free, and as governor they picked "thirty-five battles, thirty-five victories Nolichucky Jack." Since Governor Jack was seeking Benjamin Franklin's help with Congress, he tactfully changed the state's name to Franklin.

Congress wasn't interested. The North Carolina Assembly, watching all that good land disappear, changed heart and repealed its act, but the over-mountain men—reinforced by land speculators—refused to give way. Finally Sevier was overthrown by North Carolina authorities, who managed to seize him and even planned to shoot him, but he escaped. And when a few years later Tennessee became a state, he became its first governor.

TENNESSEE HISTORICAL SOCIETY   TENNESSEE HISTORICAL SOCIETY

James Robertson

At 28 James Robertson turned his back on the settled lands of North Carolina and rode over the hills to Watauga. He could as yet neither read nor write, but now as his bride taught him it was as if his mind developed a new dimension. By the force of his expanding personality Robertson became the leader of the isolated egalitarian commonwealth. When a few years afterward John Sevier settled there, he at once sensed Robertson's great abilities, and they became friends for life.

The Father of Tennessee, Robertson was later called. In 1779 he led the first advance party into middle Tennessee, moving through the Cumberland Gap and along Boone's Wilderness Road, then southwest to the French Lick that would one day become Nashville.

His main party followed by river, down the length of the Tennessee and then up the Ohio and the Cumberland. The ordeal of their four-month voyage by flatboat and pirogue was the Old Southwest's *Mayflower* epic—in the snarling winter, ambushed by Indians, wrecked by surging currents, these 200 men and women under Colonel John Donelson lost 38 of their number before the anxious Robertson could welcome them.

Two of Robertson's sons and his brother were killed in Indian attacks, yet he could still treat the Indians fairly. As a just mediator between them and the settlers he was unequaled.

The Shelbys

Father to son, Evan to Isaac Shelby, they spanned the gap from the French and Indian War to the War of 1812. These Shelbys were frontiersmen-soldiers, stocky men of great strength and endurance, casual, brave, aggressive. Evan, the father, had come from Wales to wander through Pennsylvania as a fur trader. He had marched with Braddock and endured that bloody afternoon on the Monongahela with a pioneer's frustration and despair. Before the Revolution the Shelbys moved to what became East Tennessee, and in 1779, the year before Isaac and John Sevier smashed Ferguson's Tory army at King's Mountain, Evan led an expedition against the Chickamauga Indian towns on the lower Tennessee. After Sevier's term as governor of Franklin, the settlers elected Evan to succeed him, but he declined.

After the Revolution Isaac (shown above) moved to Boonesborough, and on Kentucky's admission to the Union he became the first governor. Years later the outbreak of the War of 1812 found him governor again. But after the Indians massacred several hundred Kentuckians at River Raisin, he took the field with a regiment of 4,000 volunteers and marched to the invasion of Canada. His regiment saw service in Michigan and fought in the Battle of the Thames. At the war's end Shelby began a flamboyant state tradition by making each man in his regiment a colonel.

SPENCER COLLECTION, N.Y. PUBLIC LIBRARY

Paul Revere engraved this view of Boston, a citadel of the conformists, in 1773 for the Royal American Magazine.

The Right Side of the Hedge

Samuel Sewall would have found frontier life as repellent as did his contemporary Cotton Mather, who asserted that those who swarmed into the new settlements "were got unto the Wrong Side of the Hedge." Sewall arrived from England in 1661, at the age of nine, to a Boston that was being transformed from a settlement into a town. Townsman he would remain for his ensuing 69 years, his most venturesome journeys judicial excursions to Dedham or Marblehead.

Unlike more adventurous souls who were probing west, forever seeking something better, Sewall felt that the seaboard he knew and loved was quite good enough. For over half a century he kept a diary that is a unique record of seventeenth-century daily living. Although written in Boston it might equally have been written in London. Sewall is a Puritan Pepys, with equal curiosity, an equal pleasure in the brightness of the moment, and with a similarly amorous nature held in check by a more rigid ethos. Sewall observes eclipses, the return of the robins in a snowstorm, the first "chipper" of the swallows. He notes that the governor's hat blew off, that at night there was "a great Uproar and Lewd rout in the Main Street." He plants two locust trees and two elms, and speaks to Sam Haugh who has got a maid with child but "cannot discern that any impression was made on him."

When he dreams it is not of Indians but of being chosen lord mayor of London. He amuses himself by speculating on such topics as whether Negroes will be white in the Resurrection. He enjoys evenings of pleasant company, with raisins and almonds and wine on the table, and particularly with women present. Sewall liked a good funeral. His diary is full of the accoutrements of grief—rings, gloves, scarves. He was married three times and had fourteen children by his first wife. Most of his days he lived at Cotton Hill on Tremont Street—quite far enough west for him.

MUSEUM OF FINE ARTS, BOSTON

Boston's Samuel Sewall, rather stiffly painted by the eighteenth-century portraitist John Smibert, was typical of those conservative citizens of the East coast cities who looked west and quickly averted their eyes.

The Wise Doctor Looks Ahead

There were times when it seemed to His Majesty's Deputy Postmaster and Manager in all the Provinces and Dominions on the Continent of North America that common sense was the least common of commodities. Benjamin Franklin since his appointment in 1753 had reorganized the whole American postal service. The mails sped three times a week to New York now, instead of crawling once. A letter could go to Boston and bring back its answer within three weeks. The Philadelphia post office had become the center of a network binding all the colonies together, a symbol of their necessary further unity. But did those bickering provincial assemblies see it? The postmaster general turned to his desk, picked up a quill, and wrote down another Poor Richard saying for his current almanac. "He that best understands the world least likes it."

Just as he had founded the American Philosophical Society so that there might be some community of intellect in the colonies, so one day for more practical reasons there would have to be some sort of political community. *How* was of course the problem. He had labored this point with Governor Shirley on his last visit to Boston. Sitting in the reception room of Shirley Place, with its green and gilded pilasters and great Venetian window that looked out over the formal garden to the harbor islands, the two men had talked over the whole matter of colonial unity. Franklin agreed with Shirley that America was as much a part of the British empire as any home county. But those English politicians who insisted on regarding the colonies as cows to be milked for England might be forced to realize some day—to put it crudely—that the cows could suckle each other.

Shirley wanted Parliament to do the unifying, to take the responsibility for defense and for imposing taxes, and once for all to put the bickering assemblies in their place. The trouble with the plan, Franklin told Shirley, was that it simply would not work. Any forthcoming union would have to be voluntary and originate in the colonies by their own agreement, with their own money. Otherwise there would be dissension and worse. Parliament didn't know enough about American conditions to do the regulating. America was a willing part of the empire, but it was also a land in itself that would have to act for itself.

With the French threatening to hem the English colonies within a great bow from the Mississippi to the St. Lawrence some type of combination was becoming a practical necessity. Facing the prospect of another French war, the Board of Trade in 1754 called the Albany Congress to renew the Iroquois treaty, but inevitably the question of strategic unity overshadowed Indian affairs. Preparatory to the Congress, Franklin had written his *Short Hints towards a Scheme for Uniting the Northern Colonies*. It was his idea that the union should be determined by the Albany commissioners representing the assemblies of New York, Massachusetts, New Hampshire, Pennsylvania, Maryland, Connecticut, and Rhode Island.

The plan was approved by all the commissioners present, but this generous view was not yet possible for the myopic individual assemblies: each one rejected the Albany proposals. In after years Franklin was convinced that his plan had offered the only real alternative to revolution. "But," as he remarked, "history is full of the errors of states and princes."

He could see a unified America, in Milton's antique phrase, "as an eagle mewing her mighty youth," if only England, or the colonies themselves, for that matter, could look beyond the Atlantic

LIBRARY OF CONGRESS

JOIN, or DIE.

To underline his plea for colonial unity, Benjamin Franklin designed his famous rattlesnake device (left) in 1754 for his Gazette. By 1762, when Mason Chamberlin painted him in wig and ruffles, observing his lightning detector, Franklin was a most influential colonial spokesman in London.

These four illustrations, from an engraving called Poor Richard Illustrated, *have mottoes taken from Franklin's* Almanac.

seaboard. To endure, this land must grow. What was needed now were western colonies beyond the mountains, two of them for a start in that rich land between Lake Erie and the Ohio River. As Franklin tried to explain in his *Plan for Settling Two Western Colonies in North America,* written shortly after the Albany Congress, such new colonies would not only give the English room to expand, but they would throw up a barrier to further expansion by the French.

America was like a vast unplanted field. Scatter some fennel seeds and soon the field would be all fennel. Scatter the American land beyond the mountains with men, and the population would double every 25 years. Left to themselves the older colonies would expand by inches, but expansion

now had to be by miles. Plow the lands to the west, sow them with transplanted Englishmen, and the harvest would astonish the world. That was the way Benjamin Franklin saw it—twenty years before the American Revolution.

In the years that Franklin spent in London as agent for the Pennsylvania Assembly after 1757, he never lost his conviction that local government in a united America with American representation in the English Parliament would create the most impressive political combination in the world. Rational discussion should be able to clear away preliminary misunderstandings.

The years, even with their increasing colonial solidarity, brought him slow disillusionment while they also brought him a sage's fame. Learned men

STOKES COLLECTION, N.Y. PUBLIC LIBRARY

The two pictures at left demonstrate the virtues of industry, while the pair at right show the perils of sloth and waste.

from the continent asked on arrival in England to see Dr. Franklin. The scientist-philosopher became the first American to be accepted in the European fellowship of knowledge. He was made a member of the Royal Society, and St. Andrews and Oxford awarded him doctor's degrees. Georgia, New Jersey, and Massachusetts appointed him their agent. In England he was considered the unofficial ambassador of America, and his friends and confidants were among the great of the land. Few London figures were better known.

To Franklin the casual way in which a heedless British government was undermining the empire he believed in seemed catastrophic. Always he kept the diminishing hope that common sense—in the shape of a new monarch or ministry—might pre-

vail. But even as it had been in America a generation earlier, that sovereign virtue was lacking.

The First Continental Congress left Franklin still persuaded that intelligent men on both sides of the Atlantic could resolve the approaching conflict. He sailed from England in March, 1775, just one day before his friend Edmund Burke made his great speech on conciliation in the House of Commons. The day of the explosion at Concord and Lexington found him at sea.

Franklin's beloved Philadelphia was by the time of the Revolution the first city in population in the colonies. Quick to care for its indigent and sick, the city supported a House of Employment and Almshouse (left) and the Pennsylvania Hospital (right), which Franklin helped to found in 1756.

PRINTS DIVISION, N.Y. PUBLIC LIBRARY

Robert Rogers

Anything the Indians could do Robert Rogers could do as well or better. He could travel faster afoot, by canoe, or on snowshoes, endure more on as little food. He was a better leader, a better scout, a much better shot, and equally good at scalping. On the bloody northern frontier between Canada and the colonies in the middle of the eighteenth century no name commanded more awed respect than that of Rogers. He knew that intermediate wilderness from Lake George to beyond Lake Champlain as if it were the palm of his hand. Rogers' Rangers in their tawny buckskins and Lincoln green were the terror of the woods.

He had grown up in a New Hampshire frontier village and as a young man had smuggler's dealings with the French and Indians, picking up their speech. Though he acquired some learning—in later life he even wrote a play—he found his deepest release in forest warfare.

In the French and Indian War his Rangers harried the French, ambushing their scouting parties, snatching messengers and patrols from under the walls of Ticonderoga. His most celebrated feat was the destruction of the scalphung Abenaki nest on the St. Francis, headquarters of the bloody raids against New England. The hardships of his subsequent retreat down the Connecticut Valley with the French in pursuit became a legend. Only his iron will held the starving survivors together.

At the war's end, under Amherst's orders, Rogers and his Rangers took possession of Detroit, the farthest west that British forces had yet penetrated.

He-Who-Does-Much
Oversees the
Mohawk Frontier

But for the formidable Iroquois, the French could have completed their great arch of fortifications from Quebec to New Orleans. The Mohawk Valley, the one break in the Appalachian chain and a gateway to the West, was, however, denied them by the English-Iroquois alliance.

That this alliance endured, that—in the Indian phrase—its links were kept bright, was due to William Johnson. He, the genial young Anglo-Irishman, had arrived in the valley as a trader and astonished both Indians and whites by trading honestly. The Indians of the Six Nations came first to respect and then to love him.

Johnson liked Indians and their ways. He treated them as equals, learned their language, sat at their campfires, wrestled with their braves, mated with their squaws. The Mohawks made him a war chief, calling him Warraghiyagey, He-Who-Does-Much. When he established his domain at Johnson Hall, his Mohawks moved their tribal fire there, camping on his grounds hundreds at a time and wandering through the place at will.

Johnson became a fabled figure in the valley—the wealthiest colonial of his day, lord of hundreds of thousands of acres, casual dispenser of feudal munificence at Johnson Hall, sole successful military commander in the disastrous year of Braddock's defeat, major general of militia, superintendent of Indian affairs, and the second baronet to be created in America.

Even after his death the Mohawks kept the blood-bond, following his Loyalist son to Canada. History always has its perhapses, yet if it had not been for Warraghiyagey the Midwest might well be, even today, a French-speaking area.

Through his friendship with the Iroquois, Sir William Johnson kept the vital Mohawk corridor open to English settlement and closed to the French. This newly discovered portrait, attributed to Matthew Pratt, was painted about 1772.

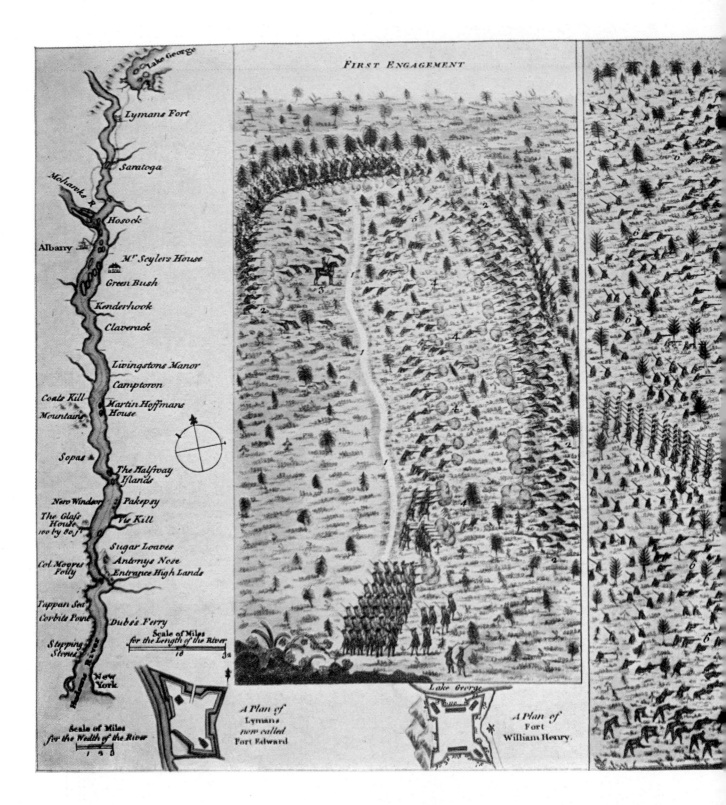

The Battle of Lake George

COLLECTION OF MRS. JOHN NICHOLAS BROWN

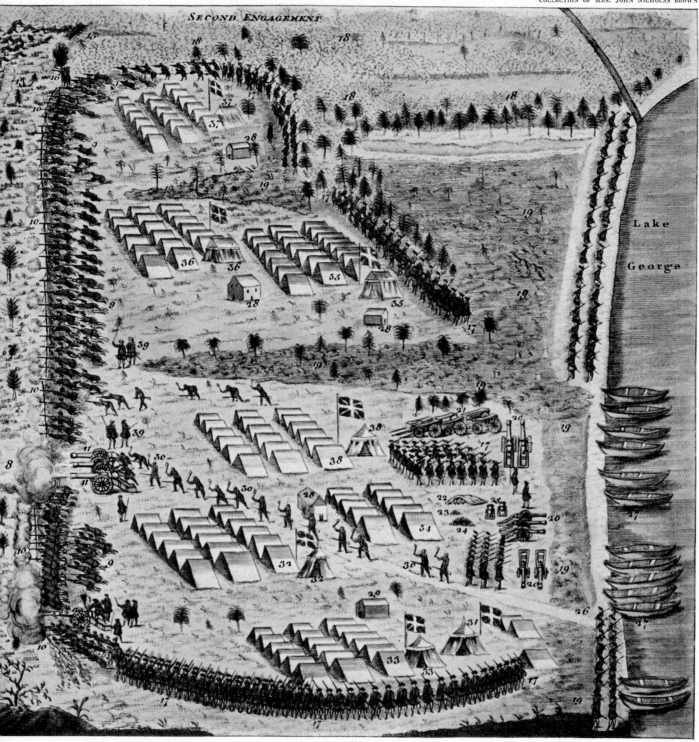

In 1755, during the French and Indian War, Johnson marched on Crown Point with an army of colonials and Mohawks. Reaching Lake George, he was attacked by the French-Indian force of Baron Dieskau, as shown in this 1756 English engraving. At left, blue-clad colonials, the "bloody morning scout," are ambushed and "doubled up like a pack of cards." Dieskau then struck Johnson's camp (right), but artillery repulsed his regulars—now the French are in blue—and a counterattack routed them. Dieskau was captured, but the victorious Johnson gave up his attempt on Crown Point.

99

Colonel Washington of the Virginia militia, by C. W. Peale.

Wilderness Command

The candle flame sputtered as the young militia colonel in the sodden blue tunic read and then signed the capitulation terms. Not ungenerously the French had granted his garrison full honors of war, allowing them to march out with drums beating, colors flying, and all the belongings that they could carry. The Indians would be restrained as far as possible.

George Washington had done his best, but this was the sorry end of Governor Dinwiddie's 1754 expedition into the Ohio country. The ignominious surrender of the swampland stockade aptly named Fort Necessity was merely the climax of a chain of misfortunes. Supplies and reinforcements had failed, there was never enough food or ammunition, transportation kept breaking down, the volunteers refused to co-operate with the Virginia militia, his Indians had deserted. And finally Colonel Washington saw his forces driven into the marshy rectangle of Fort Necessity, outnumbered three to one by the French and Indians, a third of his effectives out of action, all the horses and cattle killed, food almost exhausted, their powder soaked by the driving rain. At the last the survivors had got into the rum supply. There was no alternative but to give up his sword.

The Virginia House of Burgesses thanked him for his services, but when the less thankful Dinwiddie divided his troops into independent companies and offered him a mere captaincy, he resigned. The martial career he had planned, the King's commission, a scarlet tunic to replace the militia blue, had gone aglimmering. Nevertheless, when Major General Edward Braddock arrived in Virginia with his regulars the following year to demonstrate to the colonial amateurs how an Ohio campaign should be conducted, Washington's interest and military ambitions revived. And when the British general flatteringly offered to make him an aide-de-camp on his staff, Washington was glad to accept.

Braddock was a parade-ground soldier who in his 45 years of army life had seen no real combat. His secretary, William Shirley, son of the Massachu-

WISCONSIN STATE HISTORICAL SOCIETY

setts governor, described him as "most judiciously chosen for being disqualified for the service he is employed in."

Washington at 23 had an inherited pride in British arms and a still-awed respect for the professional soldier, but the progress of Braddock's train from Alexandria over the Alleghenies toward the distant goal of Fort Duquesne filled him by degrees with disillusion and dismay. These close red lines would not be able to meet the challenge of the forest, and the plump Guards officer who commanded, riding in his carriage as the drums beat the *Grenadier's March,* would not learn and could not be told.

When Braddock's mobile column of 1,500 finally crossed the Monongahela ford a few miles below Duquesne, Washington watched them pass, the scarlet and pipe-clayed ranks bright against the forest greenery, the sun sharp on water and bayonets and helmet brass. Afterward the Virginian aide said it was the most thrilling sight of his life.

Half an hour after the ordered lines disappeared into the woods, disaster struck. Suddenly the advance guard came face to face with a war party

Trying to rally his redcoats, Braddock was mortally wounded (above) and aide-de-camp Washington had two horses shot from under him. Of 1,459 British troops, 977 were casualties.

of some 300 Indians led by a French officer who, on sighting the redcoats, gave the signal for his men to fan out. In the first exchange of volleys the officer and several dozen Indians fell, and for that brief moment the battle was in the balance; but the Indians rallied, took cover on the heights, and began picking off the massed British ranks. On three sides the English were hemmed in, enfiladed by invisible fire, their mounted officers the first to fall. Unpracticed in cover and deployment, they tried to hold their ground, waiting for the enemy to form a line of battle, and endured the slaughter until flesh overcame discipline and the disaster became a rout.

Braddock, never lacking in courage, was shot through the lungs while attempting to rally his men. George Washington managed to bring him back across the river. "Who would have thought it?" the dying general kept asking.

101

W. H. ROBERTSON-AIKMAN

John Forbes

Fortunately, some men learned the lesson of Braddock's defeat, and Brigadier John Forbes was one of them. This genial, adaptable Scotsman had served in America as adjutant general and in 1758 was appointed by Pitt to renew the drive against Fort Duquesne. He was slowly dying during the campaign and had to direct his command from a litter, but he could truthfully say, "my sickness has not retarded my operations one single moment."

At the outset he was faced with the usual difficulties of stalled supplies, delayed reinforcements, and indifferent provincials, all compounded by the stupidities of his quartermaster general. Washington joined him as colonel in command of the Virginians, and although he and Forbes had a difference of opinion as to the route, the latter came to rely on the Virginia colonel.

The force of over 5,000 provincials and 1,400 Scots Highlanders was slow in starting and it was not until September that it finally got under way. Mindful of Braddock's mistakes, Forbes made his way by cautious stages, setting up provisioned blockhouses at intervals. He had considerable success, too, in detaching the Indians from their French allies.

Caution and the November rains held Forbes back. He was about to go into winter quarters at Loyal Hannon, fifty miles east of Duquesne, when he learned from stragglers of the plight of the French garrison, supplies exhausted and deserted by the Indians. A light force that he sent forward found the fort destroyed. Control of the upper Ohio Valley passed to the English without a shot.

Advance into Ohio Country

Forbes' second-in-command, the man he relied on most, was Henry Bouquet, lieutenant colonel of the Royal Americans, a regiment composed largely of Pennsylvania Germans. The Swiss-born Bouquet had served in the Dutch Army and had been made captain commandant of a regiment. In 1755 the British offered him command of the new Royal American Regiment.

Bouquet was free of the caste rigidity of the military mind. He treated colonial officers and troops with as much consideration as if they were regulars, he was open to advice, and was particularly interested in developing tactics of forest combat. Whenever he could he observed the Indians and their ways, becoming a skilled Indian fighter.

Five years after he watched the smoking ruins of Duquesne with Forbes, he was marching again toward the fort, now rebuilt and renamed Pitt. Pontiac's savage uprising, following the French peace, saw the English garrisons of ten western forts massacred and Fort Pitt besieged.

Jeffery Amherst, the British commander in chief, sent Bouquet with two under-strength Black Watch battalions and some Pennsylvania volunteers as a relief expedition. North of Braddock's old ground, at Bushy Run, Bouquet found himself surprised by a superior force of Indians. Leading his men in a bayonet charge he reached high ground, where he fought surrounded for seven hours—twice as long as Braddock—until nightfall. In spite of heat, thirst, and fatigue his men kept up their courage and their confidence in him.

Morning brought a renewed attack. Knowing that the Indians were waiting for the first sign of retreat, Bouquet drew back his two forward companies as if in panic, spreading the flanking troops in a thin fixed line. As soon as the whooping Indians swarmed into the gap, the two companies dodged back under cover to close it. Once within the circle the Indians were cut down from all angles before they could reload or fire. Those who managed to escape were broken fugitives, and the threat to the upper Ohio Valley collapsed. Bouquet's Bushy Run victory—the most closely contested battle ever fought between Indians and whites—opened the way for the westward-moving settlers.

PENNSYLVANIA HISTORICAL AND MUSEUM COMMISSION

Like Forbes, Swiss soldier of fortune Henry Bouquet (above) learned well the lesson of Braddock's disaster. After being ambushed at Bushy Run near Fort Pitt in 1763, he nearly annihilated his foe. The next year he cowed the Seneca, Delaware, and Shawnee tribes at a council on the banks of the Muskingum River (below), opening the way for the surge of settlers into the Ohio country.

LIBRARY OF CONGRESS

103

ALAN F. KIRBY COLLECTION, LAFAYETTE COLLEGE

BUILDING A NATION

DANIEL Boone and James Harrod had proved before the Revolution how determined settlers were to enter the trans-Allegheny West. No matter what government ruled America, they would have continued to enter it, for no barriers could hold them back. But in the forty years after 1775, the West was thrown open under circumstances almost ideally free and systematic, through a series of events involving the labors and farsighted dreams of many men.

One was a Virginian, George Rogers Clark, whose daring made certain that the close of the Revolution would find all of the Old Northwest in American hands. One was a Bay State clergyman, Manasseh Cutler, who prodded the Continental Congress into passing the Northwest Ordinance. A farsighted President, Thomas Jefferson, a Haitian patriot, Toussaint L'Ouverture, and some determined British statesmen created a situation which compelled France to sell the Louisiana country. The Revolutionary veteran Anthony Wayne and the land-greedy territorial governor William Henry Harrison gave the Indians two stunning defeats which made border settlers fairly secure. And a little group which included the obsessed Connecticut genius John Fitch, the genial Virginia tavern-keeper James Rumsey, and the masterful New York organizer Robert Fulton, brought steamboats into existence. Planners of roads and canals, builders of the Conestoga wagon, back-country smiths who made the "Kentucky rifle" and the well-balanced, keen-edged American axe, all lent their contributions, too.

Whether the Revolution is viewed as a struggle for autonomy, a civil conflict, or a social upheaval, it must also be seen as a war which changed the destiny of the West. Saratoga and Yorktown were no more decisive than King's Mountain and the capture of Vincennes. For at King's Mountain in 1780 the Carolina backwoodsmen, attacking a Tory force of equal numbers in a strong position, prostrated the southern Loyalists, turned Cornwallis back, and proved the Americanism of the border country. Earlier, Vincennes determined the character of the map of the West which would be laid before the peacemakers when they finally met around a table in Paris.

The West saved itself for the United States during the Revolution. While the red-haired, six-foot surveyor George Rogers Clark and his little band of frontiersmen were saving the Old Northwest, the Old Southwest was preserved by the determined little communities which had sprung up before and during the war: Boonesborough, Harrodsburg, Watauga, and other settlements, under such leaders as Isaac Shelby, John Sevier, and James Robertson.

Boonesborough endured its first Indian siege in 1777, the year before Clark surprised Kaskaskia. The next year Boone, while a prisoner of the Indians, found the Delawares and Shawnees in the Ohio country assembling for a new attack and escaped and ran 160 miles in four days to warn the settlers. Simon Girty, the "white savage," helped invade Kentucky, and Harrodsburg was closely beset. Farther south Alexander McGillivray, with a British commission, led the warlike Creeks against the border, and the Cherokees abetted them in their forays. In the Watauga district wise, honest James

Robertson lost a brother and two children—one son, as he pathetically wrote McGillivray, being "uncommonly Massacred." Yet the backwoods folk not only held on, but increased their numbers and advanced. In the year of King's Mountain Robertson, "the father of Tennessee," led a large party to the point where the Cumberland bends northwest to flow into the Ohio, and founded Nashville. In East Tennessee the thickening inhabitants meanwhile began to plan the separate state which they blocked out just after the war—the short-lived Frankland, or land of the free, which was renamed Franklin. On foundations laid during the Revolution, Kentucky developed so fast that it entered the Union in 1792; Tennessee followed four years later.

No task of the new American government was more imperative than to gain control of the lands in the Old Northwest and then organize them for settlement. In short, it had to form colonies under its own tutelage, but on a better basis than Great Britain had done. Some of the states, like Virginia, had huge western claims; some, like South Carolina, minor claims; and some none at all. Maryland led the non-claimant sisters in laying down a clear ultimatum: unless the lands were surrendered, there would be no Union. New York gallantly cleared the path in 1780 by ceding its cloudy western titles to the Continental Congress, and by the end of 1786 all the other claimants had followed. The primitive national government thus had at its disposal a vast domain, by far its principal asset. But how should the lands be distributed to settlers? How should the domain be governed? And what about removing or at least quieting the Indians?

The settlers of the two regions were of picturesquely divergent types. From Kentucky southward true backwoods folk like the parents of Davy Crockett and Abraham Lincoln, drawn from varied stocks, made their clearings and erected their cabins. In the Northwest the first inhabitants were mainly New Englanders, who moved westward after filling up the best lands of Maine, New Hampshire, and the Mohawk Valley. They were thriftier than their southern neighbors, more interested in education and community life, and hostile to slavery. In the Northwest the newcomers wanted farms of moderate size; in the Southwest—especially after Eli Whitney's gin made cotton profitable—they preferred large plantations.

A land system for the pioneers came first. Revolutionary veterans, European immigrants, keen Yankee traders, Scotch-Irish, Quakers, and Germans from Pennsylvania and North Carolina—all wanted clear titles. By the Ordinance of 1785 Congress divided the public lands into townships six miles square to be subdivided into 36 sections of one square mile. Land was to be auctioned to individuals at not less than a dollar an acre, and four sections in each township were to be reserved for the support of schools. This was good as far as it went; but when Rufus Putnam's Ohio Company obtained 1,500,000 acres, with a speculative interest in a much larger tract, its energetic agent Manasseh Cutler saw that further action was needed.

Before settlers would really buy lands in the wilderness, a system of government must be devised. So it was that the freedom which the pioneer impulse always fostered found a striking new development. Responding to Cutler and others, Congress passed the Ordinance of 1787, creating the territory north of the Ohio, which might presently be carved into five new territories. The Ordinance provided for a steady progression through three stages of government to complete self-rule as a new state; and this state was to be equal in all respects to the older members of the Union. The pioneers thus won a principle of novel power: where European nations, in establishing colonies, had kept them politically and economically dependent, the United States made them equal partners. And the Continental Congress by a momentous clause forever debarred slavery from the Northwest.

Beyond this, until the threat from actual or potential foreign foes—Indians, British, Spanish, and French—was ended, the West could never grow satisfactorily. In time of war or tension foreign agents incited the tribes to attack American settlements. The British, holding on to their northwestern posts at Niagara, Miami, and Detroit, were especially troublesome. Spanish power, controlling the mouth of the Mississippi, could always throttle the western economy, while France was so strong and so militant that her reappearance in North America was constantly dreaded. During Washington's presidency the young republic made some progress in reducing these dangers. When northwestern tribes rose and whipped Arthur St. Clair's little army, "Mad Anthony" Wayne took a new force, crushed the savages at Fallen Timbers in 1794, and by the Treaty of Greenville the next year obtained a surrender of practically the whole Ohio country. In 1794 John Jay's celebrated treaty had also ended British tenure of the northwestern posts.

The greatest threat of all, however, remained. Foreign possession of New Orleans and the west bank of the Mississippi had made for constant plots and ebullitions of disloyalty in the Southwest. Americans did not greatly mind Britain's hold on Canada, for England was a kindred and generally reasonable country. But they disliked the Spaniards and barely tolerated them because Spain was weak. They feared this weakness would lead to some disastrous event, and in 1800 it did. Spain suddenly transferred the wide Louisiana reaches to France, where Napoleon was indulging in dreams of an American empire, and a wave of apprehension and anger rolled through the western settlements. That wave in itself did something to effect the swift change of Napoleon's plans. Jefferson rose to the crisis by persuading Congress to vote 80,000 troops and fifteen Mississippi gunboats, and wrote grimly of an impending Anglo-American alliance.

When Napoleon decided to sell the Louisiana territory, the United States not only doubled its area by a stroke of the pen—all the anxieties that had enveloped the West disappeared, pioneers planned and toiled in a fresher atmosphere, the demand for internal improvements became clamorous, and men looked more than ever to far-off prairies, rivers, and mountains. The new century saw a fast-swelling tide of population seeking roads to the fertile territories just opened, from Wisconsin to Alabama. And the roads were there, in great parallel highways. The Boston-Albany road by 1805 connected with the Mohawk Turnpike and Genesee Road across northern New York; the Catskill Turnpike ran farther south; Forbes' Road across Pennsylvania was filled with vehicles and herds; that other memorable military artery, Braddock's Road, was equally useful; and the road down the Great Valley to Cumberland Gap debouched into the Wilderness Road across Kentucky. America was moving westward—ever westward.

The best symbol of the nation's pioneer vigor was to be found in the homely, ingenious devices for carrying the human throng to the great West. The stagecoach, rattling over the eighty-foot National Road that was begun in 1811; the Conestoga wagon, bright blue beneath, bright red above, with white canvas on hoops sheltering its long, boat-shaped body; the steamboat *New Orleans* that Nicholas Roosevelt spent $38,000 to build and ran from Pittsburgh to the city of her name—these most fitly represented the impulse that was building a greater America.

ALLAN NEVINS

EXECUTIVE MANSION, RICHMOND

George Rogers Clark

George Rogers Clark, Frontier Leader

Of the little boys scribbling on their slates in the one-room schoolhouse on the Mattaponi, two were to write their names in the history of the future United States. One of them, James Madison, would eventually become President. George Rogers Clark, long before that day, would secure the American heartland, the Northwest Territory, for his country.

George Clark was born at the edge of the Virginia settlement, with the Blue Ridge Mountains on his western horizon. Westward he turned as soon as he was old enough to strike out for himself, wandering through the wilderness to the Falls of the Ohio, surveying, hunting, meeting the men of the frontier. Kentucky became his new home and Harrodsburg, the wilderness capital southwest of Boonesborough, his base.

The indefinable quality that makes a man a leader was his gift at birth. When he was only 24 years old, in the second year of the Revolution,

he was commissioned a major and given charge of the defenses of Virginia's Kentucky region. The "year of the bloody sevens," 1777, saw Indian war parties equipped with British guns, hatchets, and scalping knives, stalking the frontier settlements. Raid after raid was sent out from the English fortress post at Detroit, and from Kaskaskia, Cahokia, and Vincennes in Illinois. It was Clark's audacious idea to lead an army against these latter posts, to thrust his way into the prairie country, and to strike at the British jugular.

He managed to convince Patrick Henry, and the Virginia governor gave him what scanty support he could. Clark had hoped for a force of up to a thousand men, but when he started out a year later from Corn Island at the Falls of the Ohio the best he could muster was about 175 frontiersmen, enough for four small companies.

They voyaged by flatboat down the Ohio to its junction with the Tennessee; then, with their scant

Clark's conquest of the Illinois country tended to neutralize England's key outpost at Detroit (above, sketched in 1780). The Indians that the British had armed were loath to tangle with Clark's fierce Long Knives, few in number as the latter were.

supplies on their backs, they plunged across prairie and forest to Kaskaskia. In spite of the change of regime, Kaskaskia—the oldest settlement in the western country—had remained a French town even to its commandant, who, with the habitants, had merely transferred his allegiance to the English.

Clark and his men found the fort indifferently guarded by local militia and stormed it at midnight on July 4, 1778, in an action so sudden that there were no casualties, and the commandant was captured in bed with his wife.

Kaskaskia's casual habitants were readily persuaded to transfer their allegiance to the Americans, as were those of Cahokia and Vincennes, and Clark's skeleton force found itself in complete control of the Illinois region. The control was temporary, however. Lieutenant Colonel Hamilton, the British commander at Detroit, led a counter-expedition of 500 which at the outset of winter recaptured Vincennes from the handful of soldiers

left behind. In the spring he planned mopping-up operations against the Americans.

Clark met this challenge with a plan so bold that it bordered the foolhardy—a forced winter march with his remaining 170 men against Vincennes.

In the rain of a February afternoon he set out on an incredible 180-mile trek over prairie and swamp. The men marched and slept wet. For miles they waded waist-deep through flooded bottom land, Clark in the lead singing, cajoling, if necessary taunting them on, or in a final desperate gesture smearing his face with powder and giving the Indian war whoop. The last two days they had no rations at all.

His desperate gamble paid off. Feigning a much larger force, he surprised the garrison and overawed Hamilton into surrendering. As the double line of redcoats filed out the mud-coated, famished Americans trudged in, too weary to grasp the symbolism of their feat.

Commonwealth of Massachusetts.

By His EXCELLENCY

JAMES BOWDOIN, Esquire,

Governour of the Commonwealth of Massachusetts.

A Proclamation.

WHEREAS information has been given to the Supreme Executive of this Commonwealth, that on Tuesday last, the 29th of August, being the day appointed by law for the sitting of the Court of Common Pleas and Court of General Sessions of the Peace, at Northampton, in the county of Hampshire, within this Commonwealth, a large concourse of people, from several parts of that county, assembled at the Court-House in Northampton, many of whom were armed with guns, swords and other deadly weapons, and with drums beating and fifes playing, in contempt and open defiance of the authority of this Government, did, by their threats of violence and keeping possession of the Court-House until twelve o'clock on the night of the same day, prevent the sitting of the Court, and the orderly administration of justice in that county:

AND WHEREAS this high-handed offence is fraught with the most fatal and pernicious consequences, must tend to subvert all law and government; to dissolve our excellent Constitution, and introduce universal riot, anarchy and confusion, which would probably terminate in absolute despotism, and consequently destroy the fairest prospects of political happiness, that any people was ever favoured with:

I HAVE therefore thought fit, by and with the advice of the Council, to issue this Proclamation, calling upon all Judges, Justices, Sheriffs, Constables, and other officers, civil and military, within this Commonwealth, to prevent and suppress all such violent and riotous proceedings, if they should be attempted in their several counties.

AND I DO hereby, pursuant to the indispensible duty I owe to the good people of this Commonwealth, most solemnly call upon them, as they value the blessings of freedom and independence, which at the expence of so much blood and treasure they have purchased—as they regard their faith, which in the sight of GOD and the world, they pledged to one another, and to the people of the United States, when they adopted the present Constitution of Government—as they would not disappoint the hopes, and thereby become contemptible in the eyes of other nations, in the view of whom they have risen to glory and empire—as they would not deprive themselves of the security derived from well-regulated Society, to their lives, liberties and property; and as they would not devolve upon their children, instead of peace, freedom and safety, a state of anarchy, confusion and slavery,—I do most earnestly and most solemnly call upon them to aid and assist with their utmost efforts the aforesaid officers, and to unite in preventing and suppressing all such treasonable proceedings, and every measure that has a tendency to encourage them.

GIVEN at the COUNCIL-CHAMBER, in Boston, this second day of September, in the year of our Lord, one thousand seven hundred and eighty-six, and in the eleventh year of the Independence of the United States of AMERICA.

JAMES BOWDOIN.

By his Excellency's command.

JOHN AVERY, jun. Secretary.

BOSTON: Printed by ADAMS and NOURSE, Printers to the GENERAL COURT.

A proclamation issued by the Massachusetts governor, condemning the "treasonable proceedings" of Shays' regulators.

Harvard-educated Nathan Dane helped to draft the Northwest Ordinance of 1787 and wrote its no-slavery provision.

A Troubled Nation Writes a Constitution

The "regulators"—armed men with sprigs of hemlock in their hats who rode into Worcester for Court Week—were there "to prevent the sitting of any court that should attempt to take property by distress." They had had enough of foreclosures and debtors' prisons in the thin days following the Revolution. Sons of Liberty many of them had been, soldiers at Bunker Hill and Saratoga and Yorktown. Daniel Shays, their leader, had been a captain in the Continental Army. Let Governor James Bowdoin call them "a despicable, degenerate mob." They had not fought a war to bind themselves afterward to the rich Boston merchants.

Shays' Rebellion, which began in western Massachusetts, was essentially a debtor's revolt. Unlike other state assemblies the Massachusetts legislature had been hesitant in issuing paper money. It took hard currency to pay debts in the Bay State, even when the lack of it drove farmers to the wall and

debtors to jail or over the border. Such farmer-populist demands for cheap money would occur again and again in the West in the years to come.

Shays himself was remarkable only in that he embodied and organized this protest. After his men had made unsuccessful forays in the eastern part of the state, he attempted with 1,200 casuals to seize the United States arsenal at Springfield. Governor Bowdoin sent out a relieving force of 4,400 militiamen under General Benjamin Lincoln, who made a surprise attack in a snowstorm on the unregulated regulators, taking 150 prisoners and scattering the rest. The rebellion collapsed, and Shays himself escaped into New Hampshire.

Shays' Rebellion, like a theorem in political geometry, demonstrated anew the need for a strong central government. A decade under the Articles of Confederation had reduced the United States to the point of thirteen-starred anarchy. Each state

110

An advocate of expansion and popular rule, James Wilson urged the Convention to vest executive power in one person.

Virginia's George Mason refused to sign the Constitution, but soon saw his ideas incorporated in the Bill of Rights.

could and did print its own money, erect tariff barriers against the outside world and its neighboring states, nullify any national law it chose. There was no Supreme Court to interpret laws, no executive to enforce them, and Congress could neither tax nor compel. The war debt was vast and credit in Europe dead. A rope of sand, men called the government contemptuously.

Yet for all its hesitancies this shadowy government did produce in the *Ordinance for the Government of the Territory of the United States, North-West of the River Ohio* the first outline of the sovereign nation, a document second in importance only to the Declaration of Independence and the Constitution.

At the close of the Revolution, when Great Britain rather surprisingly ceded her land east of the Mississippi, seven states entered their overlapping claims to that region. Virginia claimed the entire Ohio Valley by right of George Rogers Clark's conquests, New York demanded all the region between the Great Lakes and the Ohio River through treaty

with the Iroquois. Massachusetts, Connecticut, the Carolinas, and Georgia in turn asserted their claims. Finally, as a way out of this contention, New York relinquished her land claims to the general government, and the other states—with some reluctance—did the same.

Through the Northwest Ordinance Congress established the way in which this new public domain of one to two hundred million acres was to be opened up and governed. Immediate pressure had come from the Ohio Company, made up of Revolutionary veterans for the most part, looking for land in the West, but the Ordinance itself owed much to Jefferson's proposals of a few years earlier. Slavery was to be excluded from the new domain, a governor and three judges appointed, and provision made for dividing the region into from three to five districts that in the course of their growth and development could each be admitted to statehood. In 1787 there were a number of delegates to the Constitutional Convention who would have preferred to supplant the fiberless Confederation with three

111

separate republics—New England, the Middle States, and the South—but as a barrier to such fragmentation there loomed the glimpsed unity of the whole country as represented in the Northwest Ordinance.

In 1783 Congress, sitting in Philadelphia's State House, had been driven out of the city by a surly mob of half-drunken soldiers demanding their back pay. The Pennsylvania authorities made no effort to intervene, and the alarmed congressmen fled to Princeton. It was a sorry conclusion to a Congress that had promulgated the Declaration of Independence seven years before, but indicative enough of the low esteem to which the national government had fallen.

Yet the necessary remedy came about more by chance than intent. In trying to resolve their conflicting state interests, delegates from Virginia, New York, New Jersey, Pennsylvania, and Delaware met at Annapolis in 1786 to work out some sort of common commercial policy. The convention was itself contrary to the Articles of Confederation, though this seemed a petty legalism to a disorganized country flooded with paper money. Although the Annapolis Convention failed, it led to the calling of the great convention of the following year that was to frame the Constitution of the United States. The old Congress, in spite of Annapolis' illegality, accepted proposals for making such changes "as shall . . . render the federal Constitution adequate to the exigencies of Government, and the Preservation of the Union."

The 55 delegates to the Constitutional Convention were aware of their hour of decision. In a world where monarchy was the norm, their task was to erect on the ruins of the Confederation a republic that, as James Madison said, might "decide forever the fate of Republican government." James Wilson felt that for the first time since the creation of the world "America now presents a people assembled to weigh deliberately and calmly and to decide leisurely and peaceably upon the form of government by which they will bind themselves and their posterity." Some there were, nevertheless, who still felt that the forms of state were best preserved in a constitutional royal house. There was even a rumor current that a son of George III was to be offered the American throne, and several Americans—it was said—had sounded out Prince Henry of Prussia. At the Convention's end a lady asked Franklin: "Well, what have we got, Doctor, a republic or a monarchy?" "A republic," he told her, "if you can keep it."

The men of the Convention were among the ablest and most experienced that the embryo nation could muster, with Washington as presiding officer imparting his own aloof dignity to the proceedings. Though the delegates had been called merely to amend the Articles of Confederation, they soon moved boldly to create an entirely new state form. The constitution that they developed, with the defects of the Articles of Confederation in mind, was essentially practical, and its basis was political rather than economic.

Their resolution "that a *national* Government ought to be established consisting of a *supreme* Legislative, Executive and Judiciary" became the basis of all subsequent deliberation. The problem was how to create such a government and yet preserve the identity of the states within the federal structure. So sharp was the cleavage between advocates of state sovereignty and of nationalism that at times the Convention seemed on the point of breaking up.

Most troublesome of all was the election question. The large-state party wanted members of the new Congress to be elected by popular vote and in proportion to the population. The small-state group wanted state equality in Congress and election by the state legislatures. Both sides finally found a way out in the Great Compromise which gave proportionate representation to the House and equal state representation in the Senate. The Convention's highest hurdle was surmounted.

The Articles of Confederation had acted on the states. The Constitution was to act directly on the individual, making him aware of himself for the first time as an American citizen. For the chief quality of the new government would be national, with a sense of American strength and unity that would be felt the more strongly in the West, where state and parochial loyalties dissolved in the surge of the frontier.

At the beginning of the Constitutional Convention Benjamin Franklin had noticed the rayed outline of a sun embossed in the leather back of General Washington's chair and had wondered in his whimsical-skeptical way whether it was rising or setting. At the conclusion of the sessions he knew, he wrote, that the sun was rising.

NEW-YORK HISTORICAL SOCIETY; COURTESY *Life*

ART COMMISSION OF NEW YORK; COURTESY *Life*

As secretary of foreign affairs, John Jay of New York was dismayed at the weakness of the Articles of Confederation. He worked tirelessly for ratification of the Constitution; the Federalist papers dealing with foreign relations are his. He became the Supreme Court's first chief justice.

AMHERST COLLEGE

Alexander Hamilton (above) was instrumental in the calling of the Constitutional Convention. He wrote more than half of the brilliant Federalist papers in defense of the new Constitution and in 1788 almost single-handedly persuaded a reluctant New York state convention to ratify it.

A scholar of the science of government, future President James Madison (left) led the fight for a strong national organization. His "Virginia Plan" called for a government with "positive and compleat authority in all cases which require uniformity," and a vigorous executive and judiciary.

LIBRARY OF CONGRESS

The New Government

To the farmers of western Pennsylvania distilling had become as much a natural right as life, liberty, and the pursuit of happiness. They reacted to the new federal government's tax on whiskey as they had to the Stamp Act thirty years before. They tarred and feathered revenue agents, rode them out of town, set their barns ablaze, and seized federal mails. In 1794 United States authority in the four western counties had ceased to exist.

President Washington, facing the first direct challenge to his authority, was also faced with the problem of the Northwest beyond, where overmountain settlers had become so disaffected by the savagery of Indian attacks and the lack of support from the federal government that they had made tentative approaches both to the English and the Spanish. The 1790 expedition under Josiah Harmar that Washington sent out against the Ohio

At left is an oath of submission signed by participants in the Whiskey Rebellion. Below, Kemmelmeyer's painting shows President George Washington at Fort Cumberland, Virginia, reviewing the troops called up to suppress the rebellion.

HENRY FRANCIS DU PONT WINTERTHUR MUSEUM

Recognizes the West

NEW-YORK HISTORICAL SOCIETY

Indians had been repulsed. A second, led by Arthur St. Clair, suffered a humiliating rout the next year at the hands of Little Turtle, and the Americans lost almost as many men on that black day as Braddock lost on the Monongahela. A third and much tougher regiment, the Legion, was now in the Ohio Valley under command of Anthony Wayne. Although the Pennsylvania rebellion had cut off Wayne's supplies, Washington nevertheless ordered him to attack. At the Battle of Fallen Timbers the Legion shattered Little Turtle's forces and removed the Indian threat to the Ohio country.

Boldness also succeeded in ending the Whiskey Rebellion when Washington, acting on Hamilton's advice, sent 15,000 militia troops across the Alleghenies. Faced with this show of authority, the awed insurgents gave up without firing a shot. The Northwest was now secure.

After their defeat at Fallen Timbers the Indians signed the Treaty of Greenville, ceding southeastern Indiana and southern Ohio for $9,500 in annuities. An unknown artist depicts Wayne, surrounded by his staff, dictating terms.

General "Mad Anthony" Wayne was sent by Washington to avenge the defeats of Harmar and St. Clair by the shrewd and eloquent chief Little Turtle. Near Ohio's Maumee River his Legion routed the Indians in the Battle of Fallen Timbers.

CHICAGO HISTORICAL SOCIETY

Jefferson Purchases Louisiana

Political parties, in the modern sense, developed in the young republic during the presidency of John Adams; growing apace was the political cartoon, usually scurrilous. This Federalist example shows Jefferson pulling down the pillars of government erected by Washington and Adams, as the American eagle protests. Radical "Mad Tom" is assisted by the devil and fortified with a brandy bottle.

I t was "not our interest," Thomas Jefferson wrote sometime before he was President, "to cross the Mississippi for ages!" That farther stretch of continent seemed as little pertinent to the United States at the beginning of the nineteenth century as Antarctica seemed early in the twentieth. The Mississippi River, however, was vital. For the settlers of Tennessee, Kentucky, and Ohio it remained the one highway to the outside world. In 1799 they had shipped down the river 120,000 pounds of tobacco, 10,000 barrels of flour, 22,000 pounds of hemp, and 500 barrels of whiskey.

Since the cession of Louisiana by France to Spain during the French and Indian War the port metropolis of New Orleans had remained French in aspect, Spanish in control. But Spanish control of the strategic city was not oppressive. Americans were allowed to navigate the Mississippi at will and to deposit their goods in New Orleans warehouses duty-free for shipment overseas.

When Napoleon by his Brumaire *coup d'état* became First Consul, he revived not only the state but the old Bourbon dream of empire. Urged by Talleyrand, who had spent the Terror period in America, he now sought the return of Louisiana to France. The Bourbon arc was to have stretched from Canada to New Orleans, but Napoleon conceived of an easier southern arc from New Orleans across the French islands of the Caribbean to the homeland. Spain did not value Louisiana greatly, and in any case the Spanish government could scarcely stand up to the victor of Marengo. By the secret Treaty of San Ildefonso, Spain—with a few Italian provinces for a sop—retroceded Louisiana to France a few months before Jefferson became President. And before the transfer was made public, Spanish agents closed the mouth of the Mississippi River.

To Jefferson, now in the President's house, this seemed an alarming foretaste of things to come. He knew that American frontiersmen would not stand quietly by while their river outlet was sealed off by a foreign garrison. With French control would come French troops and then, most likely, war. Fearful of this possibility, Jefferson gave his minister to France, Robert Livingston, the special mission of sounding out the First Consul as to whether he would at least consider an American offer for New Orleans and Florida before he took possession of Louisiana.

Napoleon, engaged in putting down Toussaint L'Ouverture's revolt in Haiti, was not interested, for he then viewed the reconquest of that island as a prelude to Louisiana's occupation. The perdurable Talleyrand received Livingston with the minimum of civility, and during the summer of 1802 a large-scale French expedition for Louisiana was made ready at the Dutch town of Helvoet Sluys. Livingston could not even approach Talleyrand to suggest the ten-million-dollar offer that Jefferson had authorized him to make.

Yet before the year's end disaster in Haiti altered the whole prospect of a French transatlantic empire. One French army had been almost destroyed in the capture of the "gilded African," and now Napoleon learned that a second occupying army had melted away in a yellow fever epidemic. The Haitian bastion was becoming a grave, and without the intermediate island Louisiana was useless. Napoleon knew when to cut his losses.

To his surprise Livingston soon afterward encountered a more affable Talleyrand, and surprise changed to amazement when the latter asked casually what the United States would be willing to give for the whole Louisiana territory. The American minister's first cautious reaction was to say that his country merely wanted New Orleans and Florida, but he and the minister plenipotentiary, James Monroe, realized at once the scope of this incredible offer. It was almost too much to hope for. Livingston is said to have remarked exultantly that the addition of Louisiana would place the United States among the first-rank powers. After some initial bargaining the two ministers bound their country to pay fifteen million dollars, and France—against all promises made to Spain—ceded Louisiana to the United States.

The Louisiana accession doubled the country's territory, adding the land from which thirteen states would eventually be carved. Yet the acceptance of the French offer by his envoys put Jefferson in a dilemma. He had early sensed the needs and the importance of the West. Even while his agents were in Paris he had been arranging an expedition to explore the source of the Missouri. The westward-moving pioneers—not the caste-conscious eastern Federalists—were the sort of men who had elected him President.

Yet desirable and necessary as the possession of Louisiana might be, did he as President have the right to acquire this land with the stroke of his pen? There was nothing in the Constitution to give him such authority, and only two years before he had written that when a government assumed undelegated powers its acts were "unauthoritative, void, and of no force." His chief quarrel with the Federalists had been that they were usurping powers not specified in the Constitution. Again and again he had maintained that such loose construction would destroy the Union. In his belief the Constitution had to be interpreted strictly, as it was written. If it were to be implied for the sake of present convenience that the federal government could acquire territory merely because this had not been specifically forbidden in the Constitution, then his principle that the federal government was one of enumerated powers would have to be replaced by Hamilton's doctrine that the national government could assume whatever powers seemed necessary.

LOUISIANA HISTORICAL SOCIETY ; COURTESY *Life*

As a practical man sympathetic to the West, Jefferson knew that the possession of Louisiana was vital to the future of the country. But on the other hand, if one President began to undermine the Constitution, there was always an additional step for some successor to take, and who knew where it might end?

The only solution seemed to be to alter the Constitution. Jefferson considered asking Congress for an amendment which would give the federal government authority to purchase new territory. When Livingston and Monroe in Paris learned of this they were aghast. They urged Jefferson to sign the treaty at once before the mercurial First Consul changed his mind, for by the time Congress passed an amendment and the individual states got around to ratifying it, Napoleon might be off on a new adventure. The occasion was too tremendous to let it be overweighed by scrupulosity.

Jefferson knew they were right. Reluctantly he signed the treaty, admitting as he did so that "the Executive . . . have done an act beyond the Constitution." He warned his friends not to bring up constitutional problems, and Congress he begged—in an argument that might have been plotted by his old enemy Hamilton—to disregard "metaphysical subtleties." Troubled by the precedent he had established, Jefferson trusted "that the good sense of our country will correct the evil of loose construction when it shall produce its ill effects."

The Louisiana Purchase was a continuation of the formative process that began with the Northwest Ordinance, and Jefferson's principle of strict construction and his belief in the Union as a compact among the original states would be from this time on overshadowed by the larger pattern of the nation.

The extent of Louisiana was itself a mystery. How far west did it go? Did it include Texas? Livingston questioned Talleyrand as to the boundaries. "I do not know," the wily cripple answered him, "You must take it as we received it." Livingston, pressing him further, asked him how much France had meant to take. "I do not know," Talleyrand replied.

Signaling the greatest triumph of Jefferson's administration, the Louisiana Purchase was formally completed by this ceremony in New Orleans on December 20, 1803; the Stars and Stripes are run up as the French guard fires a salute.

NEW-YORK HISTORICAL SOCIETY

Aaron Burr

The new American republic had taken Rome as a model, with its senate, its neoclassic capitol, and its planned imperial city. And as an ironical complement it had in Aaron Burr its Catiline. Alexander Hamilton remarked that while Jefferson's principles were bad, Burr had none at all. Deft, brilliant, unscrupulous, Burr ended his political career when, as Vice-President, he killed Hamilton in their Weehawken duel. After that he became the pure schemer, though the thread of his schemes has never yet been wholly unraveled.

Burr left for New Orleans, visiting every adventurer and malcontent of any prominence along the way. War threatened then with Spain over the Floridas, and it is probable that Burr had plans for an invasion of Mexico. Earlier he had secretly approached the British minister, asking for funds to aid a revolution in the Southwest, though whether he intended any direct action against the United States is doubtful. He was, however, in close contact with General James Wilkinson, who was later shown to have been in the pay of Spain.

The following year Burr gathered a task force on an island in the Ohio belonging to the wealthy eccentric Harman Blennerhassett. His intention was either with Wilkinson's connivance to set up a Southwest empire, or to make himself Emperor of Mexico. In any case, as soon as the expedition got under way Jefferson had Burr arraigned for high treason. Although Burr managed an acquittal, it was clear that he had no popular backing. The shabby episode was a ringing proof of the loyalty of the western states to the Union.

119

Expansionist Dreams and War in the West

ad Anthony Wayne was dead and Fallen Timbers a fading memory. By piecemeal grant and purchase the tribes of the Northwest were being forced farther and farther back into the contracting northern oval of the Indiana Territory. Against this relentless process the Shawnee chief Tecumseh, with massive undercover British support, spent the years just before the War of 1812 building up a confederation that for a while threatened the whole American territorial advance.

Intelligent and brave, a man of superb bearing, Tecumseh was a gallant adversary and the most formidable Indian leader to appear since Pontiac. He and young Lieutenant William Henry Harrison, Wayne's aide, had fought at Fallen Timbers and had met at Greenville, where Tecumseh contemptuously refused to sign the treaty. In their middle years they were to meet again in the final Indian challenge of the Old Northwest—Tecumseh commander of the tribes in alliance with the British-Canadian forces; Harrison, a general and governor of the Indiana Territory, now commander in chief of the Army of the Northwest.

The war began disastrously for the Americans with the surrender of Detroit by the senile General William Hull and the destruction of General James Winchester's army the following winter after a rash unsupported march to River Raisin. But by autumn Harrison had retaken Detroit and advanced into Canada in pursuit of the British under the incompetent General Henry Proctor. The two forces finally engaged at the Thames River in a quick, bloody American victory in which Proctor fled and the dauntless Tecumseh stayed to be killed. The disillusioned tribesmen crept back to make their peace with Harrison. No longer would they be a threat to the American occupation line moving on now from the Wabash to the Illinois.

LIBRARY OF CONGRESS; COURTESY *Life*

SIGMUND SAMUEL CANADIANA GALLERY, ROYAL ONTARIO MUSEUM; COURTESY *Life*

Thinking Canada ripe for the plucking in 1812, an American army gained a toe hold at Queenston across the Niagara River (above, Americans in red). But it was wiped out when New York militia reinforcements refused to leave their state.

The illustration at left shows the death of the great Shawnee chief Tecumseh at the Battle of the Thames. Harrison's victory was total, and after Tecumseh's demise the remnants of his shattered Indian confederacy deserted the British.

William Henry Harrison (right) knew how to get the most from his frontier militiamen. In 1811, at Tippecanoe Creek, Indiana Territory, he fought Tecumseh's one-eyed brother and acquired a nickname that took him to the White House.

FRANCIS VIGO CHAPTER, D.A.R., VINCENNES

Henry Clay's American System

In bearing he was the incarnation of the nascent century. The previous century's neoclassic balance had given way to the flowing hyperbolic periods that came to him so easily. When he spoke to the House of Representatives, ladies fluttered in the galleries. A speech could last three or four days. Oratory was on its way to becoming a national vice.

His portraits show him dressed in sober frock coat and skin-tight trousers, the high wing collar above the black stock cornering his cheeks and forcing his head back in a stylized imperious stance. Sometimes he holds a quill in his right hand, or else his two hands poise in eloquent gesture duplicated afterward in a hundred books of elocution. At his feet lies the globe-symbol, and behind him are the Stars and Stripes. Here is the statesman-politician in the new romantic mold—Henry Clay, "Harry of the West."

Clay was the first great leader and spokesman of the West, marking in his emergent person the decline of the Tidewater hierarchy that had from the beginning dominated the young republic. In 1797, at the age of twenty and with no more capital than a law license, he had made his way through the Cumberland Gap to Lexington, Kentucky. There he quickly established himself as a brilliant trial lawyer. His driving interest, however, was in politics, in the national scene. In 1811, after two interim appointments to the Senate, he was elected to the House of Representatives, where he became in his first term Speaker and leader of the young southern and western War Hawks who were to force a reluctant Madison into the war against England. He declared confidently that the Kentucky militia alone could take Montreal and Upper Canada. The irregular course of the war sobered and matured him, bringing out the conservative side of his nature that would prevent him from ever attaining the close identification with the common man that his rival Andrew Jackson did.

European imports of American food surpluses had ceased after the fall of Napoleon, and the ensuing depression of 1819 led Clay to evolve a system of economic self-sufficiency as an answer to the paradox of bankruptcy in a land of plenty. Looking for an American prosperity independent of world markets, he plumped for an alliance between the undeveloped West and the industrial North.

On March 30 and 31, 1824, Clay made his classic two-day speech in which he explained and urged on the country his American System. In it he advocated a planned national economy, developed and regulated by the federal government. To the government would fall the burden of internal improvements, a mighty network of roads and canals which would speed the agricultural products of the West to the eastern cities. A high tariff would enable American industries to develop behind a protective wall and at the same time would furnish funds for necessary public works. In this way the United States, insulated from the vagaries of European markets, would be able to develop an internal stability of exchange. Tariffs would protect both industry and agriculture, federal highways would connect them. Let American farmers wear American cotton spun in American mills! Let American cotton spinners and mechanics eat western food and drink western whiskey! With the country stimulated by a growing population, with the domestic market constantly expanding, the American System promised to link all sections of the United States together in a prosperous, mutually dependent whole.

In its time and place Clay's system was a tremendous concept, no narrow nationalism but a vision of a continent. His high rhetoric even then encompassed a future when "the wave of population, cultivation, and intelligence shall have washed the Rocky Mountains and have mingled with the Pacific." But though the West honored him, the frontiersmen and the men from the slashes never responded to Clay's dignity and polished phrases the way they did to Jackson's earthy manner.

More than anything else in his long political career Clay wanted to become President. Five times he was an aspirant. But directly or indirectly the shadow of his great rival was always too much for Harry of the West.

This life-size portrait of Henry Clay, by John Neagle, includes symbols of Clay's statecraft (right), American System (left), and life as a gentleman-farmer (background).

MUSEUM OF THE CITY OF NEW YORK

DeWitt Clinton

and the Big Ditch

NEW-YORK HISTORICAL SOCIETY

Up and down the Mohawk Valley the canal barges passed like meadow ships, just above the level of the marsh grasses and hardhack and buttonbush. Silhouetted against sky and summer greenness, moving at three miles an hour, they formed a gay background of blue, orange, and red to the sober reapers in the August fields. Yet the slowness of the placid scene was deceptive. Twenty thousand barges a season traversed the canal, from 31-ton passenger packets to bullheads of 72 tons carrying freight.

The Grand Canal, Governor DeWitt Clinton called this cherished dream of his; his opponents had labeled it Clinton's Gutter. To those living in the new towns along its banks it was the Can-awl. The Erie Canal, however called, was the greatest piece of engineering that had yet been undertaken on the continent, a prodigious man-made waterway linking Lake Erie and the Atlantic Ocean. Forty feet wide, four feet deep, and 362 miles long, it was eight years in the building. Finished a year after Henry Clay's American System speech, it became a practical demonstration of his theory.

Pennsylvania and Virginia had had visions of a

New York Governor DeWitt Clinton, by staunchly support-
ing the building of the Erie Canal, gave impetus to western
settlement. This portrait was done by John Wesley Jarvis.

Anthony Imbert's painting shows a flotilla from Albany and points west, in New York Harbor in 1825 to open the Erie Canal officially and set off the "Grand Canal Celebration."

westward canal, only to come up against the rugged reality of the Appalachian barrier. New York state alone, with its natural highway of the Mohawk Valley, held the possibility of water access to the West. President Jefferson had considered a New York canal a harebrained scheme. President Madison was more sympathetic, but he could not persuade Congress to expend government funds on the project. DeWitt Clinton, now mayor of New York city but still pursuing his canal dream, was all for having New York state do the job, and in 1817 he stumped the state and got himself elected governor on a pro-canal platform. To his sanguine mind the canal would not only pay for itself out of tolls but free the state's inhabitants forever from all personal and real estate taxes.

The sole precedent for such large-scale public works was the new federal road from Cumberland, Maryland, to Wheeling. No state government had ever attempted what Governor Clinton was now undertaking, but he kept his promise, and the Fourth of July following his election the first shovelful of earth was turned over for his Grand Canal.

One side effect of the "Big Ditch" project was the initial wave of mass immigration that would within a short time double the population of New York city. Irish laborers swarmed overseas, enticed by the promise of "meat three times a day, plenty

of bread and vegetables, with a reasonable allowance of liquor, and eight, ten, or twelve dollars a month wages." At year's end over 3,000 of them were digging the canal bed, quartered in their sleazy compounds, working their dawn-to-sunset day.

Even the panic year of 1819 left Governor Clinton undaunted. And as the work progressed, doubters—centered chiefly in New York city—diminished while new towns were springing up along the canal route.

October of 1825 saw the final canal link and the first water caravan from Lake Erie to the sea, with Clinton himself leading the ceremonial flotilla in the canalboat *Seneca Chief*. That nine-day voyage, punctuated by the daily roar of cannon and the nightly flare of burning tar barrels, reached its convivial climax in New York, where a procession five miles long marched down Broadway to the Battery to welcome the nautical governor.

Before long the Erie Canal was to become the gateway through which immigrants poured into Michigan, Wisconsin, Indiana, and Minnesota, breaking the monopoly Kentucky and Tennessee had once held on the West.

125

MELLON COLLECTION, NATIONAL GALLERY OF ART

Old Hickory, Western Hero

I cannot believe," Henry Clay wrote with wistful petulance, "that the killing of 2,500 Englishmen at New Orleans qualifies a person for the various, difficult, and complicated duties of the chief magistracy."

He never could understand the source of Andrew Jackson's appeal. Clay knew himself to be more intelligent and a more astute and experienced political leader with a larger grasp of state affairs, yet the militia general, on the strength of a useless victory, would march triumphantly to the White House, thrusting Harry of the West and his ambitions aside. The explanation, though it escaped Clay, was a simple one. Clay was indeed the spokesman for the West, and respected as such. But Jackson in his violent self *was* the West. Frontiersmen, settlers, rivermen, farmers, the mechanics of the cities, saw themselves reflected in the personality of Jackson. They identified themselves with him as they never could with Clay.

Old Hickory was the first American President to have a nickname, the first people's President, the dynamic self-made man. And, more than a man, he became the embodiment of a myth evolved out of the obscure needs and frustrations and dreams of ordinary and anonymous men.

Jackson, who had probably never read a line of poetry, represented the new romantic movement on a practical level, the Byronic hero emerging into politics with energy and natural instinct as opposed to the ambiguities of formal learning. The country's first six Presidents were of eighteenth-century cast, in which reason dominated the course of human events. Proportion, neoclassic in form, had been the key, whether in the Roman conception of a senate or the plan of Monticello. Jackson's election was a romantic revolution, the moving-on of the time spirit from static reason to dynamism.

To men of the West the Harvard background of the Adamses was corrupt, the eastern-seaboard civilization under the influence of Europe corrupt,

Andrew Jackson, sketched here by Thomas Sully, came to the White House in 1829 as the very embodiment of the hard-handed men of action from the frontier who had driven to the Mississippi and were soon to push far beyond it.

tradition itself corrupt. What a man knew with his heart was enough. A man of right instinct was more to be trusted than an educated man. In Jackson "the farmer-soldier" the westerners found reassurance, a consciousness of their own innate worth whatever their lack of learning or property, and the conviction that the future of America lay in the rough hands of men like themselves.

Even though the myth would have had Jackson a plain dirt farmer leaving the plow handle at his country's need, he was in actuality, like Clay, a plantation owner whose farming was done by slaves. Both men paralleled each other in their early careers and in their way of life. Nine years before Clay, the young Jackson, with the rudiments of common law in his head and a few books in his satchel, made his way through the Cumberland Gap to the new settlements beyond. His Nashville was much like Clay's Louisville, his Hermitage like the latter's Ashland. Both men made money on land speculations. Both gambled, drank, fought duels, raced horses. Both belonged to the ruling caste of that somewhat raffish post-frontier Tennessee-Kentucky society. But where Clay had a hankering for a Federalist past to which he would conform, Jackson neither hankered nor reflected. He was all action. There was in him the combination of leadership and will to power that one finds in men of destiny, men who—depending on circumstances—make or wreck empires.

In the War of 1812 Jackson, commanding the Tennessee militia, had avenged the Fort Mims Indian massacre and overrun the Creek territory in southern Alabama. But it was as the victor of the Battle of New Orleans, fought fifteen days after the peace treaty had been signed at Ghent, that Jackson made his reputation and became a legend.

That triumph on the plains of Chalmette was so overwhelming that even today it still seems mysterious. For here some 5,000 haphazard American militiamen defeated a larger force of Wellington's Peninsular veterans, killing and wounding over 2,000 of them, while the American losses were a mere 8 killed and 13 wounded.

According to the legend this resounding victory was made possible by the iron will of General Jackson, infused through the ranks of Kentucky hunters who made up the bulk of his army. These men could shoot out a squirrel's eye at fifty yards. By their steady battle courage and superb marksmanship they picked off the victors of Badajoz and Salamanca, until the British fled the field. Eighteenth-century professionalism with its disciplines was no match for men made hardy and self-reliant by the life of the frontier. The free Kentucky hunter, contemptuous of uniforms, discipline, and training, proved himself at New Orleans the master of scores of European mercenaries. Songs were written about him.

The facts of the Battle of New Orleans are as astonishing as the legend. Bounded by a cypress swamp on the left and a river levee on the right, the main British force launched a direct attack on the Americans sheltered behind an earth wall. To cross the muddy ditch in front of the American lines the British commander had prepared fascines of sugar cane. When the redcoats were in position to move, it was discovered that both fascines and ladders to scale the American rampart had been forgotten. General Gibbs, commanding the assault, halted his troops in mass formation to wait for them. About the British troops a pale January dawn was breaking, and a breeze was tearing away ragged patches of the protecting fog. Time was running out for the British. Gibbs finally sent his men forward in a bravely foolish gesture. Booming American cannon and volleys of rifle fire picked them off like so many decoy ducks. Only a handful of British reached the breastworks before the order for retreat had to be given. At battle's end 500 redcoats who had saved themselves by feigning death rose from the fields like ghosts to surrender.

In any version the Battle of New Orleans was an American triumph, a restorative to national pride shaken by the dreary course of the war. It marked a turning point, as if in final decision the national consciousness turned westward. Jackson the Giant Killer became a folk hero.

In the 1824 presidential election Jackson, though receiving a plurality of the votes, lost in the House of Representatives to John Quincy Adams. Four years later in the first grass-roots presidential campaign he defeated Adams by both a popular and electoral majority.

From a 500-mile radius the common people (as Adams called them) converged on Washington for Old Hickory's inaugural. After the ceremony the crowds surged through the gates into the White House. Damask chairs bore the marks of muddy boots, glass and china crashed in the surge toward the refreshments, women fainted, men fought, punch was carried out in buckets. It was more than another generation since Washington's courtly levees—it was another age.

To Jackson the Bank of the United States was a symbol of plutocratic corruption he was determined to destroy. In 1832 he vetoed Clay's bill to renew its charter. In this cartoon Jackson (left) attacks the many-headed Bank hydra with the stick of his veto. The largest head is Nicholas Biddle, the Bank's president; the others represent state branches. He is assisted by Martin Van Buren (center) and Seba Smith's comic character, Major Jack Downing.

NEW-YORK HISTORICAL SOCIETY

PORTRAIT OF THE EASTERN FRONTIER

RESERVE DIVISION, N.Y. PUBLIC LIBRARY

Aquatint after Karl Bodmer's 1833 sketch, depicting a road west through the Alleghenies.

About 1850, the story goes, Henry Clay was on his way to make a speech to a group of mountain people and halted for a while at Cumberland Gap. Why did he linger, someone asked. "I am listening," he said, "to the tread of the coming millions."

Whether or not Clay made such a statement, there is no disputing the phenomenon that gave those words meaning. In the last decades of the eighteenth century and well into the nineteenth, thousands upon thousands of restless Americans turned their backs on the East and its security, packed up their pitifully few possessions, and set off in search of a dream. The beckoning call of cheap land and the elusive promise of a new life drew them like a magnet into the trans-Appalachian West, and on they came, by ones and twos and scores, along the tangled trails, over mountains that seemed to go on forever, down river valleys that wound toward the sunset. The journey's end they punctuated with log cabin and rough forest clearing. But in truth it was not the end—only the first leg of a trek that would go on until others of their sort reached the Pacific. Even while a generation was growing up on the rim of the Mississippi Valley, pushing its roots deep and creating a new form of American life, a few men were moving on, west again into the limitless lands where no white people had settled before.

By Foot, Mule, and Wagon

"Travel this Day along a verey Bad hilley way," one early pioneer wrote of the rugged journey on foot and mule over the mountains. These vivid eyewitness sketches were done by Joshua Shaw about 1820.

MUSEUM OF SCIENCE AND INDUSTRY

BOTH: METROPOLITAN MUSEUM OF ART

Before bridges spanned the turbulent streams, travelers had to rely on such primitive ferries as the flat-bottomed scow depicted in Paul Svinin's water color (above) of a scene on the Susquehanna River.

Below, the spirit of light-hearted frivolity that reigned at wayside inns is recaptured in another Svinin water color. The Russian artist, who visited America during the years 1811–13, traveled from Maine to Virginia.

COLLECTION OF HERMAN P. DEAN

At Every Stop, Signs of Change

In 1821 Felix Achille Saint-Aulaire rode down the Ohio River and paused opposite Guyandotte, West Virginia, to picture himself and his dappled horse on the north bank of the main water route to the West. The river craft shown in his water color include three flatboats (left), a keelboat (right center), and portending the future, an early western side-wheel steamboat chugging upstream.

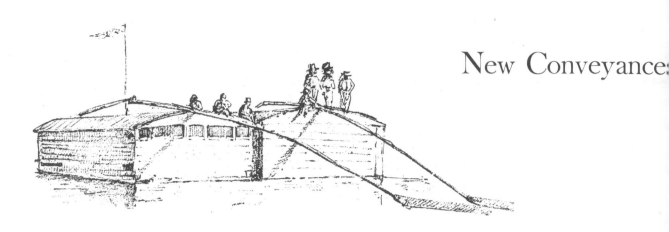

Heavy cargoes were carried on the cheap interior water routes by a variety of craft, shown on these pages in contemporary sketches by the French naturalist Charles Lesueur. Some passengers used the faster keelboat (left); but the cumbersome flatboat (above and below) served as log cabin, fort, country store, and floating barnyard for westward-bound pioneer families.

Ply the Waterways

Flatboat construction, at ten degrees above zero, is illustrated in Lesueur's 1831 sketch at right. Capable only of traveling downstream, these flatboats were sold for their timber at journey's end. Below, en route to his Utopian colony at New Harmony, Indiana, Robert Owen's "boat load of knowledge" is halted while a floating bridge is removed from the ice-choked Ohio River.

The Forest Gives Way to Farms

Cumberland Valley settlers had to be on constant alert against Indian attacks such as the 1796 raid on a Tennessee station so vividly depicted in the drawing at left.

Eager to plant a crop, farmers displayed "an unconquerable aversion" to forests. George Harvey's 1840 water color (right) shows how trees were killed by girdling, then burned.

Timber cleared from the land was used to fill nearly every wilderness need, from split-rail fence to log cabin. The 1822 English view below shows a typical raw farmstead.

KENDALL, *Life of Gen. A. Jackson*, 1843

HUDSON'S BAY COMPANY

Any Gathering Becomes a Social Occasion

ART MUSEUM, RHODE ISLAND SCHOOL OF DESIGN

The convening of court often provided early Americans with an excuse for a get-together, a "frolicking time" as the 1849 painting at left suggests.

A camp meeting (below, left) was one remedy for wilderness isolation. Even skeptical Mrs. Trollope said that it was "like standing at the gate of heaven and seeing it opened to you."

At right, fun-loving boatmen and cigar-smoking women kick up their heels to a lively reel in the Natchez ballroom sketched by Charles Lesueur in 1830.

Pennsylvania settlers make sport of work at a "Flax-Scutching Bee" (below) painted by Linton Park. The big paddles had other uses than the removal of woody elements from flax.

LIBRARY OF CONGRESS

MUSEUM OF NATURAL HISTORY, LE HAVRE

COLLECTION OF EDGAR WILLIAM AND BERNICE CHRYSLER GARBISCH, NATIONAL GALLERY OF ART

Frontier voices were strident and loud enough to be visible.

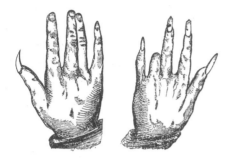

Scarred weapons of the western fighter (useful for gouging).

A Crockett character downed potent drinks with composure.

Only in Crockett's West could one find "ring-tailed roarers."

Vol. 1.] "*Go Ahead.*" **[No. 2.**

Davy Crockett's ALMANACK,
OF WILD SPORTS IN THE WEST,
And Life in the Backwoods.
CALCULATED FOR ALL THE STATES IN THE UNION.

1836

Col. Crockett's Method of Wading the Mississippi.

NASHVILLE, TENN. PUBLISHED FOR THE AUTHOR.

Davy Crockett was a full-blown legend even while he lived. As hunter, coonskin philosopher, and representative to Congress from Tennessee, Crockett personified the frontier. His exploits and tall tales were widely publicized in a series of hilariously illustrated Crockett almanacs—forerunners of the modern comic book—which first appeared in the West in the 1830's. The 1836 Nashville almanac shown above appeared the same year that Crockett died fighting at the Alamo.

Frontier free-for-alls were justly famous for their disregard of life and limb.

Neither bears nor wolves could intimidate this intrepid "Heroine of Kaintuck."

Travel was a problem easily solved by men who were "half-horse, half-alligator."

NEW-YORK HISTORICAL SOCIETY

New Cities
Dot the Landscape

Towns mushroomed in the wake of the Erie Canal, opened in 1825. Some days as many as fifty boats were lined up at the locks in Lockport (left), waiting to go through.

Its "most animated and bustling" wharves made New Orleans the undisputed capital of Mississippi Valley trade. The aquatint (right) by W. J. Bennett was done about 1840.

Smoke-belching steamboats made the Pittsburgh of 1849 (below) a river metropolis. The "Gateway to the West" was a vital link between overland routes and western rivers.

ABOVE AND BELOW: STOKES COLLECTION, N.Y. PUBLIC LIBRARY

ACROSS THE MISSISSIPPI

O F ALL the men who prepared the way for permanent settlement of the West, a special place of honor belongs to the trans-Missouri "mountain men." Like the hunters, trappers, and traders, scouts and Indian fighters, their mark on the land was evanescent. But they did more than any other group—far more than the government, in fact—to find usable paths through the vast rugged expanse of the Rockies, the Sierras, and adjoining lands. They spied out the fertile valleys and oases of a forbidding wilderness. And they produced some commanding figures, many of whom later became settlers, Indian agents, and local leaders.

Over the entrance to Far Western history—a grand archway opening into a magic land—rises the Lewis and Clark Expedition, the fruit of Thomas Jefferson's imaginative thinking over a period of twenty years. The sober, scientific-minded Meriwether Lewis and the bluff, adventurous William Clark wrote a chapter of exploration as memorable as those of La Salle, Alexander Mackenzie—the Canadian who was the first white man to cross the continent—or Livingston. In some respects the enterprise of 1804–06 surpassed these other exploits, for it showed more planning and less improvisation. It united wilderness skills, the best instruments and technological apparatus of the time, geographic knowledge, and scientific aims with courageous direction. Fundamentally, its chief result was to reveal a great natural pathway, from the Missouri to the Columbia, across America.

Lewis and Clark brought back reports of streams teeming with fish: pike, bass, catfish, trout, perch, and others. They noted the abundance of wild fruit: Osage plum, wild grapes and cherries, gooseberries, and currants better than those in the East. For much of the way they were surrounded by game—deer, elk, buffalo, antelope, and bighorn; ducks, geese, and plover. But what especially attracted the notice of Americans back East were their notes on furs. Small furry animals were found everywhere. The bears, although dangerous, had fine pelts; and as Lewis and Clark went westward, the otter population increased. Above all, they expatiated on the beaver, which along some stretches of the upper Missouri were more numerous, larger, fatter, and with thicker fur than any they had previously seen.

It is not strange that as Lewis and Clark neared civilization on their return, one of their company begged permission to leave, join two trappers, and return up the Missouri. This was John Colter, as honest and intelligent a frontiersman as Boone or Kit Carson, and a man for whom, as another trapper wrote, danger "had a kind of fascination." Lewis and Clark supplied him with powder, lead, and other articles for a two-year sojourn, and he became a true explorer. In 1807, going down the western side of what is now Wyoming and returning to the Missouri headwaters a little to the east, he became the first white man to traverse the Yellowstone Park district.

Partly because of the pleasing pen of Washington Irving, the fur story to most Americans means John Jacob Astor; but admiration for the enterprise which he and his men showed in planting Astoria at the mouth of the Columbia should not blind anyone to the transiency of his foothold on the Pacific.

Mountain man Joe Walker as he appeared in the Rockies in 1837.

Astor, already rich from fur trading in the Great Lakes region, was one of the men excited by the Lewis and Clark reports. The logical way to enter the country they had explored was by parties based on St. Louis, but the jealous hostility of the traders already established there made this a dangerous undertaking. Bold imagination went into Astor's alternative plan for a busy emporium on the Oregon coast, served by a line of posts all across the West and connected by ships with the eager Chinese market. It should have succeeded. But with the War of 1812 Astoria was taken over by the rival British concern, and a better man than Astor came on the scene. The wise, farsighted Canadian Dr. John McLoughlin, who supplanted Astoria with Fort Vancouver, fairly earned the title of Father of Oregon by his activities as trader, farmer, lumberman, colonizer, and friend of the Indians.

The really potent American organization in the Far West, which in its day of glory scattered pathfinding agents all over unknown regions, was the Rocky Mountain Fur Company which William Henry Ashley and Andrew Henry founded in 1822. Henry had led the first party of trappers to winter west of the Rockies in 1810–11. With Ashley, a man of many enterprises, he brought about a revolutionary approach to the problem of collecting the furs. They had to depend on their own trappers, since the best skins were taken only in winter and most Indians recoiled from the rigors of snow-choked ravines and icy streams. Instead of scattering fortified posts over the West, the company established an annual "rendezvous" to which its hundred or more trappers, with a motley crew of Indians, Mexicans, French-Canadians, and others, flocked to drink whiskey, run races, fight, gamble, and exchange furs for money and goods before dispersing again.

The mountain men who crisscrossed the West for beaver, penetrating all its recesses so that gentlemen in New York, London, and Paris might wear glossy hats, led what Irving called "a life of more continued exertion, peril, and excitement" than perhaps any others of their time. For their toils and hardships they found compensation in absolute independence; the loneliness of their existence was brightened by passionate absorption in its chances. At any moment they might light on a glade of rich spoils. They took their lives in their hands, for a treacherous savage, an outlaw, a fall from a rock, or an untended illness would leave their bones to whiten on the ground. But the solitude, the scenery, the adventure, and the exultation of overcoming obstacles fascinated them as the sea fascinated the sailor.

The Rocky Mountain Fur Company, its founders and successors, gave the Old West some of its greatest names. Two that hold an immortal partnership in our history were Jedediah Smith and Thomas "Broken Hand" Fitzpatrick. Smith made the first effective discovery of South Pass and was the first explorer of what Frémont later aptly termed the Great Basin between the Rockies and Sierras. The first American known to enter California from the east, by way of Great Salt Lake and the Mojave Desert, he was also the first to quit it by heading east, scaling the mountains into Utah. His investigations of the Snake and Columbia valleys gave the government information which supplemented that of Lewis and Clark. The number of his adventures and the scope of his achievements gave him an apparent longevity he did not have—he was only 32 when he was killed on the Santa Fe Trail. Fitzpatrick, who with James Bridger and others took over the old Ashley-Henry interests in 1830, became in time the greatest of all leaders of emigrant trains, exploring parties, and military expeditions. As for Jim Bridger, who once said that in seventeen years he had never tasted bread, the long list of his exploits began with his discovery of Great Salt Lake in 1824.

The last great rendezvous took place in 1838. That year the twilight had begun to fall on the whole fur trade, for the beaver supply was failing and London had already witnessed the introduction of the irresistible silk hat. When the fur trade sank, one of the great economic forces in North American history came to an end. It had done much to develop Canada, and in the United States its influence was many-sided. By its systematic if unlawful distribution of liquor and other demoralizing goods among the Indians, it accelerated their deterioration. Its dependence on bulky goods for trade gave early encouragement to steamboating on the Missouri and Yellowstone. Under John Jacob Astor and William Henry Ashley it brought private enterprise and the government into partnership in developing the West, for Astor in particular, always influential in Washington, got federal agencies to withdraw from fur-trading activities and persuaded Congress to erect legal barriers against the Canadian companies. But above all, before the mountain men disappeared, they made the wilderness pathways, the great natural wonders, and the best sites for settlement fairly well-known. Bridger or Fitzpatrick, sitting on the ground, could draw a better map of the West with a charcoal stick than any cartographer in the land; and they and their associates could lead newcomers anywhere with assurance.

Thus the settlement of the region was facilitated, and the advent of pioneer farmers who wrote the most heroic chapters of constructive effort turned the Old West into the New West. Rich free lands, the challenge of new scenes, and the opportunity to rear free institutions exercised their immemorial spell. The missionaries came, and after them the hardy colonizers.

For the first time, stoutly built wagons spanned long wilderness stretches without previous roadmaking. Bonneville had taken wagons across Green River in 1832. The missionary Marcus Whitman, traveling with his bride in 1836 to Oregon, determined to drive vehicles clear through to the Columbia. When a companion declared at Fort Hall that either he or the troublesome cart must quit, Whitman took the cart and pushed on with it to Fort Boise. A statue reared to him in Philadelphia fittingly shows him standing beside a sturdy wagon wheel. By the time Whitman made this pioneer journey to Oregon, planting his mission at Walla Walla, the states along the Mississippi were filling up. Illinois in 1840 had 476,000 people, and Missouri 384,000, while every year the westward-moving tide along the Erie Canal and the Ohio grew. It was certain that as men heard more of the lands beyond "The Great American Desert"—their gigantic forests, the incredibly rich soil, the rivers choked with salmon, the meadows waiting for livestock—many would overleap the barriers between.

Tyler was hardly in the White House, Victoria barely on her throne, when the torrent began. In May, 1841, the Bartleson-Bidwell party was crossing the Missouri with Fitzpatrick in the lead. The following year a larger party, inspired by the missionary Dr. Elijah White, was moving toward Oregon, and in 1843 there were greater parties yet. By then the paths were firmly established. Along the Sweetwater, through South Pass, across Green River, past Bridger's Fort, and on to Fort Hall—this was the accepted way. Until 1849 the Oregon Trail, traversed by tens of thousands of emigrants, was one of the chief settlement roads of our history. Then suddenly it became a gold-seekers' road—the Oregon and California Trail. Meanwhile, in 1847 the Mormon exodus to Utah began. An epic movement was uniting the West to the East just as the bonds between North and South appeared to be breaking.

ALLAN NEVINS

John Ledyard, would-be circumambulator of the earth.

A First American Look
at the
Pacific Northwest

I am going in a few days to make a tour of the globe from London east on foot." It was 1786, and John Ledyard, a 35-year-old Connecticut Yankee, had a grandiose idea to bring fortune to himself and glory to his newly established nation. He would make his way across Europe and Asia, take boat to the Pacific shore of North America, and walk across the unexplored wilds of that continent to the eastern states.

It was the fantastic climax of a dream, born eight years before in the legendary, fog-hung waters of the north Pacific. There, as a corporal of marines on Captain James Cook's final voyage of discovery, Ledyard had gone ashore in March, 1778, at Nootka Sound on Vancouver Island, and "though more than 2,000 miles distant from the nearest part of New England," had been "painfully afflicted" by the realization that he was on his home continent.

Ledyard returned to Connecticut to write a book about his experiences and try to interest others in building an American trading post on the Northwest coast. There was a fortune to be made in sea-otter furs, he argued, and he told how Captain Cook's men had picked up furs from the natives for scraps of metal and sold them for huge profits in China. But the Pacific shore, still a vague line on maps, was too remote for moneyed men on the Atlantic, and in 1784 Ledyard journeyed to Europe to find more venturesome backers. In Paris he met Thomas Jefferson, the new American minister, and told him of his dream to link the western wilderness with the East.

The visionary Jefferson had had a similar idea and had already suggested to George Rogers Clark an overland expedition to the Pacific Ocean. He encouraged Ledyard, but could find him no money, so the indomitable Yankee set off alone to walk to his goal.

It was a wild, half-formed scheme, but by March, 1787, Ledyard could write to Jefferson from St. Petersburg that, though he had but two shirts, "and yet more shirts than shillings," he was being kicked from place to place and had every expectation of being kicked around the globe. He got as far as Yakutsk, Siberia, when Russian merchants, convinced that he might after all prove a threat to their Alaska fur trade, prevailed upon Catherine the Great to have him arrested as a spy and deported.

His dream of bringing the United States to the Pacific was ended for Ledyard, who died the next year in Cairo. But it lived on, and others soon began to understand the erratic genius of this first American who had seen the Northwest coast and realized what opportunities it held.

This first view of Nootka, later a rendezvous for sea-otter traders, was painted by John Webber, official artist with Captain Cook, and shows the wild shore as Ledyard saw it in 1778.

Captain Gray Claims the Columbia

The published account in 1784 of Captain Cook's last voyage confirmed John Ledyard's report of the vast wealth to be made from Northwest sea otters. Aroused at last, the mercantile nations of the world sent ships racing to Nootka Sound, and among them were two American vessels, the *Columbia Rediviva* and the sloop *Lady Washington*, dispatched by a group of Boston merchants.

Thanks to the deaf ear they had turned to Ledyard, the Americans were late arrivals, and found the British and Spaniards already in contest over the ownership of Nootka. The U.S. traders stayed out of the argument, and in the summer of 1789, the *Columbia,* under Captain Robert Gray, went on to China with a cargo of otter skins which had cost a chisel apiece. In August, 1790, laden with tea that had been exchanged for the furs, Gray brought his ship back into Boston harbor, the first American sea captain to sail around the world.

The building of the sloop Adventure, *with Captain Gray giving his orders to the carpenter, is shown in this original sketch by George Davidson, a member of Gray's crew, done on Vancouver Island in 1792. The* Columbia *is at anchor in the cove.*

The venture lost money for its backers, but Gray, who now knew the trade items most valued by the natives, thought he could do better a second time. In September, 1790, he sailed again, his hold filled with sheet copper, cheap cloth, and iron. Throughout 1791 he cruised the present-day Canadian and south Alaskan coasts, swapping for pelts and pausing to build a smaller ship, the *Adventure*, which could trade in shallower water.

In the spring of 1792, Gray turned the *Columbia* south toward an unknown land whose stormy and inhospitable coast had in the past rebuffed both traders and explorers. Somewhere along this shore, obscured by mists and thunderous waves, legend located the mouth of a fabled "River of the West" which white men had never seen, but which, Indians told them, rose in the "Rock Mountains" at the center of the continent.

More interested in trading than discovery, Gray sailed along the stern coast, looking for a cove in which to anchor, and one day passed a British captain, George Vancouver, bound for Nootka to make peace with the Spaniards. Vancouver was also on a voyage of discovery, but he told Gray that he had

LEFT & RIGHT: COLLECTION OF DR. GRAY H. TWOMBLY; COURTESY FRICK ART REFERENCE LIBRARY

observed nothing important farther south. Gray nosed on in that direction, however, and two days later, on May 11, 1792, his lookout spied the surf of a great river breaking over a bar. "A spacious harbor abrest the Ship," wrote the fifth mate, seventeen-year-old John Boit, in his journal. "Haul'd our wind for itt, observ'd two sand bars making off, with a passage between them to a fine river . . . Captain Gray named this river *Columbia's.*"

Gray remained on the newly discovered river for nine days, trading with Indians who were, Boit noted, "all in a state of Nature." At last he sailed for the Orient, exchanged $90,000 worth of otter for Chinese goods, and continued home to Boston with a fat profit for his three-year voyage.

Months after Gray left the Columbia River, Vancouver's men found it too, and ascending it in a small boat for a hundred miles, claimed it for Great Britain. But Gray had been there first, and the log of his ship eventually helped to establish his country's claim to Oregon. Meanwhile, in the wake of his profitable voyage, a stream of Yankee ships headed for the Pacific, and by the beginning of the nineteenth century the sea-otter trade was almost exclusively American. Between the busy waters of the Northwest coast and the United States, however, still stretched half a continent, in foreign hands and unexplored.

OREGON HISTORICAL SOCIETY

Captain Robert Gray, 37 when he discovered the Columbia, typified the autocratic Yankee sea captain whose harsh treatment of natives often provoked attacks on fur-trading ships.

Another drawing Davidson made in 1792, titled "Capt. Gray obliged to fire upon the natives who disregard his orders to 'Keep Off,'" shows an attack on the Columbia *in Juan de Fuca Strait by a force of coastal Indians wearing conical hats.*

William Clark, painted by Charles Willson Peale.

The Odyssey of
Lewis and Clark

The purchase of Louisiana from France in 1803 provided President Thomas Jefferson with the opportunity to achieve the dream he had long held and had once discussed with John Ledyard in Paris: that of sending an expedition across the continent to the Pacific. The new acquisition, doubling the territory of the United States, had rolled the nation's border to the Rocky Mountains, beyond which lay the Northwest country of the Columbia River, not yet the property of any one power. From the Mississippi to the ocean it was all unexplored,

Meriwether Lewis, also by C. W. Peale.

and Jefferson ached to know what lay there.

There were other reasons for such an expedition, the chief one of which was to find an overland route from the Missouri to the Columbia. British North West Company fur men were pushing rapidly west across Canada. One of them, Alexander Mackenzie, had reached the Pacific north of Vancouver Island in 1793, and others were threatening to come south to the Columbia. A transcontinental route through U.S. territory, Jefferson reasoned, would make more secure the Northwest

sea-otter trade for the United States and might also divert the inland beaver trade from Canadian to eastern American markets.

To lead the expedition Jefferson chose his private secretary, Captain Meriwether Lewis, 29, of the 1st Regiment of Infantry, and George Rogers Clark's younger brother William, 33, a 2nd lieutenant in the Corps of Artillerists (he signed himself captain on Jefferson's authority). On May 14, 1804, the 43-man "Corps of Discovery" started the long trip west from St. Louis.

The expedition, composed of hardy Kentucky hunters and frontiersmen, French boatmen, and soldiers in leather collars with their hair in pigtails, moved up the Missouri River and spent the first winter among Mandan and Minnetaree Indians near present-day Bismarck, North Dakota. Here, at the last outpost of white civilization, they added an interpreter, Toussaint Charbonneau, and his Shoshone wife, Sacajawea, to the party. In the spring of 1805 they pushed off into unexplored country, entering a land of marvelous new sights.

Still following the Missouri, they crossed dry, windy plains, teeming with buffalo, and badlands and canyons filled with antelope, deer, and elk. Beyond the trappers' legendary Roche Jaune River, the Yellowstone, they saw and passed the Milk, the Judith, which Clark named for his future wife, and the Marias, which Lewis named "in honour of Miss Maria W—d," though "the hue of the waters . . . but illy comport with the pure celestial virtues and amiable qualifications of that lovely fair one." At night on the plains, the ground rumbled and shook from the herds of buffalo, and once a bellowing bull

crashed through their camp and trampled two guns. The party had narrow escapes from "white bears" (grizzlies) and rattlesnakes, endured mosquitoes and cloudbursts, and was almost sunk by rapids. Still in present-day Montana, they portaged around the awe-inspiring Great Falls and were intrigued by animals that were strange to them, the prairie dog and bighorn sheep. Then they passed the Gates of the Mountains and the age-old Indian war ground at the Three Forks of the Missouri.

Near today's Montana-Idaho border they followed the narrowing Jefferson River to what they wrongly thought was the source of the Missouri. One man straddled the little stream and "thanked his god that he had lived to bestride the mighty & heretofore deemed endless Missouri." Looking for horses with which to portage across the mountains to the nearby headwaters of the Columbia, which they thought would be navigable, they made their way over the Lemhi Pass on the Continental Divide and met Sacajawea's people, the Shoshones, who provided them with mounts and a guide.

The guide, an old man whom they called Toby,

HISTORICAL SOCIETY OF MONTANA

took them to the canyon of the Salmon River, whose ruggedness forced them back. Moving north on a long detour, they entered the land of the Flatheads, who, like other tribes, found Captain Clark's Negro servant, York, the most interesting member of the expedition. Finally turning west again, they crossed the snowclad Bitterroot Mountains on an Indian trail, running out of food in the "Steep & ruged" wilderness and in desperation eating their horses to keep alive. Emerging on the western slope, among friendly Nez Percé Indians in Idaho's Weippe Prairie, they gorged on camass bulbs which made them sick and on dog meat which they found surprisingly good. They built canoes again on the banks of the Clearwater River and sped down it and the Snake, floating finally out on the broad current of the Columbia near present-day Pasco, Washington. Harassed by squat, smelly, fish-eating Indians who tried to steal their possessions, they navigated the Columbia's treacherous rapids and passed the Cascade Range.

The climax came one day when the canoes were plowing through rain, fog, and high-rolling waves

near the mouth of the Columbia. For a moment the mist cleared, and the men sighted the Pacific. "O! the joy," Clark wrote in his diary. On the Oregon shore they built a fort and a salt cairn and wintered. Clark cut his name on a pine tree and added, in case they failed to make it back, "By Land from the U. States in 1804 & 1805." They celebrated Christmas and New Year's among flat-headed coastal Indians, who made life miserable by pilfering their supplies and left some of the men with venereal disease.

In the spring the expedition turned back, reaching the Nez Percés again and recrossing the Bitterroot Mountains. Near present-day Missoula, Montana, they decided to try new routes and divided the party into several groups. Lewis took a short cut to the Missouri and, near the river he had named for "Miss Maria W—d," got into a fight with Blackfeet and almost lost his life. Clark tried the Yellowstone, had some of his horses stolen by Crows, and went down the stream in dugouts. Near the rendezvous where all the parties met again on the Missouri they had an elk hunt during which Lewis was accidentally shot in the buttocks.

On their way down the Missouri they began to see the first signs of the new day to which their expedition would give birth. Coming up the stream, farther west than any known white men besides themselves had yet ventured, were small groups of American fur trappers, beginning to probe toward the headwaters of the Missouri. John Colter, who had served the expedition as a hunter, caught the new fever and asked to be allowed to turn back to the West with two of the trappers. The captains gave him permission, and the expedition members wished Colter godspeed as he headed back to the wilderness from which they had just emerged.

On September 23, 1806, grimy, bearded, and bursting with marvelous tales of things no white man had ever seen or heard of, the rest of the explorers reached St. Louis. The expedition had been a huge success. At a total cost of about $39,000, and with the loss of only one man, it gave Americans for the first time an idea of the resources that lay between the Mississippi River and the Pacific Ocean.

"Lewis and Clark Meeting the Flatheads," by Charles M. Russell, portrays the historic event of September 4, 1805, on the headwaters of Montana's Bitterroot River. Clark called the Indians "Tushepaus" who, he reported, "receved us friendly."

INDEPENDENCE HALL COLLECTION

Into the Rockies

Zebulon Pike, painted by Charles Willson Peale.

Two months before Lewis and Clark's return to St. Louis, another American expedition had left that city to explore the southern reaches of the new Louisiana territory. It was led by a 27-year-old 1st lieutenant named Zebulon Montgomery Pike, and there was more to it than met the eye.

Pike was an obedient and trusting officer of General James Wilkinson, the governor of upper Louisiana and a master of treachery and deceit who, as later years would reveal, never failed to put his own interests ahead of those of his country. In 1805 he had sent Pike to explore the headwaters of the Mississippi River and to warn British traders off U.S. soil. Pike reached Leech Lake in present-day Minnesota, decided mistakenly that it was the true source of the Mississippi, and returned to St. Louis in April, 1806.

Probably without Pike's knowledge, General Wilkinson in the meantime had become involved

JAMES, *An Account of an Expedition*, 1822

On Pike's second expedition west in 1806 his party made its way across broken table lands like those shown in this 1822 engraving, as it approached the Front Range of the Rockies.

in a variety of schemes for personal enrichment and glory. He was dabbling privately in the Missouri River fur trade, planning to send secret agents to the Northwest to trade with the Indians and gather geographic knowledge for his own use, and had joined a conspiracy with Aaron Burr to erect an independent empire in the Southwest. To secure information about that part of the continent, he ordered Zebulon Pike off on a second expedition.

Pike's written orders were to explore the headwaters of the Red and Arkansas rivers. But southwest of the new U.S. border, zealously guarded by Spanish troops against curious Americans, lay Santa Fe and the gold mines of Mexico. In secret instructions Wilkinson apparently also directed Pike to get himself arrested by the Spaniards and taken to Santa Fe so that he could spy on that city.

Neither President Jefferson nor his secretary of war were aware of this venture when Pike and 22 men left St. Louis in July, 1806. They ascended the Osage and Arkansas rivers and on November 15, in present-day Colorado, sighted a mountain on the horizon "like a small blue cloud." Gradually the majestic Front Range of the Rockies rose before them, and after reaching it, Pike tried in vain to climb the tall "blue" peak which was afterwards to receive his name. Turning away, he moved through the snow-covered mountains, suffering intensely from cold and hunger, and had to abandon temporarily some of his men whose feet had become so frozen that they could travel no further.

Crossing the Sangre de Cristo Range, he finally arrived on the upper Rio Grande, where he erected a stockade of cottonwood logs. He was now in Spanish territory and, under the pretext of collecting a debt due an Illinois merchant, sent a member of his party down river to Santa Fe. This man conveniently let the authorities there know where Pike had built a fort, and soon Spanish soldiers arrived to arrest the Americans and take them to Santa Fe.

The Spaniards treated Pike courteously, and after sending him to Chihuahua for further questioning, allowed him to return across Texas to Louisiana. By the time he reached the States, the Burr conspiracy had blown up, and Wilkinson, who had turned on Burr, had been relieved as governor. Pike's information, useless now to his former commander, played a far more important role in lifting for all Americans more of the mist that had obscured the Far West.

INDEPENDENCE HALL COLLECTION

Stephen Long

One official government explorer who might better never have gone west was Major Stephen H. Long of the U.S. Corps of Engineers. In 1820 Long set off to explore the headwaters of the major rivers that rose in the central Rockies. His report of the country he saw was so negative that it accomplished the opposite of what it was supposed to, and for many years, in effect, ended further government interest in the trans-Mississippi West.

Long's party of nineteen men, including a botanist and an official artist, left the Missouri on June 6, 1820, and followed the Platte River and its southern branch across the plains to the Colorado Rockies. Near present-day Denver its members gazed upon the peak which was later named for Long, and moving along the base of the mountains, came to Pikes Peak. Succeeding where Pike had failed, three of Long's party, led by the botanist, Dr. Edwin James, climbed the mountain—the first men known to do so. At the Arkansas the expedition divided into two groups and returned home down that river and the Canadian.

On his arrival Long submitted to the government a lengthy and unflattering description of the arid plains country he had traversed, including such comments as "it is almost wholly unfit for cultivation, and of course uninhabitable by a people depending upon agriculture for their subsistence." As a result, the area became fixed upon maps and in people's minds as "The Great American Desert," and for years Long's dismal report discouraged potential settlers as well as any congressional proposals for developing the region.

COLLECTION OF MRS. PETER A. JAY; COURTESY FRICK ART REFERENCE LIBRARY

John Jacob Astor, fur-trade capitalist, as portrayed by Gilbert Stuart.

Astor Seeks a Fur-Trade Monopoly

To some Americans of daring and enterprise, the new West which the explorers had found was a land of opportunity, and they were not long in accepting its challenge. The stories that Lewis and Clark brought back with them of regions "richer in beaver and Otter than any country on earth" excited adventurous men in St. Louis and along the Mississippi, and frontier traders and fortune seekers began moving up the Missouri River to try their luck on the streams of the West.

A few of them, like the experienced Indian traders Manuel Lisa and Andrew Henry, established log posts deep in the little-known wilderness,

on the Big Horn River in Montana, at the Missouri's Three Forks, and on the Snake River in eastern Idaho. Other men—like John Colter, who found Yellowstone Lake; George Drouillard, who explored much of present-day Wyoming; and a fabulous trio of Kentucky hunters named John Hoback, Edward Robinson, and Jacob Reznor, who made the Jackson Hole area their home—hunted beaver alone or in small groups across thousands of square miles of previously unknown territory. At one time or another, most of these men narrowly survived adventures with grizzly bears or hostile Indians, and some died horribly

158

or simply vanished in the unknown mountains.

The most dramatic hardships of all were experienced by a group of men sent to the mouth of the Columbia River by John Jacob Astor of New York in 1810. Astor was born in Waldorf, Germany, in 1763, and after coming to the United States at the age of 21, had entered the Great Lakes fur trade where he made a fortune. Lewis and Clark's report of rich beaver country in the Far West provided him with a vision of empire similar to that once dreamed by John Ledyard. The difference was that Astor had the resources, and he set out to convert the Pacific Northwest into a monopoly for his newly established Pacific Fur Company. He organized two expeditions, one to go by sea and the other overland, to the Columbia River, where they would build a post, gain control of both the coastal and inland trade, and ship their furs to China.

Difficulties plagued the project from the start. The members of the sea expedition, who sailed from New York in September, 1810, aboard the *Tonquin,* fought with the ship's captain throughout the voyage around the Horn, and at the entrance to the Columbia eight men were lost trying to cross the treacherous bar. After landing a shore party to construct a post, which was called Astoria, the *Tonquin* left for the north to engage in the coastal trade. At Nootka this part of Astor's project collapsed when all the crew was massacred by natives, and the ship blown up.

The land expedition, which departed from St. Louis in March, 1811, under one of Astor's partners, Wilson Price Hunt, was equally unfortunate. Its members, the first to try to cross the continent after Lewis and Clark, intended to follow that expedition's general route, but growing alarmed at the tales they heard of hostile Blackfoot Indians, they left the Missouri and headed across the plains on horseback. Reaching the Snake River, which they thought was navigable, they abandoned their horses and started down the stream in canoes. Wild rapids and awesome canyons through which no white man had ever been before showed them their error, and after one man had drowned, they struck out across the Idaho desert on foot. Suffering dreadfully from hunger and thirst, they tried to find their way in small, desperate bands through the terrible wilderness of Hell's Canyon, and after tragic wanderings, during which some men died, became crazed, or were abandoned, the ragged survivors finally straggled into Astoria.

Their hardships did them little good, for they found upon arrival that a great Canadian explorer, David Thompson, had already established a network of British posts in the interior. Soon these rivals came sweeping down the Columbia with news of the outbreak of the War of 1812. Threatened by a British sea attack, the Americans sold Astoria to the Canadians' North West Company and withdrew from the Oregon country. The Pacific Northwest remained exclusively in British hands for a decade, but in the end, the vision of Astor and the hardships and suffering of his men established another basis for a U.S. claim to the area.

Fort George, as the British rechristened Astoria, was only a rude fur-trading outpost when artist Henry Warre painted it.

Mountain Men Invade "The Shining Mountains"

For a time, American interest in the Far West was diverted by the War of 1812 and Indian troubles, but with the return of peace, interest in the fur regions quickened again. St. Louis, on the edge of the frontier, became a booming trade center, home of the nation's principal fur companies and the outfitting base for westbound expeditions.

The goal of most men was still the almost legendary beaver country of the Rockies and the Columbia River, from which Astor's men had been driven, but the continued hostility of the fierce Blackfoot and other tribes along the upper Missouri blocked the river route to the Northwest and for a while kept Americans on the east side of the mountains. In the meantime, independent "freemen" trappers in small canoes and pirogues journeyed adventurously up the western tributaries of the Mississippi and Missouri as far as they dared go, trapping on their own and trading with friendly Indians. Some of them came floating safely back to St. Louis with small packs of furs to show for their efforts, but many others were swallowed up by the vast land and were never heard from again.

Larger expeditions, financed and led by experienced men with more capital, also had their troubles. Some of the most determined ventures were conducted by members of the distinguished Chouteau family, long pioneers in the St. Louis fur trade. Old Auguste Chouteau, still alive in the second decade of the nineteenth century, had accompanied the expedition up the Mississippi from New Orleans that had founded St. Louis as a frontier fur post in 1764, and his younger brother Pierre had arrived not long afterward. Both men had become important and wealthy Indian traders on the lower Missouri, and now an Auguste and a Pierre of a new generation endeavored to carry the family's activities into more distant and more profitable regions.

Pierre, Jr., focused his interests on the upper Missouri, but his activities were hampered considerably by belligerent Indians who did their best to prevent him from trading with their enemies. Auguste turned his attention to the Southwest and in 1815, in partnership with Jules De Mun of St. Louis, attempted to open trade with Indians on the Arkansas River. He had bitter fights with Pawnees and Comanches and eventually reached the trapping grounds of the Sangre de Cristo Mountains, only to be arrested by Spaniards who took him to Santa Fe and confiscated all his property.

In time, the persistence of both of the younger Chouteaus was rewarded, and their many trading activities added to the wealth and reputation of the family. Pierre became one of the principal leaders of the powerful American Fur Company, which for years dominated the Rocky Mountain trade, and Auguste, as proprietor of successful posts in the present-day states of Kansas and Oklahoma, served the government as a commissioner in Indian treaty negotiations.

During the intervening years, the Columbia country had beckoned other men. In 1822 General William Ashley and Andrew Henry of St. Louis

CONTINUED ON PAGE 164

Wide, silent rivers, as pictured opposite by George Caleb Bingham, were highways to the West for independents as well as traders such as young Auguste Chouteau (below).

MISSOURI HISTORICAL SOCIETY

DETROIT INSTITUTE OF ARTS

CITY ART MUSEUM OF ST. LOUIS; COURTESY *Life*

The keelboat, shown at right in an 1832 lithograph, was the sturdy mainstay of the upper Missouri River fur trade. It was more often propelled upstream by pole and rope than by sail.

OVERLEAF: *In his eyewitness painting of hunters, "Setting Traps for Beaver," artist Alfred Jacob Miller caught the uncomfortable loneliness of the fur trapper's job in the Far West. Working in icy water, often in perilous Indian country, men set their traps in the streams after sunset.*

OVERLEAF: COLLECTION OF MRS. CLYDE PORTER

CONTINUED FROM PAGE 160

undertook to pierce the Indian barrier on the Missouri. To their men, who included Jim Bridger, Jedediah Smith, William Sublette, Tom Fitzpatrick, and many others destined to become famous mountain men, the partners offered a unique arrangement. They would be supplied with arms and equipment and would be expected to assist in the normal duties of labor and defense, but they could keep one half of their furs to sell as their own. The idea proved a good one, stimulating the trappers to greater boldness.

During 1822, members of the expedition reached Montana's Musselshell River, but the next year defeats by Blackfeet and Arikaras forced them back down the Missouri. Taking to horses, they crossed the plains, and at last their luck changed. Early in 1824 a group under Jedediah Smith found the great South Pass over the Continental Divide. Along Wyoming's Green River they made a rich beaver haul, and some of the men took the valuable furs back to St. Louis.

News of the Pass and the new Wyoming beaver country excited Ashley, who hastened to the Green River with a pack train of supplies. While his men finished their spring hunt, he built "bullboats" of willows and buffalo hides and set off down the river on an exploring trip. The tumultuous voyage through fearsome gorges and churning rapids almost cost him his life, but eventually he climbed out of the canyon and returned to the place where he had left his goods. There, on July 1, 1825, his own men and trappers who converged on the area from all over the West joined him in a rendezvous.

Ashley bought their furs at rates well below St. Louis prices, charged them dearly for supplies, and returned to the States a rich man. But the mountain men were satisfied too. They had grown used to the wilderness and had no desire to return to civilization. By bringing a market place to them, Ashley saved them the time and expense of a long trip home, and the summer rendezvous, as a trading mart and breathing spell from the tensions of a year in the wilds, became an annual event. But the mountain man, wild and free, was destined to survive only as long as the beaver and a market for it held out, and by 1840 the end was in sight.

BOATMEN'S NATIONAL BANK, ST. LOUIS

Expedition supplies and rendezvous goods, first packed on horses and mules, were carried largely by wagon after 1830. In 1837 Alfred Jacob Miller painted the caravan at left, led by the Scottish adventurer Sir William Drummond Stewart (on white horse), near the forks of the Platte.

The rendezvous was a bartering place for trappers and friendly Indians; it was also a rollicking, sometimes violent holiday of gambling, racing, tall-tale telling, wenching, and colossal drunks. Miller's painting below is set in the splendor of the Wind River Mountains in what is now Wyoming.

COLLECTION OF EVERETT D. GRAFF; COURTESY *Time*

The Remarkable Jedediah Smith

At the 1826 rendezvous Ashley sold out his interests to three of his most capable field captains, Jedediah Smith, William Sublette, and David Jackson. Smith was one of the most remarkable trappers in the West, a brilliant explorer and leader of rough mountain men as well as a devoutly religious Christian. It was said that he carried a rifle across his saddle and a Bible in his pack. He was also a young man, having enlisted with Ashley in 1822 when he was 23 years old. His nine short years in the mountains, before his death in 1831, were packed with adventures in every part of the West.

In 1823 Smith had barely survived a massacre of fifteen of Ashley's men by Arikaras on the Missouri River in present-day South Dakota. In the following year, after having found South Pass, he led seven men to Idaho's Snake River, becoming the first American to return to the waters of the Columbia basin since the departure of the Astorians ten years before. He found the region being trapped without competition by the Hudson's Bay Com-

pany, which had merged with the old Canadian North West Company in 1821. Falling in with a British brigade, he followed it back to its home post in northwestern Montana, studying the country through which he traveled and causing consternation to the British traders.

Back at the Americans' rendezvous, he described the routes he had found to his partners, who planned to move into the Columbia country. Then in the summer of 1826 he headed in a new direction, hoping to find good beaver lands in the Southwest. At the head of a column of trappers, he blazed a trail through the Utah wilderness, and after ferrying the Colorado River near present-day Needles, California, rode across the Mojave Desert and the San Bernardino Mountains to the Pacific coast.

The Mexican authorities in southern California were struck dumb by the appearance of the bearded American hunters from the interior of the continent, and thinking them spies, tried to detain them. Smith finally marched his men into the San Joaquin

Frederic Remington depicted Jedediah Smith's party crossing the burning Mojave Desert during the 1826 trek to California.

Valley and left them to hunt while he returned to the 1827 rendezvous. Scaling the Sierra Nevada Mountains and almost dying of thirst as he struggled across the burning Nevada and Utah deserts, he reached the Great Salt Lake in time for the rendezvous which was gathering nearby. At the rendezvous he enlisted reinforcements for his men in California, and taking a new route through Utah, arrived back on the Colorado River. There he narrowly escaped death again when Mojave Indians massacred ten of his men while he was ferrying the river. Without horses, Smith led eight survivors in a grueling trek across the Mojave Desert to the Mexican settlements. He had difficulties once more with the authorities, but was finally allowed to rejoin his hunters in the San Joaquin Valley and head them north through unexplored wilderness toward Oregon and the mouth of the Columbia River.

The difficult journey through forests, swamps, and precipitous mountain ranges came to an abrupt halt when Umpqua Indians in Oregon fell on the party and killed everyone but Smith and two companions. The survivors made their way to the Hudson's Bay Company's Fort Vancouver on the Columbia, and eventually Smith traveled across Washington, Idaho, and Montana to rejoin his partners, who had given him up for lost.

In 1830 Smith, Jackson, and Sublette sold their interests to five of the leading mountain men, including Jim Bridger and Tom Fitzpatrick, and returned to St. Louis. The three partners had led brigades through almost the entire West, leaving their names on a multitude of terrain features and accumulating a vast store of geographic knowledge that would serve future generations of trappers, official government explorers, and settlers.

Sublette soon returned to the West, where he built the famous Fort Laramie; but Jedediah Smith's adventurous career was rapidly nearing its end. In 1831 he entered the New Mexico trade and started down the Santa Fe Trail with a caravan of goods. Near the Cimarron River Comanches caught him out ahead of his party, searching for water. Smith died alone and his body was never found. It was an irony of fate that most of his records were also lost, and his fellow countrymen soon forgot his name. But his reputation lived on among other mountain men, and from them came eventual recognition of his achievements.

HISTORICAL SOCIETY OF MONTANA

Jim Bridger

Of all the mountain men who made the Rockies their home, no man better personified the wilderness-wise hunter and trapper than Jim Bridger. "Old Gabe," as he was known to his fellow mountaineers, was only eighteen when he joined Ashley in 1822, and for almost fifty years he roamed the plains and mountains as a trapper, Indian fighter, guide, and Army scout.

His exploits were legendary in his own time, and some of his stories of wonders he had seen were disbelieved until other men found them to be true. In 1824 he discovered the Great Salt Lake, whose saline properties made him think that it was an arm of the Pacific. Later, his tales of Yellowstone's geysers and mudpots were also ridiculed as tall stories.

As one of the partners of the Rocky Mountain Fur Company, he led his brigades through the lands of Blackfoot, Crow, and other hostile tribes, learning the ways of the wilderness until he was a match for any Indian. In 1843, anticipating the westward migration of settlers, he built Fort Bridger near the Green River as a trading post for covered-wagon pioneers crossing the plains. Difficulties with the Mormons, who thought he was inciting the Utes against them, forced him from the area, but he returned in triumph in 1858 and led Army troops into Salt Lake City to establish federal authority.

In later years Bridger became a celebrated guide and scout for many government explorers and Army expeditions. Failing eyesight finally forced his retirement to a farm in Missouri, where he died in 1881.

Missions in the Northwest

ROYAL ONTARIO MUSEUM

The fierce Cayuse brave Tomakus, painted above by Canadian artist Paul Kane, was one of the leaders of the Whitman massacre. The Oregon Trail parallels the fence in the contemporary, pre-massacre view of the Whitman mission below.

OREGON HISTORICAL SOCIETY

Although the Oregon country was still dominated by the Hudson's Bay Company, by treaty it belonged jointly to the United States and Great Britain, and increasing American interest in its possession was reflected by the appearance in the mountains in 1832 of a group of new arrivals. This was a party of 110 men led by Captain Benjamin L. E. de Bonneville, on leave from the U.S. Army. Bonneville claimed to be on a private fur-trading venture, backed by eastern financiers, but his exploring activities led some to believe that he was secretly gathering information for the government.

As a fur trader, Bonneville was outmaneuvered by more experienced brigade leaders of the Rocky Mountain Fur Company and the American Fur Company. But he built forts on the Green River and the Salmon River in eastern Idaho, sent a trapping party under Joseph Walker on an exploring trip to California, and twice journeyed down the Snake River to the Columbia. The British traders at Fort Walla Walla were concerned by his appearance so deep within the territory they had long considered their own, and they refused to sell him supplies or allow Indians in the area to trade with him. Faced by starvation, he finally withdrew without offering competition to the British. After three years in the mountains he returned to the East with little to show for his efforts; but a best-selling book by Washington Irving about his travels and adventures helped to stimulate further interest in the country he had seen.

The British continued to fear U.S. trappers, but a threat to their hold on Oregon soon developed from a different direction, and in the end another breed of American pioneer won the region from them. In 1831 four Nez Percé Indians from Idaho who accompanied an American Fur Company caravan to St. Louis exhibited curiosity about Christianity and asked about a "book" that gave directions for reaching the white man's heaven. The visit of these Indians from the west side of the Rockies received wide publicity in church papers and kindled a missionary zeal among the different religious sects. The *Christian Advocate* thundered, "Let the Church awake from her slumbers and go forth in her strength to the salvation of those wandering sons of our native forests." Funds were raised and volunteers enlisted to convert the Northwest tribes, who were pictured as "searchers after the truth."

Beginning in 1834, parties of dedicated missionaries journeyed west each year with pack trains bound for the fur rendezvous. From that point they traveled on to Oregon with Hudson's Bay brigades, small groups of trappers, or even with Indian bands and settled in the wild country, hundreds of miles from each other, to build missions for the conversion of the different tribes.

The most famous missionaries, Marcus Whitman and Henry Spalding, traveled west in 1836 with their wives, the first white women to follow the overland trail to Oregon. The Spaldings settled among the Nez Percés near present-day Lewiston, Idaho, while the Whitmans built a mission for the Cayuse tribe in the Walla Walla valley of southeastern Washington. At first both couples found the Indians friendly and eager for instruction, but difficulties soon arose. The Protestant missionaries quarreled among themselves and with Catholic priests who arrived from Canada, and the Indians became confused. Then, in letters back home, the missionaries wrote glowing descriptions of the country and urged settlers to come and join them. Whitman even traveled east one year and guided an emigrant party back to Oregon himself. The British had not expected this development. Soon the swelling tide of new arrivals tipped the scale against them, and in 1846 Oregon became American. But the covered-wagon trains rolling across their lands had made the Indians restless. The missionaries, they felt, had become more interested in taking their country from them than in teaching them Christianity. In an attempt to head off trouble, an Indian agent arrived from Washington with a code of laws which allowed the missionaries to whip the Indians for offenses.

This only made matters worse, and in 1847 an epidemic of measles, which claimed the lives of many Cayuses at the Walla Walla mission, precipitated a massacre in which the Whitmans and twelve others were killed. The Spaldings and other missionaries in the interior abandoned their stations, and for a while that part of the Northwest was unsafe for whites. But the stream of settlers which the missionaries had started toward the West continued to increase and eventually doomed the Indians.

Harper's Magazine, 1892

Nathaniel Wyeth

In the summer of 1832 a strange party of greenhorns turned up at the trappers' rendezvous. It was led by Nathaniel J. Wyeth, a Cambridge, Massachusetts, ice merchant and partner of Frederic Tudor (*see* page 228), who believed that great opportunities existed in Oregon. Wyeth's interest in the Northwest had been aroused by a New England schoolteacher, Hall J. Kelley, who had been urging Americans to take possession of Oregon, and Wyeth planned to erect a post on the Columbia and enter the salmon and fur trades. He enlisted about 24 recruits and in the spring started for the West.

Sickness and discomfort on the trip across the plains disillusioned more than half the party, and at the rendezvous they turned back. The rest went on with Wyeth and reached Fort Vancouver in October. Although he was hospitably received by Dr. John McLoughlin of the Hudson's Bay Company, Wyeth had a dispiriting winter. A supply ship sent to him from Boston was wrecked in the Pacific, and he soon found it impossible to compete with the strongly entrenched British. Still his fertile mind envisioned other opportunities, and in the spring he started home with a plan to become a supplier to American trappers.

He returned to the West the next year with a caravan, but the trappers refused to buy his goods. To dispose of them, he built a trading post, Fort Hall, near present-day Pocatello. Once more he visited the Columbia, hoping to salvage something; but McLoughlin could make no agreements with him, and Wyeth went back to the ice business in Cambridge.

NEW-YORK HISTORICAL SOCIETY

TEXAS STATE CAPITOL

Davy Crockett

"I promised to give the Texians a helping hand on the high road to freedom," wrote Davy Crockett. With his heroic death in the Alamo in March, 1836, the nation lost one of its most irrepressible folk heroes, a coonskin-capped frontier humorist who symbolized America's westward march.

A Tennessee backwoodsman born in 1786, Crockett tried to make a living as a farmer, but he was unable to stay put and kept moving west to new settlements. As a mighty hunter and boaster, this "half-horse, half-alligator" claimed to have killed 105 bears in less than a year. He fought in the Creek wars under Andrew Jackson, but later, when elected to Congress, opposed almost every measure that Jackson, as President, proposed.

His tall tales filled the Capitol with laughter, but he finally got under Jackson's skin, and the administration helped defeat him in 1834. The westering urge rose in him again, and deciding that Tennessee no longer needed him, he struck out across Arkansas to help Texans gain their independence. A final entry in a diary he supposedly kept during the siege of the Alamo read: "Pop, pop, pop! Bom, bom, bom! Go ahead! Liberty and independence forever!" To a mourning nation, it summed up the indomitable spirit of this colorful pioneer.

Jim Bowie

Jim Bowie, another defender of the Alamo, was a tall, open-hearted frontiersman with a generous nature and a courtly, gallant manner. But he had a sudden and fierce temper and he strode across the Southwest with a terrible knife that made his name more legend than fact even while he lived.

Born in Georgia about 1796, he prospered in land and lumber speculations and is said to have trafficked in slaves along the Gulf coast with Jean Lafitte, the Barataria pirate. His interests carried him to Texas in the 1820's, where he married and was granted provisional citizenship by the Mexican government. He became a noted knife duelist, and in 1830, according to legend, an Arkansas smith named James Black fashioned him a massive knife with which he killed three men in one fight. The weapon and the man gained immediate fame, provoking a demand for the manufacture of thousands of knives "like Bowie's."

When the struggle for Texas independence began, Bowie became a colonel in the Texas army. At the Alamo he commanded the volunteers, but early in the siege broke his hip and was confined to a cot. When the Mexicans finally swarmed into the room where he lay, it was said that he killed nine of them before he was overpowered.

TEXAS STATE CAPITOL

LIBRARY OF CONGRESS

Stephen Austin

Stephen F. Austin was the first man to open the door of Texas to American settlers, and by adroit leadership he held it open until the Texans won their independence. Born in Virginia in 1793, he spent his early life in Missouri, Arkansas, and Louisiana, working as a manager of lead mines, director of a bank, judge, newspaper employee, and member of Missouri's territorial legislature.

After the financial panic of 1819, his father, Moses Austin, obtained a grant of land between the Brazos and Colorado rivers in Texas, but died before he could colonize it. Young Stephen carried on, inducing American families to enter the new country. In the swelling tide of immigration, he was often caught between the anti-Mexican feelings of the colonists and the fears of the Mexican government over their growing disloyalty. But Austin held absolute authority over the colony and by tactful administration guaranteed permission for an uninterrupted flow of settlers into the area.

When the Texas revolution finally came, he went to Washington to enlist support for his people, then ran unsuccessfully against Sam Houston for the presidency of the new Republic. His term as Houston's secretary of state was cut short by his untimely death in December, 1836, at the age of 43.

Sam Houston

The Battle of San Jacinto on April 21, 1836, gave Texas independence and its most popular hero, the towering and resolute Sam Houston. "Straight as a majestic Indian, a most perfect specimen of physical manhood," this 43-year-old frontier soldier and statesman had already had a full life. He had lived with Cherokees, fought Creeks with Jackson, served two terms in Congress, and been governor of Tennessee. When his bride left him in 1829, he resigned from the governorship and went back to the Cherokees, who changed their name for him from "The Raven" to "The Big Drunk."

In 1833 Houston went to Texas. Allying himself with the Texan cause, he became a delegate to a settlers' convention and in 1835 was made commander in chief of the Texas army. At San Jacinto he was shot in the ankle, but his 783 troops crushed Santa Anna's army to the cry "Remember the Alamo!" paving the way for his election as first president of the new Republic. He was re-elected, and after Texas became a state in 1845, served in the U.S. Senate until 1859. Another term as governor ended with his being deposed in 1861 when he refused to swear allegiance to the Confederacy. He died two years later, respected by friend and foe for his fearless courage and integrity.

171

BROWN BROTHERS

Kit Carson was America's ideal of the frontier hero.

Pathfinder to "The Pathfinder"

In October, 1826, a newspaper in Franklin, Missouri, carried notice of a one-cent reward for the return of a runaway saddler's apprentice, "Christopher Carson, a boy about sixteen years old, small of age, but thick set." No one claimed the reward, and the runaway, bound for Santa Fe with a trading expedition, went on to the West to become America's most famous guide and Indian fighter.

As a frontiersman, Kit Carson was no more daring than many other mountaineers. His adventures could be matched by those of lesser-known colleagues. In physical appearance, also, he was anything but the ideal image of the traditional western fiction hero, for he weighed only about 145 pounds and had short legs which Mrs. Frémont once observed were "unmistakably bandy-legged." But he had a noble and chivalrous character, was "brave as a lion," and, most important, he had the good fortune to become the guide of one of the West's best publicists, John C. Frémont, whose reports of his exploring expeditions made the "clear steady blue-eyed" Carson into a national hero.

Kit was born in Kentucky in 1809 and was raised in a frontier settlement in Missouri. Orphaned in childhood, he missed a formal education and remained illiterate most of his life. As soon as Mexican independence made the Southwest more hospitable to Americans, he decided to run away from the saddler's bench and see the world. The trader's trail to Santa Fe seemed the most logical, handiest road to adventure, and he took it. After arriving in New Mexico, he headed at once for Taos, which had become an outfitting center for trappers. In 1829 he joined his first expedition, a long trapping tour under Ewing Young that took him across the Arizona and southern California deserts to the San Joaquin Valley, fighting Indians along the way.

Returning to Taos in 1831, he followed Tom Fitzpatrick and Jim Bridger through the Rockies, becoming a free trapper and engaging in some hair-raising Indian fights that provided writers with epic material about him. When beaver became scarce in western streams, he turned to supplying buffalo meat for Bent's Fort on the Arkansas, and in 1841 took his daughter by an Arapaho woman to a school in the States. On his way back to the West he met Frémont, who was about to start on the first government exploring expedition to the Rockies since Long's trip in 1820. "I told Colonel Frémont that I had been some time in the mountains and could guide him to any point he wished to go," Carson said, and he was hired to lead the man who became known as the Pathfinder. After their return, Frémont's report of their journey to South Pass dramatized Carson's courage and ability and made him a nationally celebrated figure.

His fame soared as he guided Frémont on a second expedition in 1843–44 which took them to Salt Lake, the Columbia, and California. A year later they were back in California on a third trip and this time they were plunged into the middle of the dramatic conquest of that Mexican territory. After initial American successes, Carson started east with dispatches, but General Stephen Watts Kearny halted him and requisitioned him as a guide back to California. Carson fought in the battle of San Pasqual, and to save Kearny's command, crawled through the enemy's siege lines to bring help from San Diego.

In March, 1847, he rode across the United States with news of California events and was greeted in Washington as a hero by President Polk, who appointed him a lieutenant in the Mounted Riflemen. He made another round-trip ride between California and Washington the following winter and after the war retired to a farm near Taos.

Carson's later years were equally active. As an Indian agent and military leader, he broke the power of the Navajos and campaigned against Apaches, Kiowas, and Comanches. During the Civil War, he organized New Mexican troops for the Union and in 1865 was brevetted a brigadier general. Three years later this remarkable man died in Fort Lyon, Colorado, an honored American who had made a successful transition from mountain man to citizen and builder of the West.

This view shows the exciting climax—"Santa Fe in sight!"—of a trading caravan's 750-mile journey from Missouri.

PIERCY, *Route from Liverpool*, 1855

An 1855 view of the Missouri crossing at Council Bluffs shows the start of the Mormons' long trail to Salt Lake.

The Mormon Vision

To a British visitor, Mormon leader Brigham Young looked like "a gentleman farmer in New England . . . affable and impressive, simple and courteous" with "no signs of dogmatism, bigotry or fanaticism." To others of his time, he was a man with a towering self-righteousness and sense of power, a spiritual zealot who invited persecution. Whatever view contemporaries took, history recognizes Young as a capable, strong-willed organizer who led his people "up into the mountains, where the devil cannot dig us out," and showed Americans that the supposedly barren and sterile West could, after all, be inhabited by a persevering and enterprising people.

As president of the Mormons' guiding council, Young became leader of the church at its most critical moment. In Ohio, Missouri, and Illinois growing congregations of adherents sought sanctuary, only to be hounded by local politicians and mobs. When the Prophet Joseph Smith was murdered in a Carthage, Illinois, jail in 1844, the 43-year-old Young gathered up the disorganized factions of the faithful and in the dead of winter moved them in dazed groups across Iowa to temporary refuge on the lands of the Pottawatomie Indians. Here on the Missouri River frontier of the nation he decided on a bold move to take his people beyond the reach of persecution, outside the borders of the U.S. to Mexican territory.

"The Upper California, O that's the land for me, It lies between the mountains and the great Pacific sea!" the Mormons sang hopefully, and in the spring of 1847 Young started west across the plains with an advance group of 148 pioneers to find a site. Behind him, near present-day Council Bluffs and at several points in Iowa, he left groups of Mormons to establish provisioning farms for the stream of faithful which would follow to the new Zion he planned to establish in the West.

The valley of the Great Salt Lake, "stretching in still and solitary grandeur," had been familiar for years to trappers, but when Young reached the mountains overlooking it and proclaimed it as the Promised Land, some of his followers were appalled by its desolation. Nevertheless, "When I commune with my own heart," one of them wrote, "and ask

174

LIBRARY OF CONGRESS

Vermont-born Brigham Young started life as a carpenter and glazier. He abstained from tobacco and liquor, and "baked potatoes with a little buttermilk" were his favorite food. But he shocked the nation by espousing polygamy and was survived by 17 wives and 47 children.

myself whether I would choose to dwell here in this wild looking country amongst the Saints surrounded by friends . . . or dwell amongst the gentiles with all their wealth and good things of the earth . . . the soft whisper echoes loud and reverberates back in tones of stern determination; give me the quiet wilderness. . . ."

On July 24, 1847, the little company began its settlement and within a month, under Young's vigorous direction, had "broke, watered, planted, and sowed upwards of 100 acres with various kinds of seeds; nearly stockaded with adobies one public square," and erected "one line of log cabins."

Other companies soon arrived from Iowa, and later the original settlers were joined by brigades of Mormons pulling their belongings across the plains on creaking handcarts. There was hardship and death on the trail, suffering and heartbreak in Salt Lake City from drought and crop-destroying crickets, but the colony prospered, and two years after its establishment Forty-Niners on their way to California found it a flourishing city of 5,000.

The treaty ending the Mexican War ceded the Utah territory to the United States and returned the Mormons to the authority of Washington. As swarms of converts migrated to Utah, ugly quarrels broke out between them and non-Mormon emigrants, culminating in the arrival of U.S. troops to restore order. The Mormon practice of polygamy was under constant attack until it was abandoned in the 1890's; but in the face of all problems, Brigham Young's community thrived and grew.

A MANIFEST DESTINY

DESTINY was a word always on the lips of men interested in western affairs. Horace Greeley, who urged young men to go west and grow up with the country, visited San Francisco in 1859 and concluded that her position "fixes and assures her destiny as the second city of America." Much earlier the politician-editor John O'Sullivan had made his famous boast that it was "Our manifest destiny . . . to overspread the continent allotted by Providence for the free development of our yearly multiplying millions." The nation long had its narrow-gauge thinkers who thought it impossible or undesirable that the flag should ever reach the Pacific. But the West responded eagerly to ebullient men like Thomas Hart Benton—for thirty years senator from frontier Missouri, a sturdy expansionist who stood for the acquisition of California, homestead legislation, and a Pacific railroad, and who was proud of his early championship of peaceable plans for obtaining Texas and Oregon. "Five and twenty years ago I put those two balls in motion!" boasted Benton in 1844. "Solitary and alone I did it! Millions now roll them forward!"

A majority of frontiersmen not only believed in expansion, but were ready to use some violence to effect it. They had an inarticulate sense of what Harriet Martineau called "the depth of futurity" before them, "wherein to create something so magnificent as the world has scarcely begun to dream of." They took that idea as justification for a rough clearance of Indians from their path. Westerners raised the clamor that made the acquisition of Louisiana imperative; they tilted the scales for the War of 1812, with its possibilities of conquest in Canada; they abetted Stephen F. Austin in his plans for redeeming Texas by "spreading over it North American population, enterprise, and intelligence," as he put it; eyeing the Oregon country, they raised the cry of "54°40' or fight"; and with some exceptions, they gave the Mexican War their hearty support.

If the pioneers had read de Tocqueville, they would have endorsed his remark that their continuous westward thrust had a "providential solemnity," for the hand of God seemed to push them forward. It is true that Manifest Destiny had its sordid, demagogic, and brutal aspects. Its worst side appeared in Andrew Jackson's rough use of troops in removing the Creeks and Cherokees west of the Mississippi; in some of the pressures which brought on the Mexican War; in such episodes as the lawless uprising of the Bear Flag settlers in California; and in the piratical crimes of the filibusters who raided Central America under William Walker. But it also had its healthy and constructive side, and a certain idealism. Such men as the resolute, patient Moses and Stephen F. Austin, anxious to plant a civilization equaling that of their ancestral Connecticut in the wilderness, and Sam Houston, a statesman as well as the military hero of San Jacinto, had their vision.

It was a vision of immense empty plains turned over to contented farmsteads and ranches with peacefully grazing herds; of western forests dotted with clearings for cabins; of trails converted into glistening railroad lines, with towns strung like beads along them; of churches and colleges rising in the former solitudes. The social ideals of far-western leaders like Marcus Whitman, James King of William, the California editor slain for his fearlessness, and Mirabeau B. Lamar, who became president of the Texas Republic, were those familiar to earlier pioneers—equal opportunity, free enterprise, democracy, and faith in the common man. The leaders had to fit their political system to new environments, adapting it to vast distances, to motley conglomerates of people including Mexicans, Asians, and Kanakas, to an embarrassing remoteness from eastern authority, to painful shortages of capital, and to the occasional need for vigilantes.

At least a half-dozen gripping and colorful stories fit themselves into the pattern of Manifest Destiny. One was the government's exploration of the huge trans-Missouri region, probing the grimmest natural obstacles that pioneers had yet met—extreme southwestern heat and northern cold, deserts, canyons, and lava beds, the steep sierra and trackless forests of Douglas fir, ponderosa pine, and sequoia. Lewis and Clark had mapped one rim of the area. Zebulon M. Pike found Pikes Peak and wandered in erratic fashion down to the Rio Grande and back. Major Stephen H. Long, heading an expedition in 1820, had done the West a disservice by reporting the Great Plains "almost wholly unfit for cultivation" and labeling them on his map the "Great American Desert." Then in 1842 the government placed Thomas Benton's son-in-law, the scientifically trained John C. Frémont, in charge of a new exploring party to the Rockies, a journey quickly followed by another across the Sierras into California.

But the story of exploration was a mere prologue to others. Continued emigration along the Oregon Trail raised the population in the Columbia River valley well above 10,000 by the end of the forties. This stream of settlers made it possible to persuade Great Britain to give up her claim to the north bank of the Columbia, while Benton helped Polk convince Congress that it should yield everything above the 49th parallel. This peaceable division of Oregon in 1846 was creditable to both nations, and equally creditable was the rapid march of Oregon Territory, a singularly orderly frontier community, to statehood in 1859. An unforgettable story was that of the Santa Fe Trail, which ran from Independence, Missouri, to the New Mexican capital. At its apogee long parallel lines of covered wagons by the hundreds, drawn by mules and oxen, rolled southwest bearing as much as a quarter-million dollars' worth of merchandise for Mexican markets. Nothing had ever been seen on the continent like these wheeled cargoes, whose morning starts Josiah Gregg vividly described:

"All's set!" is finally heard from some teamster—"All's set!" is directly responded from every quarter. "Stretch out!" immediately vociferates the captain. Then the "heps" of drivers—the cracking of whips—the trampling of feet—the occasional creak of wheels—the rumbling of wagons—form a new scene of exquisite confusion. . . . "Fall in!" is heard from headquarters, and the wagons are forthwith strung out upon the long inclined plain.

But the greatest stories of the rounding-out of the United States centered in the Mexican War and the Gold Rush. The annexation of Texas was the result of an inevitable, irresistible population movement. President Polk would have preferred the peaceful purchase of the other southwestern areas. California, which Mexico left unused and ill-governed, an unrealized asset of civilization, was the richest domain. For this Polk would have paid forty millions, and he exhausted the resources of diplomacy. When he said "The cup of forbearance has been exhausted," the war began.

It was primarily a war for and by westerners, for the pioneer states embraced it eagerly while older parts of the Union hung back. From Texas and the Mississippi Valley came almost 50,000 volunteers, while the thirteen original states averaged only 1,000 apiece. The regular Army at war's outbreak numbered only 7,365 men, and the resounding American victory at Buena Vista, in which 4,800 men defeated 15,000, was fought primarily by volunteers, young men from Mississippi and Kentucky, Illinois and Indiana. The principal war hero, Zachary Taylor, an unlettered Kentucky-reared soldier who never saw West Point, had spent his life on the frontier, all the way from the Seminole country to the upper Mississippi and the Ouachita. And while these contingents were winning victories in Mexico, other volunteers under Stephen Watts Kearny and Alexander Doniphan were making their truly astonishing marches.

Gold did not make California. The steady influx of trappers, traders, ranchers, and farmers had raised the white population to 8,000 by 1845. Nevertheless, the day when John A. Sutter's foreman, James Marshall, building a sawmill for the captain, espied gold in a Sacramento Valley stream has rightly been regarded as the most dramatic in California history. It lifted the region out of the Arcadian Age; it gave headlong acceleration to its development; and it placed before the newcomers problems of control and order which no American pioneer community had ever faced on such a scale.

Bayard Taylor in his classic picture of California in 1849 laid emphasis on the hodgepodge of nationalities who rushed to this Golconda. They embraced the Moor and the Polynesian, the Australian and the Chinese, the Frenchman and the Turk. "Our own countrymen seem to lose their local peculiarities in such a crowd," he said, "and it is by chance epithet rather than by manner that the New Yorker is distinguished from the Kentuckian, the Carolinian from the down-Easter, the Virginian from the Texan." Men rushed in by the two great trails and all their cutoffs, by the fever-haunted route across the Isthmus, by ship around Cape Horn, and from across the Pacific. Sailors deserted their vessels; Mexicans took the desert roads up from Sonora. Taylor noted the general democracy among the Americans, but he was also struck by the recklessness and criminality. "It was curious to see how men hitherto noted for their prudence and caution took sudden leave of these qualities."

Within this turbulence men of brains and character gradually took charge. Lawlessness was too expensive to be endured. The methods of the vigilantes of 1851, purging San Francisco of its worst outlaws, were rough but salutary. Already, under the Compromise of 1850, California had become a state, with one of the best constitutions in the Union.

The Mexican War and Oregon settlement almost doubled the area of the nation, adding 1,200,000 square miles. These events gave America its richest mines, its most magnificent forests, its finest potential orchards, and, though men would take long to find them, its largest reservoirs of oil. But the Far West was to offer another great gift. It was to enrich the imagination of America and the world, for a magical light was soon to invest it. Everywhere that people read books and looked at pictures, they would see it as the Far West of Bret Harte and Mark Twain, of the big trees, the Grand Canyon, and the Yellowstone geysers, of the sea entrance that Frémont had called the Golden Gate, of the mighty cliffs, waterfalls, and rock domes of the Yosemite that so excited John Muir that he could not sleep, of new cattle ranches and wheat empires, of mile-high Lake Tahoe and the flower-carpeted desert. In this appeal to the imagination it fulfilled its greatest destiny.

ALLAN NEVINS

One of Pattie's narrow escapes, from his Personal Narrative, *shows him rescued from starvation in the wild Southwest.*

James Ohio Pattie: American Marco Polo

In a limited way James Ohio Pattie was an American Marco Polo, with a touch of Gulliver and Baron Munchausen thrown in. His six years of wandering through the Southwest were an incredible composite of adventure and suffering, and he explored the country widely, found many routes across that harsh land for later travelers, and wrote descriptions of the mild and healthy region of California which helped awaken the interest of his fellow Americans in that far-off Mexican territory.

Pattie's rambling journey, which was essentially a succession of mishaps, disasters, and miraculous escapes, began in company with his father, Sylvester Pattie. Both were restless frontiersmen and before the War of 1812 had moved from Kentucky to Missouri. After the death of his wife, Sylvester took the twenty-year-old James Ohio as a companion, and in 1824 they set off together up the Missouri River to try their luck on a trapping expedition to the Rocky Mountains.

Stopped at Council Bluffs because they had forgotten to get a trapping license, the Patties joined, instead, a trading caravan for Santa Fe and started across the plains through the territory of treacherous Pawnees, Arikaras, Crows, and Comanches. They were attacked several times, and two members of the party were scalped, but Pattie's closest call came from a wounded grizzly bear.

The company finally reached Santa Fe, and while waiting for permission to trap in Mexican territory, Pattie joined a group sent to rescue several women from a band of Comanches. This was successfully accomplished, and one of the captives, retrieved "without any clothing," turned out to be "a beautiful young lady, the daughter of the governor." In time she formed a warm attachment for Pattie and helped make his stay in Santa Fe more pleasurable.

When they received their licenses, the Patties set off for the Gila River, and in the wilds of present-day New Mexico and Arizona fought Indians, had their horses stolen, almost starved to death, and experienced one adventure on top of another. One night Pattie awoke to find a panther within six feet

180

of him. "I raised my gun gently to my face, and shot it in the head," he said. Another day he came on the butchered remains of a companion killed by Indians and reported that "His head, with his hat on, was stuck on a stake."

After varying fortunes Sylvester Pattie gave up trapping to manage a copper mine, and James Ohio joined a new party, most of whom were soon wiped out by Papagos Indians. Shortly afterward he had another narrow escape when Mojave Indians shot sixteen arrows through his blanket during the night. Unharmed, he continued with an outfit under Ewing Young, explored the Colorado River past the Grand Canyon, and rambled from the Yellowstone to the Arkansas. When his party returned to Santa Fe with $20,000 worth of beaver skins, a new governor seized the furs and left Pattie penniless.

After a trading visit to Chihuahua and Sonora he was trapping again along the Rio Grande. This time he got two arrowheads in his body from unfriendly Apaches. Sylvester, meanwhile, gave up mining when a clerk absconded with $30,000 he had saved from his profits, and the two reunited but luckless Patties blazed a route to the lower Colorado, had more troubles with Indians, and almost drowned in a flood. Trying to cross the lower California desert, they nearly died of thirst before they were saved by Indians from a mission.

The Mexicans threw them into jail, and the long-suffering elder Pattie finally died. James Ohio was sent to San Diego, but was freed during a smallpox epidemic when the Mexican governor learned that he possessed some vaccine which his father had carried with him. He traveled up and down California, inoculating 22,000 persons with vaccine replenished from some of those whom he had inoculated. Later he joined a revolution against the governor and then turned on the leader of the revolt. When he had had enough of California, he sailed for Mexico, where he had to borrow money to return home.

In 1831 Pattie published an account of his *Unheard of Hardships and Dangers,* but his later life is obscure, and he is believed to have died a forgotten man, trying to return to the scene of his adventures. "This man," a companion wrote, "left my camp in the Sierra Nevada Mountains, amidst the deep snows of the terrible winter of 1849–50 . . . I suppose he perished in the deep snows, or was killed by Indians."

Century Magazine, 1890

John Bidwell

John Bidwell was only 21 when he fell victim to the California fever. In 1839 he left Ohio for Missouri with $75 in his pocket, a knapsack on his back, and "no weapon more formidable than a pocketknife." A claim-jumper stole his Missouri land, but when he heard a returned trapper extol the "perfect paradise and perpetual spring" of California, he determined to go there instead. Forming a Western Emigration Society, he enlisted 500 others to join him. Most of them backed out, and at the rendezvous only 69 men, women, and children showed up, but Bidwell's group was nevertheless the first of any size to cross the plains to the Far West.

The party left the Kansas frontier on May 19, 1841, and followed the trappers' route along the Platte River. At Soda Springs the group divided, half of the emigrants turning north to Oregon, the rest, under Bidwell, without a guide and knowing only "that California lay to the west," struggling across the desert. They abandoned their wagons, killed their oxen and mules for food, and in October wandered into the Sierra Nevada Mountains. After losing hope of ever finding their way out of the wilds, they suddenly emerged in the San Joaquin Valley, still thinking that it was another 500 miles to California.

The emigrants set to work erecting homes, and before long other parties of settlers followed them into California. Bidwell went to work at Sutter's Fort, later joined the Bear Flag Revolt, and then, turning to ranching and politics, played a leading role in guiding California to statehood.

181

Stephen Watts Kearny was an able and efficient commander who died in 1848 from a fever contracted on his long campaigns. One unit of his "Army of the West" was Doniphan's Missouri volunteers, shown (right) charging the Mexicans.

America's expansionists saw that California was ripe for the plucking. Far removed from its weak parent government in Mexico, it was without authority, finances, or an effective army; and in 1846 its valleys were filling with American settlers and retired trappers, busily talking independence with the native Californians.

No one sensed the opportunity more than ambitious, 32-year-old John Charles Frémont, who in December, 1845, had entered northern California on his third exploring expedition. Back east trouble with Mexico was brewing, and the seething tensions he found in the province convinced Frémont that he was the right man in the right place at the right time.

In the spring Mexican officials ordered him to take his armed band of mountain men out of California. Frémont obeyed sullenly, but denounced the order as an insult to himself and his country.

Near Klamath Lake he was overtaken by a secret agent whose dispatches from Washington induced him to return to the Sacramento Valley, and his reappearance there encouraged an impetuous group of settlers to rise against the Mexicans and capture the village of Sonoma. Frémont threw aside all pretense of neutrality and on July 4, 1846, aided the rebels in raising a "grizzly bear" flag and proclaiming a California Republic.

The new nation and Frémont's hopes for sole glory were both short-lived. Three days later, with war underway between the U.S. and Mexico, an American squadron under Commodore John Sloat occupied Monterey. Sonoma and San Francisco were also claimed. Frémont and his motley group of Bear Flaggers joined Sloat's successor, Commodore Robert F. Stockton, and completed the conquest of northern California.

To win the southern part of the province Stock-

HUGHES, *Doniphan's Expedition*, 1850

LIBRARY OF CONGRESS

John C. Frémont (above) clashed with Kearny over his highly controversial role in the California revolt. Public sympathy in his court-martial for disobedience helped make Frémont the first Republican candidate for President in 1856.

ton mustered in Frémont's men, including Kit Carson, as Navy Mounted Riflemen and sent them by ship to San Diego. During the voyage Carson and his companions were miserably seasick, but they regained their land legs, occupied San Diego without difficulty, and in August helped Stockton take Los Angeles. By the middle of the month the conquest of the entire province of California seemed to be accomplished.

Unaware of this quick success, a large "Army of the West" under Stephen Watts Kearny, a veteran of the War of 1812, was on its way overland to California. Kearny's troops included regular Army dragoons and a boisterous, undisciplined unit of Missouri volunteers under Alexander Doniphan, a tall frontier lawyer and militia commander. Another battalion was forming in the Iowa camps of Mormons who were waiting to go to Salt Lake.

Kearny's regulars and rawboned volunteers fol-lowed the Santa Fe traders' route across the Southwest, suffering from heat, thirst, and sickness on the plains. They passed Bent's Fort and on August 18 entered Santa Fe without firing a shot. In the captured capital Kearny divided his army, and while he hurried on to California with his dragoons, sent Doniphan and his Missourians, about 900 strong, on a side-expedition to Chihuahua.

The Missouri farm boys and frontiersmen, calling themselves "ring-tailed roarers," fought their first battle near El Paso, drove off a larger Mexican force, and stormed into the city as conquerors. Continuing south across the desert, they reached the outskirts of Chihuahua and found an army of more than 4,000 men waiting for them with ropes with which to tie them up and march them as captives to Mexico City. The Missourians were uncowed. On February 28, along the Sacramento Creek, they routed the Mexicans in a wild, three-hour battle,

183

TITLE INSURANCE AND TRUST COMPANY, LOS ANGELES

Commodore Robert F. Stockton, fighting his battles ashore,
captured Los Angeles to complete the conquest of California.

and the next day entered Chihuahua.

Soon after he left Santa Fe in September, 1846, and began his grueling march across the seared, rugged wastes of New Mexico and Arizona, General Kearny met Kit Carson. The scout was racing east, carrying word of the swift and apparently successful conquest of California by Stockton and Frémont. Cheered by this information, Kearny now looked forward to heading a peaceful occupation of the captured territory. He sent three of his five companies of dragoons with all of his wagons back to Santa Fe, and giving Carson's dispatches to another rider, requisitioned the mountain man to lead him and the rest of his command—about 100 men—on to California. Carson guided them west along the Gila River route that trappers had followed for years, but the arduous journey over rough and inhospitable country was too much for the Army men and their mounts. Mile after mile of bone-dry desert took its toll of their mules and horses, and many of the men had to plod on by foot, fighting thirst and exhaustion.

At the Colorado River they met some cowboys with disquieting news. Native Californians in the settlements farther west had risen in revolt against the occupation forces of Stockton and Frémont and had recaptured Los Angeles, Santa Barbara, and San Diego from the Americans. Kearny's weary band, small in numbers and poorly mounted, realized they would probably have to fight before they reached the coast.

Plunging into the worst portion of the journey, they pushed on through the fierce heat and sand of southern California's desert. More of their mounts died, and some could be moved only "by one man tugging at the halter and another pushing up the brute by placing his shoulder against its buttocks." They finally reached a ranch owned by an Englishman, who told them that Stockton's sailors had retaken San Diego and were trying to gather horses for an attack on Los Angeles. But the road to San Diego was held by Californians who would have to be cleared away before Kearny's troops could join Stockton.

On December 4, 1846, the men moved gamely ahead again, and the following day scouts reported a force of California horsemen blocking the road at a town called San Pasqual. Kearny thought the

184

This spirited view shows the desperate combat between Kearny's dragoons and tall-hatted Californians at San Pasqual.

enemy might disperse if he presented a bold front, so the next morning at dawn he ordered his worn, bedraggled troops to attack. The battle was short and furious. In the first moments an advance unit of Kearny's men riding into the Californians was cut to pieces and its commander killed. As Kearny's main force came up, the Californians started to withdraw, then turned around and charged the Americans. The fight became a wild melee of men afoot and on horse, swinging sabers and rifles against lances. Finally the Californians moved off, but eighteen Americans were dead, and Kearny and many others were wounded.

The battered army struggled on about ten miles, still harassed by mounted Californians who seemed to be gathering for another fight. At last Kearny halted and ordered Carson and two others to try to get through the Californians' lines to bring reinforcements from Stockton. The messengers crawled safely past the enemy during the night, and soon afterwards 180 of Stockton's command arrived to break the siege and help rout the Californians.

Early in the new year a combined force of sailors, dragoons, and American settlers went on to defeat a California force at the San Gabriel River, and on January 10, 1847, they re-entered Los Angeles without opposition. Californian resistance melted away, and by the Treaty of Cahuenga the Mexicans surrendered the province to the Americans.

The occupation of the new territory was marred by an inter-service rivalry between Stockton and Kearny, in which Frémont played a self-aggrandizing role. Kearny had President Polk's authorization to command the occupation forces and organize a civil government, but Stockton refused to recognize the Army leader's authority, and moving on his own, installed the willing Frémont as governor of the captured province. In February a new commodore arrived to replace Stockton, and the orders he carried confirmed Kearny's position. Frémont was sent east where a court-martial found him guilty of insubordination. After his departure his nemesis, Kearny, was able to govern until the civil authorities took over.

California Compromise

In 1849 the territory which had been peopled almost overnight with hordes of gold-hunters applied for admission as a free state. California's request stirred a crisis which most Americans had long been hoping to avoid, and the entire nation turned toward Washington as one of the most notable debates in Senate history got underway.

Northern senators urged adoption of the Wilmot Proviso to bar slavery from all lands obtained from Mexico. In reply, angry southerners attacked the proposal as an invasion of sacred rights and threatened to resist its enforcement "to any extremity." One heated charge brought forth another, and each day threatened to engulf the country in disunion and disaster.

On February 5, 1850, the 72-year-old Henry Clay rose with his last compromise. Already mortally ill, he had said "I feel myself quite weak and exhausted this morning," but he was still able to enthrall the galleries with his brilliant two-day speech. Admit California as a free state, he urged, divide New Mexico and Utah into territories whose settlers could decide for themselves whether to become free or slave. Abolish the slave trade in the District of Columbia, and strengthen the Fugitive Slave Act.

His proposals heightened the debate. John C. Calhoun of South Carolina was too old and weak to deliver an answer, but a colleague read his speech while the southern leader, swathed in flannels, remained in his seat and listened to his own words of wrath and defiance. Extreme northerners were also opposed, but for different reasons. Finally, on March 7, New Hampshire's Senator Daniel Webster broke the stalemate. "I speak today for the preservation of the Union," he began. " 'Hear me for my cause.' "

The other senators listened, and the Compromise of 1850, as proposed by Clay, was passed. The crisis was ended, and the Union temporarily saved.

Henry Clay speaks on the Compromise of 1850. Listening are Calhoun (standing, third from right); Benton (seated, second from right); and Webster (seated, with head on hand).

LIBRARY OF CONGRESS

CALIFORNIA HISTORICAL SOCIETY

On the eve of the Gold Rush, San Francisco in 1847 (above), painted by French artist Victor Prevost, reflected its antecedents as the sleepy Mexican village of Yerba Buena.

Below, the San Francisco of 1850 was the bustling gateway to the gold fields. A forest of masts stood in the harbor, where ships had been deserted by sailors for the diggings.

COLLECTION OF MRS. CELIA TOBIN CLARK

Gold Is Found
and a
Nation Goes Wild

EDWARD EBERSTADT & SONS

John Sutter (above) helplessly watched gold seekers despoil his property. To artist Charles Nahl, a miner in 1850, "Sunday Morning in the Mines" (right) was a comic interlude.

John August Sutter was a short, fat, kindly man whom everyone in California knew for his hospitality. He had come to America from Switzerland in 1834, and catching the western fever, had traveled across the plains to Oregon. In time he arrived in the Sacramento Valley, where the Mexican governor welcomed his plan to develop the country and granted him some land. Sutter built a fort, and gathering Indians, Hawaiians, and white settlers around him, established a colony called New Helvetia which he ruled like a feudal baron.

Early in 1848 he began building a sawmill on his property, along the south fork of the American River. On the morning of January 24 a mechanic from New Jersey named James Marshall saw something glint in the water. Stepping down into the ditch he picked up a shiny nugget, and all day he

and the camp housekeeper at the mill boiled the bit of metal in a kettle of lye. When it failed to tarnish, Marshall gathered more of the glistening flakes and specks, wrapped them in a rag, and on January 28 took them to the fort. Sutter examined them. "Yes, it looks like gold," he agreed. "Come, let us test it."

Gold it was indeed, and the two men were unable to keep their secret. Laborers at the fort heard the rumor first and deserted their work; then the report spread to nearby settlements and on to the coast. By summer whole towns were emptied by a fevered rush to Sutter's land. Men abandoned their families, left homes and trades, jumped ships in the harbors. In Monterey, wrote the alcalde, "A whole platoon of soldiers from the fort left only their colors behind," and he added that some people

E. B. CROCKER ART GALLERY

were going even on crutches, and one had been carried to the mines on a litter.

Six months later a report to Congress by President Polk confirmed the news to the world, and the greatest gold rush in history was on. From the East an army of Americans stampeded for California, crossing the plains in wagons, on mules, and afoot, following every route that the pioneers had blazed. Others went around Cape Horn by ship or hurried across the continent at Panama or Mexico. At the diggings they were joined by Australians, Peruvians, pigtailed Chinese, and men from every land that had heard the news. By the end of 1849 California's population had jumped from 20,000 to nearly 100,000, and the biggest waves of newcomers were still to arrive.

The discovery that made fortunes for many

ruined Sutter. There was neither law nor force to restrain the prospectors. They overran his land, butchered his cattle, and destroyed everything that he had labored to build. By 1852 he was bankrupt. Afterward he pleaded for redress, and California granted him a pension of $250 a month. But it ended in 1878, and the man who had once been known for his open-armed hospitality died two years later in a little town in Pennsylvania, still petitioning Congress for the return of his lost acres. James Marshall, who had discovered the gold, fared even worse. He died in poverty, selling his autograph to support himself.

OVERLEAF: *American democracy followed the people west and soon took on a frontier flavor, captured by George Caleb Bingham in his painting "The Verdict of the People."*

189

BOATMEN'S NATIONAL BANK, ST. LOUIS; COURTESY *Life*

John Brown: Terrible Avenger from Kansas

Some people thought he was a madman, some thought him a hero and a saint. John Brown of Osawatomie roared out of Kansas like a tornado, a specter to a nation divided, a symbol of all the tensions over slavery that the California compromise could not still for long.

This tall, angular man with the zeal of an Old Testament prophet was precipitated on the national scene by a new conflict over western territory. The midwestern frontier was filling up, and population pressures drove settlers in ever greater numbers toward the new lands of the West. When Congress in 1854 attempted to organize Kansas and Nebraska into new territories, the old argument over slavery erupted again, now far more seriously.

By repealing the Missouri Compromise of 1820, which would have made both territories free soil, Congress directed that the matter should be decided by vote of the new settlers. This started a bitter race into the lands by partisans of freedom and

METROPOLITAN MUSEUM OF ART; COURTESY *Encyclopaedia Britannica*

John Brown's terrorist activities in Kansas and his later spectacular raid on Harper's Ferry shocked conservatives in both the North and South; but to some radicals he was "Saint John the Just." John Steuart Curry painted him as a frightening, avenging figure (right).

slavery. Among the armed men who came, ready to vote or fight, were John Brown and his five sons.

Brown was 55 years old. He had been born in Torrington, Connecticut, but like his father he became a drifter, moving from one town and trade to another. For a time a drover and traveling salesman, he had also operated a tannery in Pennsylvania. When his piety turned him against slavery, he became an abolitionist and an agent of the Underground Railroad. The Kansas-Nebraska Act infuriated him, and in 1855 he headed for Kansas, bound on a holy mission to drive slaveowners out of the new territory.

With his sons he organized a band of abolitionist irregulars at Osawatomie and soon became the terror of proslavers. Armed with pistols, Sharps rifles, and Navy cutlasses, they rode against slaveowners at night and hid out during the day. When slavers sacked the free-soil town of Lawrence, Brown and his men cried "blood for blood" and hacked five southerners to death on Pottawatomie Creek. A posse which set out to get Brown found itself surrounded and was forced to surrender to him.

Eventually Brown struck into Missouri, where he freed eleven slaves. President Buchanan offered a reward of $250 for his capture, whereupon Brown printed handbills offering 25 cents for Buchanan, and taking the slaves he had freed, rode off to Canada with a plan for his wildest and most daring scheme.

On the night of October 16, 1859, wearing a bushy beard for a disguise, he entered Harper's Ferry, Virginia, with a "liberating army" of eighteen men and seized the U.S. arsenal. Barricading himself in the building, he waited for nearby slaves to revolt and join him. Instead he was surrounded by militia and a company of marines, under Colonel Robert E. Lee, who finally stormed into the arsenal and beat Brown to the floor. By then ten of his men, including two sons, were dead or dying.

Brown, convicted of treason and murder, was led to the scaffold wearing what an observer of the execution described as "a grim & greisly smirk." In Kansas a farmer scrawled in his diary, "Osawatomie Brown, he'll trouble them more when his Coffin's nailed down." It was true. Even northern newspapers denounced his rash deed, but the motive behind it lived on in men's consciences, and soon northern armies were marching to war singing of John Brown's body and soul.

W. BIRNEY, *J. G. Birney*, 1890

James Birney

Not all of the men who opposed slavery and fought its extension into the new western territories came from the North. James G. Birney was a southerner who had once been a slaveowner himself. He ran an abolitionist newspaper and twice ran for President of the U.S. as an antislavery candidate.

Unlike many abolitionists who condoned violence and thought that slavery could not be ended by constitutional means, Birney believed in appealing to reason. In both Kentucky and Alabama he owned Negroes, but he came to abhor the institution of slavery and thought it could be ended by emancipating slaves and sending them to special colonies in Africa. As a first step he tried to have the Alabama legislature prohibit further importation of slaves, but he made little progress and in 1832 returned to Kentucky.

Resentment against his views soon forced him to move to Ohio, but even there he found opposition. The offices of his weekly newspaper, *The Philanthropist*, were twice raided, and one time he retreated to his home to defend his life, if necessary, with "about forty muskets and double-barreled shotguns" that were kept in the house.

In 1837, as an officer of the American Antislavery Society, he moved to New York, where he continued his calm appeals to men's humanity. In both 1840 and 1844 the Liberty party made him its candidate for President. A fall from a horse in 1845 paralyzed him and ended his public career, and he died in 1857. By then louder and less dispassionate voices had succeeded his in the fight to end slavery.

COLLECTION OF FREDERICK HILL MESERVE

Bloody Kansas
and the
Little Giant

The storm that turned Kansas into a tragic dress rehearsal of the Civil War was started by a bull-necked little man from Illinois. Senator Stephen A. Douglas stood only five feet four inches tall, but he had a powerful and fearless personality, and his admiring followers called him the "Little Giant" and the "Steam Engine in Britches."

Born in Vermont in 1813, Douglas moved west to rise rapidly in politics as a frontier lawyer, judge, and congressman. By the time he was 34, he was chairman of the Senate's important Committee on Territories. He had married the daughter of a North Carolina slaveholder, but as a westerner he was more interested in expansionism than in the problem of slavery, which he dismissed as one that would take care of itself.

In 1854 he became involved with Chicago businessmen in plans for a transcontinental railroad to California. The South proposed running the line from Memphis through Texas and New Mexico, but Douglas wanted it to follow a more northerly route from his own Illinois. Such a line would, of course, have to cross the Indian lands of the central plains—long avoided by settlers and still without any form of government—and to advance his project Douglas startled the country by proposing the Kansas-Nebraska Act to organize those territories.

His inability to gauge the depth of people's passions over slavery led to trouble. As a self-made man of the West, Douglas believed in the squatter law of the pioneer, and he advocated "Popular Sovereignty," as he termed it, to let the settlers decide by fair and peaceful vote whether the area would become free or slave.

The strife and bloodshed that followed appalled him. Nebraska was unsuited to slavery, but Kansas quickly became a bitter battleground. Bands of

Though he could strike the pose of a fighting gamecock, Douglas tried to compromise in the Clay tradition. But times had changed, and his solutions failed to save the Union.

194

The Battle of Hickory Point was typical of the Kansas guerrilla raids. S. J. Reader, a free-soiler, made this sketch of his companions firing on a slavers' settlement in 1856.

Missouri "border ruffians," pledged to the South, swarmed into the territory to stuff ballot boxes and intimidate free-soilers. The North was equally active, and Emigrant Aid societies in New England sent settlers by the hundreds to the contested land. When violence broke out, abolitionist minister Henry Ward Beecher added fuel to the fire by subscribing to rifles, known as "Beecher's Bibles," for the northern emigrants.

Douglas watched the spectacle of "Bleeding Kansas" with increasing dismay, but he clung to the hope that a fair vote in time would bring peace. Eventually it seemed that he might be right. Partisan emigrants continued to swell the ranks of the bushwhackers, but it soon became evident that they would be outnumbered by settlers from the midwestern states who had not come to fight over slavery, but were simply hungry for new land. Since most of them were from free-soil backgrounds, it was obvious that in a fair vote they would tip the scales decisively against slavery. By 1857 a proslaver in Kansas wrote to a friend, "Trains upon trains are pouring in from every quarter, but particularly from Free States. I had once thought, as I used to write you, that Kansas would be a Slave State; but I am now forced to alter my opinion . . . Our ferry boats are busily engaged, from daylight until dark, in carrying over trains, and the proportion of Free-Soil to Pro-Slavery emigrants is as fifteen to one."

Despite the preponderance of free-soilers, an 1857 convention rigged by slavery advocates wrote a constitution guaranteeing slavery in Kansas. Douglas knew that a fair vote would defeat it, and

he asked President Buchanan to submit it to the people. Three southern states threatened to secede if Buchanan listened to Douglas. In all probability secession would have failed at this time, and many men believed that a determined show of force by Buchanan might have averted the Civil War that came three years later. But the President was a weak, timid man. He turned a deaf ear to Douglas and instead asked Congress to admit Kansas as a new state under the proslavery constitution.

Douglas viewed the President's action as a betrayal of the Kansas-Nebraska Act's promise of popular sovereignty. "By God, sir!" he announced, "I made James Buchanan, and by God, sir, I will unmake him!" He proceeded to do just that, leading a dramatic fight in Congress that struck down the fraudulent Kansas constitution and ended Buchanan's chance for renomination in 1860.

The struggle over Kansas had a number of aftereffects. Suddenly sectional lines were more rigidly drawn, while the positions men took on the slavery issue hardened. A schism developed between Democrats of the South and West, which was to become an open breach by 1860. And the great debate elevated Stephen A. Douglas to national rather than regional prominence, a fact which was to be of considerable significance just one year later, when an obscure Illinois lawyer named Abraham Lincoln challenged him to a series of debates on the questions that Kansas had raised.

CHICAGO HISTORICAL SOCIETY

Lincoln of Illinois

Douglas' Kansas-Nebraska Bill had been bitterly opposed by many northern political leaders who denounced it with such epithets as "an enormous crime" and "a criminal betrayal of precious rights." They particularly resented Douglas' use of the westerners' traditional respect for self-government and popular expression as a means to get votes for his bill, and in 1854 some of them had banded together to form what became the Republican party, which would fight the further extension of slavery.

In 1857 the Supreme Court shocked the North with the Dred Scott decision which, among other things, ruled that the federal government had no right to bar slavery from the territories. This and the debate over the Kansas constitution drove hundreds of thousands of people into the ranks of the new party, including an inconspicuous Illinois lawyer, Abraham Lincoln.

Lincoln had been in and out of local politics, and in 1847, as a Whig congressman, he had gained some attention by his embarrassing "spot resolutions" which asked President Polk to state exactly where and on whose territory the Mexicans had first shed the American blood which Polk claimed as his reason for war. After that Lincoln had voted for the unsuccessful Wilmot Proviso which would have prohibited slavery in any new territory.

In his frank, sincere way the tall, ungainly Lincoln quickly appealed to Illinois Republicans. On slavery he said: "I hate it because of the monstrous injustice of slavery itself. I hate it because it . . . enables the enemies of free institutions, with plausibility, to taunt us as hypocrites—causes the real friends of freedom to doubt our sincerity." On the Kansas-Nebraska Act he said: "Wrong; wrong in its direct effect, letting slavery into Kansas and Nebraska—and wrong in its prospective principle, allowing it to spread to every other part of the wide world where men can be found inclined to take it."

Lincoln's words struck deep to the heart of peo-

Lincoln partisans were to make much of their candidate's rail-splitting background. The full-length portrait of him at left was used as a Republican campaign poster in 1860.

ple's thinking, and in 1858 Illinois Republicans pitted him against Douglas for the Little Giant's seat in the Senate. The campaign that ensued was the most famous in U.S. history.

Both men were westerners raised in the rough-and-tumble school of frontier politics, and both reflected their section's ideals of federal union and nationalistic expansion by people who believed in self-government. But Lincoln's roots were deeper in the pioneer heritage of the Midwest, and he better understood the forces that were driving the nation apart. As an axeman and son of an axeman, he had learned to carve a home in the wilderness, and when he spoke, he represented the pioneer folk and emigrants from Europe who had cleared the forests of the Northwest, built new cities, educated their children, and, as free men, competed with each other for the mastery of new commerce and industry. To these people the territories of the West meant continued opportunity to expand toward the Pacific, taking their way of life with them. But Lincoln saw that the Dred Scott decision and the Kansas-Nebraska Act would raise a barrier to that advance. All the unorganized land of the West was at stake, and the two sections competing for it were his own and the slaveowning South.

" 'A house divided against itself cannot stand,' " he said in his acceptance speech at Springfield on June 17, 1858. "I believe this government cannot endure permanently half slave and half free . . . . I do not expect the house to fall; but I do expect it will cease to be divided. It will become all one thing, or all the other."

A friend called it "a damned fool utterance," but the speech swept the nation and served notice that a new major political figure had appeared. Lincoln, the railsplitter, the raw, gaunt "wilderness" lawyer, a poor man, unattractive physically and virtually unknown in national politics, had laid open the issue for all to see, and when he dared to challenge Douglas to a series of campaign debates, the Little Giant had to accept.

Throughout the summer and autumn, the two men appeared on Illinois platforms, and the entire country followed their arguments. Lincoln first showed that the South's opposition to Douglas' popular sovereignty policy made it an insecure basis for the establishment of free states. Then, at Freeport, he forced Douglas to say that, despite the Dred Scott decision, free-soil settlers in territories could still exclude slavery by "unfriendly legislation" and the use of local police powers.

This statement won Douglas re-election to the Senate, but at the expense of his chances for the Presidency in 1860. The South was horrified at his defiance of the Supreme Court and turned away from him almost to a man. It split the Democratic party irretrievably in two and, as the nation's great-

Below, Lincoln rises at the Charleston, Illinois, debate to make a point. The tall backwoods lawyer often put the formidable Douglas (at Lincoln's right) on the defensive.

THE RAIL CANDIDATE.

An 1860 anti-Republican cartoon depicts Lincoln straddling his party platform, carried by a Negro and Horace Greeley.

est crisis approached, left it without any real unifying force.

The presidential conventions of 1860 were held in an atmosphere of tension and excitement. In the South political leaders talked increasingly of secession, of establishing a new nation that would guarantee their "peculiar institution" of slavery. The North replied with great rallies in support of the Union and its preservation. On both sides militia companies were forming, and in the sound of their marching feet men could feel the impending climax of years of bitterness and wrangling.

In May the Republicans gathered at Chicago in a new auditorium called the "wigwam" which had been specially built for their convention by local political clubs. The leading candidate was Senator William H. Seward of New York, who had angered the South in 1858 by prophesying an "irrepressible conflict" that would make the country all slave or all free. Despite his condemnation of John Brown a year later he was still objectionable to the South, and many moderates at the convention, hoping

desperately to save the Union, preferred a less controversial candidate.

The first ballot was a surprise to the nation. Seward had 173½ votes, almost 60 less than the number required to win. In second place, with 102 votes, was not one of the other leading candidates who were well known in the East, but Abraham Lincoln, the Illinois lawyer whom Stephen Douglas had beaten only two years before. The delegates knew little about Lincoln except that he was opposed to slavery and had made some telling points during his debates with Douglas. But on the second ballot his name began to take hold, and he picked up 79 new votes. On the third ballot the opponents of Seward, agreeing that Lincoln had the fewest enemies, combined to give him the nomination.

The Democrats, meanwhile, were reaping the unhappy harvest of the Lincoln-Douglas debates. In their convention at Charleston, South Carolina, delegates of eight slave states walked out when the majority voted to support the stand which Douglas had taken during his debate with Lincoln at Free-

198

port, backing the rights of free-soil settlers. After much bickering and a move to Baltimore the rest of the delegates nominated Douglas. The southerners put up their own candidate, John C. Breckinridge of Kentucky; while a fourth convention of older men who hoped to solve matters by avoiding all mention of slavery in their platform established a Constitutional Union party and nominated John Bell, an undistinguished, 63-year-old former senator from Tennessee.

In the ensuing campaign the Republican party was no longer the fledgling that it had been in 1856, and the contest quickly became one between Lincoln and all the other candidates. Southerners knew that he was the man to beat, and they worked up a hatred and contempt for his homespun ways and physical appearance, sneering at him as a third-rate, slangy lawyer, and complaining that he looked like an African gorilla. Others attacked the Republican platform, which had been broadly written to attract voters with varying interests. Lincoln, they said, was an issue-straddler leading a motley group of backers down a lunatic road of many different campaign promises, including a protective tariff for the East and Middle West, "free homes for the homeless" in cities, and a Homestead Act for settlers in the West.

Against this opposition Lincoln made little headway in the South or in the border states. But in the North, Republican newspapers, led by Horace Greeley's *Tribune,* played up "Honest Abe," the railsplitter from a log cabin, the plain man of the common people, who was known for his integrity and fair dealing and was just the man to calm the troubled nation and save the Union. Republican organizations formed "Wide Awake Clubs" for him, and their members in military caps and capes marched through the streets of northern towns and cities at night, carrying flaming torches and singing a campaign song that started off "Old Abe Lincoln came out of the wilderness."

Lincoln himself ran a restrained and dignified campaign, and in the end his frontier background helped carry the election for him. He lost the South and won the Northeast, as expected, but the margin of his victory was supplied by the democratic-minded western states, in each one of which he triumphed over Douglas by a narrow lead. The expansionist people of that area welcomed the Republicans' backing of such western aims as the

Homestead Act. What was far more significant for the nation's immediate future was the fact that they had followed Lincoln and in doing so had finally cut their last ties to a Democratic party dominated by slavers and compromisers with slavery. Their new, lusty settlements were now allied, economically and politically, with the industrial East.

Lincoln's victory made secession inevitable. On December 20, 1860, South Carolina left the Union. By February 1 six other states had followed its lead, and a week later the Confederate States of America was formed at Montgomery, Alabama. The timid Buchanan did nothing to interfere, preferring to leave the problem to his successor.

In his inaugural address Lincoln made a final plea to the South: "In your hands, my dissatisfied fellow-countrymen, and not in mine," he said, "is the momentous issue of civil war. The government will not assail you. You can have no conflict without being yourselves the aggressors." On April 12 the South gave its answer by firing upon Fort Sumter in Charleston Harbor.

South Carolina's governor threatened to call a secession convention if Lincoln won. The convention met, and on December 20, 1860, this Charleston extra announced the result.

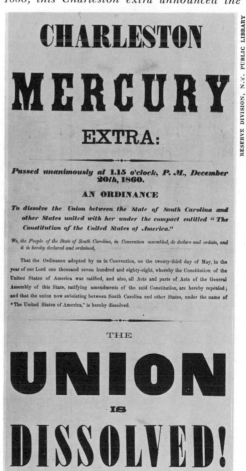

RESERVE DIVISION, N.Y. PUBLIC LIBRARY

The hopeful search for Utopia was reflected in this frontispiece to Francis Bacon's *Instauratio*.

THE PROMISED LAND

Man and the dream went hand in hand, throughout the centuries of human existence. The vision was one of a land flowing with milk and honey, a magical place of permanent peace and abundance where, some dared hope, "you never have to work at all, not even mend your socks." Here, in excerpts from the literature which inspired the explorers and pioneers, and from their own diaries and letters, is a concept of that western continent which suddenly emerged from the mists of the unknown and burst upon an expectant world as a materialization of the dream.

FROM DREAM TO REALITY

The records tell how great a power your city [Athens] once brought to an end when it insolently advanced against all Europe and Asia, starting from the Atlantic ocean outside. For in those days that ocean could be crossed, since there was an island in it in front of the strait which your countrymen tell me you call the Pillars of Hercules [Straits of Gibraltar]. The island was larger than Libya and Asia put together . . . Now on this Atlantic island there had grown up an extraordinary power under kings . . . and besides that, within the straits, they were lords of Libya so far as to Egypt, and of Europe to the borders of Tyrrhenia. All this power, gathered into one, attempted at one swoop to enslave your country and ours and all the region within the strait. . . . there was a time of inordinate earthquakes and floods; there came one terrible day and night, in which all your men of war were swallowed bodily by the earth, and the island Atlantis also sank beneath the sea and vanished. Hence to this day that outer ocean cannot be crossed or explored, the way being blocked by mud, just below the surface, left by the settling down of the island.

PLATO
Timaeus, 4th century B.C.

Moreover [the King of Denmark] spoke of an island in that ocean discovered by many, which is called Vinland, for the reason that vines grow wild there, which yield the best of wine. Moreover that grain unsown grows there abundantly, is not a fabulous fancy, but, from the accounts of the Danes, we know to be a fact. Beyond this island, it is said, that there is no habitable land in that ocean, but all those regions which are beyond are filled with insupportable ice and boundless gloom . . .

ADAM OF BREMEN
Descripto Insularum Aquilonis,
written before 1076

Zipangu [Japan] is an island in the eastern ocean, situated at the distance of about fifteen hundred miles from the mainland, or coast of Manji. . . . They have gold in the greatest abundance, its sources being inexhaustible, but as the king does not allow of its being exported, few merchants visit the country, nor is it frequented by much shipping from other parts. To this circumstance we are to attribute the extraordinary richness of the sovereign's palace, according to what we are told by those who have access to the place. The entire roof is covered with a plating of gold, in the same manner as we cover houses, or more properly churches, with lead. The ceilings of the halls are of the same precious metal; many of the apartments have small tables of pure gold, of considerable thickness; and the windows also have golden ornaments.

Travels of Marco Polo, 1295

[St. Brendan] desired to leave his land and his country, his parents and his fatherland, and he urgently besought the Lord to give him a land secret, hidden, secure, delightful, separated from men. Now after he had slept on that night, he heard the voice of the angel from heaven, who said to him, "Arise, O Brenainn," saith he, "for God hath given thee what thou soughtest, even the Land of Promise." . . . and he goes alone to Sliab Daidche and he saw the mighty intolerable ocean on every side, and then he beheld the beautiful noble island, with trains of angels [rising] from it.

Book of Lismore, 15th century

I perceive your great and noble desire to go to the place where the spices grow. . . . From the city of Lisbon due west there are 26 spaces marked on the map, each of which contains 250 miles, as far as the very great and splendid city of Quinsay. . . . its name means City of Heaven, and many wonderful things are told about it and about the multitude of its arts and revenues. . . . from the island of Antilia, which you know, to the very splendid island of Cipango there are ten spaces. For that island abounds in gold, pearls, and precious stones, and they cover the temples and palaces with solid gold. So through the unknown parts of the route the stretches of the sea to be traversed are not great. Many things might perhaps have been stated more clearly, but one who duly considers what I have said will be able to work out the rest for himself.

TOSCANELLI
Letter to Columbus, 1474

The course was west-southwest, and there was more sea than there had been during the whole of the voyage. They saw sandpipers, and a green reed near the ship. Those of the caravel *Pinta* saw a cane and a pole, and they took up another small pole which appeared to have been worked with iron; also another bit of cane, a land plant, and a small board. The crew of the caravel *Niña* also saw signs of land, and a small branch covered with berries. Everyone breathed afresh and rejoiced at these signs. After sunset the Admiral returned to his original west course. . . . As the caravel *Pinta* was a better sailer and went ahead of the Admiral, she found the land and made the signals ordered by the Admiral. . . .

The vessels were hove to, waiting for daylight; and on Friday they arrived at a small island . . .

Presently they saw naked people. The Admiral went on shore in the armed boat . . .

Having landed, they saw trees very green, and much water, and fruits of diverse kind.

The Journal of Christopher Columbus,
October 11–12, 1492

IMPRESSIONS OF A NEW LAND

Perhaps . . . it may not displease you to learn how his Majesty here [Henry VII of England] has won a part of Asia without a stroke of the sword. There is in this kingdom a Venetian fellow, Master John Caboto by name, of fine mind, greatly skilled in navigation, who . . . set out from Bristol, a western port of this kingdom, and passed the western limits of Ireland, and then standing to the northward he began to sail toward the Oriental regions . . . having wandered about considerably, at last he struck mainland, where, having planted the royal banner and taken possession on behalf of this King, and taken certain tokens, he has returned thence. . . . And they say that it is a very good and temperate country, and they think that Brazil-wood and silk grow there; and they affirm that that sea is covered with fishes, which are caught not only with the net but with baskets . . .

RAIMONDO DE SONCINO
Letter to the Duke of Milan,
December 18, 1497

During the morning, we arrived at a broad Causeway and continued our march toward Iztapalapa, and when we saw so many cities and villages built in the water and other great towns on dry land and that straight and level Causeway going toward Mexico, we were amazed and said that it was like the enchantments they tell of in the legend of Amadis, on account of the great towers and cues [temples] and buildings rising from the water, and all built of masonry. And some of our soldiers even asked whether the things that we saw were not a dream. . . . there is

so much to think over that I do not know how to describe it, seeing things as we did that had never been heard of or seen before, not even dreamed about.

BERNAL DIAZ DEL CASTILLO
The Discovery and Conquest of Mexico, 1519
Translated by A. P. Maudslay

And sayling forwards, we found certaine small rivers and armes of the sea, that fall downe by certaine creekes, washing the shoare on both sides as the coast lyeth. And beyond this we saw the open countrey rising in height above the sandie shoare, with many faire fields and plaines, full of mightie great woods, some very thicke, and some thinne, replenished with divers sorts of trees as pleasant and delectable to behold, as is possible to imagine. . . . neither doe we thinke that they partaking of the east world round about them, are altogether voyd of drugs or spicery, and other riches of golde, seeing the colour of the land dothe so much argue it.

GIOVANNI DA VERRAZANO
Letter to the King of France, 1524

In the first province, there are seven very large cities, all under one ruler, with large houses of stone and lime. . . . the doorways to the best houses have many decorations of turquoises, of which there is a great abundance, and the people in these cities are very well clothed.

FRAY MARCOS DE NIZA
Report to the Viceroy of Mexico,
September 2, 1539

203

It now remains for me to tell about the Seven Cities, kingdom and province, of which the father provincial gave Your Lordship an account. Not to be too verbose, I can assure you that he has not told the truth in a single thing that he said, but everything is the opposite of what he related, except the name of the cities and the large stone houses . . . The Seven Cities are seven little villages.

FRANCISCO VÁSQUEZ DE CORONADO
Letter to the Viceroy of Mexico,
August 3, 1540

. . . we have discovered the maine to bee the goodliest soyle under the cope of heaven, so abounding with sweete trees, that bring such sundry rich and pleasant gummes, grapes of such greatnesse, yet wilde, as France, Spain, nor Italie have no greater, so many sorts of Apothecarie drugs, such severall kindes of flaxe, & one kind like silke, the same gathered of a grasse, as common there as grasse is here. And now within these few dayes we have found here Maiz or Guinie wheate . . . [and] the continent is of huge and unknowen greatnesse, and very well peopled and towned, though savagely, and the climate so wholsome, that wee had not one sicke since we touched the land here.

RALPH LANE
Letter to Hakluyt, September 3, 1585

I have also sent your Honor of the oare, whereof I knowe some is as rich as the earth yeeldeth . . . we were not able to tarry and search the hils . . . but we saw all the hils with stones of the cullor of Gold and silver.

SIR WALTER RALEIGH
The Discoverie of Guiana, 1596

. . . those kingdoms are so delicious & under so temperat a climat, plentifull of all things, the earth bringing foorth its fruit twice a yeare, the people live long & lusty & wise in their way. What conquest would that bee att litle or no cost; what laborinth of pleasure should millions of people have, instead that millions complaine of misery & poverty!

PIERRE ESPRIT RADISSON
Voyages, 1658–1660

SETTLEMENTS ON THE SHORE

And, cheerfully at sea,
Success you will entice,
    To get the pearl and gold,
    And ours to hold,
VIRGINIA,
Earth's only paradise.

MICHAEL DRAYTON
To the Virginian Voyage, 1605

Lift up your eyes and see that brightnesse of Virginia's beauties: which the Mountaines lift up themselves alwayes with wilde smiles to behold sending downe silver streames to salute her, which powre themselves greedily into her lovely lap, and after many winding embracements, loth to depart, are at last swallowed of a more mightie corrivall, the Ocean. . . . Virginia . . . easily would give entertainment to English love, and accept a *New Britan* appellation, if her Husband be but furnished out at first in sortes and sutes, befitting her marriage solemnitie: all which her rich Dowrie would maintayne for ever with advantage.

SAMUEL PURCHAS
Purchas His Pilgrimage, 1613

And of all the foure parts of the world that I have yet seene not inhabited, could I have but meanes to transport a colonie, I would rather live here than any where: and if it did not maintaine it selfe, were wee but once indifferently well fitted, let us starve. . . . here every man may be master and owner of his owne labour and land; or the greatest part in small time. If hee have nothing but his hands, he may set up this trade; and by industrie quickly grow rich; spending but halfe that time wel, wch in England we abuse in idlenes . . .

JOHN SMITH
A Description of New England, 1616

The place they had thoughts on was some of those vast and unpeopled countries of America, which are fruitfull and fitt for habitation, being devoyd of all civill inhabitants, wher ther are only salvage and brutish men, which range up and downe, litle otherwise then the wild beasts of the same. This proposition being made publike and coming to the scaning of all, it raised many variable opinions amongst men, and caused many fears and doubts amongst them selves. . . .

It was answered, that all great and honourable actions are accompanied with great difficulties, and must be both enterprised and overcome with answerable courages. It was granted the dangers were great, but not desperate; the difficulties were many, but not invincible. . . . all of them, through the help of God, by fortitude and patience, might either be borne, or overcome.

WILLIAM BRADFORD
Of Plimmoth Plantation, 1630

And as I have, here in New Sweden, in the short time since I came here and with this small and weak people, begun to lay the foundation, which I hope to continue during the time that remains for me here and to bring it so far that Her Royal Majesty shall get so strong a foothold here in New Sweden that (in case the means will not be lacking) it will increase more and more as time goes on through God's gracious help and will be incorporated as an everlasting property under Her Royal Majesty and the Swedish Crown. . . . It is therefore my humble prayer and request that when this

my term of three years is over I may be relieved and allowed to return again to Her Royal Majesty . . . and my Fatherland, especially since I am no longer young and since the greatest part of my days have been hard and toilsome. . . . I hope that, with God's help, the one who succeeds me will have less toil than I have had.

JOHAN PRINTZ
Report to the Queen of Sweden, 1644
Translated by Amandus Johnson

. . . threw the lead in fourteen fathoms, sandy bottom, and smelt the land, which gave a sweet perfume . . . This comes from the Indians setting fire, at this time of year, to the woods and thickets, in order to hunt; and the land is full of sweet-smelling herbs, as sassafras . . . When the wind blows out of the northwest, and the smoke is driven to sea, it happens that the land is smelt before it is seen.

DAVID DE VRIES
Short Historical and Journal-Notes, 1655

This island [Manhattan] is about seven hours' distance in length, but it is not a full hour broad. The sides are indented with bays, coves and creeks. It is almost entirely taken up, that is, the land is held by private owners, but not half of it is cultivated. Much of it is good wood land. The west end on which the city lies, is entirely cleared for more than an hour's distance, though that is the poorest ground; the best being on the east and north side. There are many brooks of fresh water running through it, pleasant and proper for man and beast to drink, as well as agreeable to behold, affording cool and pleasant resting places, but especially suitable places for the construction of mills . . .

JASPER DANCKAERTS
Journal of Our Travels
in New Netherland, 1679

I shall say little in its praise, to excite desires in any, whatever I could truly write as to the Soil, Air and Water: This shall satisfie me, that by the Blessing of God, and the honesty and industry of Man, it may be a good and fruitful Land.

WILLIAM PENN
Some Account of the Province of Pennsilvania, 1681

And those who came were resolved
    to be Englishmen
Gone to the World's end,
    but English every one,
And they ate the white corn-kernels,
    parched in the sun,
And they knew it not,
    but they'd not be English again.

STEPHEN VINCENT BENÉT
Western Star

INTO THE WILDERNESS

The fourteenth of March [1669], from the top of an eminent hill, I first descried the *Apalatæan* Mountains, bearing due West to the place I stood upon: their distance from me was so great, that I could hardly discern whether they were Mountains or Clouds, until my Indian fellow travellers prostrating themselves in Adoration, howled out after a barbarous manner, *Okée poeze,* i.e. *God is nigh.*

JOHN LEDERER
The Discoveries of John Lederer, 1672

A bird's-eye view of the whole region east of the Mississippi . . . offered one vast expanse of woods, relieved by a comparatively narrow fringe of cultivation along the sea, dotted by the glittering surfaces of lakes, and intersected by the waving lines of rivers. . . . Centuries of summer suns had warmed the tops of the same noble oaks and pines, sending their heats even to the tenacious roots, when voices were heard calling to each other, in the depths of a forest, of which the leafy surface lay bathed in the brilliant light of a cloudless day in June, while the trunks of the trees rose in gloomy grandeur in the shades beneath. . . . presently a man of gigantic mould broke out of the tangled labyrinth of a small swamp, emerging into an opening that appeared to have been formed partly by the ravages of the wind, and partly by those of fire.

"Here is room to breathe in!" exclaimed the liberated forester, as soon as he found himself under a clear sky . . .

JAMES FENIMORE COOPER
The Deerslayer

The Lands we travelld over to day till we had crossed the Laurel Hill (except in small spots) was very mountainous and indifferent, but when we came down the Hill to the Plantation of Mr. Thos. Gist, the Ld. appeard charming; that which lay level being as rich and black as any thing coud possibly be; the more Hilly kind, tho of a different complexion must be good, as well from the Crops it produces, as from the beautiful white Oaks that grows thereon . . . The Land from Gists to Crawford's is very broken, tho not Mountainous; in Spots exceeding Rich, and in general free from Stone.

GEORGE WASHINGTON
Journal of his trip to the Ohio Valley, October 13, 1770

1775, Mon. 13th—I set out from prince wm. to travel to Caintuck . . .

fryday 24th—we start early and turn out of the wagon Road to go across the mountains to go by Danil Smiths we loose Driver Come to a turable mountain that tired us all almost to death to git over it and we lodge this night on the Lawrel fork of the holston under a granite mountain and Roast a fine fat turkey for our suppers and Eat it without aney Bread.

April Saturday 1st—This morning there is ice at our camp half inch thick we start early and travel this Day along a verey Bad hilley way cross one creek whear the horses almost got mired some fell in and all wet their loads . . .

Saturday 8th—We all pack up and started crost Cumberland gap about one oclock this Day Met a good many peopel turned back for fear of the indians but our Company goes on Still with good courage . . .

WILLIAM CALK
Diary, 1775

Thus we behold Kentucky, lately an howling wilderness, the habitation of savages and wild beasts, become a fruitful field; this region, so favorably distinguished by nature, now become the habitation of civilization . . . where wretched wigwams stood, the miserable abodes of savages, we behold the foundations of cities laid, that, in all probability, will rival the glory of the greatest upon earth . . .

DANIEL BOONE
*in John Filson's The Discovery, Settlement,
and Present State of Kentucky, 1793*

Women and children in the Month of Decembr Travelling a Wilderness Through Ice and Snow, passing large rivers and Creeks, without Shoe or Stocking, and barely as many raggs as covers their Nakedness . . . Here is Hundreds Travelling hundreds of Miles, they know not what for Nor Whither, except it's to Kentucky . . . the Promis'd Land . . . the Land of Milk and Honey.

MOSES AUSTIN, *1796*

More than half of those who inhabit the borders of the Ohio, are again the first inhabitants, or as they are called in the United States, the *first settlers*, a kind of men who cannot settle upon the soil that they have cleared, and who under pretence of finding a better land, a more wholesome country, a greater abundance of game, push forward, incline perpetually towards the most distant points of the American population, and go and settle in the neighbourhood of the savage nations, whom they brave even in their own country . . .

Such were the first inhabitants of Kentucky and Tennessea, of whom there are now remaining but very few. . . . They have emigrated to more remote parts of the country, and formed new settlements. It will be the same with most of those who inhabit the borders of the Ohio.

F. A. MICHAUX
*Travels to the West
of the Allegheny Mountains, 1802*

But what words shall describe the Mississippi, great father of rivers, who (praise be to Heaven) has no young children like him! An enormous ditch, sometimes two or three miles wide, running liquid mud, six miles an hour: its strong and frothy current choked and obstructed everywhere by huge logs and whole forest trees: now twining themselves together in great rafts, from the interstices of which a sedgy lazy foam works up, to float upon the water's top; now rolling past like monstrous bodies, their tangled roots showing like matted hair; now glancing singly by like giant leeches; and now writhing round and round in the vortex of some small whirlpool, like wounded snakes. The banks low, the trees dwarfish, the marshes swarming with frogs, the wretched cabins few and far apart, their inmates hollow-cheeked and pale, the weather very hot, mosquitoes penetrating into every crack and crevice of the boat, mud and slime on everything: nothing pleasant in its aspect, but the harmless lightning which flickers every night upon the dark horizon.

CHARLES DICKENS
American Notes, 1842

Here was a thing which had not changed; a score of years had not affected this water's mulatto complexion in the least; a score of centuries would succeed no better, perhaps. It comes out of the turbulent, bank-caving Missouri, and every tumblerful of it holds nearly an acre of land in solution. I got this fact from the bishop of the diocese. If you will let your glass stand half an hour, you can separate the land from the water as easy as Genesis; and then you will find them both good: the one to eat, the other to drink. The land is very nourishing, the water is thor-oughly wholesome. The one appeases hunger; the other, thirst. But the natives do not take them separately, but together, as nature mixed them. When they find an inch of mud in the bottom of a glass, they stir it up, and then take a draught as they would gruel. It is difficult for a stranger to get used to this batter, but once used to it he will prefer it to water. This is really the case. It is good for steamboating, and good to drink; but it is worthless for any other purpose, except for baptizing.

MARK TWAIN
Life on the Mississippi, 1874

ACROSS THE WIDE MISSOURI

The object of your mission is to explore the Missouri river, & such principal stream of it, as, by it's course & communication with the waters of the Pacific Ocean, may offer the most direct & practicable water communication across this continent, for the purposes of commerce.

THOMAS JEFFERSON
Instructions to Lewis, June 20, 1803

Great joy in camp we are in *view* of the *Ocian,* this great Pacific Octean which we been so long anxious to See. and the roreing or noise made by the waves brakeing on the rockey Shores (as I suppose) may be heard disticly.

WILLIAM CLARK
*The Journals of Lewis and Clark,
November 7, 1805*

. . . stupendous & solitary Wilds covered with eternal Snow & Mountain connected to Mountain by immense Glaciers, the collection of Ages & on which the Beams of the Sun makes hardly any Impression . . . The Weather was often very severe, cloathing all the Trees with Snow as in the Depth of the Winter & the Wind seldom less than a Storm we had no Thunder, very little Lightning & that very mild; but in return the rushing of the Snows down the Sides of the Mountains equalled the Thunder in Sound, overturning everything less than solid Rock in its Course, sweeping Mountain Forests, whole acres at a Time from the very Roots, leaving not a Vestige behind; scarcely an Hour passed, without hearing one or more of these threatening Noises.

DAVID THOMPSON
*Description of crossing the
Canadian Rockies in 1807*

We climbed mountains so high that I would never have believed our horses could have got over them. . . . We experienced the greatest difficulty in going onward because the steep rocks and the precipices projected to the very edge of the river. . . . A black-tailed deer was killed which made us a sumptuous feast. . . . Snow fell so densely on the mountains where we had to go that we could see nothing a half-mile ahead of us. . . . The previous evening, a small beaver was caught. We had nothing more to eat. I killed another horse. . . .

On the 4th [of December], it was necessary to leave the banks of the river and to climb the mountains. . . . Although we marched all day, we were, because of the meanderings of the river, only four miles from our encampment of the preceding night.

On the 5th the abundant snow did not allow us to see three hundred feet ahead of us. . . . A horse with his pack fell some hundreds of feet in depth, but was not hurt. The weather was much less severe in the valley than on the heights. It rained there. . . . I killed another horse.

WILSON PRICE HUNT
*Diary of his overland trip
westward to Astoria in 1811–12*

It is, that I may be able to help those who stand in need, that I face every danger—it is for this that I traverse the Mountains covered with eternal Snow—it is for this that I pass over the Sandy Plains, in heat of Summer, thirsting for water, and am well pleased if I can find a shade, instead of water, where I may cool my overheated Body—it is for this that I go for days without eating, & am pretty well satisfied if I can gather a few roots, a few Snails, or, much better Satisfied if we can affod our selves a piece of Horse Flesh, or a fine Roasted Dog . . .

JEDEDIAH S. SMITH
Letter to his brother, December 24, 1829

From the surface of a rocky plain or table [Yellowstone's Upper Geyser Basin], burst forth columns of water, of various dimensions, projected high in the air, accompanied by loud explosions, and sulphurous vapors, which were highly disagreeable to the smell. . . . The largest of these wonderful fountains, projects a column of boiling water several feet in diameter, to the height of more than one hundred and fifty feet . . . accompanied with a tremendous noise. These explosions and discharges occur at intervals of about two hours. . . . The Indians who were with me, were quite appalled, and could not by any means be induced to approach them. . . . They believed them to be supernatural, and supposed them to be the production of the Evil Spirit. One of them remarked that hell, of which he had heard from the whites, must be in that vicinity.

WARREN ANGUS FERRIS
Life in the Rocky Mountains, 1834

These are the gardens of the Desert, these
The unshorn fields, boundless and beautiful,
For which the speech of England has no name—
The Prairies.

WILLIAM CULLEN BRYANT
The Prairies, 1833

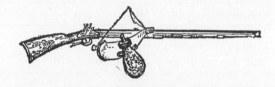

Killing buffaloes, hunting wild horses, sleeping every night on the ground for a whole month, and depending from day to day for the means of existence upon the deer, wild turkey, and bears which the rifles of their own party can alone procure, are matters of thrilling interest to citizens who read of them in their green slippers seated before a shining grate, the neatly printed page illuminated by a bronze astral lamp.

PHILIP HONE
Diary, April 14, 1835

We all crossed the river and galloped away a couple of miles or so, when we mounted the bluff; and there was in full view of us a fine herd of some four or five hundred buffaloes, perfectly at rest . . . we advanced within a mile or so of them in full view . . .

At this instant we started! . . . and away all sailed, and over the prairie flew in a cloud of dust which was raised by their trampling hoofs.

I dashed along through the thundering mass as they swept away over the plain, scarcely able to tell whether I was on a buffalo's back or my horse—hit, and hooked, and jostled about, until at length I found myself alongside of my game, when I gave him a shot as I passed him. . . . I beheld my huge victim endeavoring to make as much headway as he possibly could, from this dangerous ground, upon three legs.

I galloped off to him, and at my approach he wheeled around and bristled up for battle; he seemed to know perfectly well that he could not escape from me, and resolved to meet his enemy and death as bravely as possible. . . .

The party met from all quarters around me and my buffalo bull, whom I then shot in the head and finished.

GEORGE CATLIN
Letters and Notes on the
North American Indians, 1842

Buffalo Bill, Buffalo Bill,
Never missed, and never will,
Always aims and shoots to kill
And the company pays his buffalo bill.

Song of the Union Pacific Railroad Workers

And the Rocky Mountains, with the grand, aromatic forests, their grassy glades, their frequent springs, and dancing streams of the brightest, sweetest water, their pure, elastic atmosphere, and their unequalled game and fish, are destined to be a favorite resort and home of civilized man. I never visited a region where physical life could be more surely prolonged or fully enjoyed.

HORACE GREELEY
An Overland Journey, 1860

I turn round and round irresolute sometimes for a quarter of an hour, until I decide, for the thousandth time, that I will walk into the southwest or west. Eastward I go only by force, but westward I go free. Thither no business leads me. It is hard for me to believe that I shall find fair landscapes or sufficient wildness and freedom behind the eastern horizon. I am not excited by the prospect of a walk thither; but I believe that the forest which I see in the western horizon stretches uninterruptedly toward the setting sun, and there are no towns or cities in it of enough consequence to disturb me. Let me live where I will, on this side is the city, on that the wilderness, and ever I am leaving the city more and more and withdrawing into the wilderness. I should not lay so much stress on this fact if I did not believe that something like this is the prevailing tendency of my countrymen. I must walk toward Oregon and not toward Europe.

HENRY DAVID THOREAU
Walking, 1862

Room! room to turn round in,
   to breathe and be free,
To grow to be giant,
   to sail as at sea
With the speed of the wind
   on a steed with his mane
To the wind, without pathway
   or route or a rein.
Room! room to be free
   where the white border'd sea
Blows a kiss to a brother
   as boundless as he;
Where the buffalo come
   like a cloud on the plain,
Pouring on like the tide
   of a storm-driven main,
And the lodge of the hunter
   to friend or to foe
Offers rest; and unquestion'd
   you come or you go.
My plains of America!
   Seas of wild lands!
From a land in the seas
   in a raiment of foam,
That has reached to a stranger
   the welcome of home,
I turn to you, lean to you,
   lift you my hands.

JOAQUIN MILLER
Kit Carson's Ride, 1871

ON TO EL DORADO

Bear me from that distant strand,
Over ocean, over land,
To California's golden shore—
Fancy, stop, and rove no more.

PHILIP FRENEAU
The Power of Fancy, 1770

It is on the stroke of seven; the rushing to and fro, the cracking of the whips, the loud command to oxen, and what seems to be the inextricable confusion of the last ten minutes has ceased. Fortunately every one has been found and every teamster is at his post. The clear notes of the trumpet sound in the front; the pilots and his guards mount their horse, the leading division of wagons moves out of the encampment, and takes up the line of march, the rest fall into their places with the precision of clock work, until the spot so lately full of life sinks back into that solitude that seems to reign over the broad plain and rushing river as the caravan draws its lazy length toward the distant El Dorado. . . .

But the picture, in its grandeur, its wonderful mingling of colors and distinctness of detail, is forgotten in contemplation of the singular people who give it life and animation. No other race of men with the means at their command would undertake so great a journey; none save these could successfully perform it with no previous preparation, relying only on the fertility of their invention to devise the means to overcome each danger and difficulty as it arose. They have undertaken to perform, with slow moving oxen, a journey of two thousand miles. The way lies over trackless wastes, wide and deep rivers,

rugged and lofty mountains, and is beset with hostile savages. Yet, whether it were a deep river with no tree upon its banks, a rugged defile where even a loose horse could not pass, a hill too steep for him to climb, or a threatened attack of an enemy, they are always found ready and equal to the occasion, and always conquerors. May we not call them men of destiny? They are people changed in no essential particulars from their ancestors, who have followed closely on the footsteps of the receding savage, from the Atlantic sea-board to the valley of the Mississippi.

JESSE APPLEGATE
A Day with the Cow Column in 1843

Nov. 20 [1846]
  Came to this place [now called Donner Lake] on the 31st of last month. It snowed. We went on to the pass. The snow so deep we were unable to find the road, when within 3 miles of the summit. Then turned back to this shanty on the Lake. . . . We now have killed most part of our cattle having to stay here untill next spring & live on poor beef without bread or salt. It snowed during the space of eight days with little intermission, after our arrival here. . . .
[December] 25th
  Snowed all night & snows yet rapidly. Great difficulty in geting wood. John & Edwd. has to get it. I am not able. Offered our prayers to God this Cherimass morning. The prospect is apalling but hope in God. *Amen.*

PATRICK BREEN
Diary of a member of the Donner Party

A low, undulating line of sand-hills bounded the horizon before us. That day we rode ten hours, and it was dusk before we entered the hollows and gorges of these gloomy little hills. At length we gained the summit, and the long-expected valley of the Platte lay before us. We all drew rein, and sat joyfully looking down upon the prospect. . . .

Before sunrise in the morning the snow-covered mountains were beautifully tinged with a delicate rose-color. A noble spectacle awaited us as we moved forward. . . . For one instant some snowy peak, towering in awful solitude, would be disclosed to view. As the clouds broke along the mountain, we could see the dreary forests, the tremendous precipices, the white patches of snow, the gulfs and chasms as black as night, all revealed for an instant, and then disappearing from the view.

On the day after, we had left the mountains at some distance. A black cloud descended upon them, and a tremendous explosion of thunder followed, reverberating among the precipices. In a few moments everything grew black, and the rain poured down like a cataract. . . . The clouds opened at the point where they first had gathered, and the whole sublime congregation of mountains was bathed at once in warm sunshine. They seemed more like some vision of eastern romance than like a reality of that wilderness . . . On the left the sky was still of an inky blackness; but two concentric rainbows stood in bright relief against it, while far in front the ragged clouds still streamed before the wind, and the retreating thunder muttered angrily.

FRANCIS PARKMAN
The Oregon Trail, 1847

We have had a vary Surveare goald Feaver In this Cuntry tha are grate miny pople twok it and is goin to Calafornia To be Cured Som staret and got Cured before tha gut thare and Come back the Colery was So bad a mongse the emigrants that a grate miny Died on the rod the Colery has bean wors than it iver bean Noin tha have bean from two to three hunard Died in Sent Luis in one Day and is bad yet the goald feve is vury Cachen but i Dont think i will take it. . . . we are not trying to git rich for if we shod get rich we Cod not take it with us when we dy it is not worth a man while to lay up tresors on erth we beter lay then in heavn whare morth will not eat then nor theave brake throgh.

WILLIAM M. MILLER
Letter, July 1, 1849

The whole country from San Francisco to Los Angeles, and from the sea shore to the base of the Sierra Nevadas, resounds with the sordid cry of "*gold!* GOLD! GOLD!" while the field is left half planted, the house half built, and everything neglected but the manufacture of shovels and pickaxes.

The [San Francisco] Californian,
May 29, 1848

It seemed that every rock had a yellow tinge, and even our camp kettle, that I had thought in the morning the most filthy one I had ever seen, now appeared to be gilded—and I thought with more than one coat. During the night, yellow was the prevailing color in my dreams.

JOHN M. LETTS
California Illustrated, 1852

Out in Oregon I can get me a square mile of land. And a quarter section for each of you all. Dad burn me, I am done with this country. Winters its frost and snow to freeze a body; summers the overflow from Old Muddy drowns half my acres; taxes take the yield of them that's left. What say, Maw, it's God's country.

A MISSOURI FARMER

The men and boys are all soaking wet and look sad and comfortless. The little ones and myself are shut up in the wagons from the rain. . . . take us all together we are a poor looking set, and all this for Oregon. I am thinking while I write, "Oh, Oregon, you must be a wonderful country."

AMELIA STEWART KNIGHT
Diary, June 1, 1853

Who cares to go with the wagons?
Not we who are free and strong;
Our faith and arms, with right good will,
Shall pull our carts along.

A Mormon Song, 1856

THE COURSE OF EMPIRE

Westward the course of empire
    takes its way;
The four first acts already past,
A fifth shall close the drama with the day:
Time's noblest offspring is the last.

GEORGE BERKELEY
*On the Prospect of Planting Arts
and Learning in America, 1752*

There is America, which at this day serves for little more than to amuse you with stories of savage men and uncouth manners, yet shall, before you taste of death, show itself equal to the whole of that commerce which now attracts the envy of the world.

EDMUND BURKE
*Second Speech on Conciliation
with America, March 22, 1775*

I must soon quit the scene, but you may live to see our country flourish; as it will amazingly and rapidly after the war is over; like a field of young Indian corn, which long fair weather and sunshine had enfeebled and discolored, and which in that weak state, by a sudden gust of violent wind, hail, and rain, seemed to be threatened with absolute destruction; yet the storm being past, it recovers fresh verdure, shoots up with double vigor, and delights the eye not of its owners only, but of every observing traveler.

BENJAMIN FRANKLIN
Letter to Washington, March 5, 1780

Not to-day, nor to-morrow, but this government is to last, I trust, forever; we may at least hope it will endure until the wave of population, cultivation, and intelligence shall have washed the Rocky Mountains and mingled with the Pacific. And may we not also hope that the day will arrive when the improvements and comforts to social life shall spread over the vast area of this continent? . . . It is a peculiar delight to me to look forward to the proud and happy period, distant as it may be, when circulation and association between the Atlantic and Pacific and the Mexican Gulf shall be as free and perfect as they are at this moment in England or in any other country of the globe.

HENRY CLAY
Speech of January 31, 1824

The possible destiny of the United States of America—as a nation of a hundred millions of freemen—stretching from the Atlantic to the Pacific, living under the laws of Alfred, and speaking the language of Shakespeare and Milton, is an august conception. Why should we not wish to see it realized? America would then be England viewed through a solar microscope; Great Britain in a state of glorious magnification.

SAMUEL TAYLOR COLERIDGE
Table-Talk, April 10, 1833

Most of this vast waste of territory belongs to the Republic of the United States. What a theme to contemplate its settlement and civilization. Will the jurisdiction of the federal government ever succeed in civilizing the thousands of savages now roaming over these plains, and her hardy freeborn population here plant their homes, build their towns and cities, and say here shall the arts and sciences of civilization take root and flourish? yes, here, even in this remote part of the great west before many years, will these hills and valleys be greeted with the enlivening sound, of the workman's hammer, and the merry whistle of the plough-boy. But this is left undone by the government, and will only be seen when too late to apply the remedy. The Spaniards are making inroads on the South—the Russians are encroaching with impunity along the sea shore to the North, and further. North-east the British are pushing their stations into the very heart of our territory, which, even at this day, more resemble military forts to resist invasion, than trading stations. Our government should be vigilant. She should assert her claim by taking possession of the whole territory as soon as possible—for we have good reason to suppose that the territory *west* of the mountain will some day be equally as important to a nation as that on the east.

ZENAS LEONARD
Narrative of his adventures, 1839

. . . our manifest destiny [is] to overspread and to possess the whole of the continent which Providence has given us for the development of the great experiment of liberty and federated self-government entrusted to us.

JOHN LOUIS O'SULLIVAN
New York Morning News,
December 27, 1845

The *untransacted* destiny of the American people is to subdue the continent—to rush over this vast field to the Pacific Ocean—to animate the many hundreds of millions of its people, to cheer them upward. . . . to agitate these herculean masses—to establish a new order in human affairs . . . to regenerate the superannuated nations—to stir up the sleep of a hundred centuries—to teach old nations a new civilization—to confirm the destiny of the human race—to carry the career of mankind to its culminating point—to perfect science—to emblazon history with the conquest of peace—to shed a new and resplendent glory upon mankind—to unite the world in one social family.

WILLIAM GILPIN
A published letter, 1846

But there are soldiers of peace, as well as of war; and though no waving plume or floating ensign beckons them on to glory or to death, their dying scene is often a crimson one. They fall, leading the van of civilization along untrodden paths, and are buried in the dust of its advancing columns. No clarion's note wafts the expiring spirit from earth to heaven; no monument marks the scene of deadly strife; and no stone their resting place. The winds, sighing through the branches of the forest, alone sing their requiem. . . . The achievements of your pioneer army, from the day they first drove back the Indian tribes from your Atlantic sea-board to the present hour, have been the achievements of science and civilization over the elements, the wilderness, and the savage. The settler, in search of a new home, long since o'erlapped the Alleghanies, and, having crossed the great central valley of the Mississippi, is now wending his way to the shores of the Pacific; the forest stoops to allow the emigrant to pass; and the wilderness gives way to the tide of emigration. . . .

During the two and a quarter centuries since Jamestown and Plymouth Rock were consecrated by the exile, trace the footsteps of the pioneer, as he has gone forth to found new States, and build up new empires. In these two and a quarter centuries, from an unbroken forest, you have a country embracing almost every variety of production, and extending through almost every zone. The high regions of the North have scarcely thrown off their icy mantle, while the Southern reaper is preparing for his harvest home.

The morning sun tips your Eastern hills, while the valleys of the West repose in midnight darkness. In these two and a quarter centuries, a whole continent has been converted to the use of man, and upon its bosom has arisen the noblest empire on the globe.

GALUSHA A. GROW
Speech in the House of Representatives,
March 30, 1852

There is a power in this nation greater than either the North or the South—a growing, increasing, swelling power, that will be able to speak the law to this nation, and to execute the law as spoken. That power is the country known as the Great West . . . There, is the hope of this nation.

STEPHEN A. DOUGLAS, 1860

Nothing less than a continent can suffice as the basis and foundation for that nation in whose destiny is involved the destiny of mankind. Let us build broad and wide those foundations; let them abut only on the everlasting seas.

IGNATIUS DONNELLY
Congressional Globe, July 1, 1868

LAND OF OPPORTUNITY

The time will . . . come when one hundred and fifty million men will be living in North America, equal in condition, all belonging to one family, owing their origin to the same cause, and, preserving the same civilization, the same language, the same religion, the same habits, the same manners, the same opinions, propagated under the same forms. The rest is uncertain, but this is certain; and it is a fact new to the world, a fact that the imagination strives in vain to grasp.

ALEXIS DE TOCQUEVILLE
Democracy in America, 1835

We must always bear in mind the peculiar and wonderful advantages of *country,* when we examine America and its form of government; for the country has had more to do with upholding this democracy than people might at first imagine. Among the advantages of democracy, the greatest is, perhaps, that *all start fair* . . . But it is the *country,* and not the government, which has been productive of such rapid strides as have been made by America. Indeed, it is a query whether the form of government would have existed down to this day, had it not been for the advantages derived from the vast extent and boundless resources of the territory in which it was established. Let the American direct his career to any goal he pleases, his energies are unshackled; and, in the race, the best man must win. There is room for all, and millions more.

CAPTAIN FREDERICK MARRYAT
Diary in America, 1839

. . . our blood is as the flood of the Amazon, made up of a thousand noble currents all pouring into one. We are not a nation, so much as a world.

HERMAN MELVILLE
Redburn, 1849

The United States themselves are essentially the greatest poem. In the history of the earth hitherto the largest and most stirring appear tame and orderly to their ample largeness

215

and stir. Here at last is something in the doings of man that corresponds with the broadcast doings of the day and night. Here is not merely a nation but a teeming nation of nations.

WALT WHITMAN
Preface to Leaves of Grass, 1855

Since the days when the fleet of Columbus sailed into the waters of the New World, America has been another name for opportunity. . . . What the Mediterranean Sea was to the Greeks, breaking the bond of custom, offering new experiences, calling out new institutions and activities, that, and more, the ever retreating frontier has been to the United States directly, and to the nations of Europe more remotely. And now, four centuries from the discovery of America, at the end of a hundred years of life under the Constitution, the frontier has gone, and with its going has closed the first period of American history.

FREDERICK JACKSON TURNER
*The Significance of the Frontier
in American History, 1893*

Give me your tired, your poor,
Your huddled masses,
    yearning to breathe free,
The wretched refuse of your teeming shore.

Send these, the homeless,
    tempest-tossed, to me;
I lift my lamp beside the golden door.

EMMA LAZARUS
Inscription on the Statue of Liberty

. . . the American beams with a certain self-confidence and sense of mastery; he feels that God and nature are working with him.

GEORGE SANTAYANA
Character and Opinion in the U.S., 1920

. . . most Americans are born drunk; and really require a little wine or beer to sober them. They have a sort of permanent intoxication from within . . .

G. K. CHESTERTON
*New York Times Magazine,
June 28, 1931*

The American people never carry an umbrella. They prepare to walk in eternal sunshine.

ALFRED E. SMITH, 1931

I speak of new cities and new people.
I tell you the past is a bucket of ashes.
I tell you yesterday is a world gone down,
    A sun dropped into the West.
I tell you there is nothing in the world
    only an ocean of tomorrows, a sky
    of tomorrows.

CARL SANDBURG
Prairie

It wasn't Indians that were important, nor adventures, nor even getting out here. It was a whole bunch of people made into one big crawling beast. . . . It was westering and westering. Every man wanted something for himself, but the big beast that was all of them wanted only westering. . . . When we saw the mountains at last, we cried—all of us. But it wasn't getting here that mattered, it was movement and westering.

We carried life out here and set it down the way those ants carry eggs. . . . The westering was as big as God, and the slow steps that made the movement piled up and piled up until the continent was crossed.

Then we came down to the sea, and it was done. . . . There's a line of old men along the shore hating the ocean because it stopped them. . . .

But that's not the worst—no, not the worst. Westering has died out of the people. Westering isn't a hunger any more. It's all done.

JOHN STEINBECK
The Red Pony, 1937

I believe that we are lost here in America, but I believe we shall be found. . . . I think that the true discovery of America is before us. I think the true fulfillment of our spirit, of our people, of our mighty and immortal land, is yet to come.

THOMAS WOLFE
You Can't Go Home Again, 1940

West is a country in the mind, and so eternal.

ARCHIBALD MACLEISH
Sweet Land of Liberty, Collier's, 1955

COLLECTION OF HARRY T. PETERS, JR.

John Gast's 1872 painting gives romantic expression to a consistent theme in American literature, to a thought frequently seen in pioneer journals, diaries, and letters—the idea of a "manifest destiny" which would transform the sprawling continent into a great new nation. Americans were convinced that they had found the promised land. And quite possibly they had.

SHOWING THE WORLD

NO DANGER, no distance, no obstacle detains them," wrote Brissot de Warville of the Americans in 1791. The real motto of the country, said the English editor Charles Mackay sixty years later, is "Go ahead" and its chief boast is its go-ahead spirit. As the republic grew, it took pride in showing the world what Americans could accomplish and betrayed a keen sensitiveness to world opinion of its character. To many foreigners, the Yankee seemed addicted to boasting—but why not, the Swedish novelist Frederika Bremer asked. "He is a man who can rely upon himself; and he is a citizen of a great nation designed to be the greatest on the face of the earth."

America found a variety of ways of displaying its traits, achievements, and aims to the world, and of seeking the approbation of other peoples. It could export political ideas, as it did in the days of Washington, Jefferson, and Jackson and was still doing in the times of Lincoln and Woodrow Wilson. Quite early in its history, it could point with pride to the inventions of Benjamin Franklin (his stove, the lightning rod, an improved clock) and of Benjamin Thompson, Count Rumford (an equally famous stove, an improved lamp, a broad-rimmed wheel for vehicles, and a drip coffee pot), while acclaiming the contributions both men had made to pure science. It found eager foreign readers for its literature, from Washington Irving, James Fenimore Cooper, and Edgar Allan Poe onward. It could point out that its people enjoyed greater general well-being, social equality, and freedom than other peoples. It could send citizens abroad as sailors and traders, to settle in every port; as students, like George Bancroft, John Lothrop Motley, and Longfellow; and as artists, making Italy a home of American sculptors and painters. It could send its missionaries abroad—orthodox evangelists to Africa and the South Seas, Mormons to find recruits in Britain and Scandinavia. And it could invite visitors to its shores and wait in anxious anticipation to hear the judgments of Harriet Martineau, Charles Dickens, and Matthew Arnold.

When Americans bent themselves to "showing the world"—a work that began with Pocahontas' visit to London and was in full swing when Andrew Carnegie wrote *Triumphant Democracy*—they went at it with the same enterprise and confidence that conquered the frontier. The maritime and commercial activities of the country had a pioneer spirit. The unconventionality of many American contrivances and ways revealed the same impulse. And our democracy, which impressed Europe more than anything else, was the democracy of a pioneer land.

It must never be forgotten that America had a sea frontier no less than a land frontier; and it was on the ocean that Europe first met the American in large numbers. The seas were filled almost as rapidly with mariners as the forest with settlers. Half a century after the 180-ton *Mayflower* crossed the Atlantic, Massachusetts Bay boasted 430 ships up to 250 tons able to make better crossings, and pigtailed American seamen were becoming familiar in every port from Jamaica to the Baltic. Adventurous Yankee skippers early found new paths of commerce. Blazing the triangular route, they gave the

West Indies lumber, grain, and meats, France and Spain dried cod and barrel staves, and the English public Madeira wine, Cadiz salt, and Valencia oranges.

Moreover, American shipbuilders were quick to give the world a memorable advance in design. Captain Andrew Robinson of Cape Ann made history when in 1713 or 1714 he devised a sharp-lined vessel of two-masted fore-and-aft rig, with a forward jib, whose swift, graceful glide over the water at her launching brought from an onlooker the jubilant shout: "See how she scoons!" The schooner was born, and this Yankee craft was so handy in short-tack sailing and could be managed with such small crews that Europeans adopted it for coastal work all the way from Lisbon to Stockholm. In time, four-masted schooners built in New England yards carried the American flag from Pacific ports to Australia and China, while later still, the six-or-seven-masted schooner of steel hull became a familiar sight on the oceans of the world. But the proudest early American merchantmen were the great ships in the East India and Oriental trade. They made the names of farsighted owners like Elias Hasket Derby and Thomas Handasyd Perkins internationally famous, and produced long-remembered captains like Robert B. Forbes. These masters had to be merchants, navigators, diplomats, and fighters all in one. Some of them, like Richard J. Cleveland, whose *Narrative of Voyages and Commercial Enterprises* chronicled "captivity, robbery, imprisonment, and ruin" as well as great successes, held graphic pens. They brought home silks and china, spices and nankeens, coffee and Oriental styles in art; sometimes a Chinese wife.

One nation after another learned that the American seaman could, when he had to, become an unsurpassed fighter. More important in the Revolution than John Paul Jones' spectacular exploits were the feats of the privateersmen, who made the schooner their favorite vessel. By the end of 1777 commissions had been issued to 174 shipowners, and a Parliamentary inquiry the following year revealed that privateers had taken or destroyed 733 British vessels. When Cornwallis surrendered, the United States had nearly 450 privateers under commission. Later the French learned something of American intrepidity. Never were smarter single-ship actions fought than those in which, during the short naval war of 1798, Thomas Truxtun and the *Constellation* bested the *Insurgente* and *Vengeance*. The turn of the Barbary pirates came a few years later. Stephen Decatur's hand-to-hand fighting, Edward Preble's bombardments of Tripoli with the *Constitution,* and William Eaton's capture of Derna after an epic march from Egypt, gave the Mediterranean three new heroes.

Primarily, however, the sea frontier was a theater of peaceful enterprise. The first vessel to show the Stars and Stripes off London after the Revolution was apparently the *Bedford* of Nantucket, laden significantly with 487 butts of whale oil. From the day in 1690 when a Nantucket man, watching a pod of whales at play offshore, exclaimed, "There is the green pasture where our children's children will go for their bread," the seamen of this Quaker island began venturing to far waters. Nantucket and New Bedford whalers were the first sailors of any country to frequent Davis Strait and Baffin Bay; they made the Falkland Islands their base while Great Britain still thought it too remote to be annexed; and they almost turned Callao into a New England port. British and other foreign ships, sailing into unknown South Pacific or polar havens and preparing to claim the new lands, more than once were astonished to see a Yankee whaler already lying snugly there.

In one distant sea after another—in the South Pacific, on the stormy Japanese coast, off Kamchatka, and deep within the Arctic itself—Yankees found great quantities of whales and led the world in their capture. At the close of the Mexican War the United States had almost 700 whalers at sea, against only 14 under the British flag. In the 1860's the depletion of their prey, the destruction of ships by Confederate cruisers, and the rise of petroleum united to ruin the industry. But before it passed from the scene it had done a great deal for ocean exploration. Compared with the wilder, wider whaling voyages, the runs of the Black Ball, Red Star, and even the Collins liners, connecting New York and Liverpool, seem tame. And before the industry died, it had yielded another memorable achievement in marine design—the Yankee whaleboat. This, the fruit of a century of trial and experience, was widely regarded as the best small boat ever made. Light, speedy, easily maneuvered, so shrewdly designed that its crew were placed in the best positions for their diverse tasks, it rode almost any wave and met every other test imposed upon it.

Like the schooner and whaleboat, the clipper ships that reached their apogee between 1845 and 1860 embodied qualities peculiarly American. Other nations, particularly the British, had built good clipper ships, but they sacrificed carrying capacity for speed. The object of the great American builders was to preserve cargo space and attain still greater speeds. Henry Eckford, William H. Webb, Jacob Westervelt, and George Steers all launched famous ships; and Steers in time gave the country the cup-winning yacht *America*. The famous *Rainbow* in 1845 utilized the revolutionary ideas of an even bolder designer, John W. Griffiths. It was Donald McKay, however, Nova Scotian by birth but Bostonian by early adoption, who placed the finest thoroughbreds on the ocean. When his *Sovereign of the Seas* made 3,539 miles in thirteen days, he said, "A pretty good ship, but I think I can build one to beat her"—and he did. What the East Indiaman was to the British marine, clippers like the *Flying Cloud* and *Northern Light* were to the American.

In many of their creations, as Europe began to see by 1860, Americans particularly valued swiftness, dexterity, and grace. They preferred flexibility and daring to solidity and safety. American locomotives, for example, were nicely adapted to the peculiarly rough conditions of the frontier. They had to meet sharper curves, steeper hills, and poorer roadbeds than those of Europe, and American designers created engines suited to the work demanded of them. American frame houses were quite unlike the structures of thick timber, brickwork, or masonry familiar in Europe. They were light, well-balanced, and well-braced, economizing on the costliest American item, labor, as well as on materials. American farm implements showed the same tendency. When an American and a British threshing machine were put in competition at Kelvedon, England, in 1853, the Yankee model, though only half the weight of its rival, separated grain three times as fast. Commented the London *Times:* "The American farmer demands and gets a machine which does not ruin him to buy nor his horse to pull about . . . Nothing can better illustrate the difference in mechanical genius in the two countries." And just ahead lay the skyscraper, a pioneering creation which did much to advertise American ingenuity and boldness to the whole world.

Fundamentally, American progressivism, passion for change, and belief in the future could all be related to the democracy of the country. "I have shown," wrote de Tocqueville, "in what way the equality of conditions leads every man to investigate truth for himself." It led, that is, to independence of thought and action, to originality, and to emphasis on the pragmatic. Americans could "show the world" because their institutions gave them the freedom and self-confidence to do so.

ALLAN NEVINS

NATIONAL GALLERY OF ART

Spreading the
Gospel of Freedom

English-born Tom Paine (left) came to America in 1774, a partisan of the Revolution, and wrote Common Sense *and* The Crisis *for the cause. By 1787 he was back in England.*

An easy-going poet and Army chaplain during the Revolution, Joel Barlow (below, left) went to France to speculate in real estate, but stayed to strike a blow for liberty.

In 1781, when John Paul Jones sat for a portrait by Charles Willson Peale (below, right), he hoped for another Navy command. He never received it or his six years' back pay.

MASSACHUSETTS HISTORICAL SOCIETY

INDEPENDENCE HALL COLLECTION

The first important export of the new American nation to the rest of the world was an exciting if highly volatile product called *res publica*, and in its behalf enthusiastic Americans fanned out over Europe. They were of all kinds—poets and philosophers, rogues and radicals, soldiers and sailors—but all were imbued with the republican idea: that the proper function of government is to guarantee equal rights and opportunity for all.

At first, oddly enough, they were petted and admired even by royalty. The French court made much of Captain John Paul Jones, and he was knighted by Louis XVI for having brought confusion to France's ancient enemy, England. Jones wanted nothing more than command of an American ship, but Congress had scrapped the American Navy. He would not return to his Virginia plantation, for he detested slavery; but Catherine the Great of Russia had work for him. She gave him the rank of rear admiral and sent him to fight Turks in the Black Sea, where his republican ideas soon caused a clash with a parcel of intriguing princelings.

Meantime in England Whig leaders wined and dined Tom Paine and Joel Barlow, for they hoped with their help to push through long-overdue parliamentary reforms. When the republican idea caught fire in France and touched off the French Revolution, Paine and Barlow, like two old war horses, sniffed the smoke and decided that the times called for their persuasive pens. Paine's pamphlet *The Rights of Man* was followed by Barlow's *Advice to the Privileged Orders*, which argued the doctrine that human rights must outweigh property rights. Both had a wide circulation; but in England even Whig reformers had begun to go slower. Paine and Barlow left England for France, where they were named honorary Citizens of the Republic. Lafayette presented Paine with the key to the Bastille, and he was elected to the Constitutional Convention. Barlow, too, played an important role in framing the new French Constitution.

For their pains, these republicans suffered sorely. Jones died in obscurity in Paris in 1792; his remains were not brought home until 1905. Paine, jailed during the Reign of Terror, was ignored by the American minister, and returned to America to die an impoverished outcast. Barlow, maligned for his views by John Adams, later died of pneumonia in the wintry wastes of Poland, on a fruitless mission to Napoleon on behalf of his country.

COIN GALLERIES

Lewis Littlepage

In 1781 Lewis Littlepage, an eighteen-year-old clerk serving under John Jay, the American minister in Madrid, grew fretful. At home boys his age were fighting for freedom, and he yearned to do the same. He persuaded the King of Spain to let him join an expedition against Majorca, and, as aide-de-camp to the Duc de Crillon, he was wounded at the siege of Port Mahon. When Jay demanded that he return to Madrid, Littlepage answered, "My military Quixotism is not yet abated," and joined Crillon at the siege of Gibraltar. Here he won a reputation for bravery and the friendship of Lafayette and the Prince of Nassau. He was a captain in Nassau's regiment at Constantinople in 1783; next year Poland's King Stanislas invited him to Warsaw.

At 24 Littlepage was chamberlain of Poland, where his services earned him the Cross of the Order of Saint Stanislas (above). He concluded a treaty with Catherine of Russia, was a secret envoy to the court of France, fought with John Paul Jones on the Black Sea, and was a special agent in Spain. Recalled to Warsaw in 1790, he fought as a major general against the invading Russians. When in 1794 Kosciuszko led a revolt, Littlepage joined him as commander in chief of the troops on the Prussian front. He lost a battle, however, and was nearly hanged. He was too hot for Warsaw, too hot for Vienna and St. Petersburg, while Paris and London, suspicious that he was a Russian agent, refused him entry.

In 1801, weary, he came home to die. At his order, all his papers were burned, and he remains today an almost entirely obscure figure.

223

U.S. MARINE CORPS

Led by William Eaton, marines marched "to the shores of Tripoli" to win the Corps' first glory.

To the Shores of Tripoli

Around 1800 the Barbary States of the North African coast existed almost solely by piracy. The Dey of Algiers, the Bey of Tunis, and the Pasha of Tripoli, satraps of the decaying Ottoman Empire, exacted tribute from every possible foreign government as their price for permitting commerce in the Mediterranean. It was as though an obstacle course had been set up to determine whether or not a nation was a self-respecting power. England and France alone had passed the test. They stood for no nonsense from the pirates, and they stood by, amused, to see how the young United States would react.

In 1787 Congress had submitted to Morocco, paying out $80,000. In 1796 Joel Barlow had gone to Algiers to ransom some hundred American seamen from slavery for $40,000 and an annual tribute of $25,000. When payment was made in 1800 by Captain William Bainbridge of the frigate *George Washington,* the Dey insolently ordered that his own tribute to the Sultan of the Ottoman Empire be taken on board and carried to Constantinople—and that Bainbridge haul down the U.S. flag and hoist the Dey's in its place while on this humiliating errand. Europe smiled.

Next year the Pasha of Tripoli, greedy for still more cash, hacked down the flagstaff of the U.S. consulate and declared war. That did it. Jefferson ordered the tiny American Navy to the Mediterranean, and the issue was joined. At first it was a war of naval duels in which, typically, Tripolitan vessels were sunk or sent running without the loss of a single American. By 1803 the Mediterranean squadron numbered nine ships, with 214 guns. That summer the *Philadelphia,* the unfortunate William Bainbridge commanding, ran aground in the harbor of Tripoli while chasing a blockade runner and, ringed by gunboats, was obliged to surrender. The Tripolitans set about refitting her.

In February, 1804, Lieutenant Stephen Decatur

224

The Navy frigate Philadelphia, *captured and converted into a raider by the Barbary pirates, is set ablaze by Lieutenant Stephen Decatur and his daring crew in the harbor of Tripoli, February 16, 1804. Decatur's men row safely away at left.*

and a plucky crew slipped into the harbor under cover of darkness. They made fast Decatur's *Intrepid* to the *Philadelphia*, scrambled overside, knifed the guards, cleared the decks, fired the frigate with gunpowder, cast off, and rowed the *Intrepid* safely out to sea while the *Philadelphia*'s burning guns were shooting their last broadside at the Pasha's castle. Europe looked on, impressed. Nelson is reported to have said that Decatur's feat was "the most bold and daring act of the age."

Five times in August and September the American squadron forced the harbor of Tripoli and bombarded the port. Meanwhile William Eaton, the American consul at Tunis, had conceived a plan. The Pasha of Tripoli, he knew, had deposed an elder brother, Hamet, from the throne. With eight U.S. marines and about 400 Greeks and Arabs, Eaton and Hamet marched over the desert to attack Derna, storm the town, and for the first time in history raise the American flag over a foreign fort. (Young Marine Lieutenant Presley Neville O'Bannon hoisted the flag and thereby inspired the author of the *Marine Hymn* with the second half of his first line.)

By spring of 1805 the Pasha of Tripoli was eager enough to sue for peace. Tobias Lear, the consul general at Algiers, signed a notably craven treaty giving the Pasha $60,000 ransom for the release of the American prisoners, while Eaton and his marines sputtered indignantly that they could have captured Tripoli and dictated their own peace on their own terms.

But the chief American demand had been achieved: henceforth no tribute would be paid to Tripoli. The United States had taken its place in the international community.

Salem's learned Nathaniel Bowditch was known to the world's seafarers for his work,
The New American Practical Navigator. *After 70 editions, it is still the standard authority.*

Merchants to the World

Scarcely had the last shot been fired in the War of Independence before American merchantmen were off to capture as much of the China and East India trade as they could. Barks and brigs from Boston, having pioneered in commerce with the Pacific Northwest, pushed on to traffic with the Chinese at Canton, exchanging sea-otter, seal, and beaver skins for tea, silk, and nankeens. The Europeans, whose China trade was carried on through subsidized and chartered monopolies, could not believe that the small Yankee ships would survive economically. Yet America's China trade grew annually.

More little ships stood out from Salem to grab off the East India trade, and so successful were they that as late as 1833 a Sumatran merchant prince believed Salem to be a rich and independent nation. Salem skippers customarily sailed east around Africa to sniff for spices among the Dutch East Indies. In 1793 one schooner sold an $18,000 cargo of pepper at a 700 per cent profit. In no time Salem had become the world's trading center for pepper.

A most remarkable aspect of this Yankee maritime supremacy was the age of the mariners. Skippers were boys about twenty; one such, an old salt of nineteen, sailed a sixty-foot sloop around the world, noting in his log that at Hawaii "the females were quite amorous." By the time they were thirty, if no Malay had stuck a kris between their ribs, they could retire, to finance their younger brothers' voyages and sip their Madeira in opulent comfort.

Elias Hasket Derby of Salem built a global business empire; the East India trade made him America's first millionaire.

A hodgepodge of national flags fly over the hongs or warehouses of Canton, the focal point of the rich China trade.

MASSACHUSETTS HISTORICAL SOCIETY

Frederic Tudor

In his way, Frederic Tudor changed the customs of mankind as much as any American before or since. As the world's first iceman, he popularized the iced drink.

Tudor was a Boston shipping clerk at thirteen; at 22 he sailed to the West Indies and, baked by the tropical heat, thought fondly of the thick ice on his father's pond, back in Saugus. If only he had some of that ice right now, to cool the drink he held in his hand. Why not ship ice here to Martinique, to Cuba, to any hot place in the world?

Back in Boston, of course, they laughed at him. Nobody had ever sold ice; hence, nobody ever could. But Tudor did. It meant years of persevering struggle while he built special ships, hit upon pine sawdust as the best insulator, tied up the ice rights in dozens of ponds around Boston, built icehouses all over the tropics, created a market, and then met the demand. In 1826 he shipped 4,000 tons of ice; by 1836 his cargoes were traveling as far as Calcutta, where a Parsi asked the captain if this strange stuff grew on trees or on shrubs. In 1849 Tudor was indisputably the world's Ice King, having shipped 150,000 tons to the East and West Indies, South America, San Francisco, and even to Persia.

By Walden Pond Thoreau watched Tudor's workmen cut the ice and reflected "that the sweltering inhabitants of Charleston and New Orleans, of Madras and Bombay and Calcutta, drink at my well . . . The pure Walden water is mingled with the sacred water of the Ganges." Tudor was more prosaic. He looked at Fresh Pond and saw "$50,000 worth of Ice."

Thar She Blows!

So be cheery, my lads, let your hearts never fail,
While the bold harpooner is striking the whale!
—Old Nantucket Song

COLLECTION OF MRS. H. CROWELL FREEMAN

Joseph Starbuck, of the famous Nantucket whaling family, from an 1847 portrait.

The golden age of American whaling lasted from the War of 1812 to the Civil War. Earlier the English had led the world in whale hunting. As late as 1815 they sent out 164 ships, some off Spitsbergen but most to the Pacific, and English warships had played hob with the American whaling fleet during the Revolution. Nevertheless, Yankee shipowners rapidly overhauled the English and, in less than a decade, seized the leadership of the whale fisheries.

Traditionally Nantucket had been the American whaling capital, and in the 1840's she was home port for more than eighty whalers; but her harbor was neither big nor deep enough, and gradually she yielded primacy to New Bedford. By the 1850's there were more than 300 whalers sailing out of New Bedford. Her skippers ranged the blue waters from Antarctica north to Kamchatka and from Chile west to the Indian Ocean. From each voyage a ship's owners counted on doubling their investment; whaling and whale products were a chief industry in Massachusetts and provided as well one

OLD DARTMOUTH HISTORICAL SOCIETY AND WHALING MUSEUM

About 1849 marine painter Benjamin Russell completed a monumental panorama, over 500 feet long, recording the in-cidents in a world cruise of the New Bedford whaler Kutusoff. *This detail shows the* Kutusoff *in the Cape Verde Islands.*

of the chief exports to the rest of the world.

It was, moreover, an industry abrim with ro-mance and adventure, or at least so it seemed to the New England farm boys hungry for the South Seas. "O the whaleman's joys! O I cruise my old cruise again!" sang Walt Whitman; "I hear the cry again sent down from the mast-head, *There—she blows!*" and he might as well have been writing advertising copy for a shipping agent's handbill.

And yet, in truth, whaling was a brutal and a brutalizing business. The owners, watching the price of sperm oil rise from less than a dollar to nearly two dollars a gallon, grew ever more rapa-cious; the skippers grew more cruel, and their crews more desperate. Theoretically each whale-man got a share of the cargo's value, but the shares were steadily shaved and other techniques invented for exploitation until it was not uncommon for a hand to owe the owners money after four years at sea. Mutiny was frequent, and desertion so routine that one American consul reported that three to four thousand youngsters were annually becoming

beachcombers on Pacific islands. Each year, as the competition grew fiercer, the skippers became more villainous. Some tarnished America's name by de-frauding the Pacific islanders with whom they dealt, and others switched their ships to the slave trade.

A sordid, foul, and degrading business it was, and all hands knew it; but just let them hear the cry, "A shoal of sperm whales! *There she blows! There she breaches!*" and everyone knew they were in for the matchless thrill of a "Nantucket sleigh ride" in a whaleboat whirled along by a harpooned sperm whale, while the waves rushed past, as Her-man Melville wrote, with a "surging, hollow roar . . . like gigantic bowls in a boundless bowling-green." And then for a few moments they could for-get the cruelty and the thievery and the terrible hardships, and those few moments they would re-member as long as they lived.

OVERLEAF: *In this print of a whaler at work the quarry is pursued as, in the background, blubber is stripped off pre-paratory to boiling it down in the smoky tryworks on deck.*

229

Fastest Ships Afloat

The most glorious chapter in American maritime history is also, ironically, the briefest. For one scant decade the gallant clipper ships ruled the sea lanes of the world. They came in answer to a demand for speed. Speed they had aplenty, and beauty as well, but all too soon they were elbowed off the trade routes, again because of the demand for faster ships. The clippers were the swiftest ships that ever sailed, but steam licked them.

They were a natural development. Speed had always distinguished American sailing vessels, from the time smugglers aboard quick, handy little cutters had outfoxed the British to avoid the hated excise tax. The War of 1812 put another premium on speed, and so later did the illegal slave traffic. In the early 1840's the sharp competition for the China trade, with bonuses for the first ships to make port with a new season's cargoes, prodded the shipbuilders still further.

The first real clipper ship—lean-hulled, streamlined, three-masted, with square sails piled high—was the *Rainbow,* out of New York in 1845. But the swiftest, best-known, and most beautiful clippers were built in Boston by Donald McKay. They were costly, but the demand for them was insistent, for soon there was not only the passage around Cape Horn to San Francisco, where there was gold, but there was also the long run to Australia, where a new colony was aborning. The clippers scudded along, up to 350 miles a day.

As with the Yankee ships, so with their Yankee crews. A committee of the British House of Commons sourly reported on the "vast superiority in officers, crews and equipment and the consequent superior success and growth of American shipping." And the historian of the British Merchant Service said, "The masters of American vessels were as a rule greatly superior to those who held similar positions in English ships."

However rueful, such admissions were unavoidable. After flying the 15,000 miles from Boston or New York to San Francisco in less than a hundred

By all odds the best designer and builder of clippers was Donald McKay. Largely self-taught, he learned his profession in New York; but all his ships were built in Boston.

days, the clipper ships would hustle to Hong Kong, where British merchants were willing to pay them three times as much as they would pay their own ships to carry tea to London. Back in London the English shipbuilders eyed them enviously.

American clippers dominated, as well, the North Atlantic packet trade. The *Dreadnought,* skippered by the celebrated Captain Samuels, who had been master of sailing vessels from the age of 21, regularly trimmed the transatlantic record.

By 1853, with the lucrative Australian trade beckoning them, the British were chartering American clippers on sight and commissioning American designers for more. McKay alone built four—*Lightning, Champion of the Seas, James Baine,* and *Donald McKay*—considered the finest clippers ever. Indeed, three of those four set records that no sailing vessel will ever match.

Meanwhile, however, steamship lines had been organized. For another few years the fleetest clippers showed the steamships their heels; but it was only a matter of time before the engine became more powerful and more reliable than the wind.

Long and low, Donald McKay's Lightning *was the fastest clipper ever built. On her maiden trip to Liverpool she ticked off 436 miles in 24 hours, a record for sailing ships.*

Converting the Heathen

In 1806 five devout Williams College students met in a meadow, as was their wont, for prayer. A thunderstorm drove them to a haystack for shelter, and there, improbably, they made a compact to dedicate their lives to the conversion of the heathen. The American foreign missionary movement had been born.

Four years later their leader, Samuel J. Mills, had prodded into being the American Board of Commissioners for Foreign Missions. In 1812 the first missionaries sailed for Ceylon and India, but meantime Mills chafed. There were so many heathen! Where to begin? While a graduate student at Yale in 1809, he had met Obookiah, a Hawaiian lad whose thirst for knowledge and experience had brought him halfway around the world, to Yale and Christianity. At that time Mills had the idea for a mission to the Sandwich (Hawaiian) Islands, where he planned to go himself until he heard an even clearer call.

There was talk at Yale of buying a colony in Africa where freed slaves might be resettled—the idea being to return them home and bring the word of God to the savages. The American Colonization Society was formed in 1817, and Mills was appointed its agent; by 1818 he and a companion were exploring the West African coast for a proper site. Having chosen what would become Liberia, they started home, but Mills died at sea.

Jehudi Ashmun, a frail young fanatic, was ready to replace him. Ashmun clearly foresaw that slavery would lead to mortal conflict. To avert it he urged that all slaves be purchased for a few million dollars and sent to found a Negro republic. A fool idea, said the government, but agreed he should go to Africa as escort for some freedmen, rescued from slave-runners, who were to join the hundred blacks already in the settlement. When Ashmun and his wife arrived in 1822, they found the colony demoralized, leaderless, and ravaged by fever.

Within a month Mrs. Ashmun was dead of fever. By the third month Ashmun, broken-hearted and sick himself, was obliged to command the defense of his disabled colony against two savage attacks by neighboring tribesmen. He had twenty strong men and one brass cannon against some 800, but each time, "with the guardianship of Divine Providence," he beat them off. A passing British man-o'-war left some seamen ashore to insure peace. Thereafter, for six years Ashmun led the colonists in building the trim village of Monrovia and becoming independent. Still sick, he came home in 1828 to die, comforted only by having helped launch a godly commonwealth.

Mills' other dream, the mission to Hawaii, was by then eight years old and prospering. Obookiah had died, like Mills, in 1818, but even in death he was an inspiration to young Yankees eager to redeem the world from sin. One man, Hiram Bingham, in 1820 led a mission of seven couples that brought Hawaii clothes, Bibles, cheese, and Puritan sex morality. The astonished Hawaiians at first liked only the cheese, but slowly there was a change.

Other Yankees, traders and seamen, had brought to the lovely islands other gifts: venereal diseases, rum, even the mosquito. Presently the Hawaiians decided that the white man's God was the best defense against the white man's evils. In 1825 the chiefs declared it was *tabu* for Hawaiian girls to consort with sailors and whaling men. This caused a Navy riot, in which Bingham was assaulted, but the *tabu* stuck. After twelve years there were 900 schools and about 50,000 scholars scattered over the islands. Soon a religious revival swept Hawaii, and the Puritan triumphed over the pagan. Bingham went home in 1841, his job done.

Liberia, founded in 1822 by freed American slaves with the aid of American missionaries, was independent by 1837.

BLACK STAR

Hiram Bingham was a resolute Vermonter who, with iron hand and stubborn devotion, brought to a pleasant pagan paradise the creed of a Calvinist Jehovah. Assailed by both traders and angry sailors, Bingham nevertheless prevailed.

Eloquent Jehudi Ashmun (above, right) wanted to resettle Negro slaves in their African homeland. If his words had been heeded, much misery might have been averted; as it was, his missionary zeal helped found the Republic of Liberia.

Obookiah (right) was seventeen when in 1809 he left Hawaii for New York. He was found weeping for his ignorance on the steps of Yale College. Once educated, he yearned to go home to convert his people, but he died too soon.

The engraving below shows a prayer meeting in an idyllic Hawaiian grove. By the 1840's Bingham and his missionaries had succeeded so spectacularly that disappointed sailors found their usual island diversions almost nonexistent.

DWIGHT, *Memoirs of Obookiah*, 1818

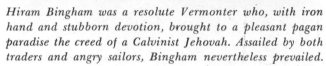

Lieutenant Charles Wilkes, USN, engraved after the portrait by Thomas Sully.

236

Charles Wilkes and His Look at the World

Just as Hiram Bingham left Hawaii, Lieutenant Charles Wilkes arrived, heading the U.S. Exploring Expedition, then three years old. The expedition had as its purpose the discovery of new whale fisheries and a safer passage for the China trade. Few other naval officers cared for such a long voyage, but Wilkes, to his great delight, was appointed. He was forty years old, a man of hot temper, and much happened during his four years at sea to scratch his temper raw.

He left New York in August, 1838, for the Azores, Madeira, and the Cape Verde Islands. That winter he rounded Cape Horn and set out due west from Valparaiso to survey the Pacific islands and chart their waters. In the Fiji Islands a lieutenant and a midshipman, the latter Wilkes' nephew, squabbled with some natives and were killed. With red in his eye, Wilkes burned three Fiji villages and killed 60 natives in reprisal. Assured by kneeling chiefs that never again would a Fiji warrior harm a white man, Wilkes pushed on to Australia.

In January, 1840, he was well beyond sixty degrees south latitude and crawling along the barrier of ice that shields Antarctica. His crew was restive as the ship passed grinding icebergs, in fog, against gale winds. With fifteen seamen on the sick list, Wilkes' medical officers urged him to turn back, and the wardroom officers agreed. But Wilkes insisted on sailing south until he had sighted the Antarctic Continent. For three weeks he kept its coast in view and then, while his crew cheered, he turned north to warmer waters.

Wilkes was not, however, the discoverer of the Antarctic shore. That honor went to a 21-year-old seal fisher, Nathaniel Palmer of Connecticut, skipper of the forty-ton sloop *Hero*, who in 1820 came upon it from the other side, by way of the South Shetlands. The *Hero* was becalmed in a fog on her return passage, and when it lifted, Palmer found himself between two Russian warships. Their commander, Bellingshausen, was astonished to find a Yankee at hand who knew the waters so well as to offer to pilot him to safe harbor. "We must surrender the palm to you Americans," he said.

Even in the face of this earlier discovery, folk were skeptical of Wilkes' claims. He went on to survey another hundred Pacific islands, chart the coast of the Pacific Northwest, scout the China seas for whale, and return after four years by way of the Cape of Good Hope; but it was not till 1911 that he was belatedly honored by having a swatch of Antarctica officially called Wilkes Land.

Fiji Island warriors brandish war clubs in a dance performed for Wilkes and members of his crew, visible at right.

Wilkes sketched his sloop, the 780-ton Vincennes, *anchored in what he called Disappointment Bay in the Antarctic.*

Barnum: Master Showman

Phineas Taylor Barnum, Connecticut Yankee, self-styled Prince of the Humbugs, was another American ambassador to the world in his own bizarre fashion. During the third quarter of the nineteenth century, the period of his greatest renown (or notoriety), Barnum was known all over the world as the foremost collector of human freaks. Whatever the monstrosity, Barnum had first call on its services for public exhibition.

Much of his success he owed to the charm of a tiny citizen of Bridgeport, Connecticut, called Charles Sherwood Stratton but by Barnum dubbed General Tom Thumb. The great showman had launched his career with such arrant frauds as a Negro slave alleged to be 161 years old, a "Fejee Mermaid," and a "Woolly Horse"; but when he found Tom Thumb he sensed that he had it made. He toured his midget through Europe, capitalizing on command performances before Queen Victoria and other royal personages until he was grossing $3,000 a day. By publishing an autobiography in 1855 he called down on his head a storm of curses, especially from English editors, for he confessed that he had gulled the public. Still his fame grew. He was admired the more for insisting that "There's a sucker born every minute."

His second tour of Europe with Tom Thumb proved his point, for it was more successful than his first. He even found time to tour himself, giving a lecture on "The Art of Money-Getting," a thoroughly cynical sermon by what *The Times* of London described as "the most adventurous and least scrupulous of showmen." When the Prince of Wales, later to be Edward VII, came to the U.S. in 1860, Barnum's American Museum was the only place of public amusement he visited. But Barnum was not there. "We have missed the most interesting feature of the establishment," said the Prince. In 1889, when Barnum toured his circus in England, a group of English public figures honored him as America's most representative man.

Advertising his American Museum, Barnum trumpeted such attractions as "Shaking Quakers" and a "Circassian Family Groupe." He bragged that, even at two bits a head, he consistently outdrew the free-of-charge British Museum.

LIBRARY OF CONGRESS

Commodore Matthew Perry, younger brother of the hero of Lake Champlain, Oliver Hazard Perry, won fame on his own as the astute diplomat who opened Japan for the world.

In the spirit of America's Manifest Destiny, J. G. Evans titled his painting (right) of Perry's black-hulled fleet "Commodore Perry Carrying the 'Gospel of God' to the Heathen."

Commodore Perry Opens Japan

When Commodore Matthew Calbraith Perry set out from Annapolis on the steam frigate *Mississippi* in 1852, his mission was considered so important that President Fillmore and the secretary of the navy were both on hand to see him off. His orders were to secure what only a few Dutch and Chinese had been able to get before him—free and friendly access to the mysterious and inhospitable empire of Japan. His expedition, he knew, was virtually an act of aggression, for six years earlier Commodore Biddle had sailed two American warships up Yedo (now Tokyo) Bay on a similar mission, was forbidden to land, and was told, "You must depart as quickly as possible and not come any more to Japan." The Gate of the Sun had been slammed shut and locked.

To a cocky young nation, such a stand was intolerable. When word came that crews off Yankee whalers had been jailed, Yankee tempers rose. Perry proposed to halt such practices and to open ports. "Invasion of Japan!" shouted New York newspapers; but in London *The Times* asked "whether the emperor of Japan would receive Commodore Perry with the most indignation or most contempt."

Perry, "Father of the Steam Navy," had supervised the building of the Navy's first steam vessel, a paddle-wheeler called the *Fulton,* and he had planned the Navy's first steam frigates, the *Mississippi* and the *Missouri.* Under his command the *Mississippi* had swiftly silenced the forts at Vera Cruz in the Mexican War, and it was logical to pair them again for this consequential mission.

Perry had done considerable homework before he left. He knew the Japanese loved ritual, so he

CHICAGO HISTORICAL SOCIETY

Commodore Perry

Interpreter H. Portman

Lt. Oliver Hazard Perry

Captain Joel Abbott

planned some ceremony of his own. He knew they swore by prestige; he proposed to outface them. He knew they had been exclusive; he would be more so. If they chose to lie, he had a few fibs up his own sleeve.

In Hong Kong he joined with the steam frigate *Susquehanna* and the sloops *Saratoga* and *Plymouth*, engaged S. Wells Williams, a missionary, to accompany him as interpreter, and resolutely he ordered his squadron into the Sagami Sea. With thick coal smoke pouring from its funnels, his flagship led the way up Yedo Bay. "As the squadron sailed up the coast," said the official historian, "eight or ten junks hove into sight. . . . The *Mississippi*, in spite of a wind, moved on with all sails furled at the rate of eight or nine knots, much to the astonishment of the crews of Japanese fishing junks . . . who stood up in their boats and were evidently expressing the liveliest surprise at the sight of the first steamer ever beheld in Japanese waters."

Japanese guard boats circled warily around the black-hulled American warships, but they were warned off by U.S. marines baring their steel. When the vice-governor of Uraga attempted to parley, Perry deputed a lieutenant to meet with him; next day the governor himself rated only a captain. In reply to the Japanese insistence that the Americans go to Nagasaki, Perry, through his spokesmen, stated that he had a letter from the President to the Emperor, that if a suitable person were not sent to receive it "he, the commodore, would go on shore with a sufficient force and deliver [it] in person, be the consequences what they might." According to their custom, some "mandarins" were rowed out for an unofficial visit; but it was a Sunday, so, according to *his* custom, Perry refused to receive them.

His firmness paid off. The President's letter, he was told, would be received with fitting formality. On July 14, 1853, 300 officers, sailors, and marines moved toward shore in fifteen cutters and launches. As Perry himself (now known as Lord of the Forbidden Interior) stepped into his launch, the *Susquehanna* gave him a thirteen-gun salute. Pomp? Perry would show them pomp.

As he landed, his officers were drawn up in a double line and fell in behind him as he passed. He was preceded by two tall seamen—one with the U.S. flag and the other with Perry's—and by two boys bearing in a scarlet envelope the President's letter, which was written on vellum, bound in blue silk, and sealed with pure gold. Perry was flanked by two huge Negroes, each armed to the teeth. Gilbert and Sullivan could not have done better.

The entire procession marched to a specially constructed reception hall, where sat two Japanese princes. They were silent and motionless. So was Perry. On signal, the letters were delivered. On signal, the ships' bands struck up patriotic airs.

Perry was then told his ships should leave at once. He replied that he would leave in two or three days. When asked if he would return for his answer with all four vessels, he replied: "All of them and probably more."

He was back in the Bay of Yedo the next February with three steam frigates and four sloops of war, and sailed up to anchor twenty miles from the capital. "The whole bay," said a Japanese, "became filled with black ships." This time (March 8, 1854) Perry went ashore with 500 men and three naval bands; this time his ships fired a 21-gun salute for the Emperor and a 17-gun salute for the chief of the high commissioners. On signal, the Japanese ensign was unfurled from the masthead of Perry's flagship. It was consummate showmanship.

COLLECTION OF DE WOLF PERRY

Perry's official artist, Wilhelm Heine, recorded the historic American landing in Japan. The day was July 14, 1853; the place Kurihama, a village near the entrance to Tokyo

Bay; the occasion the delivery by Commodore Perry of President Millard Fillmore's letter to the imperial shogun; the result a treaty of "perfect, permanent, and universal peace."

There followed three weeks of glacial negotiation during which the Japanese were friendly but granted little. Perry continued firm and essayed to speed things up by tendering gifts: clocks, telescopes, a telegraph station, farm tools, one hundred gallons of Kentucky bourbon, and—best received of all—a miniature railroad complete with locomotive, tender, passenger car, and rails. Toot! went the whistle, every time the train went round a bend. The Japanese clamored for a ride: "It was a spectacle not a little ludicrous to behold a dignified mandarin whirling around . . . at the rate of twenty miles an hour . . . grinning with intense interest." Next there was an exchange of entertainments, the Japanese offering an evening of wrestling matches, featuring their massive and muscular champions, the Americans responding with a minstrel show staged by American Negro sailors. At a banquet aboard the *Powhatan* the Japanese were "uproarious under the influence of [Perry's] champagne, Madeira, and punch."

On March 31, 1854, Perry and four Japanese commissioners signed the Treaty of Kanagawa, guaranteeing help for shipwrecked Americans, access to any port for a ship in distress, restricted trade relations, and two ports with facilities for refueling. As one Japanese said, clutching Perry in an extravagant embrace, "Japan and America, all the same heart." So it seemed, as Townsend Harris, first minister to Japan, soon obtained a more comprehensive commercial treaty.

Perry's was a notable diplomatic victory and one that gained the United States enormous prestige. Six months after Perry's success, England also won some commercial rights; Russia and Holland followed. But America had showed the way.

243

OLD PRINT SHOP

The 2,856-ton Baltic, *shown in an 1855 lithograph, was one of*

The Collins Line

Harper's Magazine, 1892

Edward Knight Collins

In 1838 no maritime magnate was more successful than Edward Knight Collins, whose sailing packet ships dominated the transatlantic run. But that year, when the English steamship *Great Western* plowed from Bristol to New York in fifteen days, the portents were clear. "There is no longer a chance for enterprise with sails," said Collins; "it is steam that must win the day." By 1847 he had sold all his packets and was hard at work financing and building a steamship line. England's Cunard, with an annual £60,000 government mail subsidy, had been in business for ten years before the first Collins side-wheeler was launched, but Collins' ships—the *Atlantic, Arctic, Baltic,* and *Pacific*—were bigger, more luxurious, and faster. In 1852 the Col-

four Collins Line steam packets that ruled the Atlantic in the mid-nineteenth century before a series of tragedies doomed the line.

lins Line carried 4,306 passengers across the Atlantic to the Cunard Line's 2,969.

Their speed was hideously expensive. Collins needed a $33,000 subsidy for each voyage to meet the costly competition, and Congress was cool. A superb showman, Collins steamed his *Baltic* up the Potomac to Alexandria to show the backwoods congressmen what they would be supporting. When he won his subsidy, it seemed that American maritime supremacy was assured. Then Collins' luck ran out.

In 1854 the *Arctic* was rammed and sunk off Newfoundland; 321 passengers, including Collins' wife and two children, were lost. Two years later the *Pacific*, out of Liverpool with 45 passengers and a crew of 141, disappeared without a trace. Stub-

bornly persevering, Collins launched his biggest and showiest ship yet, the *Adriatic*, at a cost of more than a million dollars. Then she developed engine trouble, and a year passed before she was ready for her maiden voyage. There was worse to come. His subsidy was cut, and suddenly Cornelius Vanderbilt announced that he would carry the mails for less than half what Collins wanted.

Collins' hopes were pinned on the *Adriatic*, but she steamed off with only 38 passengers—a tenth of her capacity—and foggy weather kept her from breaking any records. Early in 1858 the ill-starred line collapsed. The ships were sold at auction, and by 1861 the United States had no crack entries for the fast transatlantic passenger service.

STEVENS INSTITUTE

Commodore Stevens

America's Cup

To sharpen with cloyless sauce the appetite of those visiting the first international exposition at London's Crystal Palace in 1851, a Britisher had the idea of inviting the Yankees to fetch over one of their celebrated pilot schooners to show American skill in design and navigation. The commodore of the New York Yacht Club was John Cox Stevens, of the family of Hoboken inventors and financiers. He chose instead to form a syndicate and build a yacht.

Thus the *America* was born. Her designer was 31-year-old George Steers (who also built the *Adriatic* for the Collins Line), and he modeled the schooner along clipper lines. Her concave bow with the broadest beam amidship was a departure from the traditional design of yachts. She sailed for England in June with her designer aboard her, seasick.

Once she was safely anchored in Cowes, Commodore Stevens issued a defy on her behalf, offering to wager up to 10,000 guineas ($52,500) that she would beat any "cutter, schooner or vessel of any other rig of the Royal Yacht Squadron." But the English sportsmen had seen her sailing off Cowes and they had grown cautious.

On August 22 Stevens entered the *America* in the Yacht Squadron's open race, 53 miles around the Isle of Wight, against fourteen British cutters and schooners. Late that afternoon Queen Victoria, who was on hand, was told the *America* was leading. "Which," she asked, "is second?" "Ah, Your Majesty," was the answer, "there is no second."

The America, *painted by James Buttersworth as she put out from Boston bound for her international triumphs,*

ART MUSEUM, RHODE ISLAND SCHOOL OF DESIGN

won a cup that British yachtsmen have failed to regain after seventeen attempts. Sold and resold, she sailed for both sides in the Civil War, winding up at last in an Annapolis shipyard. There in 1942 she was crushed during a storm.

247

ON TO UTOPIA

WE OUGHT to be subject to enthusiasms," Emerson wrote in his journal in May, 1845. All Massachusetts should be "agitated like a wave with some generosity, mad for learning, for justice, for philosophy, for association, for freedom, for art." A thousand voices agreed. Use Arcturus as a hitching post for ideas, accept the maxim that infinite good is yours for the asking, go out and do battle for a better world—these were the fervent doctrines of the age of reform, when Whittier sang, Theodore Parker preached, and Horace Greeley scattered his newspaper polemics broadcast over the North.

The atmosphere of the country in these decades of youthful vigor was electric. Men and women became drunk on ideas; they took an intense delight in the clash of rival schools of thought; they were tinder for the sparks thrown out by brave idealists—by Jefferson, John Taylor of Caroline, Crèvecoeur, William Ellery Channing, Margaret Fuller, and the versatile Beecher family. And what unselfish courage the best of them showed! Henry I. Bowditch, the eminent Boston physician, walking in downtown Boston one day in 1835, saw a "broadcloth mob" trying to seize William Lloyd Garrison. "Has it come to this," he exclaimed, "that a man cannot speak on slavery within sight of Faneuil Hall and almost at the foot of Bunker Hill? If this is so, it is time for *me* to become an Abolitionist." What sublime confidence they felt in their causes! "The establishment of woman on her rightful throne is the greatest revolution the world has ever known or ever will know," boasted Elizabeth Cady Stanton.

Half a dozen reasons united to make Americans zealots for reform. They regarded themselves as a people with a special mission, believing with the old colonial governor William Stoughton that "God sifted a whole Nation that he might send Choice Grain over into this wilderness." They felt that they had cast off the trammels of the past. As Jefferson put it, they had erected the standard of reason after long ages during which the human mind had been held in vassalage by kings, priests, and nobles, and they now obeyed the laws written by God in the book of nature with a pencil of sunlight. Their almost uninterrupted success in the surge across the continent made them optimistic that they could conquer any error or evil as they had subjugated beast, Indian, and forest. And the empirical approach to life that the frontier inculcated made them devotees of experiment. They experimented impartially with constitutions, religion, education, criminal codes, and party doctrines and often saw that the result was good.

Altogether, Americans had built up a great fund of spiritual energy, which they increased steadily. They were characteristically individualistic in their reforms, each leader thinking he alone saw the true path. "Not a reading man but has a draft of a new community in his waistcoat pocket," Emerson reported. People should give their best thought to the inner life and self-reform. But this seemed a selfish position to Dorothea Dix, who could not sleep when she thought of the harmlessly insane chained in cold, filthy cells, and men rotting in jail for a fifty-dollar debt. Others—Theodore Weld, the

orace Greeley, spokesman for a generation of reformers.

Grimké sisters, James G. Birney—were made miserable by the sight of fettered slaves with scarred backs. One school of abolitionists, however, believed in emphasizing moral agitation, another demanded legislative action, while free-soilers like Lincoln did not believe in immediate abolition at all.

These divergences of opinion were proof of the healthy earnestness of reform. It never lacked adherents of independent thought and sturdy self-confidence, who toiled unflaggingly and had their reward. As the historian Edward Channing says, the reconstruction of American morals made more progress in the first half of the nineteenth century than in all the preceding years since the settlement of Jamestown. This great fact puts the fanatics and eccentrics of the period into proper perspective. Every sweeping movement has its lunatic fringe, whose picturesqueness makes them seem more important than they are. William Miller, for example, who calculated on the basis of obscure Bible texts that the world would end in 1843, was an ignorant rustic of warped brain. Most people rightly disregarded his prediction of doom. Albert Brisbane's father, when told of it, ejaculated: "Damned glad of it, sir—damned glad of it! The experiment of the human race has proved a total failure!" Bronson Alcott correctly denounced the spiritualist mania of the time—really a materialist mania—as "the apotheosis of idiocy." However, as P. T. Barnum said in different terms, human credulity is boundless, and before the Fox sisters confessed that they had produced their supernatural raps by toe-cracking, they had bewildered tens of thousands. Alcott himself was too lofty of spirit, too inspired to be grouped for a moment with the spiritualists, the water-cure fanatics, or the phrenologists. But he had his lunatic moments, as his short-lived community farm of Fruitlands proved.

For at Fruitlands the horses and oxen were not to be coerced, nor the insects harassed. Nobody was to eat meat, fish, poultry, milk, cheese, butter, honey, or eggs; sugar, molasses, rice, and cotton were to be banned as the products of slave labor; and nobody was to wear wool or sleep on feathers. Instead, acorns and the Golden Age! Unfortunately, nobody would live for many weeks on acorns. Alcott gave up, as did the reformer Dr. Reuben Dimond Mussey who pointed out that tobacco was evil not only in itself, but for the thirst it produced among users. "They frequent soda fountains, and from soda water get to drinking beer, and then brandy." Stubborn evildoers continued to smoke and to drink soda water.

But the really useful reformers shook off ridicule, letting society take the good in their work and discard the bad. Dr. Sylvester Graham, for one, could easily be mocked as "poet of bran bread and pumpkins." At its worst his dietary reform must have been horrible. Greeley, who met his wife at a Grahamite boardinghouse, remarked that her addiction to extreme Graham doctrine had just one happy effect—abbreviating visits by guests. "Usually a day, or at most two, of beans and potatoes, boiled rice, puddings, bread and butter, with no condiment but salt and never a pickle, was all they could abide." But in a land of hot biscuits, salt pork, fried beefsteak, and bolted pies, Graham's prescription of whole-wheat bread, more fruits, more salads, more vegetables, and decent chewing habits was salutary. So, also, in a feminine population altogether too much enslaved by the foreign fashions of tightly laced corsets, high-heeled shoes, and skirts that swept the pavement or ballooned out over wide hoops, Amelia Bloomer did well to advertise the possibilities of dress reform.

The experiments in Utopian socialism, the idealistic co-operative communities which sprang up so numerously during the first half of the nineteenth century, had various origins. Some were religious in motive, like the colonies founded by followers of that extraordinary personage Mother Ann Lee. Celibacy, confession of sin, an ascetic mode of life combined with great industry and fine craftsmanship, belief in faith healing, community of property, aloofness from the world, and intense piety gave these bodies their distinctive character. By 1874, a century after Ann Lee came from England, the country had 58 of them. Other efforts at Utopia sprang from the doctrines of the self-made industrialist Robert Owen in England, or the soldier-count Saint-Simon and the shop clerk Charles Fourier in France. Two of the most famous, Brook Farm and the Oneida Community, may fairly be called indigenous, although the Brook Farmers had a Transcendental background, while John Humphrey Noyes had studied Owen and Fourier before taking his Vermont converts to Oneida in 1848.

Most of the communities consciously or unconsciously reflected the world-wide revulsion against the worst aspects of industrialism—its uncertainties, ugliness, brutality. Some wanted to go back to the land, others to take the good and reject the bad in the new industrial world. Many Americans felt a sense of betrayal—the early promise of beauty, prosperity, and perfect liberty in the new republic had been so bright, and the reality of want, ignorance, and anxiety in both rural and town slums was so dark! Young Horace Greeley, sensitive and emotional, had experienced a profound shock. He eloquently relates how after the Panic of 1837, living in the Sixth Ward in New York, always noted for squalor, he found extreme destitution on every side. He saw families with six or eight children burrowing in a cellar under a stable, starving, freezing, sick, and eaten by vermin; he saw three widows and three children living on the proceeds from an apple stand which yielded less than three dollars a week; he saw men who supported their families on five dollars a week, and yet gave something to the *really* poor.

Any critic can point out how certain of failure so many of the Utopian experiments were. Opportunities for success in the competitive world, the individualism that rebelled against planning and regulation, kept able men outside; the chance of an easy living brought in the crotchety, the headstrong, and the worthless. But it is important to remember how high was the goal, how gallant the effort, and how appealing the self-sacrifice.

The lusty humanitarian crusades of the period all achieved at least partial success. Reformers shortened the list of crimes punishable by death; they abolished imprisonment for debt, or lessened its rigors; they improved the penitentiaries. Meanwhile, the temperance crusade was making some gains that proved temporary, but others that were permanent. Neal Dow and his Maine law, John B. Gough and his lectures on his own fall and rise, T. S. Arthur and the combination of morality and sensationalism in his *Ten Nights in a Bar-Room,* could easily be lampooned; but they created an atmosphere which made inebriety a disgrace.

All the while, squarely in the foreground of the national life, the most powerful of all reforms, the antislavery crusade, moved inexorably forward. From that fire bell in the night, the controversy over Missouri's entrance as a slave state in 1820, its history for the next forty years was increasingly the history of the nation. When it began to make itself felt, slavery was an almost unchallenged giant; a generation later, thanks to Birney and Garrison, Benton and J. Q. Adams, Whittier and Harriet Beecher Stowe, John Brown and Abraham Lincoln—very different individuals working in diverse ways—it was tottering to its bloody downfall.

ALLAN NEVINS

LIBRARY OF CONGRESS

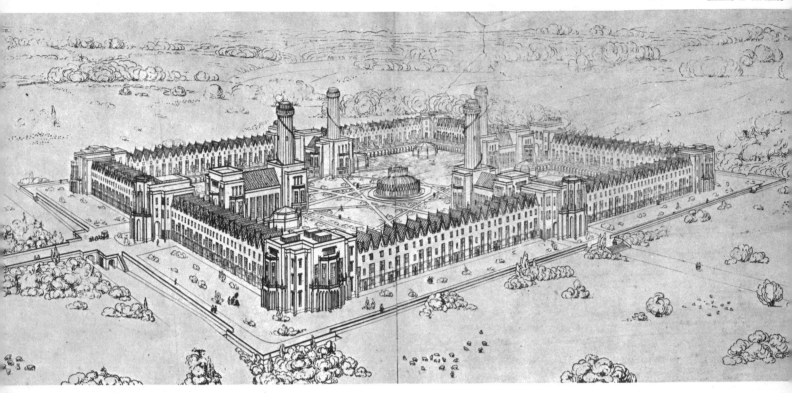

Above, New Harmony as imagined by Robert Owen and drawn by an English architect. Gabled houses and futuristic buildings would be on a square enclosing botanical gardens.

Below, New Harmony as it was, the reality less bright than the dream. French naturalist Charles Lesueur (see page 135), who had joined the colony, made this sketch in 1831.

MUSEUM OF NATURAL HISTORY, LE HAVRE

Dreams in the Wilderness

In the second quarter of the nineteenth century idealists of every kidney sniffed deep the American air and rejoiced. At last, they felt, the perfect life was just around the corner. It would come, said some, on the heels of religious reform; of dietary reform, said others; of economic or sexual reform, said still others; but each insisted that, if only his specific reform were realized, all evils would disappear and mankind would flourish. And so, periodically, they organized into contentious groups to demonstrate what the perfect life would be like.

An early and celebrated Utopia was New Harmony. It was organized in 1825 and financed by an exceedingly sweet-tempered British mill owner, Robert Owen, who was persuaded that proper environment and education would cure all ills. He had tested his theory on his Scottish mill hands, but his partners objected that his benevolence, especially in respect to child labor, grievously shaved their profits, so he sold out and turned to America.

His money bought a village and 20,000 acres in Indiana. To his dream settlement flocked, as his son later recalled, a "heterogeneous collection of radicals, enthusiastic devotees of principle, honest latitudinarians and lazy theorists, with a sprinkling of unprincipled sharpers thrown in." It failed after two years and Owen went back to England to support the co-operative movement and to pioneer in the field of workers' education.

His son Robert Dale Owen lingered at New Harmony and later edited a journal, *The Free Enquirer*, which urged a redistribution of wealth, more liberal divorce laws, and education, "the sole regenerator of a profligate age." In these campaigns he was seconded by Fanny Wright, a queenly, statuesque beauty whose own Utopia had already collapsed. In 1825 she had bought some land in Tennessee, dubbed it Nashoba, and peopled it with a few whites and some Negro slaves she had purchased and freed. The white colonists quarreled, Miss Wright was predictably accused of advocating free love, and the Negroes were sent to Haiti.

Miss Wright later took to the lecture circuit, a career then regarded, for a woman, as unthinkable. Owen, after serving two terms in Congress, embraced spiritualism.

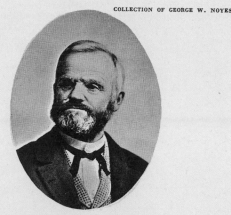

COLLECTION OF GEORGE W. NOYES

John Humphrey Noyes

It is a tribute to John Humphrey Noyes that his Oneida Perfectionist Community was based on the most explosive of theories, yet was by all odds the most successful Utopian experiment of its time. For more than thirty years it thrived on a diet of outrageously heretical principles: that all property should be shared; that sexual intercourse was no more shameful than eating or drinking, but should be freed from the "tyranny of child bearing"; that love was "something to give, not to claim"; that each was married to every other; that procreation should be planned.

Oneida was not, as was charged, a "free love" community; rather it was a brave, devout, hard-working effort to establish a heaven on earth. Economically, Oneida was a rousing success, for its products, including silks, canned goods, silverware, and traps, were much in demand. Morally, it seems likewise to have worked well, but the experiment in scientific breeding was, naturally, an affront to the world outside. Fifty-three young women of Oneida agreed in 1869 to participate in the venture if singled out for motherhood by the community's leaders, and 38 young men offered themselves as part of "any combinations that may seem . . . desirable." Fifty-eight children were born in the next ten years to 100 men and women. Outside Oneida the angry howls of complaint mounted.

In 1879 Noyes fled to Canada (presumably to the relief of his first cousin Rutherford B. Hayes, who was living in the White House). Complex marriage was abandoned, and Oneida survives as a manufacturer of silverware.

Lofty Thought, Simple Life

Gentle philosopher Bronson Alcott sits on the steps of his chapel in Concord, where he taught school. Alcott was singularly beloved, despite his irritating incompetence.

Renounce, said the New England transcendentalists, the works of the world as too materialistic. Shun the vulgar and frivolous. Seek a truly spiritual existence. The difficulty was that they were never able to agree exactly on what the spiritual existence was, for they were the most eagerly individual idealists in an age when eccentrics abounded. And so Brook Farm, their communal effort to show the way by wedding lofty thought to a simple life, was, like many other Utopias, bravely begun but regrettably brief in duration.

Brook Farm was launched in a Boston suburb by a clergyman, George Ripley, who by 1841 had tired of fashionable piety and timid, conservative theology. He discussed his plans with other transcendentalists, notably Emerson, Thoreau, and Bronson Alcott; but they were too strongly individualistic even to join him at the outset. Nathaniel Hawthorne was there, however, as was Charles A. Dana, and Margaret Fuller, the awesomely brainy feminist, showed up for a time.

Labor, capital, and culture were to be pooled. In peasant blouses the men were to divide into groups to plow, tend the cattle, and harvest, while the women in muslin or calico supervised the kitchen, the dining room, and the nursery. All were then to gather in the evening to discuss Nature, or God, or the Perfectibility of Man, or other large thoughts. It turned out that both men and women preferred the windy talk of the evening to the sweaty work of the day.

Alcott, a dedicated teacher and idealist in a materialistic age, wandered about Massachusetts, inspecting the various perfectionist phalansteries and debating where and how to set up his own. At length in 1843, with $2,000 of borrowed money, he bought a farm and founded Fruitlands, an Eden serving no meat, fish, dairy products, coffee, or tea; where cotton could not be worn because it was grown by slaves; where only "aspiring vegetables," or those that grew upward, were planted; and where no crop was harvested, because the philosophers were too much preoccupied to help their wives and children. It lasted six months, and today Alcott is remembered chiefly because his daughter wrote *Little Women*.

"Standing on the bare ground, – my head bathed by the blithe air, & uplifted into infinite space, – all mean egotism vanishes. I become a transparent Eyeball."

Nature. p. 13.

I expand and live in the warm day, like corn & melons.

Nature. p. 73.

"This is my music – this is myself."

p. 22.

Christopher Pearse Cranch studied for the ministry at Harvard, but, plunged among the local transcendentalists, he began to show a wicked sense of humor. Neglecting his sermons, he became "more and more inclined to sink the minister in the man." He wandered about with Bronson Alcott, wrote comic verses, and amused children with ventriloquism. Most engaging, he drew wonderfully barbed cartoons spoofing transcendentalist zeal. These were inspired by Emerson's essay Nature *and his* The American Scholar.

"Men in the world of today are bugs." p. 24.

ALL: HOUGHTON LIBRARY, HARVARD UNIVERSITY

HOUGHTON LIBRARY, HARVARD UNIVERS

Vegetarian Sylvester Graham

"A vegetable diet," proclaimed the chairman of a congregation of food faddists in 1850, "lies at the basis of all reform," and the loudest voice in the amen corner was that of Sylvester Graham, a skinny, voluble, cantankerous clergyman and self-appointed physician whose notions about diet, muscle-building, chastity, and the deterioration of the race won him a vast and fanatic following.

It cannot be claimed that Graham was the first American vegetarian. That distinction goes to the Reverend William Metcalfe, who landed in Philadelphia in 1817, formed the first vegetarian society, and edited the first vegetarian magazine. But if not the first, Graham was easily the most vociferous and the most influential. A Presbyterian preacher, Graham was appointed general agent for the Pennsylvania State Society for the Suppression of the Use of Ardent Spirits. While in this post he concluded that man would not crave whiskey if only he ate enough bread. Not any bread—only bread with bran in it, bread baked of unbolted flour, bread home-baked by mother.

Graham bread became a staple at all Utopian communities. As the list of his prejudices grew, more and more folk swore off liquor, tobacco, tight corsets, feather beds (they subverted chastity), hot mince pie, and water with meals. Today all that remains of his quirks is the graham cracker.

Millerite Millennium

If man can achieve perfection, there must be a moment when that perfection will be achieved. And so, in an age when eager believers devoutly anticipated the millennium, quite naturally a man arose to name the day. The man was William Miller, a New York state farmer; the day was to be April 23, 1843; the proof was deduced from the Book of Daniel, VIII and IX (Sylvester Graham cited Daniel I to show that vegetarianism was backed by Holy Writ); and the apocalyptic event was to be Christ's return to earth, preceded by a fire that would cleanse the world. On every hand the apprehensive slogan was: "What shall I do to be saved?"

Millerites were accused of clothing themselves in white ascension robes and waiting in graveyards or atop mountains for the Coming of the Lord. Whether or not they prepared, nothing much happened, and cynics were not surprised. One showed his disbelief by drawing the cartoon above, in which a man, having stocked his fireproof safe with ice, cheese, brandy, cigars, a ham, and a fan, puts thumb to nose and announces, "Now let it come, I am ready!" This ribbed not only the Millerites but also the vegetarians, the antitobacconists, and the teetotalers.

When another date—October 22, 1844—was set but went by uneventfully, Millerite meeting houses were mobbed by the disappointed faithful.

RESERVE DIVISION, N.Y. PUBLIC LIBRARY

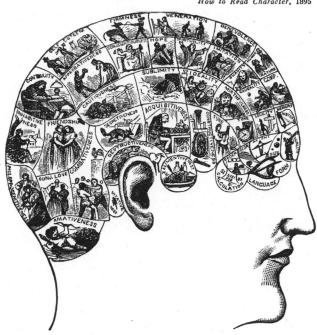

The Spirit-Rapping Foxes

In 1848 in a farmhouse near Rochester, New York, things began to shake, rattle, and roll. What was afoot? Spirits, said all the neighbors. And the two Fox sisters, prankish teenagers who seemed ever to be at the center of the raps and taps, looked on with round eyes but kept their mouths shut. Margaret and Kate were on their way to international celebrity, and the vogue for spiritualism had been born.

Their fame spread when they began to order their tapping so as to spell out spirit messages from the Beyond. By 1850 they were conducting séances in New York for $100 and up. Most of the newspapers jeered, but *Tribune* editor Horace Greeley —always generously receptive to the new, however silly—endorsed them. The eminent mystic Andrew Jackson Davis was consulted: were the Fox sisters genuine mediums? He saw no reason why not; and so Spiritualist Circles sprang up all over the country, many of them becoming "churches." It was, Margaret found, easier to get into spiritualism than to get out, and the unhappy woman took to the bottle. When she exposed the whole fraud, the faithful stood fast by their loony belief. They insisted she had been bribed or had confessed while under the influence of alcohol. In vain she gave lectures exposing spirit rappings. Finally she recanted and became a medium again to earn a living.

Orson Fowler, Phrenologist

Phrenology was born in Germany, but it was bound to thrive in ante-bellum America, where any idea aimed toward perfection was sure to be tenderly cultivated. Phrenology was a "science," yet its adepts needed no special training, and its data could be used to judge the character and ability of everyone, including political candidates. Armed with such mighty magic, might not the ideal society be attained—and soon?

The foremost practitioner was Orson Squire Fowler, whose entire training was attendance at one lecture and the purchase of an official map of the cranium. He palpated pates all over the Atlantic seaboard, his books and lectures on the science made him rich, but after a time he tired of skulls and turned to architecture. It was his conviction that all buildings should be octagonal. Around 1850 octagonal houses, churches, and schools began to go up all over New York and New England.

By 1856 a man named Henry Clubb managed to combine the octagonal house with vegetarianism. Clubb's Octagon City, Kansas, was a community limited to nonsmoking, teetotaling vegetarians who paid $1.25 an acre to cultivate wheat, uplift, and other genteel refinements. Pioneers of the New Day streamed west, the Vegetarian Settlement Company declared that stock subscriptions amounted to some $30,000, but Octagon City died a-borning.

The Abolitionists Are Heard

I *will* be as harsh as truth, and as uncompromising as justice," wrote William Lloyd Garrison. "I am in earnest—I will not equivocate—I will not excuse—I will not retreat a single inch—AND I WILL BE HEARD." So, on January 1, 1831, in the first issue of the *Liberator,* there began the grimmest struggle for reform of the century, the struggle that would culminate in the Civil War, the struggle for the abolition of slavery.

Garrison was far from the first American to oppose slavery, but he was easily the most articulate and the most uncompromising. Like all reformers who see only white and black, good and evil, Garrison warred on every attempt to find an expedient middle ground. Was the slave power spreading under the cloak of the Constitution? Then that august document was "a covenant with death and an agreement with hell" that should be burned. Indeed, he burned a copy of it at a public meeting, crying, "So perish all compromises with tyranny! and let all the people say, Amen!" He was reviled by North and South alike, mobbed, and even jailed; but he could not be silenced.

Tempers grew hotter. In Alton, Illinois, the Reverend Elijah Lovejoy on July 20, 1837, printed an editorial in the *Observer* stigmatizing slavery as a "*wrong,* a legalized system of inconceivable injustice, and a SIN . . . against God." Some three months later proslavery hoodlums wrecked his press, burned his office, and shot him dead.

If abolition were to gain ground, it needed an advocate who, with gentler arguments, could appeal to far greater numbers of people. Such an apostle appeared in 1851—a little woman, wife of a preacher, daughter of a preacher, sister of a preacher, mother of a preacher, and herself a very considerable artist. This was Harriet Beecher Stowe, who, distressed by the Fugitive Slave Act of 1850, sat down and wrote *Uncle Tom's Cabin.*

The Act stipulated that a fugitive slave, wherever he was and however long he had been free, could be seized and shipped south without trial by jury or the right to testify on his own behalf. "A filthy enactment," cried Ralph Waldo Emerson; "I will not obey it, by God!" He did not; nor did thousands of other northerners who organized an Underground Railroad by which Negroes were smuggled out of slavery and to freedom in Canada.

In June, 1851, a Washington paper, the *National Era,* began serializing *Uncle Tom's Cabin,* and it caught hold at once. Published as a book in March, 1852, it was fantastically popular—10,000 copies sold the first week, 300,000 copies the first year.

Even before the serialization of the story had been finished, an unauthorized dramatization was being performed in Baltimore. In Troy, New York, another version ran for three months, and by 1853 five companies, including one organized by P. T. Barnum, were staging *Uncle Tom* in New York. Simon Legree and his bloodhounds were the best possible arguments for abolition.

Harriet Beecher Stowe hoped Uncle Tom's Cabin *would unite North and South; in 1863 Lincoln said, "So you're the little woman who wrote the book that made this great war!"*

METROPOLITAN MUSEUM OF ART

CHICAGO HISTORICAL SOCIETY

LIBERTY LINE.

NEW ARRANGEMENT---NIGHT AND DAY.

The improved and splendid Locomotives, Clarkson and Lundy, with their trains fitted up in the best style of accommodation for passengers, will run their regular trips during the present season, between the borders of the Patriarchal Dominion and Libertyville, Upper Canada. Gentlemen and Ladies, who may wish to improve their health or circumstances, by a northern tour, are respectfully invited to give us their patronage.

SEATS FREE, *irrespective of color.*

Necessary Clothing furnished gratuitously to such as have "*fallen among thieves.*"

"Hide the outcasts—let the oppressed go free."—*Bible.*

☞ For seats apply at any of the trap doors, or to the conductor of the train.

J. CROSS, *Proprietor.*

N. B. For the special benefit of Pro-Slavery Police Officers, an extra heavy wagon for Texas, will be furnished, whenever it may be necessary, in which they will be forwarded as dead freight, to the "Valley of Rascals," always at the risk of the owners.

☞ Extra Overcoats provided for such of them as are afflicted with protracted *chilly-phobia.*

The Underground Railroad predated the 1850 Fugitive Slave Act. The Western Citizen *ran this advertisement in 1844. Companies performing the smash-hit stage version of Mrs. Stowe's book treasured a good brace of baying bloodhounds.*

CULVER SERVICE

Devil in a Bottle

Throughout the nineteenth century all reformers of good will (and a few certifiable lunatics as well) clearly perceived that the greatest hindrance to the achievement of a perfect society was booze, and so they energetically engaged to wring the republic dry. Their battle cry was "Temperance!" but what they longed for was outright prohibition. And since the need to be saved from sin is deeply ingrained in the American character, it frequently seemed that they might prevail.

There was, to be sure, cause for reformist alarm. In 1780 there were 2,579 distilleries in the infant United States, most of them doing good business. Here was a sodden situation—one that cried out for the legions of purity. The first to gird their loins were the Methodists; the Wesleyan discipline forbade the sale or use of spirits except for medical reasons. The Quakers, who likewise opposed drunkenness, added their strength, and in 1826 the American Society for the Promotion of Temperance was formed. It claimed a membership of 500,000 by 1833, and the next year boasted a million members. A temperance journal crowed that the number of American sots had been reduced from 200,000 to 125,000, and the number of moderate drinkers from six to three million.

Six drunks of Baltimore met, reformed, and launched the Washingtonian Movement of the 1840's, which was said to have returned 500,000 topers to the straight and narrow path with the help

ARTHUR, Six Nights with the Washingtonians, 1871

The terrible tale of the Latimer family, from Timothy Shay Arthur's "The Bottle and the Pledge." That first drink leads to poverty and sodden ruin. After Latimer kills his wife, he is visited in the madhouse by his forbearing children.

of such stories as that of little Hannah Hawkins, who cried: "Papa, please don't send me for whiskey today!" A children's Cold Water Army was set to marching. A spate of temperance tracts began to appear. A young journalist, Walt Whitman, wrote one called *Franklin Evans; or, The Inebriate,* but far more influential was Timothy Shay Arthur's classic *Ten Nights in a Bar-Room,* with its immortal "Father, dear Father, come home with me now . . ." (But they kept saving the same old soaks.)

All this activity resulted in a wave of prohibitory legislation. By 1855 thirteen of the 31 states had outlawed alcoholic drink. Then—as the reformers sadly wagged their heads—these virtuous triumphs were swept away by the Civil War.

Not until 1873 was the nation again in a mood for reform. A Dr. Dioclesian Lewis, homeopathist, gymnast, advocate of short skirts and enemy of corsets, urged that women could forever end the curse of drink if they would only form what he called Visitation Bands and go to sing and pray outside the saloons of their home towns. In Ohio his idea caught hold and inspired some ladies to puff up what was later described as "a whirlwind of the Lord." Before the big wind died down 25,000 saloons had been slammed shut, and 700 breweries had gone out of business. But once again the cure failed to take.

This women's crusade had, however, attracted the attention of an Illinois schoolteacher, Miss Frances E. Willard. A handsome, dedicated zealot, she rose like a rocket to the presidency of the Women's Christian Temperance Union. She died in 1898, but her imprint was on the future. When the short-lived victory came 22 years later, the white ribbons of purity waved in her honor.

Carry Nation took her membership in a Kansas local of the WCTU seriously. About to be arrested for defacing property, she cried: "Defacing! I am defacing nothing! I am destroying!" She did just that with her famous hatchet.

BROWN BROTHERS

The Weaker Sex Rebels

When this picture was taken of the Executive Committee which arranged the First International Council for Women in 1888, some of these women had been pioneering for upwards of forty years on a cheerless frontier—the fight for women's rights. Another 32 years would pass before the chief prize they sought—votes for women—would be won.

CULVER SERVICE

Temperamentally some of them were jolly souls, but on this occasion there were no smiles. Let the men do the laughing, their determined expressions seem to say; we women have work to do.

The struggle for women's rights was born out of the struggle for other reforms. Susan B. Anthony (seated, second from left) was first concerned with temperance, while her great friend Elizabeth Cady Stanton (seated, fourth from left) was originally an abolitionist who found out that women were not permitted to speak in public against slavery and began agitating against women's enslavement. As if things weren't bad enough here, May Wright Sewall (standing, fifth from left) carried the crusade abroad.

263

CULVER SERVICE

George Francis Train

"I am that wonderful, eccentric, independent, extraordinary genius and political reformer of America, who is sweeping off all the politicians before him like a hurricane, your modest, diffident, unassuming friend, the future President of America—George Francis Train!"

The speaker had reason for his self-esteem. Train had already been a shipping magnate, spurned the presidency of a revolutionary Australian republic, rejected an offer to join Garibaldi in Italy, promoted a railroad in Pennsylvania on behalf of the Queen of Spain, laid horse-car tracks throughout Great Britain, and organized the financing of the Union Pacific Railroad. Having made three fortunes, he turned to politics. In 1867 he discovered women's rights; his money backed a newspaper, *The Revolution,* edited by Susan B. Anthony and Elizabeth Cady Stanton; in 1872 he ran for the presidency on his own ticket against Grant, Greeley, and Victoria Woodhull and came in a distant last.

Suddenly he heard that Mrs. Woodhull and her sister had been jailed for printing obscenity. In his own paper he promptly printed verses from the Bible, insisting they were more obscene. He was jailed too, tried, adjudged insane, and freed. In protest, he walked out of jail clad only in an umbrella.

Afterward, Train circled the globe in record time (he had earlier inspired Verne's *Around the World in Eighty Days*), embraced vegetarianism, and lived on his lecture fees. At the end he was poor and lonely, his only friends the children he met in the park.

The Versatile Claflins

Not idealism, not a splendid vision of a perfect society, but rather a shrewd and selfish practicality inspired the seductive Claflin sisters, Victoria and Tennessee, to their celebrated romp among the assorted spiritualists, socialists, suffragists, and reformers of the 1870's.

From an obscure and raffish background of fortunetelling, mesmeric healing, medicine shows peddling bogus cancer cures, prostitution, and blackmail, the sisters burst into New York in 1868. Along the way Victoria had picked up two husbands (she kept the name of Woodhull, the first), and Tennessee one (she changed only her first name—to Tennie C.). They had fleeced chumps all over the Midwest, and now, in the big town, they set their sights on the richest one of all—Commodore Cornelius Vanderbilt, then 74 years old. Soon Tennessee was on extremely close terms with him, and by 1870 he was so docile that he backed them in an enterprise—Woodhull, Claflin & Co., Brokers—which stunned Wall Street. Victoria was 32, Tennie C. was 24, and no more alluring brokers ever operated. In three years the young financiers grossed a tidy $700,000.

Victoria had the brains; her sister's talents, while striking, were limited. And with capital the former branched out. In April, 1870, she announced her candidacy for President; a month later she published the first issue of her *Weekly,* in which she stumped for free love, short skirts, easier divorce laws, vegetarianism, world government, magnetic healing, birth control, abortion, abolition of the death penalty, an excess-profits tax, legalized prostitution, public housing, and socialism.

As editor, Victoria first tried to take over the women's rights movement and very nearly succeeded. Balked, she touched off the greatest scandal of the age by printing a story of the adulterous relationship between Henry Ward Beecher, preacher, and Elizabeth Tilton, wife of Beecher's friend and fellow reformer. The sisters were charged with obscenity and jailed. They were let go, but what saved them was Vanderbilt's death. In the ensuing fuss over his will they collared a sizable sum and took it to England, where each married well. Tennie even married a baronet. At last she was a Lady.

In Thomas Nast's pious 1872 cartoon, diabolical Victoria Woodhull is scorned by a wife who says, "I'd rather travel the hardest path of matrimony than follow your footsteps." With that burden the choice could not have been easy.

Victoria frequently announced her candidacy. The Cosmo-Political party gave way to the Equal Rights party, another of her inventions, in 1872. She fell far short of election in the year that also saw Horace Greeley lose to Grant.

BOTH : CULVER SERVICE

CITY ART MUSEUM OF ST. LOUIS

In 1871 Winslow Homer immortalized "The Country School" and, in the teacher, set a style for the idealized American Girl.

Toward an Education for All

In the first years of the nineteenth century no area of American life offered more fruitful possibilities for reform than education, and no area was more generally disregarded. In the early colonial days of theocratic New England, there were schools in every township—"it being one chief project of the old deluder Satan to keep men from the knowledge of the Scriptures"—and the colonists were required to support them; but gradually the idea had taken hold that education was a privilege, that schools were no responsibility of government, but rather of the church or of private enterprise. Some public schools were taught by ignorant bullies; others were only for pauper children; and since child labor was widespread, hundreds of thousands of children got no schooling at all. Secondary schools for boys were wretched; for girls they were almost nonexistent.

But a powerful tide was running that forced men to change their ideas about education. This was the concept of universal suffrage for white men, which between 1810 and 1830 became the law in nearly all the states. But what price universal suffrage amid universal ignorance? It was clear to a rising generation that only an educated electorate would guarantee self-government.

And now the reformers appeared: Henry Barnard, Emma Willard, Catharine Beecher, Horace Mann, and Mary Lyon. They were denounced as dangerous radicals, and their notion of taxing "one man's property to educate another man's child" met bitter opposition. But the reformers had an answer, one based on eighteenth-century French political thought—"every schoolhouse opened closes a jail." As the first battlefield they chose New England. There they could capitalize on the strong tradition of compulsory education as a public necessity, one of the ideals of the Protestant Reformation carried over from Europe on the first ships.

As a boy in Franklin, Massachusetts, Horace Mann had found the most terrifying places to be his school and his church. In school he was brutalized and beaten, in church he heard Calvinist sermons that predicted eternal damnation.

266

CULVER SERVICE

In 1848 educator Horace Mann succeeded J. Q. Adams as an antislavery Whig in the U.S. House of Representatives.

LIBRARY OF CONGRESS

Mary Lyon used quiet diplomacy to get "gentlemen of independence and repute" to finance Mount Holyoke College.

His family was poor, so he was never able to attend school for more than ten weeks in a year. Yet at twenty he showed his mettle by launching on an intensive six months' course of study that prepared him for the sophomore class at Brown, whence he graduated with high honors in 1819. A brilliant lawyer and state legislator who became president of the Massachusetts State Senate, he suddenly chucked his political career in 1837 to accept the post of secretary of the state Board of Education. Here his income was severely reduced, but his horizons limitlessly expanded. In eleven years he organized the nation's first normal schools to train teachers, got the legislature to double appropriations for public education, improved the elementary curriculum, raised teachers' salaries over 50 per cent, built fifty new high schools, and insured education for every child six months in the year.

"Be ashamed to die until you have won some victory for humanity," said Mann in 1859. His words could have served as text for Mary Lyon, one of his contemporaries.

When Mary Lyon was a small girl, her mother found her fussing with an hourglass. She was, she said, inventing a way to make more time. As it hap-

pened, she needed all the time she could find.

She was said to have mastered an English grammar in four days and a Latin grammar in three. Whenever she could, she studied, often twenty hours a day. When she couldn't study, she taught, for a salary of 75 cents a week. Should she marry? No—instead, in 1821, when she was 24, she entered a seminary at Byfield, Massachusetts, run by Dr. Joseph Emerson, an early champion of education for women. Here she met another dedicated teacher, Zilpah Grant, with whom she organized a girls' school at Ipswich. But unfortunately Miss Grant's health failed.

In 1834 Mary Lyon met with some men "to devise ways and means for founding a permanent female seminary upon a plan embracing [her] favorite views and principles." Of these, one was the hope that it might attract the daughters of the rich and yet be cheap enough for those in moderate circumstances. This was Mount Holyoke, the first girls' school to own its own buildings and equipment, which opened in 1837 with four teachers and 116 pupils. In ten years it had doubled its enrollment. Now it was possible for American women to get a collegiate education.

BROWN BROTHERS

Anne Sullivan (right) was a graduate of Boston's Perkins Institution for the Blind. At the recommendation of Alexander Graham Bell she became Helen Keller's teacher when the blind, deaf-mute child was six. As a result of their unique relationship Miss Keller (at left) learned to read, to write, and to speak, and became a figure of world renown.

Dorothea Dix, Humanitarian

On a wintry Sunday in March, 1841, Dorothea Lynde Dix, a tall, slender, retiring Boston spinster, went to the House of Correction in East Cambridge to conduct Sunday school. While there she was shown four sick persons—"harmless lunatics," she was told—locked together in one small, dark, filthy, frigid room. Miss Dix, who was at least touched with saintliness, was deeply moved. To her horror she found that they were actually being treated rather better than the mentally sick of other communities. Was it possible, she asked, that sick people were chained like animals, imprisoned like criminals, beaten, exhibited like Barnum's freaks?

Miss Dix determined to find answers to these troubling questions and, if her suspicions proved true, somehow to correct this horrible situation. Other nineteenth-century reformers and humanitarians were grappling with the problems of society's outcasts—criminals, paupered blind or deaf or mute, and pathetic idiot children. A succession of prison reformers culminated in Thomas Mott Osborne, one of many men who sensed that prisoners should be taught to be good citizens. The remarkable Gallaudets, father and two sons, established homes, schools, and churches for deaf-mutes and taught them ways of communication. Dr. Samuel Gridley Howe, whose wife, Julia, wrote "The Battle Hymn of the Republic," founded the Perkins Institution for the Blind in Boston, and through his astonishing success with such pupils as the deaf-blind Laura Bridgman, proved that the sightless could become socially and economically competent. Yet few of these crusaders had such a powerful impact on their times as did the extraordinary Miss Dix.

For two years, quietly, almost secretly, she prowled through nearly fifty prisons, jails, and almshouses in eastern Massachusetts, jotting down cold, angry notes on the treatment afforded the mentally sick. Her facts, clothed in cold, angry prose, she incorporated into a memorial to the Commonwealth that shocked legislators dumb. Her report was, of course, challenged by the petty bureaucracy which stood accused; but she had important backers—Horace Mann, Dr. Howe, and Charles Sumner—who endorsed her charges of sick men and

Dorothea Lynde Dix was a single-minded reformer who succeeded in changing, all by herself, the climate of public opinion toward the treatment of unfortunate "lunatics."

women beaten, chained, and brutalized. At once laws were passed to mitigate their condition.

Dorothea Dix turned to Rhode Island, where matters were worse, and forced improvement. In New Jersey her grim tour of inspection resulted in the building of a state asylum at Trenton. Reformers invited her to double her efforts, but the invitations were scarcely necessary to a woman of such dedication. She traveled as far south as Louisiana, west to Illinois, and in her wake left legislatures convinced, rich men persuaded, and hospitals and asylums a-borning. She even memorialized Congress and got it to legislate sale of a land grant, proceeds to go for the care of the insane; but Franklin Pierce vetoed this.

Miss Dix went to Europe and got hospitals built in Britain and an asylum in Rome. In June, 1861, she was named superintendent of women nurses of the Union Army, and for her services the secretary of war commanded that "a Stand of Arms of the United States National Colors be presented to her." Not until the age of eighty did she retire.

269

International Peace:
Pursuit of
the Elusive Vision

Beginning in the 1840's, the former blacksmith's apprentice Elihu Burritt devoted his vigorous energies to the cause of international peace.

M an's noblest dream—that war shall be abolished from the earth—is not, of course, exclusively American. And yet it fell to two nineteenth-century Americans to give the ideal a practical framework.

First came the robust, good-humored William Ladd, a New Englander who, after a comfortable and adventurous youth, at the age of forty poured himself, with wit and great personal magnetism, into the faltering peace movement. In May, 1828, he founded the American Peace Society. Indefatigably, despite failing health, he propagandized state legislatures, Congress, and even the White House. Ladd was not simply a pacifist. By delegation, petition, and political pressure he urged a concrete plan for a Congress of Nations that would provide for the general welfare, and a Court of Nations that would settle international differences judicially or diplomatically. Ladd was the first to recognize that any international court would have to be separate from the executive body. He foresaw, as well, the importance of public opinion as a bulwark of international organization, but he died in 1841, partially paralyzed, preaching to the last the dream of international amity.

Into his shoes stepped an awkward, shy, self-taught blacksmith from New Britain, Connecticut,

named Elihu Burritt. With no formal schooling, he nevertheless read and spoke more than a dozen languages when, at 27, he walked to Worcester, Massachusetts, in search of a better job and a better education. He found both and a cause as well. By 1844 he was publishing an international pacifist journal, *The Christian Citizen;* during the crisis over the Oregon boundary he peppered President Polk with peace propaganda. British pacifists had co-operated with him, so in 1846 he went to England, where he formed the League of Universal Brotherhood, under the auspices of which 40,000 British and Americans pledged total abstinence from war. He got peace messages, called "Olive Leaves," published in forty influential European newspapers, and they reached, he estimated, a million readers monthly. He organized annual peace congresses in Brussels, Paris, London, and elsewhere, and at each he backed Ladd's plan for a Court and Congress of Nations. As the only alternative, he urged workers of the world to go on strike and thus abolish war.

Back in America to campaign against the threatened Civil War, Burritt advocated the sale of public lands to pay for the freedom of the slaves, but his voice was a lonely one. After his death in 1879 his dream and Ladd's were partially realized in The Hague Conferences and the World Court.

COLLECTION OF DR. WILLIAM E. LADD

William Ladd, skipper of a brig at the age of 20, was a prosperous Maine farmer when he got the call to become an "Apostle of Peace." He became a minister at 59 and subsequently beggared himself for his splendid ideals. Neither he nor Elihu Burritt lived to see the hopeful establishment (left) of the International Court of Arbitration.

271

A TINKERING PEOPLE

I N THE Grant era the most popular sight in Washington after the Capitol and White House was the Patent Office. It did not show much originality, for its south front was a copy of the Pantheon in Rome, and its east portico was patterned after the Parthenon; but its exhibition room, 274 feet long, was lined with two tiers of glass cases holding models of thousands of inventions, ranging from steam engines to rattraps. One case contained a miniature wooden steamboat hull equipped with a false bottom, bellows, and air-bags, which was ticketed: "Model of sinking and raising boats by bellows below. A. Lincoln, May 30, 1849." When Grant took office, about 14,000 patents were being issued annually, or nearly as many as in all Europe, including Great Britain. "We are an inventive people," said his commissioner of patents. "Our merchants invent, our soldiers and sailors invent, our school-masters invent, our professional men invent, aye, our women and children invent."

The penchant of Americans for inventing in fact gave rise to many jokes. Darius Green and his flying machine, celebrated in John T. Trowbridge's poem, was outdone by the inventors of perpetual-motion devices and the geniuses who demanded patents for such schemes as the capture of tigers by pits filled with catnip and the extermination of Kansas grasshoppers by the concussion of heavy artillery. However, the whittling Yankee came by his propensity legitimately. Labor was costly in a country whose open frontier made opportunity seemingly endless, and labor-saving devices were prized and sought more than in crowded, older lands. The fluid society gave men scope for originality, and a population rich in versatile handicraftsmen, who must turn their energies to a hundred tasks, naturally made tinkering a pastime. When every pioneer farm abounded in homemade implements, every farm boy had his opportunity to design something of archetypal novelty. It was all very well to laugh at Darius Green until his name became Orville Wright. The country that gave the world the best steamboat, telegraph, sewing machine, harvester, cotton gin, and electric light might well make its inventiveness a boast.

The truest inventor is of course more than a tinkerer. He is a man possessed; he has an idea which will not let him go, as the great ideas of Arkwright and Watt, Fulton and Morse, enslaved them; he is poet, enthusiast, and crusader, enlisted with other fanatic thinkers in the army of enlightenment. One of the classic examples of this supreme type is the American martyr to invention, Charles Goodyear.

Who was Goodyear? Said friends: "If you see a man with an India-rubber coat on, India-rubber shoes, an India-rubber cap, and in his pocket an India-rubber purse with not a cent in it, that is he." His selfless dedication to the conquest of rubber for man had an almost religious intensity. Working in abysmal poverty, he boiled his rubber, baked it, smoked it, mixed it with quicklime, magnesia, and other substances, and gave it every possible mechanical treatment. He pawned nearly everything he had—once even his children's

Robert Fulton, painted by Benjamin West in 1806.

textbooks. Between 1830 and 1860 he was seldom long out of debtors' prison; his family sometimes wanted bread. Finally he hit upon the fact that sulphur had the property of hardening rubber, and the accident of touching a mixture of rubber and sulphur to a red-hot stove gave him the secret of vulcanization. But it cost him ten years more of poverty, humiliation, and frustration to perfect his process. It was symbolic of his final alternations of triumph and failure that at the Paris Exposition of 1855, for which he had borrowed money to make an exhibit, Napoleon III awarded him the cross of the Legion of Honor, and his creditors put him in jail for four days. He died leaving his wife and six children debts of $200,000; yet he had the satisfaction of knowing that he had created a great industry. Others reaped where he had sowed, but as he said philosophically, the only real tragedy was that of the man who sowed and then found that nobody reaped.

The typical American inventor, however, is to be found on a lower and more practical plane; for the most remarkable fact about our invention is the way in which it has responded to the peculiar economic demands of the social and geographical environment. The innovator makes an article for which he sees a beckoning market and expects a material reward.

The cotton gin, the reaper, and the circular saw were direct responses to public demand. Equally so was the river steamboat created by Henry M. Shreve and others. These boats had to be made of wood, the abundant raw material at hand; they had to be cheap, for snags, ice, sandbars, boiler explosions, and reckless piloting took a constant toll; they had to be able to run in close to banks; they had to be carriers of large bulky cargoes; and they had to be of such light draft that they could make fast time "on a heavy dew."

Without the quick ingenuity of American inventors, settlement of the trans-Missouri West would have been impossible. On the treeless plains, barbed-wire fencing was indispensable. To supply water in the semi-arid country, bored wells and inexpensive, durable metal windmills were equally useful. In areas of little fuel the kerosene or gasoline stove solved the problem of cooking. Not only ranchmen but westerners in general found the Colt-Walker revolver invaluable in quick defense against Indians and outlaws. Primitive appliances had sufficed to subdue the eastern woodland frontier, but invention had to bring up the newest products of the Industrial Revolution before the Great Plains were conquered.

As population grew in the United States, affording the largest and richest free-trade market in the world—a truly national market, too, when trunk-line railroads abolished local boundaries—the inventor found another special factor conditioning his work. This was the scope for quantity production. English visitors made merry, for example, over that common household device, the apple parer. England had not enough consumers of apples, apple pies, or apple butter to make it profitable, but in the United States it could be sold by the hundred thousand. So could corn shellers, peach stoners, sausage grinders. patent coffee mills, and coffee pots. Eli Whitney had the quantity market in mind when he devised the modern system of interchangeable parts, applied it to musket-making, and obtained a government contract. It was inevitable that the invention of automatic machinery to make such parts should soon follow. By 1860 Waltham had become one of the familiar names in the country—the first watches made by the new machinery, their parts perfectly standardized, appeared on the market in 1853 and began driving English and Swiss watches to the wall.

The word "market" is always closely connected with the word "invention," and most successful American innovators have had the ability to combine an original inspiration with efficient systems of manufacturing and marketing. Emerson to the contrary, the patenting of the best mousetrap will not bring the world to a man's door; the inventor must produce it in better form than others and sell it more efficiently. No doubt Americans have often exaggerated the element of mere primacy in their inventive feats. Frenchmen can say that Barthélemy Thimmonier made the first good sewing machine, Germans can point out that they first used gang saws for lumber, and Englishmen can prove that Mark I. Brunel devised machinery which cut, nailed, and finished army shoes long before Lyman R. Blake thought of the subject. Invention is usually rather a process than an inspiration, anyhow, and many brains of many nations must be pooled in it. But the pragmatic approach of Americans gave them a special talent for uniting novelty in design, skill in manufacture, and energy in marketing in one successful whole.

Thus it was that although Goodyear was no more original than the Scot, Charles Mackintosh, who pioneered in making rubber garments with such expert chemical knowledge that his name is still popularly attached to the raincoat, Goodyear's American associates and successors far outdid him. They made and sold their wares so efficiently that even in Scotland Goodyear and rubber became synonymous. Thimmonier's sewing machine, an object of mob attack in France, never attained wide use. The outstanding early American inventor in the field, Elias Howe, did much better, scoring a success in the United States after being swindled in England. But it remained for Isaac M. Singer, son of a New York millwright, unskilled laborer, and roving mechanic, to exhibit the special American combination of traits. He devised in 1851 a better machine than any predecessor, with one vital new part; by bringing about a patent pool, he put new skill into manufacture; and he was fortunate in choosing a partner, Edward Clark, who was a perfect genius in salesman-ship. The result was that by 1873 no fewer than 233,000 Singer sewing machines were sold throughout the world. An even better instance of the combination of gifts is offered by Cyrus H. McCormick. Reapers were invented far and wide, even in Algeria and Australia. But by his original invention, by the steady adoption of improvements, by manufacture with labor-saving machinery, and by new sales methods—with lavish advertising, guarantees, installment payments, and an enterprising foreign sales force—McCormick placed himself far in the van.

American inventiveness ran a wide gamut. What was more American than the lyceum of mid-century days? Or the dentistry in which we so far excelled the rest of the world? Or the network of express lines which had to be specially created to carry parcels over far-flung routes? While Barnum raised the circus to new heights of splendor and humbuggery, American systems for the training of the deaf, dumb, and blind set an improved world standard. The minstrel show, with Mistah Tambo and Mistah Bones answering the quips of the end man, struck some foreign visitors as vulgar; but a minstrel walk-around popularized "Dixie," and Stephen Foster wrote for the minstrel stage some of his best-known songs. Just how much invention and how much borrowing from "rounders" and "four old cat" went into baseball is still a matter of debate; but at any rate it had become an essentially new and thoroughly Yankee sport when New Yorkers of the Knickerbocker Baseball Club cracked out a high ball by adopting a set of formal rules in 1845. By that year any denizen of the Old World would have nodded assent to the simile, "as inventive as an American."

ALLAN NEVINS

Oliver Evans forced his many inventions on a heedless era.

Oliver Evans:
Stubborn
Mechanical Genius

If ever a man was born before his time, it was a pudgy mechanical genius named Oliver Evans, whose inventions, when they were not ignored or derided, were shamelessly stolen from under his nose. Without education or technical training, without patronage of any sort, but with incredible pertinacity, Evans designed and constructed the first vehicle ever driven by a high-pressure steam engine—and more, one which could travel over land or in the water. His contemporaries yawned.

The times were bleak for inventors. There was no patent law; indeed, patents were considered an infringement of public rights. There was very little capital to test a new gadget or promote it, and what capital there was in the young nation went in other directions. Worst of all, there was precious little sympathy for the new. A man like Evans could *know* beyond doubt that he was right, yet meet only with ridicule, no matter how persuasive his proofs.

In 1772, when Evans was seventeen years old, his brother told him how a friend had made a splendid explosion by filling a gun barrel with water, plugging the ends, and tossing it into a fire. "It immediately occurred to me," Evans wrote later, "that here was the power to propel any wagon, if I could only apply it, and I set myself to work."

Evans had never heard of Newcomen, the English blacksmith who had invented the atmospheric steam engine, nor of James Watt, who had improved it. In fact, when he read an account of Watt's engine, his reaction was, "He's doing it the wrong way!" But nobody cared about a better way. "My object," Evans wrote, "only excited the ridicule of those to whom it was made known."

Man must live. Evans got a job making wool cards by hand, invented a machine to do the job better, sold his machine to a manufacturer on condition that it be kept secret and that he be paid a share of the profits, and was at once cheated. In 1781 he entered the milling business. Mills to grind meal required four men's labor, and Evans soon invented a mill one man could run. When millers shrugged, he won a hearing from Pennsylvania legislators and convinced them that his notions had merit. Pressing his advantage, he mentioned his steam wagon. "My representations," he wrote, "made them think me insane."

More than twenty years later Evans was stubbornly demonstrating his "Orukter Amphibolos" to doubters. "I do verily believe," he wrote in 1812, "that the time will come when carriages propelled by steam will be in general use . . . traveling at the rate of fifteen miles an hour."

Evans lived to see his machinery widely adopted in flour milling (his patents were stolen right and left) and his high-pressure engines accepted.

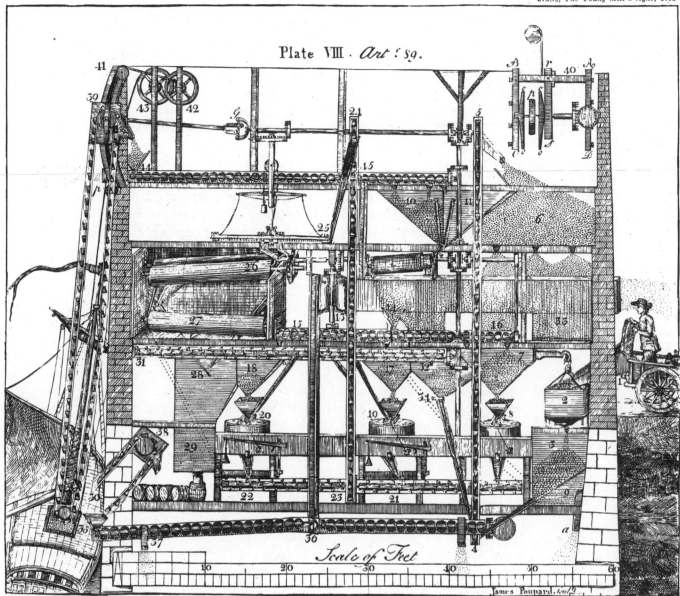

Plate VIII. *Art: 89.*

Scale of Feet

James Poupard, sculp.

The Evans gristmill needed only one operator (at right). Fully automatic, his invention eliminated the need for three other men. For years the world's first automatic plant was a commercial flop, since millers would have none of it. One of Evans' few customers was a sensible businessman from Virginia named George Washington.

The "Orukter Amphibolos," or Amphibious Digger, was a scow thirty feet long, weighing fifteen tons. Evans put this monster on wheels, sent it chuffing to the Schuylkill River, fixed a paddle wheel to its stern, and despite headwinds drove it to Philadelphia. Confronted with this miracle, wiseacres said only that the thing was too slow.

TRANSPORTATION LIBRARY, UNIVERSITY OF MICHIGAN

The Factory System Comes to America

Once the struggle for political independence had been won, Americans faced the far more difficult struggle for economic independence. With no industry of its own, agrarian America was obliged to buy nearly all its manufactured goods from England, and England meant to keep it that way.

The classic example was the textile industry. Cotton was grown in America, shipped to England where it was woven into fabrics in the mills of the nascent Industrial Revolution, and then shipped back to be sold in America—at a handsome profit. All American efforts to build competing mills failed; there was no machinery to compare with Arkwright's famous spinning frame. England refused to sell her industrial secrets, and attempts to smuggle them across the Atlantic were invariably foiled by alert agents. In vain, bounties were offered English workmen to come illegally to America.

However, the most determined police agents cannot forever confine knowledge within national boundaries. In 1788 a husky, fair-haired young Englishman named Samuel Slater read in a Philadelphia paper how a man had been paid a bounty of £100 for designing a textile machine. He decided to try it himself.

Few men could have been better trained for the venture. Slater was only twenty, but he had worked in Derbyshire cotton mills for seven years, rising to the superintendency of a hosiery mill while still an apprentice. There was no need for him to smuggle plans or models, for the technology was in his head. To gain more experience, he supervised the construction of a new Arkwright cotton factory, and in 1789, without telling even his mother, he left for London. There, assuring officials that he was a farmer, he took ship for New York. In America Slater was unique. No one else had ever seen the Arkwright machinery, much less worked it. He could write his own ticket.

He very soon found out just how valuable he was. Moses Brown, a wealthy Quaker merchant of

MARYLAND HISTORICAL SOCIETY

Providence, Rhode Island, wrote him offering all the net profits if he could work the machinery at Brown's new mill.

One look at Brown's primitive jennies and frames was enough. Slater shook his head. "They are good for nothing," he said, "nor can they be made to answer." So he engaged to build new machines, following the Arkwright patents, and added, "If I do not make as good yarn as they do in England, I will have nothing for my services, but will throw the whole of what I have attempted over the bridge."

Slater needed a machinist. Fortunately, one Oziel Wilkinson, a Quaker blacksmith, was living in Pawtucket, close by Brown's mill. He and his son David and a wheelwright, Sylvanus Brown, took Slater's designs and hewed and forged. Gradually from Slater's capacious memory there emerged a complete cotton mill, the first factory in America, on the banks of the Blackstone River. Twenty years later there were 165 mills in just three New England states, and Samuel Slater owned seven of them. Forty years later President Jackson called on Slater in Pawtucket and graciously nominated him "Father of American Manufactures."

JAMES T. WHITE CO.

Samuel Slater smuggled a cotton mill out of England in his head and brought the factory system to America. His wife first produced cotton sewing thread from Slater's yarns.

Maryland's Union textile mill (below), sketched c. 1812, typified the industrial boom during Jefferson's Embargo and the War of 1812. By 1825 the mill employed 600 workers.

William Henry

The first American to think of propelling a boat by steam—or at any rate the first to do anything about it—was a gunsmith, William Henry, of Lancaster, Pennsylvania. Such an idea could not have come more appropriately than to such a craftsman in such a community. For Lancaster, in the days before the Revolution, was a kind of commissary to the frontier, inventing and manufacturing what the frontier would need. Here was developed the light and accurate Kentucky rifle; here were built the famous Conestoga wagons that would navigate the prairie; here, sooner than in any other community, men would sense the need for power-driven craft that could negotiate the fast-running, spring-swollen inland waterways that led to empire.

At 21 Henry was a crack gunsmith. He sold rifles to Braddock and Forbes in the French and Indian War and later to colonial revolutionaries. But his interests ranged further. Intrigued by the possibilities of steam, he traveled to England in 1761 to meet and talk with James Watt and, according to tradition, designed just two years later a stern-wheel steamboat that was unsuccessfully tested in Conestoga Creek.

It is certain, however, that Henry conceived the notion of a steamboat at least as early as 1775. Not long afterward he discussed his idea with Tom Paine and got as far as drawing some plans for a paddle-wheel steamer. And to his machine shop used to come a youngster named Robert Fulton.

James Rumsey

In the fall of 1784 the innkeeper at the sign of the Liberty Pole and Flag, near what is now Berkeley Springs, West Virginia, was James Rumsey, a man of unusual charm. One day to his inn came George Washington, bound on a tour of inspection of his vast land holdings. Before long, Rumsey found occasion to confide to his guest that he had invented a marvel—a boat that would move upstream under its own power. Moreover, he proved his claim by demonstrating with a model how a paddle wheel—turned by a hand-pumped water jet—could drive poles that pushed on the stream bottom and so walk a boat forward. "An important invention," Washington wrote, which would secure "a large proportion of the produce of the western settlements. . . ."

Rumsey's ideas expanded. A year later he was considering the possibility of steam. A man who won friends wherever he went—first Washington, Jefferson, and John Marshall, later Benjamin Rush and Benjamin Franklin—Rumsey sailed to England in 1788 with their blessing to confer with James Watt. Already Rumsey had sent a boat steaming up the Potomac at three miles an hour, but in England he offended Watt's partner, Matthew Boulton, his money ran out, and with it his friends. Late in 1792 he addressed a committee of London's Society of Arts on hydrostatics. Those who heard him urged him to draft a resolution praising his own invention. While doing so, he fell dead.

COLLECTION OF MRS. BASIL M. STEVENS; COURTESY FRICK ART REFERENCE LIBRARY

John Fitch

If the Devil had really wanted to test Job, said John Fitch, he would have asked him to build a steamboat. Fitch knew what he was talking about, for he was to experience every imaginable trial during his bitter career. Yet it was he who designed and constructed the first successful steamboat in America.

He got his idea in 1785. By that time he had deserted a shrewish wife, become a successful silversmith, speculated in western lands, been captured and nearly killed by Indians, laid claim to 200,000 acres of the Northwest Territory, and come home to Pennsylvania to get rich. Out strolling one day, he conceived the idea first of a steam carriage, then of a steamboat. He had yet to see a steam engine—indeed, he didn't even know there was such a thing. Someone showed him a picture of one, and at once he built a model of a steamboat propelled by broad, flat oars and prayed Congress to support his further efforts. He was ignored. In Lancaster he called on William Henry and was staggered to learn of Henry's earlier designs. But Henry generously yielded whatever claim he had to priority.

Not so Rumsey, however, who fought Fitch every way he could. Nonetheless, with the help of a mechanic, Henry Voight, Fitch built a boat which by 1790 was in regular service between Philadelphia and Trenton. It came too early, it lost money, and Fitch, after a fruitless trip to France, went west to Kentucky where he drank himself to death.

John Stevens

The way was now clear for John Stevens, who, unlike Fitch, needed neither friends nor money since he had both aplenty. He had the ingenuity to perceive that Fitch's idea was sound, enlisted the help of his close friend and brother-in-law, Robert Livingston, and set out to beat Fitch to the prize. Since Livingston also recognized that steam power was the key to the future, their partnership swiftly became a rivalry and even more swiftly a feud which eventually led to the first federal patent law and along the way entangled the talents of Livingston's kinsman Robert Fulton.

Stevens bought a large estate in Hoboken, New Jersey, across the Hudson from Manhattan, in 1784. He also bought the ferry monopoly and engaged to make it pay by installing steam. He hired as his mechanic a man who had once worked for Fitch, and when Fitch showed up at his door one day in 1795, shabby and flat broke, Stevens sent him on his way. Meantime Livingston had gone to France, met Fulton, and interested him in the idea of steamboat passenger service. At stake was a New York state monopoly for steamboating. Livingston backed Fulton, but Stevens had his own steamer, the *Phoenix,* which he proposed to put into the Hudson River service. The *Phoenix* was ready when Fulton sent his *Clermont* to Albany and back. Rather than buck Livingston any further, Stevens sent his *Phoenix* out to sea and up the Chesapeake into ferry service on the Delaware.

BOTH: NEW·YORK HISTORICAL SOCIETY

Above is Fulton's own drawing of the Boulton & Watt engine-drive system, which powered the 100-ton Clermont *(below).*

"Toot" Fulton and His Folly

Robert Fulton packed a notable series of achievements into his fifty years. At twenty a successful Philadelphia painter, in 1786 he went to London with Benjamin Franklin's encouragement to study with another American artist, Benjamin West, and to plunge into a society half-Bohemian, half-aristocratic. Before he was thirty, he had exhibited his paintings at the Royal Academy and, as an engineer, had invented a way to lift canal boats without the use of locks and the first power shovel for digging canals. Handsome and charming, Fulton was compared to Leonardo da Vinci.

In Paris in 1797 Joel Barlow (*see page 222*) took Fulton under his wing and introduced him to Paris salons. Here he picked up a nickname—"Toot"—and a reputation as an inventive mathematician. He developed a torpedo, but abandoned it to work on a submarine, the *Nautilus*. He hoped this vessel would have "all the nerve and muscle of an Infant hercules which at one grasp will Strangle the Serpents which poison and Convulse the American Constitution." His chief concern was that the British Navy would starve America; and by promoting his belief that "The liberty of the seas will be the happiness of the earth," he got the French to finance his submarine attacks on British shipping. But the British steered clear of his *Nautilus*.

Robert Livingston, who had come to Paris to negotiate the Louisiana Purchase, now diverted Fulton from submarines and interested him in steamboats. The inventor promptly built a craft that moved up the Seine at four and a half miles per hour. Still persuaded that his submarine would insure freedom of the seas, Fulton flirted briefly with the British Admiralty; but in 1806, when the British chilled, he came home.

Livingston had a charter granting him exclusive steamboat rights on the Hudson River, but since it had only a year to run, Fulton had to hurry. Moreover, he found himself involved in the Livingston-Stevens feud, the more so because he had married Harriet Livingston soon after his arrival. But his *Katherine of Clermont*—predictably called "Fulton's Folly"—was ready for her trial by August, 1807. When she reached Albany in 32 hours, Fulton wrote, "It was then doubted if it could be done again; or if done, it was doubted if it could be of any great value."

Even though the Albany to New York service was soon profitable, it gave Fulton little joy, because his designs were stolen, and the charter invaded and finally overthrown. He lived to build many more steamboats, and died a national hero, symbol of American ingenuity.

MANUSCRIPT DIVISION, N.Y. PUBLIC LIBRARY

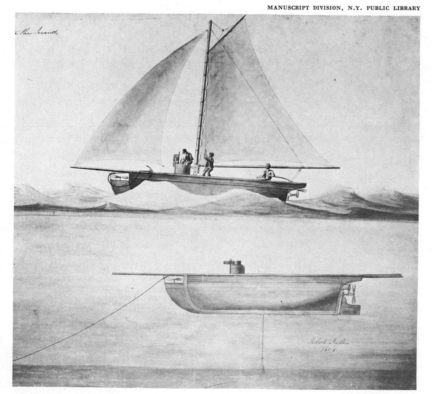

DICKINSON, *Robert Fulton*, 1913

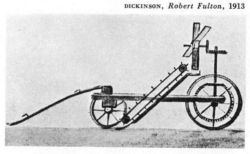

FULTON, *Torpedo War*, 1810

Fulton's Nautilus, *shown as he painted her surfaced and submerged, had a folding mast. Top, above, is his excavating machine; below, his torpedo, fired with a harpoon.*

Eli Whitney Makes
Cotton King
and Guns Cheap

YALE UNIVERSITY ART GALLERY

Eli Whitney sat for this portrait by Samuel F. B. Morse in 1822. No other American's inventions influenced the country's history so profoundly. The cotton gin fastened slavery on the South, while Whitney's system of practical interchangeable parts gave the North the industry to win the Civil War.

Two years after Samuel Slater launched the first American cotton mill, Eli Whitney, then 26, graduated from Yale. This tall, rawboned man of gentle disposition had already demonstrated to his home town of Westboro, Massachusetts, that his big hands could fix anything. He was offered a tutoring job in Georgia, and with no other prospects, he accepted it.

The job went sour, but Whitney had met Mrs. Nathanael Greene, widow of the Revolutionary general, and she invited him to her Savannah plantation. In no time he made himself indispensable as maker and mender. When some neighbors complained that it took one slave ten hours to snatch a pound of cotton lint from three pounds of seed, Mrs. Greene smiled. "Gentlemen," she said, "tell your troubles to Mr. Whitney, he can make anything." And sure enough, he could.

From a sieve, a rotating drum, a comb of hook-shaped wires, and a rotating brush he contrived in a fortnight the cotton gin, with which in an hour he did the day's work of ten men. Before he could patent his model, planters broke into his shop and copied it. Rumors spread like brushfire; so much cotton was planted that in two years the national export had risen from 138,000 to 1,601,000 pounds.

For ten years Whitney fought in the courts of cotton country for his rights; most of the $90,000 he collected went to pay lawyers. The planters, richer by millions, suddenly began to triple their price for slaves. King Cotton had been crowned.

Bitterly disappointed, Whitney went home to New Haven. What could he make that no man could copy? What he hit upon changed the northern economy quite as much as his cotton gin had changed the southern. He invented the "American system" of manufacture, by which, thanks to interchangeable parts, an unskilled worker could turn out just as good a product as a craftsman could. Without factory, machines, or workmen, Whitney got a government contract for 10,000 muskets at $13.40 each to be delivered within two years. He designed and built all the machine tools he would need for this revolutionary method of production before he hired a single workman, and though he exceeded the time limit on his first contract, by 1811 his system was functioning smoothly, and he turned out 15,000 muskets in two years. Whitney's precision machine tools, cutting metal by pattern, ushered in the age of mass production.

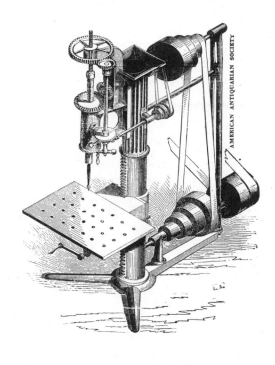

AMERICAN ANTIQUARIAN SOCIETY

A Harper's Weekly *picture shows Whitney's cotton gin in operation. Before the gin, slavery was on its last legs; then the invention of this one simple mechanical gadget raised the price of a strong slave from $500 to $1,500. "It was the cotton interest," said Daniel Webster in 1850, "that gave a new desire to promote slavery, to spread it, and to use its labor."*

The idea of interchangeable parts, made by such power-driven tools as this drill press, was not original with Whitney. In 1785 Jefferson visited a French inventor who was working on that principle; but Whitney was the first to translate a theory into a production system. He fulfilled his first gun contract at the New Haven, Connecticut, works below.

MABEL BRADY GARVAN COLLECTION, YALE UNIVERSITY ART GALLERY

BETTMANN ARCHIVE

CONNECTICUT STATE LIBRARY

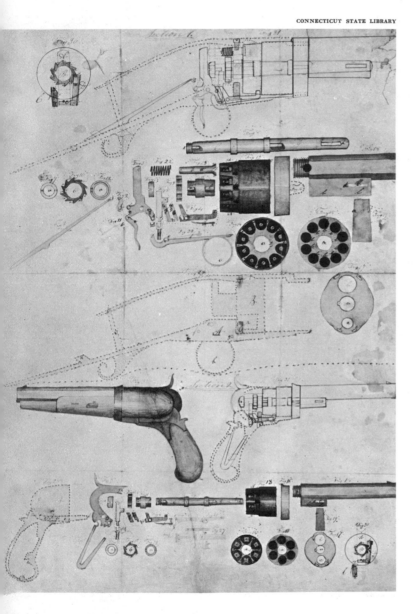

AMON G. CARTER FOUNDATION

*Samuel Colt was portrayed (above, right) holding his cele-
brated revolver, sometimes called Colt's Patent Pacifier, or,
more simply, The Difference. This weapon tamed the Plains.*

*As Samuel Colt originally envisioned his repeating pistol in
the patent drawing above, it was to have chambers for ten
cartridges. Other changes, including raising the caliber from
.34 to .44, were suggested by a Texas Ranger, Sam Walker.*

*Colt's revolver, which gave the white man a better-than-even
break against Indians, came into its own in Texas. The detail at right, from a Remington painting, shows it in action.*

286

Sam Colt's Equalizer

As Whitney's muskets led to mass production, Samuel Colt's six-shooter led to the assembly line. There was always some small boy in Colt—the older he grew, the more he wanted to play with firecrackers. After one explosive experiment had blown the windows out of his schoolroom, he was shipped to sea to keep him out of trouble. When he returned, he had with him the idea for a gun whose bullet chambers would spin into line with a fixed barrel. His father refused him the money to make a revolver from his model, so Colt went into business as "Dr. Coult of New York, London and Calcutta," demonstrator of laughing gas. He toured his attraction from Boston to Cincinnati to New Orleans and with the proceeds hired a mechanic to make him two revolvers. They were splendidly murderous. Colt took out patents and opened a factory in New Jersey.

"The first workman," he said, "would receive two or three . . . important parts and would affix them together and pass them on to the next who would add a part and pass the growing article to another who would do the same . . . until the complete arm is put together." The assembly line had been born.

The world beat no path to Colt's doorway. His gun was expensive, and the Army rejected it as "too complicated." Only in Texas, where shooting was a serious business, was Colt's revolver appreciated. The Texas Rangers ordered a hundred—not enough to keep Colt's factory from closing down.

Colt, however, went on playing with grown-up firecrackers. With some help from the inventive Samuel F. B. Morse, he designed an underwater mine that exploded on electrical impulse sent from shore by insulated cable. A vast throng gathered at Coney Island to watch him blow up an obsolete gunboat, and Colt gradually acquired some fame. Then suddenly, unexpectedly, he was rich. The Mexican War had begun, and General Zachary Taylor had found that no Texan would use any gun but Colt's. He ordered a thousand for immediate delivery. Colt let subcontracts with other manufacturers to fill the order, and before he could even build his new factory at Hartford he was receiving orders from all over the world.

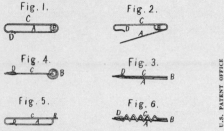

Walter Hunt

By all odds the most versatile of America's tinkering geniuses was the astonishing Walter Hunt, a New York Quaker who invented literally dozens of useful gadgets, some of them still in everyday use. The doors of the U.S. Patent Office were opened in 1790. Hunt was born six years later in upstate New York, and it was as well the Patent Office had a head start.

In 1826 Hunt invented a machine that revolutionized the flax-spinning industry. This was followed by a fire-alarm system, a knife sharpener (unimproved in five generations), a globe caster for chairs, a coal stove, a logging saw (awarded a diploma by the American Institute of Science), a flexible spring for use in belts and suspenders, an ice boat, several improvements in the manufacture of nails, three different types of inkwell, a fountain pen, many improvements in the mechanism of the repeating gun and its cartridges (ironically, since he was a Quaker, these were his most profitable inventions), the paper collar, a reversible metallic heel, and even an "Antipodean Apparatus"—a pair of shoes with suction cups for circus performers or anyone else zany enough to walk up walls and across ceilings upside down.

Hunt's sewing machine anticipated Elias Howe's by thirteen years, but he never applied for a patent. His daughter vetoed it because "such a machine . . . would be injurious to the interests of hand-sewers."

His greatest triumph came in 1849. Hunt owed a man $15. To pay him, within three hours he got an idea, made a model, and sold it for $400. It was the safety pin.

Yankee Clockmakers and Sam Slick

There were clockmakers all over colonial America, but their products—usually the tall-case or grandfather clocks—were expensive. By 1800 the clock business was at low ebb. Then a Connecticut Yankee, Eli Terry, invented the techniques that put clocks into mass production and brought the price within every family's reach.

Terry made his first clock in 1792, when he was twenty. In those days a craftsman did well to turn out one clock a month, but Terry was impatient. He began to use water power for his machinery, and by 1805 he was ready to make clocks two or three dozen at a time. Since clock movements, whether of brass or wood, had to be made by hand, his scheme was ridiculed; but Terry hired a pair of master craftsmen, Seth Thomas and Silas Hoadley, and turned out wooden-movement, tall-case clocks in batches of 500. In 1807 he contracted to make 4,000 clocks and finished the job in three years.

Terry, though successful and well-to-do, was still not satisfied. He sold his factory to Hoadley and Thomas, and in a small workshop began tinkering with designs for new cases and movements. By 1814

he had his answer—a wooden-movement shelf clock to retail at the unprecedented price of $15—and two years later he patented his design. Framed in a handsome pillar-and-scroll case, the new Terry clock revolutionized the whole business. Every Connecticut handyman blithely pirated the Terry patent, and clocks began streaming out of the Nutmeg State by the thousands.

The infant industry at once required a ready-made distribution system, and there it was—in the form of the peddler. He had already won notoriety all over the country for his unexampled skill at chaffering, for his Yankee wit, and his ways with the farmer's daughter. His goods—buttons and calicoes, needles and pins, pots and pans, ribbons and nails—he offered at a markup of 1,000 per cent, knowing that he could always clinch a sale by generously shaving his profit by half. The tall-case clock was too cumbersome by far for the average peddler, but shelf clocks were ideal. The happy union between clockmaker and peddler produced one of the most enduring figures of nineteenth-century folklore—Sam Slick of Pumpkin Crick.

A master clockmaker's skill is evident in the works of the 30-day model by Eli Terry, shown at right. Most of the movement was machined from hard wood.

Glib, nattily dressed Yankee peddlers like the one in the anonymous painting at left provided rural America with everything from clocks to candlesticks.

INTERNATIONAL BUSINESS MACHINE CORP.

COOPER UNION

Peter Cooper, in an unfinished portrait by John A. Calyo.

Hell-in-Harness

It was clear by 1830 that the steam engine—so long a symbol of folly—was here to stay and that it might even replace the horse. In that year, for the first time in America, steam pulled passengers along a railroad.

The sudden interest in railroads was aroused in part by concern over the country's new canals, in part by the booster spirit; but whatever the motive, old John Stevens of Hoboken could watch the burgeoning railroad companies with grim satisfaction. Five years before, to prove the feasibility of a steam locomotive, he had run a toy engine over a circular track laid down on his own lawn. In 1829 Horatio Allen brought back from England the *Stourbridge Lion,* a seven-ton locomotive that unfortunately proved too heavy for American roadbeds. But in August, 1830, Peter Cooper drove his *Tom Thumb* from Baltimore to Ellicott's Mills— thirteen miles in 72 minutes and back again in 57— lugging three dozen passengers in a car behind him. The railroad had arrived.

Actually, the *Tom Thumb* was less a locomotive than an improvised makeshift put together by Cooper to prove to directors of the Baltimore & Ohio that their tracks were not too sharply curved for steam engines. Cooper was an inveterate tinkerer with a dozen inventions, including a rotary steam engine, to his credit. He simply stuck his engine on a platform, attached it to a boiler with two musket barrels, contrived a blowing apparatus to keep a head of steam, and away he went.

Horatio Allen soon after designed an engine, *The Best Friend of Charleston,* for the South Carolina Canal and Railway Company; and a later Allen locomotive, the *South Carolina,* was mounted on two pivoted trucks so that it could round a sharp curve. Other engineers—notably John B. Jervis and Ross Winans—set their locomotives on rotating trucks. In 1836 Henry Campbell patented the engine with two pairs of driving wheels that came to be known as the "American type"—bigger and more powerful than any others. This was the iron horse with the snort like thunder that was to stir the imaginations of Americans for three generations. "Hell-in-Harness," it was called, and its whistle soon echoed across the land.

BROWN, *History of the First Locomotives in America*, 1874

STEVENS INSTITUTE

John Stevens' son Robert (right) cut his engineering teeth on steamboats, then turned to railroads. He improved locomotives, invented the T-rail and the track-laying method that became standard, but was too busy to take out patents. *Above*, The Best Friend of Charleston. One day its fireman, vexed with the hiss of escaping steam, squelched the safety valve and became the first casualty of American railroading.

The gaudy creature below, called the Tiger, was built in 1856 by Matthias Baldwin, a Philadelphia jeweler who switched to locomotives in the early 1830's. One of his 1836 engines, the Pioneer, was still able to roll in 1949.

COVERDALE & COLPITTS COLLECTION

ENGINES OF THIS PLAN WEIGHING FROM 37000 TO 64000 LBS.

M. W. BALDWIN & CO. LOCOMOTIVE BUILDERS,
PHILADELPHIA.

Golden Day
of the Iron Horse

E. L. Henry painted "The 9:45 a.m. Accommodation, Stratford, Connecticut," in 1867. Two years later, on May 10, 1869, a golden spike was driven into the rails at Promontory, Utah, celebrating the junction of the Central Pacific and the

METROPOLITAN MUSEUM OF ART

Union Pacific by which railroad travel from coast to coast was consummated. As a result, Americans all over the continent could join in the celebration, once or twice a day, of their most important moment—when the train came in and that lordly man, the engineer, condescended to chat with loungers at the depot, giving them a hint of what life was like in the great world outside. Those were, as Thoreau wrote, "the epochs in the village day," when the atmosphere was "electrifying."

293

BOSTON ATHENAEUM LOAN, MUSEUM OF FINE ARTS; COURTESY *Time*

Pat Lyon, Innocent Blacksmith

When Patrick Lyon commissioned John Neagle to paint his portrait, he told the artist, with a fierce pride: "I wish you to understand clearly, Mr. Neagle, that I do not desire to be represented in the picture as a gentleman—to which character I have no pretension. I want you to paint me at work at my anvil, with my sleeves rolled up and a leather apron on."

Lyon was then, in 1825, a wealthy, solid citizen of Philadelphia, well-known as a designer and hydraulic engineer who had built some of America's best and earliest fire engines. He was also the city's foremost locksmith; yet he had reason to prefer the tools of his craft to the style of gentleman.

Twenty-eight years before, thieves had stolen

These paintings reveal the humble beginnings of two craftsmen who went on to bigger and better things. Lyon's portrait (left) includes the Walnut Street jail, a bitter symbolic reminder. In the California wheel shop below, the man at left is J. M. Studebaker, who made his stake in the West before coming back to the family carriage business in Indiana.

$163,000 from the Bank of Pennsylvania, the locks of which Lyon had just repaired. At the time, Lyon was in Delaware, where he had gone to escape an epidemic of yellow fever, but he was accused of the theft by the bank's officers. He returned at once to confront those gentlemen with his positive alibi, but nonetheless he was jailed. Even when the thief was caught and had confessed, Lyon was held in jail as an accomplice. After three months he was finally released in $2,000 bail, but for seven years he suffered disgrace and poverty. Then his lawyer brought an unprecedented action—suit for malicious prosecution. A bitter trial resulted in a victory for Lyon.

It was a celebrated cause in its day. The story of Pat Lyon the Innocent Blacksmith found its way into children's books as a moral tale of virtue triumphant; but even though Lyon went on to a successful career and retired a well-to-do man, he never forgot that he had been jailed unjustly because one class—gentlemen—mistrusted another class—workmen.

COLLECTION OF EDGAR WILLIAM AND BERNICE CHRYSLER GARBISCH ; COURTESY *Life*

ADDISON GALLERY OF AMERICAN ART

Young Samuel Finley Breese Morse, seen above in a self-portrait, got the idea for the picture within a picture at right while strolling through the Louvre with his friend James Fenimore Cooper. In his painting of the famous Salon Carré he included the Mona Lisa (bottom center), Titian's "The Entombment" above it, Raphael's "Belle Jardinière," and the canvases of Claude, Poussin, Van Dyck, and other great masters which his fellow Americans had often heard about but seldom seen.

Samuel F. B. Morse and the Amazing Lightning Wire

It was characteristic of the young America that a man who had worked hard to learn the disciplines of art should believe that he could, in a trice, turn to science and conceive, develop, and perfect a complicated electrical invention. After all, had not Robert Fulton been first a painter and then an inventor? His example was before all American youth. Fulton's *Clermont* had steamed up the Hudson to Albany the same year that Samuel F. B. Morse entered Yale, and it was natural for

SYRACUSE UNIVERSITY

Morse to want to do what Fulton had accomplished.

    Morse was a successful painter when in 1832 he boarded a packet to sail home from France. The trip lasted a month, long enough to deflect him from art to science. What influenced him was a chat with a fellow passenger about electromagnetism. Michael Faraday's papers had been published earlier that year, and his experiment demonstrating how electric currents could be induced by a magnetic pole had fired the imagination of scientists everywhere. To Morse, who knew nothing of scientific theory, the conversation nevertheless suggested that if sparks could be drawn from a magnet, they could be arranged in a code and so transmit messages over a wire.

    Off and on during the next few years he tinkered with his notion, wholly ignorant of the fact that Joseph Henry had already solved the problem theoretically and that in Europe at least three men were ahead of him in practical development. In

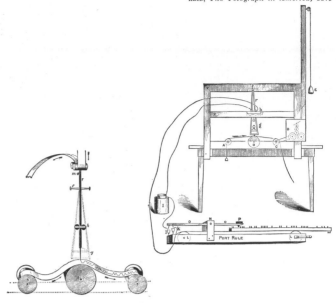

Morse's first telegraph machine (above, right) was far too complex. His receiver (detail above, left) was an electromagnet that caused a pencil to mark a tape with his early code, so intricate that no operator could memorize it.

The first news bulletins of national interest to be sent over Morse's Lightning Wire were Mexican War dispatches (left). By 1848 the Associated Press had its own wire service.

Alfred Vail (below), Morse's assistant for ten years, convinced Morse to discard his early, cumbersome transmission system for a signal key and a simple code. Vail profited but little from this and other improvements and died poor.

This photograph of Joseph Henry (below) was taken by Mathew Brady when the American physicist was beginning to be honored as he should have been years before. But he was dead before science named the unit of inductance for him.

U.S. NATIONAL MUSEUM

COLLECTION OF FREDERICK HILL MESERVE

1832 Morse was appointed Professor of Arts on the faculty of New York University. Here, after taking a few lessons in the rudiments of electromagnetism from an associate in the chemistry department, Morse was able in 1837 to send a message over 1,700 feet of wire.

This success interested a prosperous ironmaster, Stephen Vail, who offered Morse capital if he would agree to engage Vail's son Alfred as his assistant. His lucky star was now in the ascendant, for Morse could not have found a better helper. Vail would, in the course of time, simplify both Morse's code and Morse's telegraph machine—all in Morse's name; but first there was the far more important problem of how to send electrical impulses over distances measured in miles, not in feet. And for help in the solution Morse traveled to Princeton to get advice from Joseph Henry.

Henry was a physicist of extraordinary talent who had experimentally proved the theory of electromagnetic induction some months earlier than Faraday. By 1831 he had built the first electric motor and had invented the electric relay, sending impulses through a mile of wire. But temperamentally he was, unlike most American inventors, a research scientist who cared little for the practical application of his deductions. Having solved a problem, he preferred not to exploit the solution but rather to grapple with another problem. Cheerfully he explained to Morse how his relay system could send impulses for thousands of miles without loss of strength in the signal. Morse took the advice.

Now he needed money. Although Congress had years before promised $30,000 for a telegraph system that would work over 1,000 miles, not until 1843 was a grant given to finance his demonstration. The test was run between Baltimore and Washington after Ezra Cornell, the construction engineer, had strung wire from trees and poles for the forty miles, using broken bottle tops for insulators. After Morse sent the first celebrated message— "What hath God wrought?"—from the Supreme Court room in the Capitol to Vail in Baltimore, the telegraph later carried news from the Whig nominating convention.

Despite tepid interest in Washington, what was called the Lightning Wire caught on soon enough. Newspapers used it for faster news service, railroads for dispatching, and soon the promoters moved in, stringing lines all over the country.

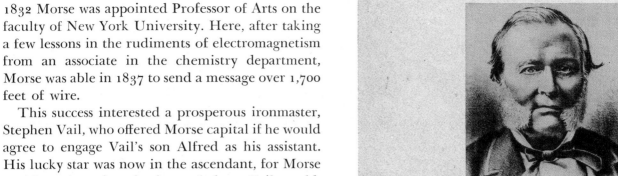

U.S. STEEL CORPORATION

Joseph Glidden

As more and more farmers fanned out across the prairies, a commonplace object—the fence —took on more and more importance. How to make cheap and efficient fences? Board blew down or burned; there was little stone. Wire, at first scarce and costly, gradually came into general use, but the trouble was that cattle gratefully rubbed against it and pushed it down. By 1867 farmers were experimenting with all sorts of prickers, spurs, and thorns. Although some of these efforts were patented, none ever went into production.

Then in 1873 at a county fair in De Kalb, Illinois, three men—Joseph F. Glidden, Jacob Haish, and Isaac Ellwood—thoughtfully eyed one of the experimental fences. Each of the three had an idea, but Glidden's was the best and the quickest to bear fruit. In October he applied for a patent on barbed wire.

Glidden was less an inventor than an inspired tinkerer. He made his barbed wire by coiling the barbs around a strand of wire with the help of an old coffee mill, winding that strand and another between a tree and the shaft of a grindstone, then twisting the two strands together by cranking the grindstone.

For $265 Glidden sold a half interest in his invention to Ellwood, owner of a De Kalb hardware store. In 1876 he sold the other half to an eastern manufacturer for $60,000 plus a royalty of 1/4¢ per pound of barbed wire made under his patent. Meantime Haish had independently designed his rival S barb. Despite bitter litigation, however, Glidden's barbed wire was in 1892 awarded what amounted to a monopoly by the U.S. Supreme Court.

299

A Revolution in Agriculture

To tame the wild prairies and make them fruitful, two things were chiefly needed: a mechanical reaper that would gather a crop in fast and a good plow that would cut a straight furrow quickly. The first appeared in 1834, the second in 1838. There was the usual time lag while folks tried to catch up with the idea that what they needed lay ready to hand, but by 1850 these two homely American inventions had wrought a revolution that transformed the western states into the richest granary in the world.

The new plow was conceived by a young Illinois blacksmith, John Deere. Wood and iron plows had, of course, been in use in America for generations before Deere came along, but his improvement was of crucial importance. The remarkably rich soil of the prairies stuck to the blade of an iron plow like glue. In vain farmers tried to lick the problem by changing the shape of the iron blade; the rich loam still stuck.

Then one day in 1837 Deere's eye was caught by the glint from the smooth, gleaming surface of a circular steel saw. Maybe, he thought, the answer lay not in the shape of the plow but in the metal of which it was made. So simple, yet when he demonstrated his new steel plow, from which the soil fell cleanly away, furrow after furrow, his witnesses were skeptical. Finally, after Deere had priced his plows as low as $10 apiece, he acquired enough orders to warrant opening a factory in Moline; and soon his plow was the most sought-after farm implement in the Midwest.

Meantime, half a continent away in the Shenandoah Valley of Virginia, a young Scotch-Irishman

Years after the event, an artist recorded his own idea of the scene that day in 1831, near Steele's Tavern in Virginia's Shenandoah Valley, when McCormick (inset, upper right) successfully tested his reaping machine. McCormick's patent for "the full and exclusive right" to his invention cost him $30.

CHICAGO HISTORICAL SOCIETY

named Cyrus McCormick had been busying himself with the problem of a mechanical reaper. It was not a new idea. His father had tried to make one, and so had a score of other men. The difference was that Cyrus McCormick's reaper worked better. He was only 22 when, in 1831, he cut six acres of grain in a meadow near Steele's Tavern in one day. But his machine was imperfect, and the neighbors were unimpressed.

McCormick took out two patents, but laid his dream aside since he was too busy with a 200-acre farm and a profitable iron foundry. Then the Panic of 1837 changed his course. When he found himself bankrupt and deep in debt, he turned to the reaper to salvage his fortune.

He improved his machine, but in those lean days precious few farmers had the dollars to buy such a luxury. Two machines sold in 1841, seven in 1842, while McCormick squirmed impatiently. At night he could scarcely sleep for his vision of something "so enormous that it seemed like a dream—like dwelling in the clouds—so remote, so unattainable, so exalted."

It was the order of a machine from Illinois that decided him. With $300 pinned in his pocket, he rode west at the age of 36, and as soon as he saw the rolling, limitless prairies he knew he had found the land where his machine would prosper. By 1847 he had hit upon a swampy, raw, ugly little town called Chicago for the site of his factory and within a few short years was on his fabulous way.

One thousand reapers were built and sold in 1851; six years later, 23,000 reapers, at a profit of better than $1,000,000. The only fly in his delectable ointment was the fact that other men were trying to horn in on his profits, claiming they had invented different, newer, or better reapers. Never was an inventor so litigious as McCormick. In 1858 he spent more on lawsuits than he collected in royalties, but, as implacable as the Grim Reaper himself, McCormick cut his competitors down. When his factory went up in smoke in the great Chicago fire of 1871, it failed to discourage him. He rebuilt it immediately and went right back to work at the age of 62.

Before McCormick, America had imported grain. In his lifetime the balance swung—and violently. Wheat filled the bottoms of American freighters bound for every port in the world. Farms had found machines.

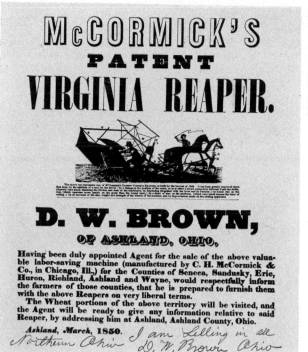

INTERNATIONAL HARVESTER CO.

McCormick had 19 assembly plants for his reapers. The poster above, advertising such a concern, bears a handwritten comment by the enthusiastic distributor. Below, an announcement of John Deere's plow exudes quiet confidence.

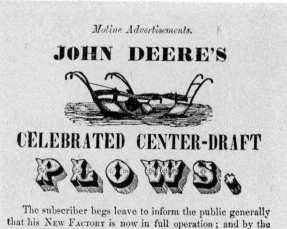

JOHN DEERE CO.

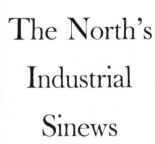

PUTNAM COUNTY HISTORICAL SOCIETY; COURTESY *Life*

The North's
Industrial
Sinews

John Ferguson Weir painted this picture of the West Point foundry in 1865. Here 3,000 cannon and 1,600,000 projectiles were manufactured for use in the Civil War. Here were produced Gouverneur Kemble's cast-iron cannon, and rifled artillery designed by John Dahlgren and Robert Parrott. In the painting a cannon is cast while Kemble, at right, watches.

303

WESTERN UNION TELEGRAPH CO. LIBRARY

The Great Eastern, *five times as big as any other ship in the world, was used to lay the transatlantic cable. Robert Dudley painted her leaving Ireland in 1865. Below, workmen splice the cable after a break.*

METROPOLITAN MUSEUM OF ART LOAN, SMITHSONIAN INSTITUTION

Spanning the Atlantic

CHICAGO HISTORICAL SOCIETY

Having made a fortune at the age of 33, Cyrus W. Field retired to travel and enjoy himself. Two years later, when a man called on him to raise money for a telegraph wire across Newfoundland, Field was noncommittal. Why should he get involved? Later, glancing idly at a map, it occurred to him that the Newfoundland telegraph might become a bridge in a far more important line. Why not a transatlantic cable?

Next day he sent off letters to Samuel F. B. Morse and to Lieutenant Matthew Fontaine Maury of the U.S. Navy. Morse, who had successfully tested submarine telegraph cable in New York harbor ten years before, heartily approved. Maury, the world's foremost oceanographer, wrote Field that he had himself just informed the secretary of the navy that the ocean floor in the North Atlantic was entirely suitable for an underwater cable.

Thus powerfully encouraged, Field emerged from retirement to become an international promoter. The year was 1854. After talking with his next-door neighbor Peter Cooper and a few other venturesome rich men, Field was sanguine enough to believe the cable could be laid in three years. In fact it took twelve and entailed protracted lobbying to get the backing of two governments and the co-operation of two navies, an apparently endless chain of calamitous disappointments, the formation of a new company every time disaster ruined its predecessor, and the incessant raising of money— $9,000,000 before he was done—even throughout the Civil War.

A cable was laid in 1858 amid an Anglo-American chorus of huzzahs, but it fizzled due to faulty insulation. Field was the only American among 500 Britishers (including the brilliant physicist William Thomson, later Lord Kelvin) when a second cable was laid in 1865. It snapped in mid-ocean. Finally, in July, 1866, the cable's end was successfully delivered to Heart's Content, Newfoundland. Field's dream was realized: America and Europe were linked together by a telegraphic marvel.

Cyrus Field was, as this picture by Mathew Brady suggests, a sensitive, intense visionary. He was also sufficiently practical to put a telegraphic cable across the Atlantic Ocean.

BROWN BROTHERS

Isaac Singer

Machines to Lighten Woman's Burden

Howe's sewing machine

In the summer of 1850 a massive, lusty man named Isaac Singer arrived in Boston to demonstrate a machine he had designed for carving wood-block type. It was not his first invention; ten years earlier he had patented a machine for drilling rock and sold his rights in it for $2,000. But despite his mechanical talent Singer was no dedicated inventor. Oddly, he preferred the life of an actor; yet that life, while glamorous, was uncertain, and Singer needed money. "I don't care a damn for the invention," he said. "The dimes are what I am after."

In Boston Singer first saw a sewing machine, which, like all the models of that time, was sadly defective. By 1850 patents had been granted to a dozen American inventors of mechanical sewing devices, of which the most important went to Elias Howe, Jr., in 1846 for his lock-stitch machine with eye-pointed needle and shuttle. Although Howe's

Howe's lonely experiments led to . . .

. . . public proof, where he excelled . . .

. . . to London, where his dreams burst.

PARTON, *History of the Sewing Machine*, 1867

He borrowed money to get home, where

. . . having sued all his competitors . . .

. . . at length he found himself rich.

machine was the best, it could sew only eighteen stitches before the cloth had to be removed for a fresh start. If Singer could design a better sewing machine, he was told, he would make more dimes in a year than he could in fifty with his type-carving device. At once he set to work, and in eleven days he had developed the first efficient sewing machine. The first of the world's important household appliances had been born.

Meantime Howe had suffered one bitter setback after another. His experiments had begun in 1843, when he was supporting a wife and three children on a wage of $9 a week. By 1845 he had built a machine which at a public demonstration in Boston outsewed five expert seamstresses; yet he sold no machines. In 1847, lured by the promises of an English manufacturer, Howe took his family to London. When the promises were broken, Howe, penniless, had to borrow money to ship his family home and pawn his machine to buy his own passage. He landed in New York in 1849, flat broke. Before long he learned that his wife was dying of tuberculosis in Cambridge and, in deep despair, he borrowed money to reach her before she died. In this black mood he first heard of Singer's success. After all his efforts, was his patent not worth something? Oppressed by his debts, he called on Singer and offered to sell his American rights in the patent for $2,000. Singer, a forthright man, answered by ordering Howe to clear out or be kicked out. This was the opening salvo in what was hailed by the press as "the great sewing machine war."

Howe first brought suit against Singer for infringement of patent, demanding $25,000. Moreover, once Singer had demonstrated that the machine could be made practical, a dozen manufacturers had appeared—so Howe sued all these as well. By 1854, having won a series of minor skirmishes against lesser manufacturers, Howe was able to force I. M. Singer & Co. to pay him $28,000 and a royalty of $10 on every machine sold thereafter.

By 1856 peace was declared. A patent pool was organized, the model for similar arrangements later to be made in the automotive, aircraft, movie, and radio industries, by which all manufacturers agreed to pay license fees of $5 to Singer and Howe alike. All the principals got rich, thanks chiefly to the acumen of Singer's partner, Edward Clark, the first man to apply installment buying, the trade-in, and advertising to sell a product on a nationwide basis.

REMINGTON RAND CORP.

Christopher Sholes

"All my life," said Christopher Latham Sholes to a friend when he was nearly sixty, "I have been trying to escape becoming a millionaire, and I think I have succeeded admirably." He was a frail man with a wistful disposition and a tendency to tuberculosis, and he dreamed of a Utopia where there would be no greed, no poverty, but only love. Oddly enough, this impractical eccentric invented the first practical typewriter. True to his unworldly ambition, he sold the rights to his invention to a pair of fast-talking promoters for about $12,000.

Sholes was not the first to contrive a machine that would write; at least fifty men had done so before him. Nor did he do the job unaided; two others, Carlos Glidden and Samuel Soulé, were in it with him. But Sholes was chiefly responsible, and the machine he built (shown above, operated by his daughter) was the first that would typewrite with reasonable accuracy, speed, and neatness.

It originated in a small machine shop on the outskirts of Milwaukee. Early in 1867 Sholes, then 48, a printer, journalist, and sometime politician, was there working with Soulé, a professional machinist, on a device that would number serially the blank pages of a book. Glidden was fussing with an idea for a mechanical spader that would, he hoped, replace the plow. One day he looked over Sholes' shoulder and said, "Why not make a machine that will write letters and not numbers only?" Some months later they had a model which was efficient enough to make a reporter say, "By jingo! It prints the lingo!"

Tableau of Inventors

A gallery of American inventors, painted c. 1860 by Schussele, shows Goodyear seated at left of the table and Morse seated at right. Peter Cooper leans over Goodyear's shoulder, and

at Goodyear's other side stands Cyrus McCormick. Elias Howe is seated at far right. To the right of the pillar stands John Ericsson, who designed the ironclad Monitor; at the left of the pillar is Joseph Henry, who anticipated Michael Faraday's discovery of induction. Over them all broods benign Benjamin Franklin, archetype of American inventors.

MELLON COLLECTION, NATIONAL GALLERY OF ART

CONQUEST OF A CONTINENT

When Richard Harding Davis went west about 1890 to inspect the hostile Indians, the desperadoes, the cattle rustlers, and the cowpunchers who so frequently shot up the county seats, what he found was a land more peaceful than Broadway. Women in Wichita wore the newest Parisian fashions and in Denver criticized the latest Howells novel. The only Wyoming bandits were lightning-rod agents. Most of the ranches that survived seemed to be owned by wealthy easterners or Britons and run on strict business principles. Some cowboys he met at a way station wanted to know the score of the Harvard-Yale game. Nearly everywhere the trunk-line railroads, advertising cheap land to Europeans, were bringing in settlers. When Davis crossed the King ranch in Texas, he felt his train slowing down. A gang of train robbers, or marauding savages? No, the engineer was worried lest he injure a valuable Hereford bull, and was running slow until he passed the animal.

The West had been really wild in 1865. In that year Leland Stanford, Collis Huntington, and their associates built another twenty miles of the Central Pacific into the forbidding reaches of the high Sierras. Grenville M. Dodge, skirmishing with Crow Indians in the Wyoming Black Hills, discovered a pass through which he later laid the Union Pacific track. New gold strikes in Virginia City made fresh "kings of the Comstock"; vigilantes in Montana still kept a wary eye on badmen; and Union and Confederate veterans began using Spencer repeaters to reduce the vast buffalo herds on the plains. Texas cattlemen, with five million longhorns on their hands, were planning the first "long drive" of massed beeves to the railheads of the Missouri Pacific. But only 25 years later the West was a tamed land, riveted down by four transcontinental railways (with James J. Hill soon to complete the fifth), dozens of cities, and a busy agricultural economy.

A series of frontiers, indeed, magically appeared in this quarter-century only to vanish still more magically, and the whole process could be summed up as the conquest of pioneer individualism by well-organized enterprise. The mining frontier, for example, brought hundreds, even thousands, of prospectors to any new strike. They wielded picks, sank their sluice boxes, panned the streams, and exhausted the surface dust and nuggets. With them came a rush of gamblers, saloonkeepers, owners of dance halls and billiard parlors, and madams with flocks of prostitutes. But when the surface wealth evaporated, powerful corporations moved in, with mining engineers trained at Freiberg or Columbia, batteries of stamps to crush the ore, and chemists versed in the best methods of extracting gold, silver, and lead. The rush into the Black Hills of Dakota in 1875–76, which brought on the Sioux War and the Custer massacre and which gave American legend such delightful properties as the Deadwood Stage, Calamity Jane, and the final appearance of Wild Bill Hickok—this was the last stand of the mining frontier before capitalism took over.

The earlier rushes to such Montana towns as Helena, Bannack, and Virginia City had been of epic proportions, but in the end Montana became the

Grenville M. Dodge, builder of the Union Pacific Railroad.

most completely corporation-controlled section of the United States.

Much the same process overtook the cattlemen's frontier. When from 1869 to 1871 the "long drive" put 1,500,000 cattle into the Abilene yards, many ranchers thought the business would last forever. Multitudes of people still believed that the upper plains were a semi-desert, where agriculture and stock-growing could never thrive. The Texans in particular took a lordly view, and Stuart Henry quotes a typical southwestern cattleman: "This ain't no country fer little two-by-four farmers. The homestead plan the guv'ment is shufflin the deck fer is the biggest skin game goin . . . The big thing about the plains is that you don't have to feed stock. It can rustle fer itself. You can yoke it up with stepmaw Nature an' the pair, if they wants to, can make the dollars crawl into yer jeans."

But more intensive organization for higher production gained the day. When men found that cattle could winter on the northern plains, eating wind-cleared buffalo grass in all but the worst seasons, a more systematic ranching arose—the type that Theodore Roosevelt practiced in the Bad Lands. Fine breeds, the Durham, Aberdeen Angus, and Hereford, supplanted the uneconomic longhorn. On the heels of these ranchers came farmers and small stockmen, encouraged by railroads which wanted their richer freight and manufacturers who supplied them with barbed wire, windmills, gang plows, and big combine harvesters.

Drawn by the immemorial lure of low-cost land, free institutions, and a better future for their children, they came in tens of thousands. Nesters building sod cabins roofed with poles, loose earth, and grass took more and more of the best lands; small stockmen fenced in the streams. The farmers indeed overdid their westward thrust, plowing up much land in western Kansas and Nebraska that was unsuited for tillage. Their pressure coincided with a series of bad years for the ranchmen, who suffered from overcrowding of the range, a worldwide drop in meat prices, restrictive federal laws, and some bitter winters. After the ranchers retreated to remote areas, the Great Plains produced far more meat than before and general crops as well. Bonanza wheat farming became big business. Millions of sturdy, independent people filled the region so lately roamed by millions of buffalo.

Each successive frontier of the last Far West had its heroes. The leaders in the final Indian wars numbered truly admirable figures on both sides: the modest, fearless George Crook, for example, who pacified the Apaches by kindness instead of cruelty, and the equally humane and statesmanlike Chief Joseph of the Nez Percés, whose fighting march of a thousand miles to take his people to safety in Canada barely failed of success. Among the railroad builders were men like Cyrus K. Holliday of Topeka, whose dream of a railway following the old Santa Fe Trail from the Missouri to the far Southwest was realized by constructive talent, industry, and enthusiasm of a rare order. This was the road which brought in over 10,000 Mennonites suffering from imperial tyranny in Russia. The mining frontier had many picturesque figures, such as the Colorado Croesus Horace A. W. Tabor, who built a famous opera house in Leadville and entertained General Grant in that richest of silver towns. It had heroes, too—none finer than Adolph Sutro, who drove a $6,500,000 tunnel into the Comstock Lode, opened a new era in mining, fought Collis P. Huntington's railroad monopoly, and eventually became mayor of San Francisco.

The long cattle trail and roundup produced so heroic a breed that the cowboy forever rides on in fiction, motion picture, and television. The heroic sheriffs and town marshals exemplified by Thomas J. Smith of Abilene, whose murder in 1896 closed a career of dauntless courage, have the same undying appeal. And there were the bold city builders like General William J. Palmer, to whom Colorado Springs, Canon City, and Pueblo are monuments.

But in the end the real hero of the last phase of the old West was the same pioneer figure as in every previous stage of American growth from Jamestown and Plymouth onward—the farmer. His problems were different when he crossed the Missouri, and he was much more the son of the Machine Age and the Railroad Age; but he had the traditional qualities of the self-reliant, liberty-loving backwoodsman. He tilled his 160 or 240 acres in resolute defiance of drought, tornadoes, and grasshoppers; he looked to his country ministers, schoolteachers, and editors for guidance; he took part in local government through the town meeting and county board of supervisors.

These men were as sternly attached to democracy as their fathers had been in the days of Jackson and Lincoln, but in defending it they had to face some quite new enemies. One special problem of the last Far West was lawlessness. Outlaws had been numerous enough along every frontier—on the Holston and along the Mississippi, for example—but they really infested the mining camps and range country of the Far West. The reasons for this are complex. Unquestionably the Kansas fighting in the 1850's, the Civil War in general, and the guerrilla phases of that war in particular had made human life seem cheap. But the main roots of the lawlessness lie deeper—in the distance of the Far West from old established centers of law and order; in the improved transport that gave every thug and cutthroat of New York, Paris, London, Naples, Mexico City, and Sydney cheap, easy transit to San Francisco; in the recklessness and the get-rich-quick mania that the speculative nature of prospecting and ranching created; and in the fact that men became accustomed to living violently in a land of Indians, grizzlies, and rattlesnakes.

Violence by the lawless begat violence by the law-abiding. The Committee of Vigilance in San Francisco offers the classic instance of a community arming itself against rampant robbery and murder. The battles of cattlemen against sheepherders, of ranchers against rustlers, of rival factions over the choice of county seats, and of jealous range groups in the Lincoln County War, which involved the New York killer Billy the Kid, left a heavy stain on the post-bellum history of the West. In the end, vigilante activity darkened rather than lightened that stain. Emerson Hough makes the shocking statement that in the decade 1876–86 the cattle-range vigilantes killed more men without process of law than were legally executed in the entire United States during the next thirty years.

Much larger problems of democracy, however, had to be faced. At the same time that the land frontier was coming to an end, when population was massing in large cities, and industry and capital were concentrating in more powerful units, historian Frederick Jackson Turner noted that "the Western pioneers took alarm for their ideals of democracy." Historically, these westerners had mistrusted government as an entity outside themselves. But now, as the conquest of the continent neared completion, they began to demand that government become a direct agency of the people—not only for their protection, but for the shaping of their destiny.

The ideas of the men and women who had opened the West now began to play an increasingly important role in the democracy which was the heritage of every American. Before the nineteenth century was done, the wave of reform which took shape in the last frontier would be felt across the land.

ALLAN NEVINS

AMERICAN ANTIQUARIAN SOCIETY

Butterfield's Stage
and the
Pony Express

News announcement about the Pony Express.

With the opening of the West, the nation faced the pressing need of long-range transportation and communication facilities. Pioneers clamored for goods and news from home, and easterners demanded a means of contact with the new areas. In 1858 the first stagecoach service started between the Mississippi and California. It was operated by John Butterfield, a New York expressman, and ran from St. Louis and Memphis across the Southwest to Los Angeles and San Francisco. Twice a week Butterfield's stages departed from each end of the line, carrying passengers at breakneck speed across nearly 2,800 miles of plains, mountains, and desert, taking 25 days for the trip.

A Pony Express to carry the mails even faster was launched in 1860 by William H. Russell—veteran operator of freight wagons on the plains. Russell bought 500 horses and set up 190 way stations at ten-mile intervals between St. Joseph, Missouri, and San Francisco. Racing in relays from station to station, the Pony Express riders, one of whom was young Buffalo Bill Cody, flew across the lonely land, braving floods, blizzards, and hostile Indians to deliver the mails from one end of the route to the other in ten days. The project proved more romantic than profitable, however, and was abandoned after the telegraph reached the Pacific in 1861.

Russell also established a stage line to California, using South Pass, but it too failed and was bought in 1862 by Ben Holladay, a more vigorous operator. Holladay expanded his lines and soon had a network of Concord coach routes covering the West. With most of the populated areas bound together, he sensed the coming of railroad competition and in 1866 sold out to Wells, Fargo for $2,500,000.

Concord coaches, two to a flatcar, were photographed in 1868 departing the Abbott-Downing Company's factory in Concord, New Hampshire, bound for Wells, Fargo in Omaha and Salt Lake City. This storied coach was the last word in western travel.

Journal of American History, 1917

BETTMANN ARCHIVE

CULVER SERVICE

William H. Russell   John Butterfield   Ben Holladay

The Deadwood Stage, with a guard riding shotgun on top, was one of the most famous lines using the Concord coach. Carrying gold and passengers, including Calamity Jane and Wild Bill Hickok, it ran the dangerous route between Cheyenne and the Black Hills mines. Paying fares sometimes participated in running gunfights with road agents and the marauding Sioux.

NATIONAL ARCHIVES

Asa Whitney's Transcontinental Dream

Asa Whitney was a New York dry goods merchant who looked so much like Napoleon Bonaparte that when he visited France on buying trips, people stopped and stared at him. Like the Emperor, he was also capable of dreaming great and daring dreams, but there the resemblance ended. Whitney was a businessman, and his visions were of peaceful and constructive projects that would advance commercial ties between countries and benefit mankind.

In 1840 he traveled to China as an agent for several New York firms. As he looked back from the great markets of Asia, eastward across the Pacific toward his own country, he began to think how advantageously a transcontinental railroad would link the Atlantic seaboard of the United States with the commerce of the Orient. Railroad building was scarcely a decade old, but there was no reason, he thought, why a line could not be pushed clear across the continent, over plains, Rockies, and deserts, to a port on the Pacific Ocean. The more he considered it, the more important it seemed, and when he re-

turned to the United States in 1844, he had a plan ready for Congress and his fellow Americans. Whitney was far in advance of his time, and the vigorous propaganda campaign he waged in behalf of his idea during the following eight years seemed fanatical and unrealistic to many of those who listened to him. Railroads were moving westward, following the pioneer settlements across the Ohio Valley toward Chicago and St. Louis, but they were expensive to build, and they advanced slowly. No line spanned the Mississippi until 1855, and it took another decade to reach the Missouri. Nevertheless, Whitney proposed a route from Lake Michigan to Oregon across land which the government could sell to settlers for funds with which to build the railroad.

The idea was sound in the East, where Congress granted large portions of the public domain to states which then gave the railroads millions of acres in alternate sections. The railroads then sold the land to settlers, using the proceeds for construction of new lines. But beyond the Missouri, Whitney's critics pointed out, his scheme would not work. The

When Congress selected a central route to the Pacific in 1862, surveying teams under General Grenville Dodge charted the path of the new Union Pacific Railroad. This contemporary lithograph shows one group at work in a mountain gap.

great, treeless plains, inhabited only by Indians, would not support settlers. Only an outright government subsidy could meet the prohibitive cost of constructing the line across the mountains.

Whitney argued back with pamphlets, letters to newspapers, speeches, and personal appeals to Congress. His eyes were fixed determinedly on the long-range benefits of the line, no matter what the immediate cost. Asia, he contended, was a huge market, scarcely touched. A transcontinental railroad would not only increase its accessibility to American businessmen, but would open a vast, new East-West trade that would extend from Europe across North America, with the United States as its booming, prosperous center.

In time, people began to question Whitney's motives, and soon many of them suspected that he was simply another land speculator. When Congress finally convinced him that it was not ready to underwrite his project, he made an unsuccessful attempt to interest England in building a line across Canada, then resignedly dropped the idea and retired to live the remainder of his life in the quiet seclusion of a country estate.

Yet in spite of his failure, his persistent campaign had made greater headway than he realized. With the admission of California and the spectacular increase of population on the west coast, many hard-headed businessmen and politicians began to agree that a transcontinental railroad was a necessity after all, and in 1853 Congress asked the Army to survey all possible routes for a line between the Mississippi and the Pacific.

The findings, presented in 1855, showed that four routes were practical—two in the north and two in the south. To appease the competing sectional interests, Stephen Douglas proposed that Congress aid three railroads: a Northern Pacific from Wisconsin to Puget Sound, a Central Pacific from Missouri or Iowa to San Francisco, and a Southern Pacific from Texas to southern California. The staggering costs of such a plan insured its defeat, yet northern and southern legislators were unable to agree on any one line. Although the transcontinental railroad was no more than the subject of partisan debate until the Civil War, the long, heated discussions increased the nation's awareness of the need for the project and settled the people's acceptance of it. With Secession, the northerners who were left in control of Congress quickly agreed on a central route, and Asa Whitney's dream of a railroad to the Pacific at last got underway.

Land sold by this ad of the Hannibal and St. Joe helped to finance its line from the Mississippi to the Missouri.

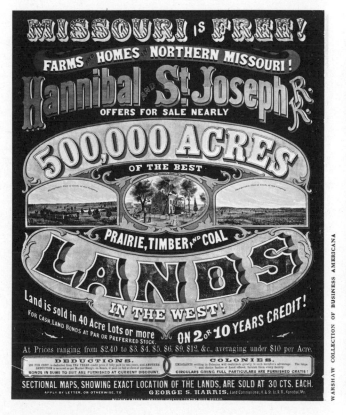

WARSHAW COLLECTION OF BUSINESS AMERICANA

Although he failed as its lobbyist, Connecticut-born Asa Whitney lived to see a railroad to the Pacific completed.

UNIVERSITY OF PENNSYLVANIA

The Red Man's Last Stand

Our chiefs are killed. . . . The old men are all dead. . . . It is cold and we have no blankets. The little children are freezing to death. My people . . . have no blankets, no food . . . Hear me, my chiefs. I am tired; my heart is sick and sad. From where the sun now stands, I will fight no more forever."

These touching and dignified words of surrender by Chief Joseph of the Nez Percés in 1877 symbolized the end of the long, dramatic struggle between red and white men for possession of the West. Though tragic in the extreme, the conflict was inevitable. Indian occupation of western lands barred the advance of miners, settlers, cattlemen, and railroad builders, and when the intruders pressed irresistibly onto the Indians' lands, resistance and savage frontier wars followed.

Hostilities flared hottest in the years immediately after the Civil War, when the nation's energies were freed for renewed western expansion. As pressure on the Indians increased, the tribes felt the squeeze on their homes and hunting grounds, and they fought back desperately. Veteran Civil War officers,

General Nelson A. Miles' heavy winter garb gave him the name Bear Coat among the Indians on the northern plains.

HISTORICAL SOCIETY OF MONTANA

sent west to crush the hostiles, rode off jauntily at the heads of columns of troopers only to find that the Indians and the difficult terrain were a match for all their past learning in orthodox warfare.

One general, the bushy-bearded George Crook, had more than his share of difficulties. Crook was a West Pointer and a veteran of Antietam, but Sioux and Cheyenne warriors mauled his forces at Rosebud Creek on the central plains. Ordered to capture the Apache chief Geronimo, he spent three futile years trying to subdue the wily Indian in the tortuous mountains of the Southwest.

General O. O. Howard, a one-armed veteran of the Army of the Potomac, fared even worse. Trying to round up Chief Joseph's Nez Percés, he was led on an exasperating chase across 1,321 miles of some of the most rugged terrain in the West, from Idaho to northern Montana, only to see his quarry finally captured by a rival officer, Nelson A. Miles.

The most unfortunate Indian fighter of all was also the most flamboyant. George A. Custer, a seasoned cavalry officer with long curls and a rakish uniform of his own design, was a reckless leader who thirsted for fame. His lack of caution led to the worst debacle on the plains, when his entire detachment of 265 men was wiped out by Sitting Bull's Sioux at the Little Big Horn in 1876.

Other military men had more success. One of them, General Miles, came west with a brilliant Civil War record. He had fought in every major battle but one with the Army of the Potomac, had been wounded four times, and had won the Congressional Medal of Honor. He campaigned for fifteen years against Cheyennes, Comanches, Kiowas, Sioux, Nez Percés, Bannocks, and Apaches. After Custer's defeat, he helped round up and punish the hostiles, and when Crook abandoned his chase of Geronimo, Miles succeeded in catching him.

In the end, the most enduring reputation was acquired by a scout rather than a general. Buffalo Bill Cody's many stirring adventures while guiding troops against the Indians brought him international fame, and when the last hostiles were subdued, his Wild West shows toured the world, a dramatic echo of the bitter campaigns that had cleared the West for the settlers.

NATIONAL ARCHIVES

Custer's difficulties with the Sioux started in 1874 when members of a reconnaissance expedition (above) which he led into the Black Hills found gold on the Indians' hunting grounds.

The slaughter of buffalo by hide hunters, shown below by Montana pioneer photographer L. A. Huffman, deprived the Indians of their food supply and hastened their collapse.

COLLECTION OF MRS. RUTH HUFFMAN SCOTT

Longghorns up from Texas

The Cattleman

McINTIRE, *Early Days in Texas*, 1902

Charles Goodnight (left) and Oliver Loving were two of the many men who opened trails north from Texas to create a great cattle empire across the West. Their long overland drives, pictured below by Frederic Remington, were romantic but rugged bouts of endurance, during which the cowboys coped with heat, thirst, Indians, and dangerous stampedes.

Charles Goodnight was a big man, six feet tall, weighing more than 200 pounds, with a short-cut beard that made him look like a larger edition of U. S. Grant. Before the Civil War, he had been a Texas freighter and a bullwhacker, and while out on the plains, had had one of his feet frozen so that he limped for the rest of his life. It failed to hobble him, for his usual place thereafter was astride a horse, first as a Texas Ranger, then as one of the Southwest's great pioneer cowmen.

Goodnight turned to cattle in 1856. At that time some five million longhorns, mostly unclaimed mavericks, roamed Texas, far from markets where men would pay $40 or more a head for them. In 1846 one Edward Piper had herded 1,000 head to the Ohio Valley; others had trailed steers to the California and Montana mines, and as early as 1858 Texas cattle had arrived at railheads in Missouri and Illinois. But "long drives" were few, and no one followed any particular trail. Goodnight helped to change that.

Far to the west, in New Mexico, Kit Carson and troops from Fort Sumner had rounded up 7,000 Navajos on a reservation. Soldiers and Indians, Goodnight reasoned, would make a rich market for beef if a man could get his cattle to them across the rough, waterless Staked Plains. When the thirty-year-old Goodnight met Oliver Loving, a trail driver in his fifties who had herded cattle north to Quincy, Illinois, and Denver, the two joined forces

and in 1866 started 2,000 head across Texas to New Mexico. They moved through dangerous Indian country and across a searing, 96-mile dry leg, but they made it to Fort Sumner, and their large profits encouraged others to follow them. Loving took stock cows and bulls farther north to Denver and Cheyenne, and this route, the Goodnight-Loving Trail, became one of the most famous in the West.

The next year Loving was killed by Comanches on the trail he had helped establish, but Goodnight went on to amass a fortune in the cattle trade. He laid out other trails and in 1877 started the JA Ranch in the Texas Panhandle, running almost 100,000 head over nearly one million acres. Crossing Shorthorns and Herefords with his scraggly longhorns, he developed one of America's finest beef herds and in 1880 organized the Panhandle's first stockmen's association to protect cattle and systematize range work. He lived a long and active life, dying in 1929 at the age of 93. Not the least of his achievements was fathering a child when he was 92.

In eastern Texas other men had been seeking ways to get their cattle to northern markets. Many tried to drive herds to Illinois, but they had trouble with irate Missouri farmers who barred their way. In 1867 Joseph G. McCoy, an Illinois meat dealer, hit on the idea of aiming the drives farther west to Abilene, Kansas, a drowsy railhead on the plains, where no one would object to the huge herds. McCoy built yards and chutes, and that year 35,000 Texas steers came bawling into Abilene. Their route followed a trail from the Red River taken two years before by a half-breed Cherokee named Jesse Chisholm. The next year 75,000 head drove the Chisholm Trail, and the tide swelled until between 1869 and 1871 nearly 1,500,000 Texas beeves reached Abilene.

Other Kansas railheads came into use, and Ellsworth, Newton, Wichita, and Dodge City all became famous cowtowns, scenes of rip-roaring blowouts when the Texas cowboys arrived with their herds. The suppression of the plains Indians opened new territory to the cattlemen, and soon Texas steers moved to markets and ranges throughout the West. But settlers also spread across the plains, bringing barbed wire and ordinances that interfered with the drives. A proposal to establish a 690-mile national cattle trail proved too expensive, and by the middle eighties, when railroads reached Texas from the north, the "long drives" ended.

KING RANCH

Richard King

In 1852 a burly steamboat captain named Richard King rode through stirrup-high grass between the Nueces River and the Rio Grande in south Texas. Three hundred years before, the shipwrecked conquistador Cabeza de Vaca had gazed on this lush prairie and written: "All over the land are vast and handsome pastures, with good grass for cattle . . ." Spanish ranchers had found his description true, but brigands and Indians had driven them away, and King found it a silent, unused land, known to Mexicans as the Desert of the Dead.

King was a tough-minded businessman who had saved some money by hard work and ambition. When he was eleven, he shipped as a cabin boy on a coastal steamer. He steamboated all over the South, and with a partner, operated his own boats on the Rio Grande after the Mexican War. But something about the grass going to waste on the Desert of the Dead told him that his fortune was now no longer on the river.

With $300, he bought 15,500 acres, and adding more land soon afterwards, started acquiring stock. During the Civil War, Union troops drove him from his property, but he came back with a pocketful of money made in cotton trading and started over again. In time, his holdings included 100,000 cattle, 20,000 sheep, and 10,000 horses. He fought rustlers and lawless elements, improved his herds with imported breeds, and during the great drives sent thousands of head of cattle over the long trails to the north. When he died in 1885, the prosperous King Ranch had grown to include more than 600,000 acres.

321

James Hill

In his youth, James J. Hill wanted to be a doctor, but he lost an eye in an accident and became, instead, a builder of railroads and empires.

A powerful man with a massive head, he started railroading in St. Paul and in 1879 began building the Great Northern from Minnesota to Puget Sound. Other lines had received land grants and government aid, but Hill depended solely on traffic revenue to meet his building costs. He was a skillful manager who supervised construction himself and kept expenses low, but to reach the Pacific, he had to populate the country through which his line ran.

He brought immigrants from Europe and gave them cheap transportation to the Dakota and Montana plains. He loaned them money, laid out model farms, and gave away imported blooded bulls. In 1893, when the Great Northern reached Seattle, its route all the way back to St. Paul served newly settled country.

Later, Hill clashed head-on with another giant, E. H. Harriman. The Supreme Court broke up his Northern Securities Co. and halted his bold dreams of monopoly, but when he died in 1916, the populated Northwest remained as his monument.

Edward Harriman

The son of an Episcopal minister, Edward H. Harriman became a sharp, ruthless speculator in railroads. At 21 he borrowed $3,000 and bought a seat on the Stock Exchange; by 35 he had purchased his first railroad; and at 49 he took over the Union Pacific, the first transcontinental line, which had since gone bankrupt.

Harriman rigged up a special train with an observation car and had himself backed over the entire UP system. When he returned to Wall Street, he put $25,000,000 into new cuts, grades, and equipment. Two and a half years later, the UP declared a dividend, and Harriman promptly used its credit to buy into other lines. He purchased 46 per cent of the Southern Pacific, but an attempt to take over the Chicago, Burlington & Quincy brought him into conflict with James Hill. The struggle between the titans resulted in the Panic of 1901, and when it was over, Harriman was part-owner of the Northern Pacific, which Hill controlled.

Harriman's activities aroused the ire of Theodore Roosevelt, and he was investigated by the Interstate Commerce Commission. At the height of public feeling against him, he died in 1909.

BROWN BROTHERS BROWN BROTHERS

Leland Stanford

Collis Huntington

In 1861 four Sacramento storekeepers decided to build a railroad to link California with the East. Leland Stanford, who sold groceries to miners, was the money man. Son of a New York innkeeper, he had come west to supply provisions to the gold fields and had made $400,000 from a lucky mine interest.

His associates were hardware dealers Collis Huntington and Mark Hopkins and a dry goods merchant named Charles Crocker. San Francisco financiers laughed at them, but an engineer showed them a route over the Sierras, and they went ahead on their own.

While Huntington raised money from Congress, Crocker imported Chinese coolies and began laying track. Hopkins kept the books, while Stanford, who had a flair for politics, got elected governor of California and passed laws to aid the railroad.

In 1869 their Central Pacific joined the westward-pushing Union Pacific, and their dream became a reality. The "Big Four" went on to build the Southern Pacific and grow fabulously rich. Stanford became a U.S. senator, established a horse ranch named Palo Alto, and founded Leland Stanford Junior University as a memorial to his son.

"I'm worn out," said Collis P. Huntington when the last spike was driven on the Central Pacific. But Huntington was a perpetual-motion machine, and his dynamic activities as a railroad magnate were just beginning.

A Connecticut Yankee, he had peddled watches in the South before coming to California in 1849 with a stock of goods to sell to miners. The hardware firm he established in Sacramento with Mark Hopkins prospered, and its second floor became the railroad's headquarters. But Huntington preferred the East, where he borrowed money and bought supplies for the line, and when the Central was completed, he stayed in New York, borrowing more money with which to go on building railroads.

As the drive wheel of the "Big Four" partnership, he bought out competition and pushed rails north, south, and east until the Central Pacific was only a part of the mighty Southern Pacific system which ran to New Orleans and St. Louis. To gain rights and grants, he lobbied in Congress and was suspected of bribery. But he ignored critics and continued to amass wealth and power. When he died in 1900, he was worth some $40,000,000.

UNION PACIFIC RAILROAD

Meeting at Promontory

During the Civil War, General Grenville Dodge built bridges and trestles and kept railroads running for the Union armies. In 1866 he returned home to Council Bluffs and found the biggest job of his life waiting for him.

Four years earlier, Congress had authorized the building of a transcontinental railroad, and in California the Central Pacific was already being pushed toward Nevada. But on the eastern end, the Union Pacific had been stalled by the war, and only forty miles of track pointed west from Omaha.

Dodge took over as chief engineer for the UP and started things moving. He hired crews of Irishmen and the first year built 266 miles of track. His problems were immense. There was no timber on the plains, and ties had to be brought from Minnesota and Michigan, sometimes at a cost of $2.50 a tie. Stone was hauled from Wisconsin, steel rails from Pennsylvania, and it took forty freight cars of supplies, fuel, and provisions to lay one mile of track. Huge herds of buffalo got in the way, and Indians who attacked the crews had to be fought off.

Still Dodge pushed west, 240 miles in 1867 and 425 in 1868. The Central Pacific topped the Sierras and was given permission to continue eastward until it met Dodge's men. Congress spurred the race by lending the companies up to $48,000 for each mile they built, and the Central Pacific's Chinese laid ten miles of track in a single day. The rails came up in a car to be seized by gangs and spiked down. "The moment the car is empty it is tipped over on the side of the track to let the next loaded car pass it, and then it is tipped back up again . . . It is a great Anvil Chorus that these sturdy sledges are playing," an observer wrote.

In the last days, the two lines were moving so fast that their graders went right past each other. But on May 10, 1869, at Promontory, Utah, Dodge's "Irish terriers" joined their rails to those of the Central Pacific, and a few days later a train was speeding passengers on the first wondrous ride across the West from Omaha to Sacramento.

A wood-burning locomotive from California (rear) approaches the UP's coal burner to bump cowcatchers in this historic view of the meeting of the rails at Promontory, Utah.

325

Big Trees
and Hidden Wealth

As the nation expanded west after the Civil War, no part of the vast land, no matter how wild or rugged, escaped the attention of fortune hunters and exploiters. While farmers and cattlemen spread through the warm valleys and across the open plains, lumbermen and miners pushed into the more formidable areas that had once turned aside even the most stout-hearted pioneers.

In the Northwest the forested wilderness was invaded by an army of loggers who set to work with axes, saws, and ox teams to cut down whole mountainsides of huge ponderosa pines and Douglas firs. Bull-team logging on skid roads gave way to donkey engines and Shay locomotives, designed to speed operations in these tallest and densest of all U.S. forests. Feverish activity opened new areas, built new towns, and established cities like Seattle and Spokane as important centers of the timber industry.

Elsewhere, the increasing capitalization needed to work the California mines forced small-time gold seekers to comb the mountains in other parts of the West for new strikes. In 1859 a few men, including a shiftless prospector named Henry Comstock, found gold in some bluish rock in Nevada, and when they sent it to be assayed, discovered that it was worth $3,000 a ton in silver. The Comstock Lode, soon bought by wealthy investors, turned out to be the richest single find in mining history.

Other strikes, in the Pikes Peak area, Idaho, Montana, and the Black Hills of South Dakota, kept the country in a frenzy of gold and silver rushes until the 1880's. To supply the diggings, merchants, farmers, and professional people followed the miners and soon dotted the West with new populated centers like Denver, Boise, and Walla Walla.

A logging crew of 34 men (above) sits for its portrait atop huge fir logs in a Washington forest in 1908. The picture was made by Darius Kinsey, a Seattle photographer.

A topographical map of 1872 shows how the four-mile-long Sutro Tunnel, one of the great engineering feats of its time, gave underground access to the fabulous Comstock mines.

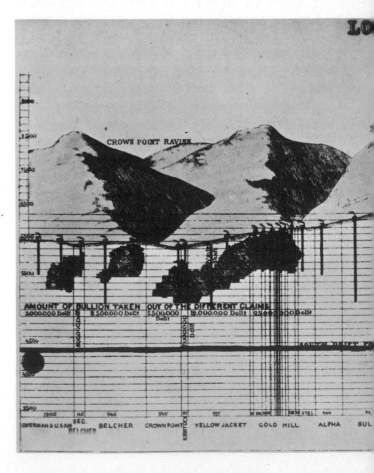

SUTRO, *Closing Argument to Aid the Sutro Tunnel*, 1872

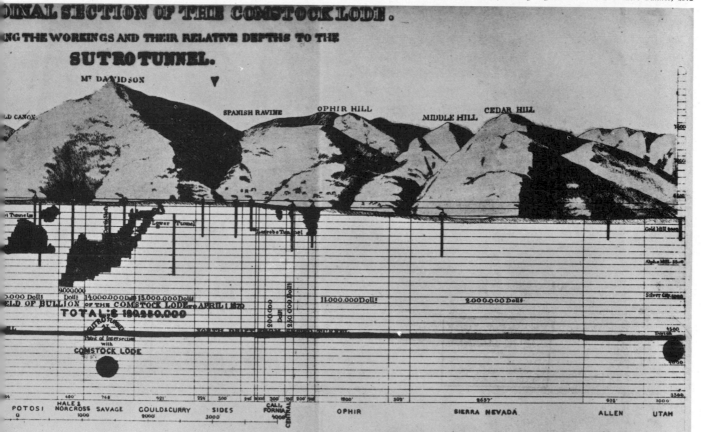

Law West of the Pecos

Jesse James was born in Clay County, Missouri, in 1847. Guerrilla fighting in the Civil War whetted his appetite for ruthless killing; after the war he went on murdering and robbing until a friend killed him in 1882 for a $10,000 reward.

James was the best-known of all the badmen in a West that bred outlaws and gunfighters. The frontier settlements of miners, railroad camps, and cattlemen provided ideal conditions for outlawry, for men were too busy seeking their own fortunes to bother with law enforcement, and hardy pioneers understood that "there's no law west of Kansas City, and west of Fort Scott, no God."

When conditions became too bad, miners' courts and vigilante groups dealt summary punishment to the worst offenders. In 1849 California miners hanged three robbers and for a while called their camp Hangtown. The pattern of San Francisco's vigilante committee was taken to Montana, where in the 1860's a ferociously mustached man hunter named John X. Beidler led the rounding up and hanging of a gang of brazen road agents.

After the Civil War, excitement-seeking veterans poured onto the plains, and wild gunplay rattled in every Kansas cattle town. Despairing businessmen hired tough gunfighters, some of them not so honest themselves, and made them marshals and sheriffs. One of them, Wild Bill Hickok, had been a Kansas guerrilla, Union scout, Indian fighter, and gun dueler. He was quick to kill, but he quieted things in Hays City and Abilene. After a stint as a performer in Buffalo Bill's Wild West Show, he was shot in the back in 1876 while playing poker in a Deadwood, South Dakota, saloon.

Wyatt Earp's Dodge City Peace Commission, looking deadly businesslike, enforced peace among the rival saloons in the "Queen of the Cowtowns." Earp is second from left, front; his chief lieutenant, Bat Masterson, is at right, back row.

KANSAS STATE HISTORICAL SOCIETY

Another lawman, Wyatt Earp, had been a stage driver and buffalo-hide hunter before becoming a marshal in Wichita and Dodge City. With the help of a lieutenant, Bat Masterson, who got his name by batting offenders over the head with a cane, Earp cleaned up those towns and struck off for Tombstone, Arizona. There he became a U.S. marshal, and with his brothers and a friend, Doc Holliday, a gambler-dentist, waged a famous sixty-second gun duel at the O.K. Corral, burying three outlaws in the town's Boot Hill cemetery.

The Southwest was the last stand of the gunfighters, and none was more celebrated than a psychopathic killer named William H. Bonney, who was born in a New York tenement in 1859. Known as Billy the Kid, he became a cowboy in New Mexico and gained notoriety as a killer during the Lincoln County cattle war. He was finally ambushed by his friend, Sheriff Pat Garrett, but before he died, he claimed boastfully that he had killed one man for each of his 21 years.

COLLECTION OF JAMES HORAN

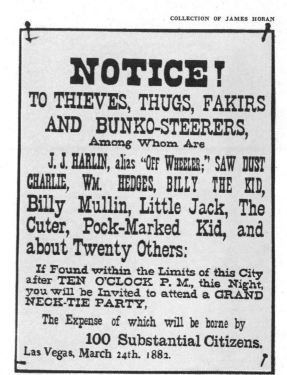

NOTICE!
TO THIEVES, THUGS, FAKIRS AND BUNKO-STEERERS,
Among Whom Are

J. J. HARLIN, alias "OFF WHEELER;" SAW DUST CHARLIE, WM. HEDGES, BILLY THE KID, Billy Mullin, Little Jack, The Cuter, Pock-Marked Kid, and about Twenty Others:

If Found within the Limits of this City after TEN O'CLOCK P. M., this Night, you will be Invited to attend a GRAND NECK-TIE PARTY,

The Expense of which will be borne by

100 Substantial Citizens.
Las Vegas, March 24th. 1882.

An 1882 poster warns badmen to get out of town.

"Law West of the Pecos" was administered by a usually whiskey-sodden justice of the peace named Roy Bean, who gave whimsical fines to offenders from the porch of his saloon in a west Texas hamlet which he named for the actress Lily Langtry.

These pioneer homesteaders in Nebraska, 1886, were typical of settlers who raised lonely sod huts on the treeless plains.

NEBRASKA STATE HISTORICAL SOCIETY

Galusha Grow, Homesteaders' Champion

Every person has a right to so much of the earth's surface as is necessary to his support," said Galusha Grow, member of Congress. Grow had been brought up on a pioneer farm in Pennsylvania and was a champion of hard-working frontier settlers. When he entered the House of Representatives in 1850, he was only 28, but he made a lot of noise in behalf of the free distribution of public land to needy settlers and he was made chairman of the influential Committee on Territories.

For ten years, Grow tried to pass a Homestead Act, but he was opposed by powerful land speculators who wanted the bill written to their own advantage and by southern legislators who feared that the Act would fill the western territories with antislavery settlers.

When Secession cleared Congress of southern members, Grow became Speaker and finally got his bill passed. His Homestead Act of 1862 provided that any adult citizen or alien who had filed his first papers could, for a $10 fee, claim 160 acres of the public domain. At the end of five years, if he had not abandoned the land for more than six months, he could secure final title.

Grow's Act was not perfect, for it limited the size of farms to uneconomic units on the arid western plains and failed to provide assistance for many poor settlers who needed it. But after the Civil War, it was the magnet that drew pioneers and veterans by the thousands to Nebraska, Iowa, and Minnesota, gradually filling up the nation's sparsely settled middle border states.

The year his Homestead Act passed, Galusha Grow lost his seat in Congress. When he returned some thirty years later, the bill he had authored had done much to settle the West.

331

Boomers, Sooners, and the Last Great Runs

As the West filled up, land-hungry pioneers pressed for the opening of the last good farming country left to the red men. The Indian Territory, still held by 22 tribes, was guaranteed "for eternity" by treaties, but bands of eager "boomers," eyeing its millions of acres of good soil, shouted impatiently, "On to Oklahoma!"

For ten years federal troops held the excited home seekers in check on the Kansas border, but they became more numerous and from time to time forced their way onto the Indian land and had to be thrown off again. Finally, in 1889, the government managed to extinguish all native claims to two unused portions of the territory and announced that the first of them would be thrown open to settlers at noon on April 22.

That morning, at least 20,000 "boomers" on horseback and in every type of wheeled conveyance waited breathlessly for miles on end along the starting line. Some "sooners" had already stolen in ahead of them to claim choice land, but the troops held the main throng back while tension mounted. At the zero hour, guns fired, and a maddened, fighting horde of men, animals, and wagons burst across the line in a great cloud of dust. Within a few hours, men had settled on 1,920,000 acres, and thousands of temporary shelters were going up over claims. That night, Oklahoma City had a population of 10,000 and Guthrie nearly 15,000. Many claims had as many as six contenders, and it sometimes took bloodshed to settle the arguments.

In time, local governments were established, and Congress created the Oklahoma Territory. Other Indian areas were opened, including the six-million-acre Cherokee Outlet, and the "boomer" rush of 1889 was re-enacted by armies of new settlers. By 1907, with 1,500,000 inhabitants, Oklahoma became a state, and the conquest of the nation's continental land mass was complete.

This famous photograph was taken an instant after the signal was given that began the mad land stampede in Oklahoma's Cherokee Outlet in 1893. Horsemen, some on blooded racers, are already streaking ahead, outstripping those in wagons.

OKLAHOMA HISTORICAL SOCIETY

End of the Frontier

With more people than supplies in the Klondike, store owners like those in Dawson (above) made small fortunes selling beer and meat to hungry miners at inflated prices. Below, lady "prospectors" on the way to the gold fields.

LIBRARY OF CONGRESS

In 1897 the nation was stirred by another dramatic gold strike, this time on a brand new frontier in the far-off, almost forgotten territory of Alaska. All during that spring, rumors trickled down the Pacific coast of a fabulously rich find on a tributary of the Yukon River which the Indians called the *Throndiuck*. In early summer two steamships from Alaska docked at Seattle and San Francisco, and the reports proved to be true. As thousands thronged the wharves in frenzied excitement, some eighty grizzled prospectors struggled down the gangways with heavy suitcases, buckskin bags, and canvas sacks bulging with half a million dollars in gold dust and nuggets. A roar went up from the crowd, and the news that crackled by telegraph and cable across the nation and around the world brought on, within a few days, a wild stampede to Alaska's "Klondike."

Treacherous Chilkoot Pass (left) was the toughest leg of the route to the Klondike.

The original strike had been made in August, 1896, in a remote, mosquito-infested part of the interior by two Indians, Skookum Jim and Tagish Charlie, and a prospector companion named George Washington Carmack. Carmack was typical of the handful of white men who were living in Alaska, the latest of America's pioneers who had pushed steadily ahead of advancing civilization to search for freedom and adventure in an unknown land. His father had crossed the plains as a Forty-Niner, and Carmack had been born near San Francisco. He had worked on ferryboats and as a dishwasher on a man-of-war and at Juneau had jumped ship and found a life of contentment as a packer, prospector, and companion of Indians in the cold northern wilds.

The Alaska through which Carmack roamed was scarcely known in the U.S. For thirty years, ever since its purchase from Russia in 1867, "Seward's Folly" had been all but abandoned by its new owner. For a while its huge expanse of 586,400 square miles was garrisoned by five small detachments of troops, and in 1869 the territory had received a visit by surveyors and a military group under General George H. Thomas, the celebrated "Rock of Chickamauga" of the Civil War.

From 1877 until 1884, what local government there was centered in a few customs agents. The wholesale slaughter of whales and seals by fleets of ships resulted in a brief flurry of attention when missionaries discovered that the Eskimo population was being deprived of its source of food and was on the verge of starvation. With Congressional aid and money from charitable citizens, reindeer were imported from Siberia, and the increasing herds managed to save the Eskimos. Then most of the nation again lost interest in the apparently valueless "northern icebox."

With the disappearance of America's own frontier, however, men like Carmack began to drift toward Alaska. Many, whose luck had played out in the mines of Montana, Nevada, Colorado, and Arizona, were still following a golden dream, and they arrived in twos and threes with tin pans and shovels. Others, fleeing civilization for a variety of personal reasons, trekked into the wilds and groped across the huge frontier, hunting and trapping for a living, following the rivers, and trading with Indians and prospectors.

Carmack's lucky strike ended the territory's slumbering isolation. "Gold! Gold! Gold! Gold!" newspapers screamed throughout the U.S., and overnight the days of '49 were relived. "Seattle," a reporter wired to New York, "has gone stark, staring mad on gold." Within ten days of the arrival of the first prospectors from the north, 1,500 people had left that city for Alaska, and thousands more were arriving daily to fight for passage to the Klondike. Behind them came an army of others from all parts of the country. In the first 24 hours after the news reached New York, 2,000 people tried to buy tickets to Alaska. In Chicago, 1,000 people a day applied for transportation at railroad and steamship offices. Everywhere, men again left their jobs, gave up businesses and homes, and set out for the distant gold fields of a virtually unknown land.

Only a small fraction of those who started made it all the way to the Klondike. Some tried to hurry across northern Canada to the Yukon, and many perished or were forced to turn back by the wilderness. Others fought their way up the long Yukon River or through the interior of Alaska, and became discouraged by the many hardships. Most of those who successfully reached the gold regions did so by crossing treacherous mountain passes in Alaska's Panhandle. One of the most popular routes led across the 3,550-foot high Chilkoot Pass, a steep slope of glistening snow and ice where, during the height of the rush, a steady column of men, each one carrying between 100 and 200 pounds on his back, struggled slowly up the mountainside, braving gale winds and the threat of sudden death in avalanches.

The Klondike in time may have yielded as much as $300,000,000, but the easiest pickings were soon exhausted, and the rush ended almost as quickly as it had begun. It served its purpose, though, in turning the nation's attention finally to the vast natural wealth of the territory. Mining, timber, and fishing industries were established, agriculture began, and civil government was expanded.

Especially during and after World War II, the remote territory's strategic geographic position gave Alaska increased importance, and a new military and defense-based civilian population helped to provide a firm foundation for the statehood which finally came in 1958. But hard on the heels of admission to the Union came the realization that for countless years in the future Alaska will continue to have wilderness to conquer and new frontiers for the pioneer spirit to challenge.

PORTRAIT OF THE WESTERN FRONTIER

SMITHSONIAN INSTITUTION

The *Yellowstone,* here passing St. Louis in 1836, took artist George Catlin up the Missouri.

Among these mountains, those that lie to the west . . . are called the Shining Mountains, from an infinite number of chrystal stones . . . which, when the sun shines full upon them, sparkle so as to be seen at a very great distance." The year was 1767, and the author, Jonathan Carver, was describing the Rocky Mountains, about which he had heard such wondrous tales from the Indians.

By the beginning of the nineteenth century not much more than a handful of white men had seen those shining mountains, but, after the journey of Lewis and Clark, more headed west, first singly, then in little groups. The first were pathfinders and trail-blazers, marking the way for those who followed in their footsteps. Some were adventurers, pulled by the lure of the wild; some sought the fur pelts that meant wealth. But all brought back a dream—a vision of the promised land that was always further west. The spark caught fire east of the Mississippi where it was getting so a man could see his neighbor's farm. Americans needed room to move around in, and that room was waiting for them across the wide Missouri. Once again the wagons were loaded, the ox teams headed west, and the first tentative probes became full-scale migrations. There was a continent to conquer and claim, out where the sun set.

337

COLLECTION OF MRS. ANGUS GORDON BOGGS

Miner Bob Pitt rides his belled horse in front of his squaw and pack mules.

LIBRARY OF CONGRESS

This 1869 prairie farmer was a symbol of industry.

A bullwhacker makes his whip sing.

© LEADER CO.

MCCOY, *Sketches of the Cattle Trade*

End of the cattle trail: an Abilene dance hall.

NEW-YORK HISTORICAL SOCIETY

Ponchos and pigtails adorned California barrooms.

NEW-YORK HISTORICAL SOCIETY

A trio of grizzled prospectors.

Where Men Were Men

Not long after the first white man succumbed to the lure of the trans-Mississippi West, that extraordinary region became a stage for some of the most colorful characters in American history. There were fur trappers and Forty-Niners, dance-hall girls and desperadoes, rustlers, cavalrymen, and, it goes without saying, cowboys and Indians. Members of this wonderfully improbable cast fanned out across prairie and desert, climbed the Great Shining Mountains, and descended into verdant far valleys. In the miner's phrase, they went "to see the elephant" to meet the implausible. Their allotted time was brief, but even before the Old West was gone, they were reincarnate in story and song.

Century Magazine, 1889

A cavalryman takes a pull at his canteen.

"Hands up!"—a Charles Russell bandit.

© LEADER CO.

HUNTINGTON LIBRARY

Buffalo chips were fuel for a prairie meal.

"I took ye for an Injin!" It was an easy mistake for these rough trappers.

OVERLEAF: High in the Wind River Mountains of Wyoming, Sir William Stewart, a Scottish sportsman, found this pristine lake in 1837. Artist Alfred Jacob Miller later painted several versions of the scene from his on-the-spot sketches.

OVERLEAF: COLLECTION OF C. R. SMITH

Strange New Animals
Stirred an
Artist's Imagination

COLLECTION OF FRANK SCHAFFER

Buffalo Calf

AMERICAN MUSEUM OF NATURAL HISTORY

John James Audubon is seldom remembered today as the hunter who tramped the Pennsylvania woods about 1804. This portrait is the joint work of his two sons.

Prairie Dog

Columbian Black-Tailed Deer

A tempting variety of fur-bearing animals lured men up the Missouri River and into the Rocky Mountains in the quest for valuable pelts. Having won fame with his *Birds of America*, John James Audubon began a study of these animals. When an octavo edition of his *Quadrupeds of North America* was issued in 1849, he noted that little had been "accomplished toward the proper elucidation of the animals which inhabit . . . our widely-extended and diversified country." An enthusiastic if sentimental observer of nature, Audubon always strove for animation in his pictures, an effect notably achieved here. After his death, the work was completed by his son John Woodhouse Audubon.

White American Wolf

The Cougar

Wolverine

343

Grizzly Bear

WALTERS ART GALLERY, © 1951 UNIVERSITY OF OKLAHOMA PRESS

WASHINGTON UNIVERSITY

The Far Outposts of Civilization

Fort Laramie on the North Platte River was a rendezvous for Indians, trappers, and emigrants. Alfred Jacob Miller's 1837 scene (above, left) is the only known interior view of the original wooden fort.

Fort Snelling (above), painted by soldier-artist Seth Eastman in the 1840's, was for thirty years the Army's farthest northwest outpost. The garrison supervised trade and protected settlers against marauding Indians.

For years Indians brought their trade goods to Fort Benton, at the head of steam navigation on the Missouri River. In 1859 Charles Wimar pictured a colorful plains caravan approaching the frontier post (left).

Trial and Triumph Followed the Long Road West

BUTLER INSTITUTE OF AMERICAN ART

An aura of promise shimmers in the setting sun as the wagon train "draws its lazy length toward the distant El Dorado." The idealized version of the Oregon Trail above was painted by Albert Bierstadt.

Above right, the sudden whirlwind of an Indian attack on the wagons is dramatized by Charles Wimar. Danger and often death awaited pioneers on their trek across savage wastes to the new promised land.

"A well . . . with hind parts of an ox sticking out. Dead oxen all around. Air foul," wrote Forty-Niner J. Goldsborough Bruff en route to the gold fields, and illustrated his point with the sketch at right.

COLLECTION OF AUGUST A. BUSCH, JR.

HUNTINGTON LIBRARY

First a House, Then a Town

CULVER SERVICE

Charles Wimar's "Turf House on the Plains" (above) was nothing but prairie sod "piled up layer on layer, and smeared over or between with a clayey mud." Yet it was home to the lonely farmer.

Spawned by cattle, gold and silver, or the railroad, such rude, brawling towns as Virginia City, Abilene, and Dodge City sprang up. At left is Deadwood, South Dakota, pictured about 1876.

Colorado boom towns like Blackhawk Point (right) had a "curious, rickety, temporary air, with their buildings standing as if on one leg [below] bald, scarred and pitted mountains," according to a visiting newspaperman's report.

COLLECTION OF ROBERT B. HONEYMAN

LIBRARY OF CONGRESS

CHICAGO HISTORICAL SOCIETY

Rails Replaced
Wagon Ruts,
And a Continent
Was Conquered

WILLIAM ROCKHILL NELSON GALLERY OF ART

Thomas Otter's symbolic painting (above) shows what might have been the last covered wagon, paced by the railroad "stretching out its iron arm to the region of gold."

A ten-minute refreshment stop on the way west often turned into the boisterous Donnybrook depicted in the 1886 lithograph (left) of travelers at a busy frontier railroad station.

A buffalo herd, reaching out to the horizon, could hold up a train for hours (right). Wanton wholesale slaughter of the beasts led to their virtual extermination by the 1880's.

SMITHSONIAN INSTITUTION

351

THE STRENUOUS LIFE

W HEN Theodore Roosevelt ranched on the Little Missouri in the early 1880's, the West was still the colorful country of Frederic Remington, Buffalo Bill, and Sitting Bull. Roosevelt lived in a cabin of hewn logs, donned a fringed buckskin hunting shirt—"the most picturesque and distinctively national dress ever worn in America"—and cultivated what he called "the stern, manly qualities that are invaluable to a nation." He did his share of bronco busting, rode with stampeding cattle, made grueling marches, and endured blistering summer heat and iron winter cold without flinching. He felled trees, shot bighorn, buffalo, elk, deer, and grizzlies, branded steers, and defied badmen. As a climactic exploit he brought some horse thieves down from the Kildeer Mountains, at the point of his Winchester, to the sheriff and law courts.

The Wild West was dying when Roosevelt returned to the East. The terrible winter of 1886–87 marked the imminent end of the cattlemen's frontier. In a bitter succession of blizzards thousands of cattle froze to death, and people died in snowbound cabins and ranch houses. The over-all loss on the high northern range was estimated at 75 per cent of the herds. T.R. caught the Northern Pacific in 1886 back to New York and the mayoralty campaign, never to return except for brief stays. Before him now lay political and social frontiers.

But had he stayed in the West he would have seen the frontier passing. Farmers and stock growers were irresistibly fencing the plains; the great corporations that alone could build railroads, open deep mines, smelt ores, and turn forests into lumber for the nation's construction industry were taking control of state after state. They were dominating legislatures, choosing governors, placing their agents in the national Senate, and even controlling the judiciary. As Roosevelt turned eastward the West was generating deep forces of unrest and formulating passionate ideas of reform; and soon the radical doctrines voiced by the Farmers' Alliances and the Populist party rode eastward too.

Roosevelt's career bridged as that of no other man's the interval between two worlds and two eras. On the Dakota frontier he had learned much that he was later to apply to politics and government. He had seen the importance of the primary canons of morality—how a frontier society could disintegrate if strict rules of right and wrong were not enforced; he had learned how vital it was to hit malefactors hard, without hesitation or compromise. He had seen how individual greed threatened the public welfare. He had grasped the fact that co-operative action and public controls become increasingly important to every community growing in complexity. From firsthand experience he knew that seemingly illimitable natural resources have their limits and require state protection. Though a thoroughgoing individualist, impatient of governmental action which coddled or fettered men, Roosevelt saw that social justice always needs fighting champions.

As T.R. found the doors of political advancement temporarily swung against him in 1893 by the inauguration of a Democratic President, and as the

Theodore Roosevelt, chief apostle of the strenuous life.

country underwent panic and depression, America celebrated the four hundredth anniversary of its discovery. As an architectural feat and an exhibition of national achievement the Columbian Exposition remains a landmark. In Chicago, which within the memory of men still living had not been even an incorporated village, rose a creation that made viewers catch their breath. The gleaming panorama of stately white buildings, monuments, fountains, and esplanades, fronting on lovely lagoons and canals, with blue Lake Michigan as background, housed the latest triumphs of art, science, and mechanics.

It did more, for Chicago, as Eugene Field observed, was "making culture hum." Meetings had been arranged of bodies devoted to social, aesthetic, and learned progress. Before the American Historical Association a young historian of Wisconsin rose to announce that the frontier as defined by the Census Bureau was dead and to assess its significance in the development of a distinctively American character.

Up to their own day, Frederick Jackson Turner told his audience, "American history has been in a large degree the history of the colonization of the Great West. The existence of an area of free land, its continuous recession, and the advance of American settlement westward, explain American development." What the successive waves of settlement did to the frontier was less important than what the frontier did to the settlers. This process was now ended. A logical line of growth, constantly reproduced in new areas, had brought the country into a perplexingly novel age. The infant communities of a frontier zone had begun with hunting and fur trading; they had progressed to stock grazing; the range had been taken over by farmers, first with simple, then variegated crops; then farming had yielded to manufacturing. So swift was the change that Turner himself, who had seen Indians and fur traders in his Portage boyhood, now knew Wisconsin as an industrial state. In the nation as a whole cities had replaced a rural civilization, and vast concentrations of capital had replaced personal enterprise. "The age of individualism," Rockefeller had said, "is gone, never to return."

Turner, now that the marching frontier had disappeared, was uncertain of the future. Industrialization, with all it meant for co-operative effort and a new social outlook, was a necessity. But Turner raised questions rather than answering them. The great masters of finance and capital were sons of a primitive democratic society. Would such men prove an incipient aristocracy, or "the pathfinders for democracy in reducing the industrial world to systematic consolidation suited to democratic control"? Would their successors try to exploit the masses or serve them? Certainly the American people had not ceased to cherish the democratic ideal. They had steadily enlarged the sphere of government in democracy. All the parties—Democrats, Republicans, and Populists—looked in the direction of wider state regulation; but Turner was apprehensive as to the growing numbers of immigrants, the power of bossism, the massive weight of the trusts.

Not so Theodore Roosevelt. To him it was crystal-clear that the government must and should assert itself aggressively to master aggregations of wealth and promote social justice. As Cleveland's second administration ended, the United States swung into a more dynamic era. Its life, its thought, its ambitions, moved faster and faster. Prosperity returned. The nation annexed Hawaii, ousted Spain from the Western Hemisphere, took Cuba under its tutelage, and established itself in Puerto Rico, Guam, and the Philippines. It was a great world power and asserted itself as such abroad. A new journalism under Hearst and Pulitzer joined the new magazines under McClure and

Munsey; a reformative spasm of muckraking shook press, pulpit, and politics; new impulses in literature appeared with Frank Norris, Stephen Crane, Hamlin Garland, and Theodore Dreiser. As the old hope of an indefinite perfectibility in American society was reborn, life seemed richer, more exciting, and more promising.

To Theodore Roosevelt this dynamic new era was completely congenial. He made himself the apostle of the strenuous life for the individual, the community, and the nation. Rising from his fame as Rough Rider and governor to the Vice-Presidency, he was made by Czolgosz's bullet the youngest President in our history. In the White House he directed his strenuosity into one central channel: he was determined that the government should control the great economic agencies, reform politics, and inspire the people of the United States to better citizenship.

The multifarious problems of the new era thus found in Roosevelt an untiring reformer and champion of national authority. Where men like Turner had questions, he had a program. Indeed, accidental President though he was, his first message to Congress in December, 1901, was almost a blueprint of what he was to accomplish in the next seven years. He not only offered legislation on the crystallizing situations of the twentieth century; by state papers, speeches, letters, and his genius for dramatic acts he quickened popular thought on them. A White House conference brought conservation into the limelight of public concern. His friendship for Booker T. Washington and a bold speech in New York in 1905 made the Negro question urgent. The Panama Canal was a contribution to national defense and commercial expansion. He coupled the voyage of the fleet around the world with earnest efforts to improve relations with Japan.

But economic problems and the control of big business were always foremost. In this area Roosevelt's central tenet was what he came to call his New Nationalism: the doctrine that the growth of interstate business made dependence on the states for regulation of monopoly, protection of women and children, and other concerns an impossibility. The interstate commerce clause of the Constitution gave Washington the sword and buckler it needed.

By the end of the second decade of the twentieth century two statesmen of the first rank, Theodore Roosevelt and Woodrow Wilson, had carried through elaborate programs of reform. They gave the nation reassurance that in the age of industrial and financial power represented by Vanderbilt, Rockefeller, Carnegie, and Morgan, the American dream of equal rights, equal opportunity, and equal justice was after all safe. With proper vigilance, the nation's leaders could conserve the immense benefits contributed by business growth and minimize the attendant evils. Though the methods of both leaders were Hamiltonian, their ideals were Jeffersonian—the ideals of the frontier. Both believed in the essential goodness of the common man, in social as well as political democracy, and in the ability of popular government to withstand any pressures. They did much to restore the faith of Americans in the great pioneering adventure that had begun in 1607 and 1620.

It was time, for in 1917 the republic had to accept immense new responsibilities. Henceforth it would find frontiers not at home, but in and even beyond the world. The challenges and opportunities were far greater, the need for faith and courage and strength more demanding than ever. For men who recognized them, the frontiers would always be there. It only remained for Americans to preserve and to bolster the spirit that had conquered those frontiers in the past.

ALLAN NEVINS

BROWN BROTHERS

The Commodore

CULVER SERVICE

I n the aftermath of the Civil War, when venality and corruption were all too frequent, the times produced a new and often ruthless kind of pioneer— the man who measured success in more and more millions of money, no matter how crude his methods in obtaining it. Fortunately the best of them took pride in constructive achievement. Of this breed, Commodore Cornelius Vanderbilt was the first spectacular example.

Starting with a New York ferryboat in 1813, Vanderbilt muscled into the steamboat business by fighting Fulton's state-protected monopoly, and even engineered a revolution in Nicaragua to protect his steamship route to California. By the end of the Civil War he had sold his steamships, turned to railroads, and was worth over twenty million dollars.

There were, he felt, too many railroads leading west from New York. It would be far better (and far more profitable) if a few strong trunk lines emerged. In his efforts to control the Erie Railroad, Vanderbilt ran afoul of three highly unprincipled men— the one-time cattle drover and full-time swindler, Uncle Dan Drew, and his lieutenants Jim Fisk and Jay Gould. The war that followed typified the times —judges and legislatures of two states corrupted, 50,000 shares of illegal stock printed and sold, a railroad looted of millions of dollars.

Vanderbilt went on to organize and operate the New York Central, while Gould and Fisk, having betrayed Drew, ran the Erie into the ground and used their winnings in an effort to corner enough of the gold in current use to force its price to extortionate levels. Thousands were ruined, and the national credit was seriously threatened, but Gould, having betrayed Fisk, cleaned up.

CULVER SERVICE

A one-time circus barker, flamboyant Jim Fisk (top) happily spent his millions on wine, women, and a Grand Opera Palace. He was murdered by a man who coveted his mistress.

Jay Gould (center), cold, shrewd, and thoroughly unpleasant, was on his own terms successful, for he came to control the Union Pacific and Western Union before he died in 1892.

Commodore Vanderbilt (left) died leaving a $105,000,000 estate. His son William (right) was famous for a remark made in an impatient moment: "The public be damned!"

Judge, 1885

Rockefeller and the Seneca Oil

In 1854 a former journalist named George Bissell was shown a bottle of what was variously called Seneca Oil or Rock Oil, for some years a favorite cure-all in medicine shows, but nothing more. Bissell sent a sample of the fluid to a chemistry professor at Yale, who described it as "a raw material from which [you] may manufacture very valuable products." He had spoken a mouthful.

Bissell, who had formed a Pennsylvania Rock Oil Company, was encouraged; but he needed great quantities of the stuff to manufacture anything, and how was he to get it? At this point his eye fell upon a label shouting the praises of a quack nostrum, and on this label was a picture of an artesian well. Of course! So he dispatched a former railroad conductor to Titusville, Pennsylvania, to see if he could not drill some oil. Folks naturally thought the venture crazy, but on August 28, 1859, the world's first oil well started gushing.

Overnight every shrewd man in the neighborhood started buying oil leases; drills were sunk in every pasture; up came the black oil, thousands of barrels a day; and down went the price, from $19.25 a barrel in January, 1860, to ten cents in October, 1861. This was Boomtown, U.S.A., and among the curious businessmen who came to inspect Titusville was a twenty-year-old commission broker from Cleveland named John Davison Rockefeller. He was appalled by the untidiness of the area; he considered how competitive production was driving the price of the smelly stuff down out of sight; and he went back to Cleveland thinking hard.

Rockefeller wanted no part of a business being whooped into prosperity by a parcel of promoters

BROWN BROTHERS

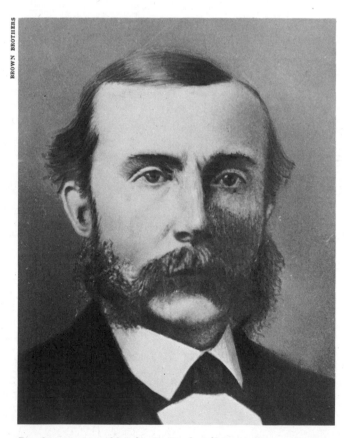

By 1872, 32-year-old John D. Rockefeller was the most important man in the booming oil industry, and the end was not in sight. Fabulous wealth gushed from blasted Pennsylvania hillsides like that at Pioneer Run (right), shown in 1865.

and part-time farmers. That was chaos, and Rockefeller wanted order. He had seen enough of the new age which was opening up for the American businessman to realize that an intelligent man, by making use of other people's ideas, energy, and capital, could also impose discipline on them. And in just 21 years he brought forth, from wasteful competition, the nation's first monopoly.

He began in 1863 by investing in an oil refinery in Cleveland, one of thirty-odd, and soon his was the biggest by far. He accomplished this magic by taking as partner the ablest refiner in the city, Samuel Andrews, by borrowing heavily from the Cleveland banks, and by using his growing power to obtain from the railroads lower shipping rates than other refiners got.

This was not out of line with prevailing practice, but it occurred to Henry Flagler, a Rockefeller associate, that perhaps it could be made even more efficient. Refiners and railroad men organized the South Improvement Company, and through it signed contracts with the Pennsylvania and New York Central railroads whereby the member companies (dominated by the Rockefeller group) received rebates not only on their own shipments of oil but on competitors' shipments.

The South Improvement agreement never went into effect, for public indignation in Pennsylvania forced its dissolution; but while it was a threat, Rockefeller's Standard Oil Company bought out practically all of its Cleveland competitors.

In the oil regions Rockefeller was hanged and burned in effigy by furious producers and independent refiners, but in vain. By 1878 interests headed by Rockefeller controlled perhaps eighty or ninety per cent of the nation's pipe lines and refineries. And in 1882 John D. Rockefeller's dream came true: the stockholders in all of those companies which were affiliated with Standard conveyed their holdings in trust to nine trustees, who would henceforth control both the price and the production of oil. At least, so they hoped.

AMERICAN PETROLEUM INSTITUTE

Andrew Carnegie put together a steel empire, sold it to Morgan, and devoted himself to philanthropy.

Andrew Carnegie: Apostle of the Gospel of Wealth

In 1849 Andrew Carnegie, thirteen-year-old messenger for a Pittsburgh telegraph company, found a draft for $500 lying in the street and, "like an honest little fellow," turned it over to the authorities.

Half a century later, in 1901, the same Andrew Carnegie sold his steel mills to J. P. Morgan for $492,000,000. Morgan, that year, had organized the United States Steel Corporation, capitalized at a toothsome $1,404,000,000—the biggest corporation

MUSEUM OF MODERN ART

Awesome J. P. Morgan was photographed by Edward Steichen shortly after "re-Morganizing" Big Steel.

thus far born. "Well, Pierpont," Carnegie said, "I am now handing the burden to you."

Between these two dates the Carnegie story was the very model of a Horatio Alger novel. But the enterprising industrialist added a surprise ending that would have astonished even Alger.

In 1889 Carnegie had promulgated a "Gospel of Wealth"—the theory that a rich man should spend the first part of his life acquiring wealth; the second part, distributing it. Before he died in 1919 Car-

negie had given away a whopping $350,000,000. Carnegie libraries sprang up in small communities across the country; colleges received grants; churches got new organs. Carnegie Institute in Pittsburgh was founded; the Peace Palace at The Hague in Holland was built; money was sprinkled across England and his native Scotland. Yet Carnegie scornfully rejected the title philanthropist. "The man who dies rich dies disgraced," he had written thirty years earlier.

Tattered Tom Makes Good

There were excellent reasons in the 1890's for thinking of the rags-to-riches story of a Carnegie as a typical Horatio Alger plot. The fact was, Horatio Alger never wrote any other kind of story. It was always the same: a poor but honest little fellow who, thanks to some fluke of good luck such as finding $500 in the street and turning it over to the authorities rather than spending it on riotous living, wins his reward by becoming president of the company after a period of dutiful, moral, hard work. According to the best estimate, Alger wrote this story 119 times. His books began to sell after the Civil War, and they were still selling well when the First World War broke out—more than two hundred million copies of them. No American author can ever have had such a pervasive influence—certainly no author who wrote so badly.

Why not? Were not his stories true to life? Look not only at Carnegie and Rockefeller; look at any successful American—Tom Edison, ex-newsboy; George Eastman, the Kodak king, once a $3-a-week insurance clerk; George Goethals, who built the Panama Canal, once an errand boy; Charles Schwab, president of Bethlehem Steel, once a grocery clerk—the list could easily be multiplied. "They can laugh all they like at Alger now," said Edward W. Bok, editor of *The Ladies' Home Journal,* "but he pulled his weight in the world when he was with us."

Alger's stories gave sustenance to an insistent dream. For despite the recurrent financial panics, despite the periods of hard times and the millions of poor on farm and in city, despite the difficulties of life and the near presence of death, the last years of the nineteenth century and the first years of the twentieth were years of confidence and optimism. Anything could happen. Any boy could be President. Wonders would never cease. And so Alger's stories not only reflected the exuberant, forward-looking spirit of their times, but they also substantially encouraged that spirit.

As for Alger himself? Educated for the ministry, he instead went to Paris for a spree. Later he drifted from one career to another, until he hit upon his happy literary formula. His writings brought him wealth, but he died in poverty as the result of spendthrift habits.

CULVER SERVICE

BRAVE & BOLD
SERIES

RLD
JR.

ALGER SERIES No.10
ONLY AN IRISH BOY
BY HORATIO ALGER, JR.

TATTERED TOM SERIES.
BY
HORATIO ALGER JR.

TATTERED TOM

LUCK AND PLUCK SERIES
BY HORATIO ALGER JR.

RAGGED DICK SERIES
BY
HORATIO ALGER JR.

SECOND SERIES
attered Tom
BOOKS.

ratio Alger Jr.

Horatio Alger's potboilers featured heroes like Ragged Dick and Tattered Tom (eight books were needed to get Tom into some respectable clothes) and others, all poor boys who rose to riches by one stratagem or another. The prolific Alger once dashed off a complete book in two weeks.

ER SERIES No.23
NEW YORK BOY
HORATIO ALGER, JR.

RK MATCH BOY

ND SERIES
& PLUCK
OOKS

ALL: CULVER SERVICE

A few rich got richer in the last quarter of the nineteenth century, but a great many poor got poorer. And it seemed to many of the latter that the men who paid salaries and fixed farm prices were ruled by Henry Ward Beecher's remark: "The man who cannot live on bread and water is not fit to live."

The times were scarred by severe financial panics and resulting wage cuts. Labor was denied the right to organize, to bargain collectively, or to seek redress of grievances. Lockouts were frequent, workers who tried to form unions were black-listed, and strikes were opposed by armed strikebreakers and even federal troops. Yet the cruel contrast between the great personal fortunes and the poverty of the worst-paid farmers and working men was an injustice that could not be ignored.

A wave of strikes hit the railroads in 1877. No unions were involved, for there were none—only angry mobs; but soon men began to join the semi-secret Knights of Labor, led by pacific, bookish Terence V. Powderly. Under him the organization won an unprecedented victory over Jay Gould's Wabash railway system in 1885, swelled to 700,000 members by the following year, and seemed likely to take over the entire American labor movement.

But a new kind of unionism which would eventually eclipse the Knights of Labor was developing under the leadership of Samuel Gompers, who

William D. "Big Bill" Haywood (top) welded the I.W.W. into a force feared throughout the West. Idealistic Terence Powderly (above) sadly watched his Knights of Labor crumble.

A bomb tossed into police ranks at an 1886 Haymarket Square rally in Chicago (below) set off a riot resulting in scores of casualties and a severe, long-lasting setback to organized labor.

Sleeping Giant

brought to the labor movement the idea of organization within a craft or trade, as against the Knights' industrial organization. In 1881 the Federation of Organized Trades and Labor Unions—parent of the American Federation of Labor—was formed.

Unhappily, a series of disasters did much to discredit honest efforts at reforming working conditions. The bomb that disrupted a rally in Chicago's Haymarket Square on May 4, 1886, gave all labor a black eye. Violence was used by both labor and management at the Homestead strike in 1892, but public opinion again turned against labor.

The Panic of 1893 precipitated the Pullman Car strike in Chicago, when the workers' pay was cut 25 to 40 per cent. The strike was smashed when President Cleveland ordered the Army to enforce a federal court injunction, and the workers' leader, Eugene V. Debs, was jailed. After the turn of the century aggressive tactics were championed by the Industrial Workers of the World—the Wobblies—under Big Bill Haywood, head of the Western Miners' Federation; but the Wobblies, like the now defunct Knights of Labor, went into rapid decline when public sentiment turned against them.

Sam Gompers, in the meantime, was slowly building his American Federation of Labor. When someone asked him what labor wanted, he was ready with his quiet answer. "More," he said.

Eugene Debs (below, addressing a freight-yard audience) was the best-loved of all American labor leaders. In 1920 he got nearly a million presidential votes while in prison.

Samuel Gompers (above) led the American Federation of Labor from 1886 until he died in 1924. Carefully avoiding left-wing agitation, he successfully fostered craft-unionism.

BROWN BROTHERS

CULVER SERVICE
CULVER SERVICE

William Jennings Bryan was the era's most magnetic orator.   *Ignatius Donnelly was an early leader of Populism's legions.*

The Voices of Reform Are Heard

For a whole generation the forces of reform tried to improve the conditions of laborers and poorer farmers. They formed associations to help immigrants, to reduce drunkenness and vice, to provide model tenements, to promote parks and playgrounds. They established settlement houses in slum districts, and under men such as Jacob Riis crusaded against slums themselves. They founded reform parties and attacked the bosses and machines which held corrupt sway in nearly all the great cities and half the states, and which were usually allied with selfish business interests. They published a clamorous succession of books, pamphlets, and articles attacking the evils of the time. And they went more and more energetically into politics.

Their greatest political effort began about 1890 with the organization of the Populist party, whose early leaders were James B. Weaver, Ignatius Donnelly, and John P. Altgeld. The Populists elected a few governors and congressmen, but no third party could hope to elect a President until it obtained control of one of the old parties. So the Populists took steps to take over the Democratic organization. In 1896, when the movement for free coinage of silver became irresistible in the West, Democrats and Populists whooped for joy and closed ranks behind William Jennings Bryan and a long list of advanced demands.

Then they began to savage plutocracy and political oppression in book and magazine. In *McClure's Magazine* and elsewhere the nation read how the trusts had grown powerful and how the bosses were subverting democracy. Ida M. Tarbell's history of the Standard Oil Company and Lincoln Steffens' *Shame of the Cities* made them national figures. Upton Sinclair's *The Jungle,* exposing unsanitary conditions and labor oppression in the meat-packing industry, scandalized every reader. Finally under Presidents Roosevelt and Wilson a long list of progressive measures became law.

The authors of the Populist platform in 1892 had called for a generous rural credit system, a graduated income tax, flexible currency, direct election of senators, shorter hours for workers, and the secret ballot. By 1914 these and many other ideas which had once seemed hopelessly quixotic were the law.

BROWN BROTHERS
HARRIS & EWING

Upton Sinclair, effective novelist and pamphleteer of reform.

Senator Robert La Follette, the Progressive party's champion.

Inventions to Order

One factor contributing to America's *fin-de-siècle* sense of optimism and confidence was that the inventions of the time were mostly well-behaved, designed for man's comfort, and yet at the same time quite miraculous. They seemed to prove that man could do anything. Jules Verne's tales were not science fiction, only glimpses of a magic wonderland that lay just around the corner.

The two greatest inventors of the day, Alexander Graham Bell and Thomas Alva Edison, were born in the same year, 1847, reached the fullness of their power at about the same time, 1875, and developed the same variety and wealth of interests.

Bell was primarily a philologist and acoustician, concerned with teaching speech. Born in Scotland, he came to America in 1870 for his health. A year later he was teaching at the Boston School for the Deaf. In his spare time he fussed with the problem of how to send several messages at once over one

AMERICAN TELEPHONE AND TELEGRAPH CO.

telegraph wire, and thought of doing it with the help of musical notes of different frequencies. A happy accident led in 1875 to the invention of the telephone, which Bell was able to demonstrate at the Philadelphia Centennial Exposition in 1876. Thereafter events moved with gratifying celerity, and by 1900 there were more than 1,500,000 telephones in America. Bell used the fortune he made to experiment in a dozen different directions, including aerodynamics and hydrodynamics.

Edison was a hard-boiled, swaggering youngster, the fastest telegraph operator of his time, who was managing the wireless facilities of the Gold Indicator Company when Jay Gould attempted his notorious gold corner in 1869. Perceiving that men would pay handsome sums for quick information about stock quotations, Edison invented an improved stock ticker, sold it for $40,000, and by 1876 was ready to open a laboratory in Menlo Park, New Jersey, where, he announced, his specialty would be "inventions to order." The performance was no less than the promise: during his lifetime Edison was awarded 1,093 patents, more than any other man has ever been granted.

He achieved what Bell had sought, a multiple telegraph; in the course of a patent war, he even invented a telephone of a different kind than Bell's; in 1878 he tackled the question of electric lighting for the home, recognized that he would have to design a lamp that would perform better and cost less than the gas jet, in 1880 patented an incandescent lamp, and within four years was manufacturing a lamp so much cheaper than gas that he had recouped all his losses to date.

He went on to invent a phonograph, an electric automobile, a motion-picture projector and camera, and a hundred other useful gadgets. As for the wealth these brought him, he said, "I want none of the rich man's usual toys. I want no horses or yachts —I have no time for them. What I want is a perfect workshop."

At left, Alexander Graham Bell at the New York end of the first New York-Chicago connection in 1892. Fourteen years before, he had foreseen most of the ramifications of commercial telephony, including the phrase "Hello, Central." At right, Thomas Edison ponders in his laboratory-workshop.

BROWN BROTHERS

Frederick Jackson Turner

Interpreting the Frontier

There was almost no end to the excitements at Chicago's Columbian Exposition in 1893. Little Egypt, with her enticing tummy-dance, called the hootchy-kootchy, attracted visiting rubes from New York to San Francisco; George Washington Gale Ferris' wondrous wheel transported hundreds of them to delightful thrills 250 feet above the Midway. Sin and sensation, equally distributed, more than made up for the fact that the Fair had opened one year too late for its purpose, which was to celebrate the four hundredth anniversary of the discovery of America by Columbus.

Curiously, however, another event took place in Chicago that year, unmarked except by historians, that was of far greater importance. It occurred on July 12, when Frederick Jackson Turner, a young history professor from the University of Wisconsin, read a paper, "The Significance of the Frontier in American History," before the American Historical Association.

Basing his remarks on a bulletin of the superintendent of the census for 1890, Turner stated that an era lasting four centuries had closed; it had closed because there was no longer an American frontier. "To the frontier," he said, "the American intellect owes its striking characteristics . . . coarseness and strength combined with acuteness and inquisitiveness; that practical, inventive turn of mind . . . that restless, nervous energy; that dominant individualism . . . and withal that buoyancy and exuberance that comes with freedom."

The pioneers would have to find new frontiers.

One of the glories of the Columbian Exposition was the Trans-

CHICAGO HISTORICAL SOCIETY

portation Building, with its gracefully decorated Golden Door, designed by the pioneer Chicago architect Louis H. Sullivan.

371

PEORIA PUBLIC LIBRARY

Frank and Charles Duryea built the first successful American gas-engined car in 1893; in 1895 a Duryea won a race against foreign cars. This 1898 model is driven by Charles.

If the America of the expanding frontier was dead, the America of expanding energy and power was just beginning to feel its oats. One proof of this, in the late 1890's, was the sudden appearance of the horseless carriage.

There was, of course, nothing particularly new about the idea of an automotive vehicle; after all, Oliver Evans had built his Orukter Amphibolos (*see* page 276) back in 1804. But by the 1890's the craze for bicycling had prepared folks for newfangled contraptions like automobiles, and it had also forced the improvement of some roads to the point where automobiles were feasible. The world's first patent for a carriage powered by an internal combustion engine had been filed by a New York patent lawyer, George B. Selden, in 1879; but Selden was shrewd enough to realize that he was far ahead of his time. He kept his patent alive by filing amendments to it and waited patiently.

Gradually experimental automobiles began to appear—the Duryea brothers' "buggyaut" in 1893, Elwood Haynes' carriage in 1894, automobiles built by Alexander Winton and Charles King in 1896, and a "quadricycle" put together by a young engineer working for the Edison Illuminating Company, named Henry Ford. The noisy, expensive contraptions became a fad among the wealthy, puttering through the countryside scaring horses and irritating hard-working, respectable folk.

At the turn of the century, motive power was still an unresolved problem. No less than six propellants were actually in use: electricity, gasoline, steam, and (more or less experimentally) compressed air, carbonic acid gas, and alcohol. Electricity was at first the most popular, for the electric runabout was silent, odorless, easy to handle, and free from vibration. It seemed, indeed, that electricity would win out, leading one journalist in 1899 to predict rashly that the city street of the future would be "almost as quiet as a country lane—all the crash of horses' hoofs and rumble of steel tires will be gone . . . the streets will appear much less crowded."

But it seemed that what the public wanted was speed, and so the electric gave way to the Stanley

The Horseless Carriage:
Buggyauts, Quadricycles,
and Black Flivvers

NATIONAL ARCHIVES

The Stanley twins, F. E. and F. O., pioneered the development of the steam-driven car—silent and swift as a dream. In 1907 a Stanley, "The Flying Teapot," reached 197 m.p.h.

Steamer, which was soon the country's most popular car. Although the halcyon year of 1899 saw less than fifty gasoline-driven vehicles in the entire country, it was not long before the gasoline engine began to forge ahead. There was no battery to recharge every night as in an electric; nor was it necessary to fire up the boiler each time a trip was contemplated, as it was in a steamer. But most important, that former Edison company employee, Henry Ford, was taking a hard look at the untapped mass market.

The steps leading to Ford's revolution began back in 1899. That year the Pope Manufacturing Company, which made the popular Columbia bicycle, was selling carriages designed by Hiram Maxim, propelled both by gas and electricity. A group of New York capitalists, headed by William C. Whitney, ordered 200 Pope electrics to serve as taxis in Manhattan. The Whitney syndicate was determined to expand; as a first step, patents were searched, and presently someone came upon No. 549,160, issued on November 5, 1895, to one George B. Selden. "The object of my invention," Selden's patent read,

"is a safe, simple, and cheap road locomotive, light in weight, easy to control, and possessed of sufficient power to overcome any ordinary inclination."

The pugnacious Maxim wanted to fight the Selden patent, but cooler heads prevailed. Why fight? Why not buy Selden out and so keep everybody happy? An amicable arrangement was worked out, whereby Selden was paid $10,000 and a promise of royalties from other manufacturers. Would they pay? Not until the courts forced them to; but one by one Winton, Duryea, and Haynes-Apperson fell in line. They were the biggest, and gradually the smaller fry followed.

All, that is, except one. Henry Ford angrily exclaimed, "Tell Selden to take his patent and go to hell with it." Protracted litigation dragged on through the first decade of the new century, and the country began to hear about the Ford Motor Com-

The FORD MOTOR CAR

In the eyes of the Chauffeur

is the most satisfactory Automobile made for every-day service. The two cylinder (opposed) motor gives 8 actual horse-power, and eliminates the vibration so noticeable in other machines. The body is luxurious and comfortable and can be removed from the chassis by loosening six bolts.

Price with Tonneau, $900.00
As a Runabout, $800.00
Standard equipment includes 3-inch heavy double tube tires

We agree to assume all responsibility in any action the TRUST may take regarding alleged infringement of the Selden Patent to prevent you from buying the Ford—"*The Car of Satisfaction.*"

We Hold the World's Record
The Ford "999" (the fastest machine in the world), driven by Mr. Ford, made a mile in 39⅖ seconds—equal to 92 miles an hour.
Write for illustrated catalogue and name of our nearest agent.

Ford Motor Co., Detroit, Mich.

Clever advertising made Ford a household word.

Speed sold cars, so this picture of Ford and Barney Oldfield straining forward in motionless autos was retouched to create that illusion.

FORD MOTOR CO.

LIBRARY OF CONGRESS

pany. To the casual eye the trial appeared to be one of a downtrodden little independent squaring off against the hobnailed boot of the oppressor, and Ford swiftly won the battle of public opinion. He was winning the battle in the market place, too; his Fords, cheap to make, easy to drive, and hardy over the long haul, had 1909 sales of $9,000,000, the next year $16,500,000.

In 1911 Ford won his court case—his machine was sufficiently different to be outside the scope of the Selden patent. So, therefore, was every other machine. The monopoly was broken.

Henry Ford was not the first to try to tap the mass market. Ransom E. Olds had begun to build the uni-

versal American car in Detroit back in 1899. With transmissions by the Dodge brothers, and engines by the Lelands, father and son, in 1901 Olds produced 425 cars that cost the buyer $650 apiece; the next year he manufactured 2,500 "merry Oldsmobiles," each of which ran smoothly and well. Here was a good, cheap, mass-produced automobile, but three years later Olds, under pressure from his backers, withdrew from the cheap car field, leaving the way open for Ford.

Ford was a good mechanic and he found himself a superlative financial partner in James Couzens. Twice, before he hooked up with Couzens, he had tried to float a manufacturing company. In 1903,

A few years after prairie schooners had negotiated the West's open spaces, the horseless carriage gave a generation once removed from pioneering the pleasures without the perils.

with a total capital of $28,000, he finally got under way. By 1913, with an open field and a remarkable automobile, the Model T, Ford was turning out 1,000 cars a day at his Highland Park plant outside Detroit. The next year the mass-production assembly line was in high gear, and bodies ("any color, as long as it's black") came sliding down chutes onto the waiting Ford chassis. Flivvers flooded the country, spawning a legion of Model T jokes and putting America, for better or for worse, on wheels.

375

The New Builders

CULVER SERVICE

BROWN BROTHERS

CHICAGO HISTORICAL SOCIETY

James Eads (top) built ironclads for the Union Army and later spanned the Mississippi at St. Louis; John Roebling (center), a German refugee, built the first American suspension bridges; Louis H. Sullivan (bottom), the first modern American architect, conceived the skyscraper in Chicago.

Part of the pioneer dream was building something new, something that would soar and arch and thrust, farther and higher than ever before. So it was with three very different Americans—James Eads, John A. Roebling, and Louis H. Sullivan.

Eads bridged the mighty Mississippi at St. Louis by flinging three great steel arches across the wide stream and thereby opening the West to uninterrupted railroad transportation. Begun in 1867, the Eads Bridge was the first to make extensive use of steel; it took seven years to build; it cost the lives of sixteen men; and it cost Eads his health, for he was wracked by consumption and worn out by the endless opposition of politicians, financial backers, and Nature herself, who even hurled a tornado at his half-completed structure. For his tenacity and vision, Eads was the first and only engineer to be elected to the Hall of Fame.

Roebling's celebrated Brooklyn Bridge was in its day an even more triumphant symbol of achievement, for it was the world's first great modern suspension span, hailed at its completion in 1883 after fourteen years of cruel labor as the "Eighth Wonder of the World." The bridge climaxed Roebling's fruitful career. Earlier he had invented the wire rope that would make possible so many spans, and he had built the breath-taking railroad suspension bridge over Niagara. But neither John Roebling, who designed the Brooklyn Bridge, nor his son Washington, who supervised its construction, could join in the celebration when it was finished. The father had died as a result of one accident; the son had been crippled by another.

It was left to Sullivan to create a structure that was uniquely American—the skyscraper. "A new thing beneath the sun," wrote Frank Lloyd Wright, who was Sullivan's draftsman when that architectural genius designed the Wainwright Building for St. Louis in 1890, "with virtue, individuality, beauty all its own . . . It prophesied the way for these tall office-building effects we now point to with pride." Sullivan was another pioneer, years ahead of his time. "Genius," wrote Frank Lloyd Wright, bitterly. "That term was enough. It damned him." Sullivan died, alone and broke, among the skyscrapers of Chicago in 1924.

Louis Sontag's painting of New York (above), "The Bowery at Night, 1895," mirrors many of the marvels of turn-of-the-century America: the electric streetcars, the thundering elevated railroad, the bright electric glare of the shops.

The official opening of Roebling's Brooklyn Bridge (below) on May 24, 1883, was a splendid gala, filling the air with fireworks, the East River with every type of craft imaginable, and bringing President Chester Arthur to bless the occasion.

T. R. and the Big Stick

Nowhere did the strenuous confidence of the times reach fuller flower than in the administration of the nation's foreign policy. Often that seemed less a policy than the impulsive striking of a truculent, jingo attitude, as a small boy might scratch a line in the dust of a back alley with his toe and snarl, "Dast ya cross that line!" The architect of this policy was none other than Theodore Roosevelt—"that damned cowboy," as the Republican boss, Mark Hanna, called him—and from the time he went careering up San Juan Hill as colonel of the Rough Riders, Roosevelt was an indefatigable apostle of the idea that might is right.

He was, moreover, entirely convinced of his moral rectitude. "I've done nothing that wasn't absolutely right and proper," he said, sublimely confident. He also believed that the civilized nations had a duty to lead backward peoples along the path of right-

At left, Teddy Roosevelt strikes a worldly pose in his White House study. Below, Judge lauds T.R.'s Big Stick diplomacy in a 1905 cartoon entitled "The World's Constable."

BOTH : CULVER SERVICE

eousness. "Chronic wrongdoing," he said in 1904, "may in America, as elsewhere, ultimately require intervention by some civilized nation." The civilized nation he had in mind, of course, was his United States, the wrongdoers, certain Latin American republics which were lax in paying debts. His corollary to the Monroe Doctrine was first used to collect customs duties in Santo Domingo, and it probably blocked European intervention in the Western Hemisphere. Yet all Latin America smarted when the principle was later evoked to justify wholesale landings of marines in Central American and Caribbean republics.

Having thus blandly rippled Uncle Sam's muscles over the whole hemisphere, Roosevelt intervened in the war between Japan and Russia, urging the combatants to make peace. Coming from the man who attacked "futile sentimentalists of the international arbitration type" because they produced "a flabby, timid type of character, which eats away the great fighting qualities of our race," this was something of a surprise; but his action won him the Nobel Peace Prize in 1906.

Late the next year Roosevelt ordered sixteen warships, their auxiliaries, and a complement of some 12,000 officers and men on the first round-the-world cruise ever undertaken by an American fleet. He was showing the world his Big Stick.

Above, the Great White Fleet steams through the Strait of Magellan on its world-wide cruise to "show the flag." Below, the irrepressible Roosevelt embraces the symbol of Peace after negotiating the end of the Russo-Japanese War.

Harper's Weekly, 1905

379

Conservation-minded T.R. saved and maintained many of the nation's natural wonders. This is Bridal Veil Falls in Yosemite.

ANSEL ADAMS, MAGNUM

A Precious Heritage
Is Preserved

Theodore Roosevelt not only retained his love for the great outdoors, he went further, insisting that the land be protected for the people's use. One of his greatest achievements as President was his eager defense of the nation's resources.

His three predecessors had set aside some 45,000,000 acres of timberland; now Roosevelt preserved, by fiat, another 148,000,000 acres. Fighting at his side was Gifford Pinchot, since 1898 chief of the Forestry Division of the Department of Agriculture. These two champions of conservation inaugurated policies of protecting the water supply of navigable streams, controlling forest fires, and regulating the cutting of timber. A White House conference called by Roosevelt in 1908 made conservation a national issue.

In 1903 Roosevelt had gone camping in Yosemite with naturalist John Muir, who was waging the battle "between landscape righteousness and the devil" in an effort to establish national parks. Roosevelt didn't need to be converted; he was already squarely opposed to the devil.

LIBRARY OF CONGRESS

Above, Roosevelt and writer-naturalist John Muir at Yosemite.

METROPOLITAN MUSEUM OF ART

Across the Isthmus

During the war with Spain the battleship *Oregon* took two months to round Cape Horn. To men like Roosevelt this trip proved that a swifter naval route between the Atlantic and Pacific was imperative for the national defense. The best route lay through the Isthmus of Panama, a territory belonging to the Republic of Colombia. Roosevelt offered Colombia $10,000,000 and an annual rent of $250,000 for a six-mile-wide strip of crucially valuable land. When the Colombian Senate delayed—hoping it would also get the $40,000,000 the United States was willing to pay the stalled French canal company—Roosevelt was apoplectic. And, characteristically, he acted. "I took the Panama Canal and let Congress debate," he recalled later.

This time there was no necessity to send marines. A revolution was hatched in Room 1162 of New York's Hotel Waldorf-Astoria, and the *coup d'état* was carried out by paid insurrectionists in Panama. Roosevelt authorized recognition of the new government a little more than an hour after receiving the news. A dream born when Balboa sighted the Pacific was about to come true.

Jonas Lie aptly titled his painting (left) of the Panama Canal construction "The Conquerors, Culebra Cut." In 1906 T.R. bobbed up at the Cut—the first President to set foot on foreign soil—to pose in a huge steam shovel (below).

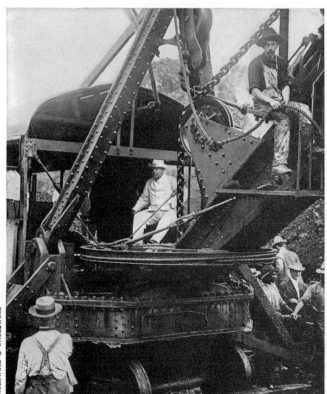

CULVER SERVICE

George Goethals

In 1880 the French began digging at Panama. They dug for nineteen years, then retired, defeated by yellow fever, malaria, graft, and bureaucracy. Then came the Americans, but not until 1907, when Roosevelt made an army officer, George W. Goethals, fully responsible for the project, was success assured.

Goethals was a good engineer, but even more important, he was a crack administrator. He had to be, for to get the canal dug required the labor of some 30,000 workers from a dozen different countries, who had to be housed, fed, amused, and kept healthy in a fetid, pestiferous climate. Gradually, from these fractious elements, Goethals molded an organization of matchless morale. The men took pride in their work. The canal was theirs.

In 1914 when the first ship sailed the forty miles from Atlantic to Pacific, Goethals was not on its bridge with the guests of honor. Instead, he was in his small personal railroad car, hard at work, appearing now on the locks at Gatun, now at Pedro Miguel, unsmiling and self-effacing as always, his bright blue eyes as always checking every detail of the operating machinery and the wave action.

"The real builder of the Panama Canal," he declared later, "was Theodore Roosevelt." For his part, Roosevelt said: "Colonel Goethals proved to be the man of all others to do the job . . . It is the greatest task of any kind." The two men understood each other perfectly. Both knew the importance of putting power in the hands of the man in charge of a job. Since both were benevolent despots, they got along very well together.

383.

UNDERWOOD & UNDERWOOD

Orville and Wilbur Wright (above, Orville at left), proprietors of a Dayton, Ohio, bicycle shop, carefully studied principles of flight by means of gliders and a wind tunnel. By the fall of 1903 they were at Kitty Hawk, North Carolina, preparing to launch a manned and powered flight.

On October 7, 1903, some two months before the Wright brothers' historic experiment at Kitty Hawk, Dr. Samuel Langley of the Smithsonian Institution made his first bid for aviation fame. After conducting successful flights with a scale model, Langley poised his full-size, 52-horsepower "Aerodrome" atop a houseboat anchored in the Potomac River. But, as shown in the picture sequence at left, his craft ran afoul of its spring catapult and plunged into the river.

The Wrights Reach for the Sky

Throughout the nineteenth century every first-rate scientist and inventor had grappled with the problem of heavier-than-air flight. In the nineties Bell, Edison, Hiram Maxim, and Samuel Langley, the secretary of the Smithsonian Institution—all had speculated and experimented, but with very indifferent success. Where men of such proven ability had failed, what chance was there for a pair of young men who were proprietors of a bicycle shop?

Some such thought must have occurred to Wilbur and Orville Wright when, in 1899, they set about solving the problem. Yet one advantage was theirs—they could profit from the mistakes of the men who had gone before them. The two most helpful failures were still in the recent past.

In 1894 Hiram Maxim constructed, for $200,000, a magnificent creature of planes and ailerons, wires and struts, driven by a 360-horsepower steam engine, far more power than would be used in an aircraft for years to come. His monster weighed four tons and boasted 4,000 square feet of wing expanse, and it looked like the box kite to end all box kites. Maxim planned to get it going along a set of rails; in fact, he had designed guide rails above the wheels to keep it from taking off on its test run. But he had so much power in his engine and so much lift in his wings that his craft smashed the guide rails and would have soared up, in ungainly fashion, if he had not switched off the power. The machine was wrecked. Maxim never rebuilt it.

Samuel P. Langley's flying machine was an improvement—at least it actually flew. After exhaustive tests he designed in 1896 a model some sixteen feet long with two pairs of wings spreading about twelve feet across. It was powered by a light little engine that generated a bit more than one horsepower. One May afternoon, accompanied by Alexander Graham Bell, he launched his unmanned craft from a houseboat on the Potomac. When it "swept continuously through the air like a living thing," Professor Langley wrote later, "I felt that something had been accomplished at last, for never in any part of the world, or in any period, had any machine of man's construction sustained itself in the air before for even half of this brief time." In November a larger model flew three-quarters of a mile; but Lang-

ley had designed no system of wing control, and it plunked ingloriously into the drink.

From these failures the Wright brothers understood that the problem of heavier-than-air flight was truly three problems: first, a light engine; second, a plane surface along which the air could stream, as it flows against the wings of a soaring hawk, and so support the combined weight of an engine and its operator; and third, a system whereby the motion of the machine could be controlled. Although their predecessors had licked the first two problems, they had ignored the third.

The Wright brothers undertook to learn the skills of gliding so that they might better understand how to design a proper flying machine. For this reason they went in 1900 to Kitty Hawk, a great stretch of North Carolina beach which was wide and windy and clear of trees. Their unmanned glider, the wings of which spanned seventeen and a half feet, flew splendidly; but when one of them lay belly-down to guide it, something went wrong.

They decided the data on aerodynamics were at fault and built a tiny wind tunnel to run tests. These led them to build longer wings and a tail plane. In March, 1903, they confidently filed for a patent, and that fall they took their new model, this time with engine attached, to Kitty Hawk. Orville was 32; he had a sense of fun. Wilbur was 36; he was a trifle more self-important. Both were dedicated and patient.

December 17 was a wintry, windy day, with clouds scudding in from the north. Five men from a U.S. lifesaving station came to help the brothers lay the track for their take-off truck. Orville squirmed his way among the wire struts and bellied down beside the motor. Wilbur, standing alongside, balanced a wing tip. Orville released the machine and it flew. The brothers took turns and made four flights. The last time the machine stayed aloft for 59 seconds while it flew 852 feet. Man had, for the first time, achieved sustained flight.

OVERLEAF: *Wilbur Wright breathlessly watches brother Orville guide their flimsy 12-horsepower contraption along a track laid on the Kitty Hawk sands and, miraculously, into the raw, gray sky. At last man had truly conquered the air.*

OVERLEAF: LIBRARY OF CONGRESS

Probing the Essence of Matter

Slowly, in this time of confident optimism, and very unobtrusively, the foundations of an American scientific movement were laid. The men responsible were wholly unknown to the public, their ideas and their experiments reached only their peers in the international scientific community, but there they were recognized as pioneers of the first importance, and they were signally honored.

Of these, probably the greatest and certainly the most obscure was Josiah Willard Gibbs, professor of mathematical physics at Yale from 1871 until his death in 1903. His celebrated phase rule, defining the laws of the equilibrium of change, was in some ways as impressive an intellectual achievement as Isaac Newton's laws of the equilibrium of motion. Gibbs' profound studies of thermodynamics were an enormous contribution to physical chemistry, and the practical applications of his theoretical work have been even more far-reaching. Quiet, gentle, urbane, and above all self-effacing, Gibbs was not widely honored by his own countrymen until his last years, and even today, ironically enough, he remains a somewhat obscure figure.

The case was different with Albert A. Michelson, the brilliant experimenter who was the first American to win a Nobel Prize in physics. Except that his goals were quite different, Michelson was curiously like his robber-baron contemporaries—intense, ruthless, and single-minded.

As a youngster, he virtually argued his way into an appointment to Annapolis. After graduating from the Naval Academy in 1873, Michelson was named to the faculty, and here he presently scored his first notable achievement: with equipment he had put together for about ten dollars, he measured the speed of light more accurately than it had ever been done before. Physicists the world over eyed his analysis with respect.

In 1880—when he was only 28 years old—Michelson took a critical look at one of the fundamental

A. Einstein
1931

assumptions of nineteenth-century physics: that all matter moves through a calm, stationary sea of "ether," the name given to an invisible, intangible medium thought to carry the waves of light and other radiation. Michelson determined to see if such a medium existed.

For his studies he perfected an ingenious and delicate apparatus—an interferometer—by which he could measure the speed of light traveling in the direction of the motion of the earth and its speed traveling at right angles, by splitting one ray of light into two parts. In 1881, very confidently, he announced that the sea of "ether" did not exist. Light traveled at the same speed, no matter in what direction.

Michelson's conclusion—strongly attacked, but finally accepted—gave a new direction to the whole study of speed and space. It led directly to the special relativity theory announced in 1905 by young Albert Einstein. But before then American physics, thanks to Michelson, was highly regarded in the international scientific community.

Michelson himself, after 1892, reared a second generation of American physicists at the University of Chicago and saw to it that a third generation would be well-disciplined. He did so by engaging young Robert Millikan as his assistant and giving him the task of educating graduate students.

Millikan was studying in Europe when, in 1896, Michelson cabled him to come to Chicago. For nearly twelve years he wrote textbooks, vetted graduate students, and raised a family. Then he turned to research. He took as his task the measurement of the charge of the electron, which, if he could do it, would establish the properties of this basic building block of matter. Many physicists, most notably those at Cambridge, had essayed the test, but all had failed. It took Millikan three years, but then, with his celebrated oil-drop experiment, he did it, and thereby won another Nobel Prize for America. His experiment clarified the photoelectric effect that had won Einstein the Nobel Prize.

These two physicists, Michelson and Millikan, had brought about an international scientific revolution. They had done it through brilliant laboratory experiments, and the result of their efforts was the opening of whole new worlds to theorists who would study the problems they posed.

At left, Nobel Prize winners Albert A. Michelson, Albert Einstein, and Robert A. Millikan, photographed in 1931. Michelson's experiments led Einstein toward his theory of relativity, while Millikan's study of the electron contributed evidence for Einstein's quantum theory of radiation.

In 1932, working under the direction of Robert A. Millikan, Carl Anderson dramatically proved the existence of an atomic particle called the positron, or positive electron. The particle is visible in the cloud-chamber photograph at right, arcing upward through a sheet of lead.

A Changing Concept: from Lone Wolf to Team Researcher

N.Y. World Telegram & Sun

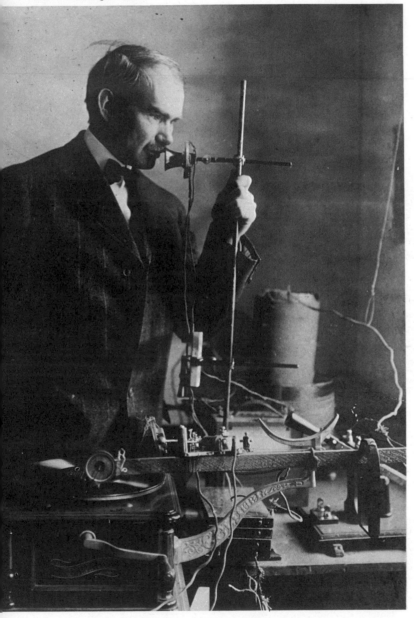

Lee de Forest's experiments in wireless signal detection resulted in the three-electrode triode, or audion tube, which revolutionized radio. This 1907 photograph shows de Forest broadcasting a news-and-music program for radio "hams."

I can fervently say," wrote Lee de Forest, "that it was Willard Gibbs' influence and inspiration which so firmly resolved me . . . to prepare myself for that project of research and invention which I had determined should be my life's work." But in fact de Forest had stubbornly made up his mind that he would be an inventor years before he studied under Gibbs at Yale. As a boy of ten or twelve he busied himself building all sorts of things—a home-made blast furnace, a toy locomotive. Always tinkering, always contriving, it was as if he had decided to include in his own lifetime every phase of American invention.

In that event, he had as well to pioneer, and this, beginning in 1900, was precisely what de Forest did. He wrote in his diary: "At last, at last, after long planning and plotting, years of study, and weeks of patient, weary waiting, I have the opportunity offered for the work that I have chosen, experimental work in wireless telegraphy!"

Actually, by 1900 de Forest was some years behind the Italian Marconi, the Germans Braun and Slaby, and the American Reginald Fessenden in radio telegraphy, and although he obtained three dozen patents in the next few years, his experiences with the promoters who exploited his inventions were so bitter that in 1911 de Forest found himself flat broke. He withdrew to California to lick his wounds and, if possible, recoup his fortunes. His best chance, so it seemed, was in an invention he had patented five years before—a three-electrode tube that he called the audion.

In San Francisco he plunged into experiments on his audion, determined to make work an anodyne for all his disappointments. In a year he had developed his tube to the point where it would amplify sound for a distance of two city blocks. American Telephone & Telegraph paid him $50,000 for the telephone rights; Western Electric paid him another $90,000 for the radio rights and then, after renegotiating, paid him $250,000 for all residual rights. The price was cheap. All electronics—radio, television, motion pictures with sound, and a dozen other developments—were to be traced ultimately back to the audion.

De Forest stayed in California, a lone wolf, busy in his laboratory, ruefully surveying the monsters that had been created out of his tube. As the years passed he took out more patents by the hundreds and was happy, working by himself.

GENERAL ELECTRIC CO.

Lee de Forest was very nearly the last of the lone wolves of technology. Irving Langmuir, eight years younger than de Forest, came along just enough later to symbolize, in his even more fruitful career, the new American scientist: an industrial scientist, functioning as part of a team.

Langmuir went to the laboratory of the General Electric Company in Schenectady, New York, in the summer of 1909. He was suspicious, and his attitude was strictly one of "show me"; for his experience was limited to teaching at the Stevens Institute, and an industrial laboratory was, in 1909, a new breed of cat. General Electric was, moreover, one of J. P. Morgan's companies. Hence, it followed—or so Langmuir imagined—that he would be assigned only some stultifying, humdrum task calculated to fill Morgan's coffers further. General Electric's executive officers (and presumably Morgan as well) were, Langmuir was to discover, far more subtle. He planned to spend only the months of his summer vacation there, but instead he stayed on for the rest of his working life.

"When I joined the laboratory," he commented later, "I found that there was more 'academic freedom' than I had ever encountered in any university. I started to work in the General Electric laboratory in 1909 on high-vacuum phenomena in tungsten filament lamps and began introducing different gases into the bulb to see what would happen, just to satisfy my curiosity . . . Some very extraordinary things happened."

One extraordinary thing was his discovery that a lamp would give brighter light longer if it were filled with nitrogen. It has been estimated that this bit of knowledge saved Americans a million dollars a night in electricity bills.

Another extraordinary thing was his discovery—with the help of a vacuum pump he invented—of how to improve Lee de Forest's audion and how, in consequence, to design the vacuum tube which is now standard in all radios.

Still another extraordinary thing was his discovery of the importance of surface chemistry: "I found that a single layer of thorium atoms on tungsten could increase the electron emission from a tungsten filament in vacuum one hundred thousand fold." His experiments in molecular chemistry led to a Nobel Prize in 1932, and in the hands of other researchers they have led to profound discoveries in medicine, biology, chemistry, and physics.

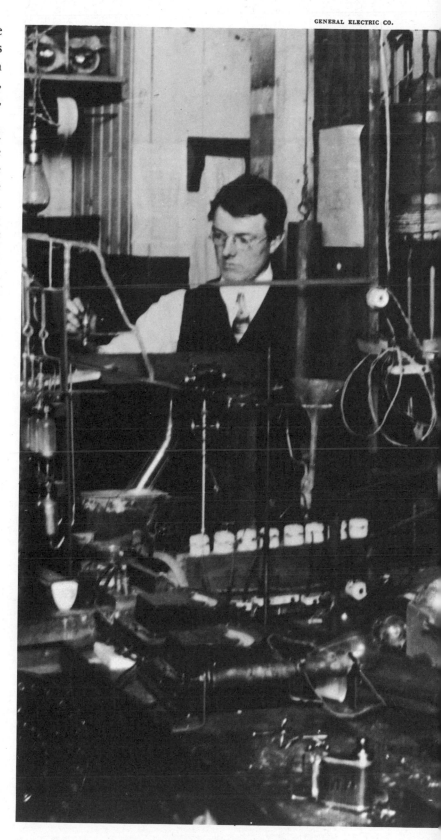

Irving Langmuir, shown in General Electric's laboratory in 1912, typified the new scientist, working as one of a team under industry's benign eye. His provocative experiments in pure science were done, he said, "for the fun of it."

The Ultimate Frontier

The uttermost horizon for the pioneer is the limitless universe of space that reaches out around the speck of cosmic dust called Earth. It is peculiarly fitting that a triumphant effort to explore this infinity should have been undertaken by the generation that lived the strenuous, confident life. The form that their effort took is the greatest astronomical observatory complex the world has ever known, perched on two California mountain tops. The intelligence that shaped it was that of a pioneering American astronomer, the explorer of the sun, George Ellery Hale. The money that built it was given by two pioneering American industrialists, Carnegie and Rockefeller.

Hale, whose photographs of the sun had won him an international reputation while he was still only 23 years old, climbed Mount Wilson in 1903 and at once sensed that climate, height, and atmosphere conspired to make the peak ideal for astral observation. When Carnegie proffered ten million dollars, the dream became a reality. Later Hale came out of retirement to seek funds from the Rockefeller Foundation for the even greater telescope on Mount Palomar.

And so the pioneer circle is completed; and at its center is a great eye, with a pupil 200 inches across, staring out into the boundless future.

BOTH : MOUNT WILSON AND PALOMAR OBSERVATORIES

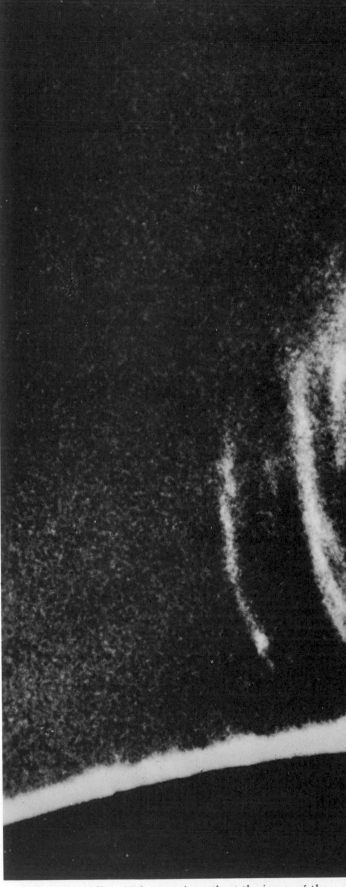

At left, George Ellery Hale peers intently at the image of the sun through Mount Wilson's 60-foot tower telescope in 1907. He served as observatory director from 1904 to 1923.

Hale's wealthy father built the young MIT student a private observatory in Chicago, where he invented the spectroheliograph with which he could analyze the sun's light.

Techniques of solar photography which Hale developed permitted pictures like the historic one above, taken in 1917, of titanic flames spurting 140,000 miles from the sun.

ACKNOWLEDGMENTS

AND

INDEX

The Editors are especially grateful to the following individuals and organizations for their generous assistance and for their co-operation in making available pictorial materials in their collections:

American Museum of Natural History, New York—Dean Amadon, Mrs. Isabelle Mount

American Philosophical Society, Philadelphia—Gertrude Hess

Chicago Historical Society—Mrs. Mary Frances Rhymer

City Art Museum of St. Louis—Charles Nagel, Merritt S. Hitt

Colonial Williamsburg, Inc., Williamsburg, Va.—Mrs. A. Willard Duncan, Alice Sircom

Edward Eberstadt & Sons, New York—Lindley Eberstadt

Filson Club, Louisville—Mrs. Dorothy Thomas Cullen

Frans Halsmuseum, Haarlem, Netherlands—Mrs. J. A. de Vries

Frick Art Reference Library, New York—Mrs. Henry W. Howell, Jr.

Colonel Edgar W. Garbisch, New York

Hispanic Society of America, New York—Clara L. Penney

Historical Society of Pennsylvania, Philadelphia—R. N. Williams 2nd

Robert Honeyman, Capistrano, Calif.

Houghton Library, Harvard University—Carolyn E. Jakeman

Hudson's Bay Company, Winnipeg—S. A. Hewitson

Henry E. Huntington Library and Art Gallery, San Marino, Calif.—Dorothy Bowen, Haydée Noya

The late James Hazen Hyde, New York

Independence National Historical Park, Philadelphia—M. O. Anderson

Indiana Historical Society, Indianapolis—Caroline Dunn

John Rylands Library, Manchester, England—Dr. E. Robertson

Kansas State Historical Society, Topeka—Robert W. Richmond

Knoedler Galleries, New York—Elizabeth Clare

Library of Congress, Washington—Virginia Daiker

Life Magazine—Dorothy L. Smith

Massachusetts Historical Society, Boston—Stephen T. Riley

Metropolitan Museum of Art, New York—Marshall Davidson, Janet Byrne, Lillian Green

Missouri Historical Society, St. Louis—Marjory Douglas, Mrs. Ruth Field

Museum of Fine Arts, Boston—Elizabeth P. Riegel

Museum of Science and Industry, Chicago—Daniel M. MacMaster

Nantucket (Mass.) Historical Association—George W. Jones

Nationalbibliothek, Vienna—Dr. Franz Unterkircher

National Air Museum, Washington—Philip S. Hopkins

National Archives, Washington—Josephine Cobb

National Gallery of Art, Washington—Perry B. Cott, Huntington Cairns, Mrs. Elizabeth Ostertag

Netherlands Institute for Art History, The Hague—H. Gerson

Newberry Library, Chicago—Ben Bowman

New-York Historical Society—Arthur B. Carlson, Betty J. Ezequelle, Geraldine Beard, Susan D. McMahon

New York Public Library—Lewis M. Stark, Mrs. Maud D. Cole, Elizabeth E. Roth, Wilson G. Duprey

New York State Division of Archives and History, Albany—Albert B. Corey

On Film, Inc., Princeton, N.J.—Tracy Ward

Old Print Shop, New York—Harry Shaw Newman, Kenneth M. Newman

Oregon Historical Society, Portland—Mrs. Nancy A. Hacker

Pennsylvania Historical and Museum Commission, Harrisburg—S. K. Stevens

Pierpont Morgan Library, New York—Herbert Cahoon

Pilgrim Society, Plymouth, Mass.—Rose T. Briggs

Rhode Island School of Design, Providence—John Maxon

Carl Selmer, Hunter College, New York

State Historical Society of Wisconsin, Madison—Paul Vanderbilt

Stevens Institute of Technology, Hoboken, N.J.—William J. Bucci

Texas State Library, Austin—Dorman H. Winfrey

Bronson Trevor, New York

U.S. Naval Academy Museum, Annapolis—Captain Wade DeWeese

Yale University Press—Arthur H. Brook

Acknowledgment is made to the University of Oklahoma Press for permission to reproduce pictures copyrighted in *The West of Alfred Jacob Miller* by Marvin C. Ross, 1951.

Color photography of paintings: Herbert Loebel, Geoffrey Clements, Eugene Cook, New York; Charles P. Mills and Son, Philadelphia; Barney Burstein, Boston; Mettee Studio, Baltimore; Jack Zehrt, St. Louis; Henry Beville, Washington; Zoltan Wegner, London.